John Lubbock, Sven Nilsson

The Primitive Inhabitants of Scandinavia

An essay on comparative ethnography, and a contribution to the history of the development of mankind

John Lubbock, Sven Nilsson

The Primitive Inhabitants of Scandinavia
An essay on comparative ethnography, and a contribution to the history of the development of mankind

ISBN/EAN: 9783337409340

Printed in Europe, USA, Canada, Australia, Japan

Cover: Foto ©Andreas Hilbeck / pixelio.de

More available books at **www.hansebooks.com**

THE PRIMITIVE INHABITANTS

OF

SCANDINAVIA.

AN ESSAY ON COMPARATIVE
ETHNOGRAPHY, AND A CONTRIBUTION TO
THE HISTORY OF THE DEVELOPMENT OF MANKIND:
CONTAINING A DESCRIPTION OF THE IMPLEMENTS, DWELLINGS,
TOMBS, AND MODE OF LIVING OF THE SAVAGES
IN THE NORTH OF EUROPE DURING
THE STONE AGE.

BY SVEN NILSSON.

THIRD EDITION,

REVISED BY THE AUTHOR, AND TRANSLATED FROM HIS OWN MANUSCRIPT.

EDITED, AND WITH AN INTRODUCTION

BY

SIR JOHN LUBBOCK, Bart. F.R.S. &c.

LONDON:

LONGMANS, GREEN, AND CO.

1868.

EDITOR'S PREFACE.

If the Science of Prehistoric Archæology had long excited as much interest in this country as it does at present, Professor Nilsson's work on the Aborigines of Scandinavia would not now be appearing in an English translation for the first time.

M. Morlot has truly observed, that the wonderful advance recently made in our knowledge of ancient men, and particularly the division of European history into the three eras, the Stone, Bronze, and Iron Ages, is 'due chiefly to the labours of M. Thomsen, Director of the Ethnological and Archæological Museum at Copenhagen, and to those of Professor Nilsson, of the flourishing University of Lund.'

Both these archæologists, however, unfortunately for us, write in languages but little understood in this country, and their labours, in consequence, have remained almost unknown. When, therefore, Messrs. Longman & Co. requested me to edit an English translation of Professor Nilsson's 'Stone Age,' I very gladly undertook to do so.

Had Professor Nilsson's object been to exalt his own reputation, he would have reprinted his book just as it stood when first published in 1838–43. In its present form, however, improved and somewhat enlarged, his work is an even more valuable contribution to our Ethnological literature.

The present translation was made in Sweden, under the immediate superintendence of the Author. It constitutes, in fact, a new edition, differing considerably, not only from the original, but also from that which was published at the commencement of last year. Under these circumstances, I have not liked to introduce too many modifications, lest, in altering the style, I might perhaps change somewhat the meaning also. Moreover, although in many places the English has a slightly foreign aspect, I do not think that the reader will find any practical inconvenience; and in the translation of a scientific work, accuracy is of more importance than style.

As this book may be read by some who have not made a special study of Prehistoric Archæology, I have prefaced it with a short Introduction, which is substantially the same as the Address which I delivered before the Archæological Institute at their London meeting in July 1866.

This is, I think, the more desirable, because no flint

implements of the most ancient, or palæolithic, types have yet been found in Scandinavia. On this point I can speak with some little confidence, having myself visited the excellent Museums of Copenhagen, Stockholm, Lund, Flensborg, and Aarhuus, besides many private collections. It seems to me, therefore, probable that Scandinavia was not peopled until the Second Stone, or Neolithic Age, which is so well treated of in the present Work.

High Elms, Farnborough, Kent:
November 10, 1867.

EDITOR'S INTRODUCTION.

PREHISTORIC ARCHÆOLOGY has but lately made good
its right to recognition as a branch of science;
and even now, perhaps, there are some who are
disposed to question the claim. We can never, it
is thought by these, become wise beyond what is
written: the ancient poems and histories contain all
that we can ever know about old times and bygone
races of men; by the study of antiquities we may
often corroborate, and occasionally perhaps even correct, the statements of old writers, but beyond this
we can never hope to go. The ancient monuments
and remains themselves may excite our interest, but
they can teach us nothing. This opinion is as old as
the time of Horace: in one of his best known Odes
he tells us that—

> Vixere fortes ante Agamemnona
> Multi; sed omnes illacrymabiles
> Urgentur, ignotique longâ
> Nocte, carent quia vate sacro.

If this apply to nations as well as to individuals—if
our knowledge of the past be confined to that which

has been handed down to us in books—then Archæology is indeed restrained within fixed and narrow limits; it is reduced to a mere matter of criticism, and is almost unworthy to be called a science.

My object in the present Introduction is to vindicate the claims of Archæology; to point out briefly the light which has, more particularly in the last few years, been thrown upon the past; and, above all, if possible, to show that the antiquaries of the present day are no visionary enthusiasts, but that the methods of archæological investigation are as trustworthy as those of any natural science. I purposely say the methods, rather than the results, because while I believe that the progress recently made has been mainly due to the use of those methods which have been pursued with so much success in geology, zoology, and other kindred branches of science—and while fully persuaded that in this manner we must eventually ascertain the truth—I readily admit that there are many points on which further evidence is required. Nor need the antiquary be ashamed to own that it is so. Biologists differ about the Darwinian theory; until very lately the emission theory of light was maintained by some of the best authorities; Tyndall and Magnus are at issue as to whether aqueous vapour does or does not absorb heat; astronomers have recently been obliged to admit an error of more than 4,000,000 miles in their estimate of the distance between the earth and the sun; nor is there any single proposition in theology to which an universal assent would be given. Although, therefore, there are no doubt great diversities of opinion among antiquaries, archæology is in this respect only in the same condition as all other branches of knowledge.

Conceding then, frankly, that from several of the following conclusions some good archæologists would entirely dissent, I will now endeavour to state briefly the principal results of modern research, and especially to give, as far as can be done within the limits of a few pages, an idea of the kind of evidence on which these conclusions are based.

I must also add, that my remarks are confined, excepting when it is otherwise specified, to that part of Europe which lies to the north of the Alps; and that by the Primæval Period I understand that which extended from the first appearance of man down to the commencement of the Christian era.

This period may be divided into four epochs :— Firstly, the Palæolithic, or First Stone Age; secondly, the Neolithic, or Second Stone Age; thirdly, the Bronze Age; and lastly, the Iron Age. Attempts have been made, with more or less success, to establish subdivisions of these periods, but into these I do not now propose to enter: even if we can do no more as yet than establish this succession, that will itself be sufficient to show that we are not entirely dependent on history.

We will commence, then, with the Palæolithic Age. This is the most ancient period in which we have as yet any decisive proofs of the existence of man. M. Desnoyers has, indeed, called attention to some bones from the Pliocene beds of St. Prest, which appear to show the marks of knives, and M. l'Abbé Bourgeois has since found in the same locality some flints, which he believes to have been worked by man; Mr. Whincopp also has in his possession a bone from the crag, which certainly looks as if it had been cut with some sharp instrument. These cases, however, are not perfectly conclusive, and as yet the implements found in the river-drift gravels are the oldest undoubted traces of man's existence—older far than any of those in Egypt or Assyria, though belonging to a period which, from a geological point of view, is very recent.

The Palæolithic Age.

As regards the Palæolithic Age, we may, I think, regard the following conclusions as fully borne out by the evidence :—

1. The antiquities referable to this period are usually found in beds of gravel and loam, or, as it is technically called, 'loess,' extending along our valleys, and reaching sometimes to a height of 200 feet above the present water-level.

2. These beds were deposited by the existing rivers, which then ran in the same directions as at present, and drained the same areas.

3. With the exception of the coast-line, the geography of Western Europe cannot therefore have been very different at the time those gravels were deposited from what it is now.

4. The fauna of Europe at that time comprised the mammoth, the woolly-haired rhinoceros, the hippopotamus, the urus, the musk-ox, &c., as well as most of the existing animals.

5. The climate was much colder than at present.

6. Though we have no exact measure of time, we can at least satisfy ourselves that this period was one of very great antiquity.

7. Yet man already inhabited Western Europe.

8. He used rude implements of stone;

9. Which were never polished, and of which some types differ remarkably from any of those that were subsequently in use.

10. He was ignorant of pottery, and (11) of metals.

I will now proceed to examine these eleven conclusions at somewhat greater length:—

1. That these beds of gravel and loam, or, as it is technically called, 'loess,' extend along the slopes of the valleys, and reach sometimes to a height of 200

feet above the present water-level, is a mere statement of fact about which no difference of opinion has arisen.

2. That these beds of gravel and loess were not deposited by the sea, is proved by the fact that the remains which occur in them are all those of land or freshwater—and not of marine species. That they were deposited by the existing rivers is evident, because in each river-valley they contain fragments of those rocks only which occur in the area drained by the river itself. As, therefore, the rivers drained the same areas then as now, the geography of Western Europe cannot have been at that period very different from what it is at present.

3. The fauna, however, was very unlike what it is now, the existence of the animals above mentioned being proved by the presence and condition of their bones.

4. The greater severity of the climate is indicated by the nature of the fauna. The musk-ox, the woolly-haired rhinoceros, the mammoth, the lemming, &c., are Arctic species, and the reindeer then extended to the South of France. Another argument is derived from the presence of great sandstone blocks in the gravels of some rivers, as, for instance, of the Somme: these, it appears, must have been transported by ice.

5. The great antiquity of the period now under discussion is evident from several considerations. The

extinction of the large mammalia must have been a work of time; and neither in the earliest writings, nor in the vaguest traditions, do we find any indication of their presence in Western Europe. Still more conclusive evidence is afforded by the condition of our valleys. The beds of gravel and loam cannot have been deposited by any sudden cataclysm, both on account of their regularity, and also of the fact, already mentioned, that the materials of one river-system are never mixed with those of another. To take an instance. The gravel of the Somme valley is entirely formed of débris from the chalk and tertiary strata occupying that area; but at a right angle to, and within a very few miles of, the headwaters of the Somme comes the valley of the Oise. In this valley are other older strata, no fragments of which have found their way into the Somme valley, though they could not have failed to do so had the gravels in question been the result of any great cataclysm, or had the Somme then drained a larger area than at present. The beds in question are found in some cases 200 feet above the present water-level, and the bottom of the valley is occupied by a bed of peat, which in some places is as much as 30 feet in thickness. We have no means of making an accurate calculation; but even if we allow, as we must, a good deal for the floods which would be produced by the melting of the snow, still it is evident that for the river to excavate its valley to a depth of more than 200 feet,* and then for the formation of so thick a bed of peat, much time must have been required. If, moreover, we consider the alteration which has taken place in the climate, as well as in the fauna, and, finally, remember also that the last eighteen hundred years have produced scarcely any perceptible change, we cannot but come to the conclusion that many, very many, centuries have elapsed since the river ran at a level so much higher than the present, and the country was occupied by a fauna so unlike that now in existence there.

6. The presence of man is proved by the discovery of stone implements (figs. 1 and 2). Strictly speaking, these only prove the presence of reasoning beings; but this being granted, few, if any, would doubt that the beings in question were men. Human bones, moreover, have been found in cave-deposits, which, in the opinion of the best judges, belonged to this period; and M. Boucher de Perthes considers that various fragments of human bone found at Moulin Quignon are also genuine. On this point long discussions have taken place, into which I will not now enter. The question before us is, whether men existed at all, not whether they had bones. On

---

* Many persons find a difficulty in understanding how the river could have deposited gravel at so great a height, forgetting that the valley was not then excavated to anything like its present depth.

Fig. 1.

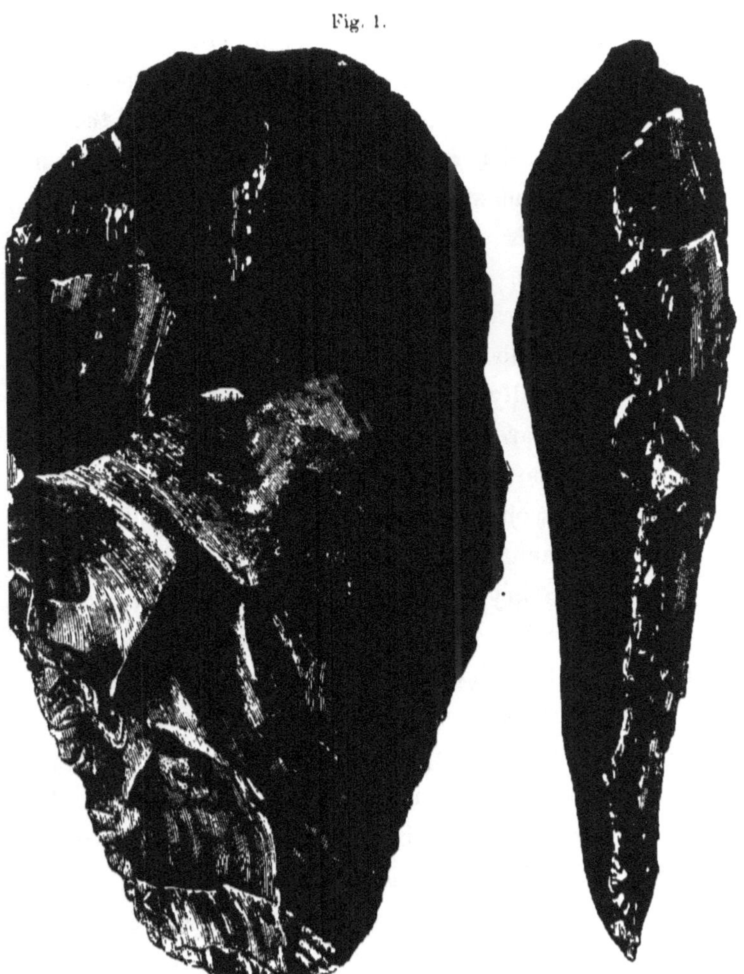

Flint Implement from St. Acheul, near Amiens.
Natural size.

the latter point no dispute is likely to arise, and as regards the former, the works of man are as good evidence as his bones could be. Moreover, there seems to me nothing wonderful in the great scarcity of human bones. A country where the inhabitants subsist on the produce of the chase can never be otherwise than scantily peopled. If we admit that for each man there must be a thousand head of game existing at any one time—and this seems a moderate allowance; remembering also that most mammalia are less long-lived than men, we should naturally expect to find human remains very rare as compared with those of other animals. Among a people who burnt their dead, of course this disproportion would be immensely increased. That the flint implements found in these gravels *are* implements it is unnecessary to argue. Their regularity, and the care with which they have been worked to an edge, prove that they have been *intentionally* chipped into their present forms, and are not the result of accident. That they are not forgeries we may be certain: firstly, because they have been found *in situ* by many excellent observers—by all, in fact, who have looked perseveringly for them; and secondly, because, as the discoloration of their surface is quite superficial, and follows the existing outline, it has evidently been produced since the flints were brought to their present forms. This is clearly shown in fig. 3 (p. xx.), which

Fig. 2.

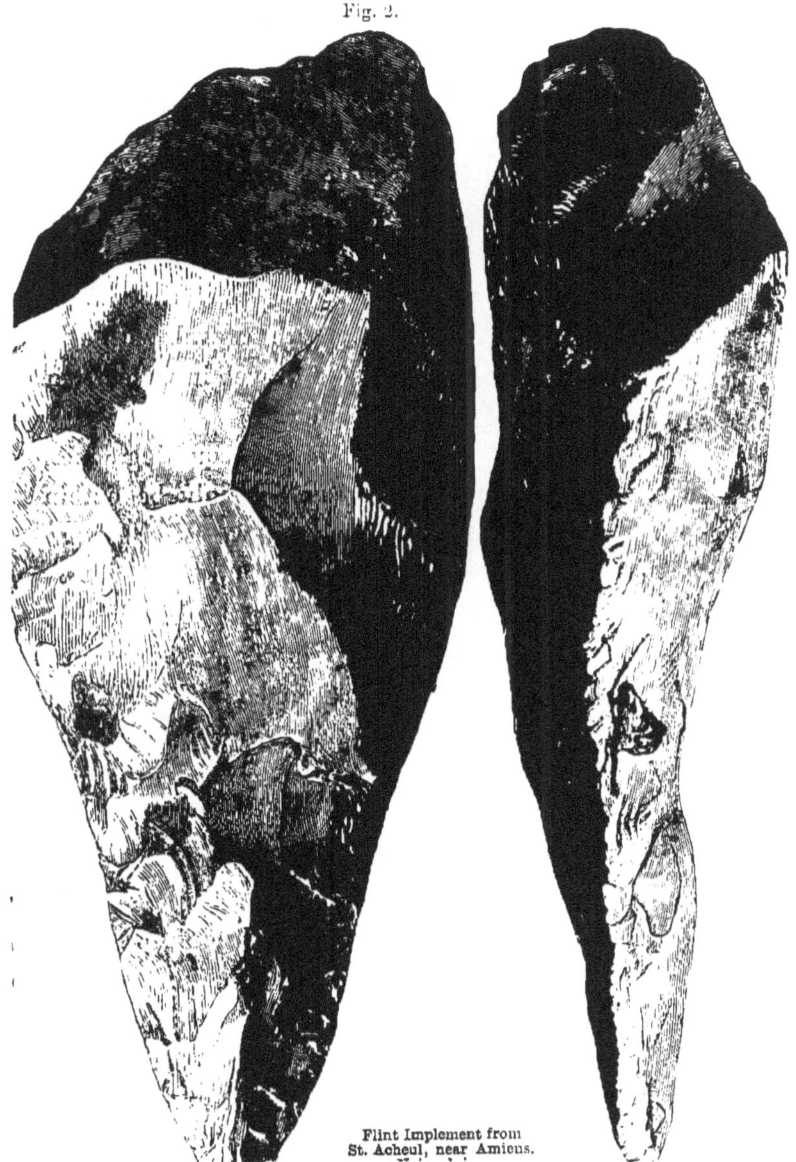

Flint Implement from
St. Acheul, near Amiens.

represents a fractured surface of fig. 2, and shows the dark natural flint, surrounded by the altered surface.

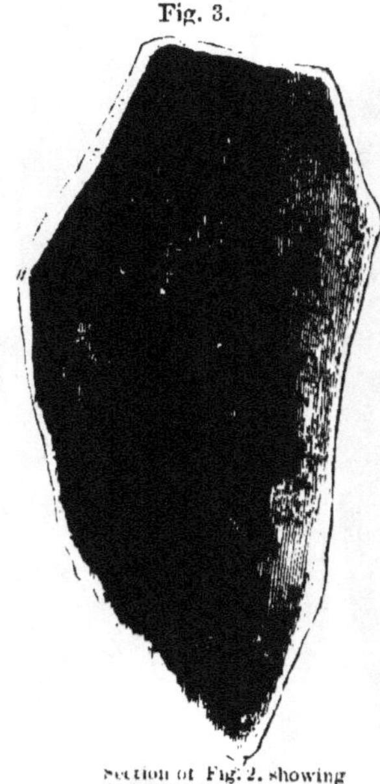

Fig. 3.

Section of Fig. 2, showing discolouration of surface.

The forgeries—for there *are* forgeries—are of a dull lead colour, like other freshly-broken surfaces of flint. The same evidence justifies us in concluding that the implements are coeval with the beds of gravel in which they are found.

8. Without counting flakes, we shall certainly be within the mark if we estimate that three thousand flint implements of the Palæolithic Age have been discovered in Northern France and Southern England. These are all of types which differ considerably from those which came subsequently into use, and they are none of them polished; we may therefore, I think, infer that the art of polishing stone implements was as yet unknown.

9 and 10. In the same manner, I think, we may safely conclude that the use of metal and of pottery was then unknown, as is the case even now with many races of savages.

Although flint implements were observed in the

drift-gravels more than half a century ago by Mr. Frere, still his observations were forgotten until the same discovery was again made by M. Boucher de Perthes. For our knowledge of the gravel-beds in which they occur, however, we are principally indebted to Mr. Prestwich. Sir Charles Lyell has the high merit of having carefully examined the facts, and given to the antiquity of man the authority of his great name; nor must the labours of Mr. Evans be passed unnoticed. To him we owe the first comparison between the flint implements of this and those of the Neolithic period.

In what precedes, I have relied principally on the researches in the river-drift gravel-beds. Much additional information has, however, been obtained by the examination of caves. Though I cannot here do justice to the numerous archæologists who have laboured at this branch of the science, I must take the opportunity of alluding to two of our fellow-countrymen, Dr. Falconer and Mr. Christy — who have recently, alas! been lost to us and to science. Mr. Busk, who had been for some time engaged with Dr. Falconer in the study of the Gibraltar caves, will publish the result of the investigations which he had left in an unfinished state, and everyone will admit that the materials could not be in better hands.

The researches carried on by Mr. Christy, in conjunction with M. Lartet, in the caves of the Dordogne, are of great interest. The general facts may be stated to be, that while thousands of implements made out of stone, bone, and horn, have been collected, no trace of pottery, nor evidence of the use of metals, not even a polished stone implement, has yet been met with. The people who lived in the South of France at that period seem, in a great many respects, to have resembled the Esquimaux. Their principal food was the reindeer, and though traces of the musk-ox, mammoth, cave-lion, as well as other animals of the quaternary fauna have been met with, it is still possible that these may not belong to the same period. These cavemen were very ingenious, and excellent workers in flint; but though their bone-pins, &c., are beautifully polished, this is never the case with their flint weapons. The habit of allowing offal and bones to accumulate in their dwellings is indicative, probably, of a cold climate.

Perhaps, however, the most remarkable fact of all is, that although in other respects so slightly advanced in civilisation, these ancient French cavemen, like the Esquimaux, show a wonderful genius for art. Many very spirited drawings of animals have been found represented on fragments of bone, stone, and horn, and M. Lartet has found in the rock-shelter at La Madelaine a fragment of mammoth-tusk, on which was engraved a representation of the animal itself.*

* See also note 7.

On the whole, these remains probably belong to an epoch somewhat less ancient than the implements of the St. Acheul gravels; from the preponderance of the remains of that animal, it has been called the Reindeer period.

The Neolithic Age.

We now pass to the later Stone or Neolithic Age, with reference to which the following propositions may, I think, be regarded as satisfactorily established :—

1. There was a period when polished stone axes were extensively used in Europe.

2. The objects belonging to this period do not occur in the river-drift gravel-beds;

3. Nor in association with the great extinct mammalia.

4. They were in use long before the discovery or introduction of metals.

5. The Danish shell-mounds, or Kjökkenmöddings, belong to this period;

6. As do many of the Swiss lake-dwellings;

7. And of the tumuli, or burial-mounds.

8. Rude stone implements appear to have been in use longer than those more carefully worked.

9. Hand-made pottery was in use during this period.

10. In Central Europe, the ox, sheep, goat, pig, and dog were already domesticated.

11. Agriculture had also commenced.

12. Flax was cultivated and woven into tissues.

13. At least two distinct races already occupied Western Europe.

1. That there was a period when polished axes and other implements of stone were extensively used in Western Europe is sufficiently proved by the great numbers in which these objects occur: for instance, the Dublin Museum contains more than |2,000, that of Copenhagen more than 10,000, and that of Stockholm not fewer than 15,000.

2. The objects characteristic of this period do not occur in the river-drift gravels. Some of the simpler ones, indeed—as, for instance, flint flakes—were used both in the Neolithic and Palæolithic periods. The polished axes, chisels, gouges, &c. are very distinct, however, from the ruder implements of the Palæolithic Age, and are never found in the river-drift gravels. Conversely, the Palæolithic types have never yet been met with in association with those characteristic of the later epoch.

Again, while the Neolithic implements are remarkably numerous in Denmark and Sweden, the Palæolithic types are absolutely unknown there. It is probable, therefore, that these northern countries were not inhabited by man during the earlier period.

3. Nor do the types of the Neolithic Age ever occur in company with the Quaternary fauna, under circumstances which would justify us in regarding them as coeval.

4. The implements in question were in use before the introduction or discovery of metal. It is a great mistake to suppose that implements of stone were abandoned directly metal was discovered. For certain purposes, as for arrow-heads, stone would be quite as suitable as the more precious substance. Flint flakes, moreover, were so useful, and so easily obtained, that they were occasionally employed even down to a very late period. Even for axes and chisels, the incontestable superiority of metal was for a while counterbalanced by its greater costliness. Captain Cook, indeed, tells us that in Tahiti the implements of stone and bone were in a very few years replaced by those of metal; a stone hatchet was then, he says, ' as rare a thing as an iron one was eight years ago, and a chisel of bone or stone is not to be seen.' The rapidity with which the change from stone to metal is effected depends on the supply of the latter. In the above case, Cook had with him abundance of metal, in exchange for which the islanders supplied his vessels with great quantities of fresh meat, vegetables, and other more questionable articles of merchandise. The introduction of metal into Europe was certainly far more gradual; stone and metal were long used side by

side, and archæologists are often too hasty in referring stone implements to the Stone Age. It would be easy to quote numerous instances in which implements have been, without any sufficient reason, referred to the Stone Age, merely because they were formed of stone. The two Stone Ages are characterised not merely by the use of stone, but by the use of stone to the exclusion of metal. I cannot therefore too strongly impress on archæologists, *that many stone implements belong to the metallic period.* Why, then, it will be asked, may they not all have done so? and this question I will now endeavour to answer.

5. The Danish shell-mounds are the refuse heaps of the ancient inhabitants, round whose dwellings the bones and shells of the animals on which they fed gradually accumulated. Like a modern dustheap, these shell-mounds contain all kinds of household objects—some purposely thrown away as useless, but some also accidentally lost. These mounds have been examined with great care by the Danish archæologists, and especially by Professor Steenstrup. Many thousand implements of stone and bone have been obtained from them; and as, on the one hand, from the absence of extinct animals, and of implements belonging to the Palæolithic Age, we conclude that these shell-mounds do not belong to that period, so, on the other hand, from the absence of all trace of metal, we are justified in referring them to a period when metal was unknown.

6. The same arguments apply to some of the Swiss lake-dwellings, the discovery of which we owe to Dr. Keller, and which have been so admirably studied by Desor, Morlot, Troyon, and other Swiss archæologists. A glance at the Table A. will show that, while in some of them objects of metal are very abundant, in others, which have been not less carefully or thoughtfully explored, stone implements are met with to the exclusion of metallic ones. It may occur, perhaps, to some, that the absence of metal in some of the lake-villages, and its presence in others, is to be accounted for by its scarcity—that, in fact, metal will be found when the localities shall have been sufficiently searched. But a glance at the table will show that the settlements in which metal occurs are deficient in stone implements. Take the same number of objects from Wangen and Nidau, and in the one case 90 per cent. will be of metal, while in the other the whole number are of stone or bone. This cannot be accidental—the numbers are too great to admit of such a hypothesis; nor can the fact be accounted for by contemporaneous differences of civilisation, because the localities are too close together; neither is it an affair of wealth, because we find such articles as fishhooks, &c., made of metal.

7. We may also, I think, safely refer some of the tumuli or burial-mounds to this period. When we find a large tumulus, the erection of which must have

been extremely laborious, it is evident that it must have been erected in honour of some distinguished individual; and when his flint daggers, axes, &c.—which, from the labour and difficulty of making them, must have been of great value—were deposited in the tomb, it is reasonable to conclude, that if he had possessed any arms of metal, they also would have been buried with him. This we know was done in subsequent periods. In burials of the Stone Age the corpse was either deposited in a sitting posture, or burnt, but rarely, if ever, extended at full length.

8. It is an error to suppose that the rudest flint implements are necessarily the oldest. The Palæolithic implements show admirable workmanship. Moreover, every flint implement is rude at first. A bronze celt is cast perfect; but a flint implement is rudely blocked out in the first instance, and then, if any concealed flaw comes to light, or if any ill-directed blow causes an inconvenient fracture, the unfinished implement is perhaps thrown away. Moreover, the simplest flint-flake forms a capital knife, and accordingly we find that some simple stone implements were in use long after metal had replaced the beautifully-worked axes, knives, and daggers, which must always have been very difficult to make. The period immediately before the introduction of metal may reasonably be supposed to be that of the best stone implements, but the use of the simpler ones lingered

long. Moreover, there are some reasons to believe that pierced stone axes are characteristic of the early metallic period.

9. Hand-made pottery is abundant in the shell-mounds and the lake-villages, as well as in the tumuli which appear to belong to the Stone Age. No conclusive evidence that the potter's wheel was yet in use has been discovered.

10. The dog is the only domestic animal found in the shell-mounds; but remains of the ox, sheep, goat, and pig appear in the lake-villages. There is some doubt about the horse; and the barn-door fowl, as well as the cat, was unknown.

11. The presence of corn-crushers, as well as of carbonised wheat, barley, and flax, in the Swiss lake-dwellings, proves that agriculture was already pursued with success in Central Europe. Oats, rye, and hemp were unknown.

12. Tissues of woven flax have been found in some of the Swiss lake-villages.

13. At least two forms of skull, one long and one round, are found in the tumuli which appear to belong to this period. Until now, however, we have not a single human skull from the Danish shell-mounds, nor from any Swiss lake-dwelling, which can be referred with certainty to this period.

The Bronze Age.

1. The Neolithic Age was followed by a period when bronze was extensively used for arms and implements.

2. Stone, however, was also in use, especially for certain purposes, as, for instance, for arrow-heads, and in the form of flakes for cutting.

3. Some of the bronze axes appear to be mere copies of the earlier stone ones.

4. Many of the Swiss lake-villages and of the tumuli belong to this period.

5. This is shown, not merely by the presence of metal, but also by other considerations.

6. The pottery of the Bronze Age is better than that of the earlier period.

7. Gold, amber, and glass were used for ornamental purposes.

8. Silver, lead, and zinc appear to have been unknown.

9. This was also the case with iron.

10. Coins were not in use.

11. Skins were probably worn, but tissues of flax and wool were also in use.

12. The ornamentation of the period is characteristic, and consists of geometrical markings.

13. The handles of the arms, the bracelets, &c., indicate a small race.

14. Writing appears to have been unknown;

15. Yet there was a very considerable commerce.

16. It is more than probable that the knowledge of bronze was introduced into, not discovered in, Europe.

1. It is admitted by all that there was a period when bronze was extensively used for arms and implements. The great number of such objects which are preserved in our museums places this beyond a doubt.

2. It would, however, be a mistake to suppose that stone implements were entirely abandoned. Arrow-heads and flakes of flint are found abundantly in some of those Swiss lake-villages which contain bronze. In these cases, indeed, it may be argued, that the same site had been occupied both before and after the introduction of bronze. The evidence derived from the examination of tumuli is, however, not open to the same objection, and in these objects of bronze and of stone are very frequently found together. Thus I have shown, by an analysis of the investigations recorded by Mr. Bateman, that in three-fourths of the tumuli containing bronze (29 out of 37) stone objects also occurred.

3. Some of the bronze axes appear to be mere copies of the stone ones. Such simple axes of iron are still used in Central Africa, where no evidence of a Bronze Age has yet been found, but in Europe they are not met with.

4. Many of the Swiss lake-villages belong to this period. The Table B. (very kindly drawn up, at my request, by Dr. Keller) places this beyond a doubt, and gives a good idea of the objects in use during the Bronze Age, and the state of civilisation during that period.

5. The absence of metal, though the principal, is by no means the only point which distinguishes the Stone Age villages from those of the Bronze period. If we compare Nidau, as a type of the last, with Moosseedorf, as the best representative of the former, we shall find that, while bones of wild animals preponderate in the one, those of tame ones are most numerous in the latter. The vegetable remains point also to the same conclusion. Even if we knew nothing about the want of metal in the older lake-villages, we should still, says Professor Heer, be compelled from botanical considerations to admit their greater antiquity.

Moreover, so far as they have been examined, the piles themselves tell the same tale. Those of the Bronze Age settlements were evidently cut with metal; those of the earlier villages with stone, or at any rate with rude and blunt instruments.

6. The pottery was much better than that of the earlier period. A great deal of it was still hand-made, but some is said to show marks of the potter's wheel.

7. Gold, amber, and glass were used for ornamental purposes.

8. Silver, zinc, and lead, on the contrary, were
apparently unknown.

9. The same appears to have been the case with
iron.

10. Coins have never been found with bronze
arms. To this rule I only know of three apparent
exceptions. Not a single coin has been met with in
any of the Swiss lake-villages of this period.

11. The dress of this period no doubt still consisted in great part of skins. Tissues of flax have
been found, however, in some of the lake-villages,
and a suit of woollen material (consisting of a cloak,
a shirt, two shawls, a pair of leggings, and two caps)
was found in a Danish tumulus which evidently
belonged to the Bronze Age; as it contained a sword,
a brooch, a knife, an awl, a pair of tweezers, and a
large stud, all of bronze, besides a small button of tin,
a javelin-head of flint, a bone comb, and a bark box.
We have independent evidence of the same fact in
the presence of spindle-whorls.

12. The ornamentation on the arms, implements,
and pottery is peculiar. It consists of geometrical
patterns—straight lines, circles, triangles, zigzags, &c.
Animals and vegetables are very rarely attempted,
and never with success.

13. Another peculiarity of the bronze arms lies in

the small size of the handles. The same observation applies to the bracelets, &c. They could not be used by the present inhabitants of Northern Europe.

14. No traces of writing have been met with in any finds of the Bronze Age. There is not an inscription on any of the arms or pottery found in the Swiss lake-villages, and I only know one instance of a bronze cutting instrument with letters on it.

15. The very existence of bronze appears to indicate that of a considerable and extensive commerce, inasmuch as there are only two places—namely, Cornwall and the Island of Banca—whence tin can have been obtained in large quantities. There are, indeed, some other places where it occurs, as, for instance, Spain, Saxony, and Brittany, but only (now at least) in small quantities, though possibly it may once have been more abundant. The earliest source of tin was not, I think, any one of those now known to us, but it is probable that, for many centuries before our era, the principal supply was derived from Cornwall. The intercourse then existing between different parts of Europe is also proved by the great, not to say complete, similarity of the arms from very different parts of Europe.

16. Finally, as copper must have been in use before bronze, and as arms and implements of that metal are almost unknown in Western Europe, it is reasonable to conclude that the knowledge of bronze was introduced into, not discovered in, Europe.

Two distinguished archæologists have recently advocated very different views as to the race by whom these bronze weapons were made, or at least used. Mr. Wright attributes them to the Romans, Professor Nilsson to the Phœnicians. The first of these theories I believe to be utterly untenable. In addition to the facts already brought forward, there are two which by themselves are, I think, almost sufficient to disprove the hypothesis. Firstly, the word *ferrum* was employed in Latin as a synonym for a sword, which would scarcely have been the case if another metal had been generally used for the purpose. Secondly, the distribution of bronze weapons and implements does not favour such a theory. The Romans never entered Denmark; it has been doubted whether they ever landed in Ireland. Yet while more than 350 bronze swords have been found in Denmark, and a very large number in Ireland also,* I have only been able to hear of one single bronze sword in Italy. The rich museums at Florence, Rome, and Naples do not appear to contain a single specimen of those typical, leaf-shaped bronze swords, which are, comparatively speaking, so common in the North. That the bronze swords should have been introduced into Denmark by a people who never

---

* The Museum at Dublin contains 282 swords and daggers: unluckily, the number of swords is not stated separately.

occupied that country, and from a part of Europe in which they are almost unknown, is, I think, a most untenable hypothesis. It is doubtless true that a few cases are on record in which bronze weapons are said to have been, and very likely were, found in association with Roman remains. Mr. Wright has pointed out three, one of which however I cannot admit. But, under any circumstances, we must expect to meet with some such cases. My only wonder is that so few of them should exist.

As regards Professor Nilsson's theory, according to which the Bronze Age objects are of Phœnician origin, I will only say, that the Phœnicians in historical times were well acquainted with iron, and that their favourite ornamentation was of a different character from that of the Bronze Age. If, then, Professor Nilsson be correct, the bronze weapons must belong to an earlier period in Phœnician history than that with which we are partially familiar.

It would now be natural that I should pass on to the Iron Age; but the transition period between the two is illustrated by a discovery so remarkable that I cannot pass it over altogether in silence. M. Ramsauer, for many years head of the salt-mines at Hallstadt, near Salzburg, in Austria, has opened not less than 980 graves in a country apparently belonging to an ancient colony of miners. The results are described and the objects figured in an album, of which Mr. Evans and I have recently procured a copy from M. Ramsauer himself. We hope soon to make this remarkable find known in a more satisfactory manner. For the moment, I will only extract the main facts which are necessary to my present argument.

That the period to which these graves belonged was that of the transition between the Bronze and Iron Ages, is evident, both because we find cutting instruments of iron as well as of bronze, and also because both are of somewhat unusual, and we may almost say of intermediate, types. The same remark applies to the ornamentation. Animals are frequently represented, but are very poorly executed, while the geometrical patterns are well drawn. Coins are entirely absent. That the transition was from bronze to iron, and not from iron to bronze, is clear; because here, as elsewhere, while iron instruments with bronze handles are common, there is not a single case of a bronze blade with an iron handle. This shows that when both metals were in use, the iron was preferred for blades. Another interesting point in the Hallstadt Bronze is the absence of silver, lead, and zinc (excepting, of course, as a mere impurity in the bronze). This is the more remarkable, inasmuch as the presence, not only of the tin itself, but also of glass, amber, and ivory, indicates the existence of an extensive commerce.

The Iron Age.

The Iron Age is the period when this metal was first used for weapons and cutting instruments. During this epoch we emerge into the broad, and in many respects delusive, glare of history.

No one of course will deny that arms of iron were in use by our ancestors at the time of the Roman invasion. Mr. Crawfurd considers them to be more ancient than those of bronze, while Mr. Wright maintains that the bronze weapons belong to the Roman period.

I have already attempted to show, from the frequent occurrence of iron blades with bronze handles, and the entire absence of the reverse, that iron must have succeeded and replaced bronze. Other arguments might be adduced; but it will be sufficient to state broadly that which I think no experienced archæologist will deny—namely, that the objects which accompany bronze weapons are much more archaic in character than those which are found with weapons of iron.

That the bronze swords and daggers were not used by the Romans in Cæsar's times, I have already attempted to prove. That they were not used at that period by the northern races, is distinctly stated in history. I will, however, endeavour to make this also evident on purely archæological grounds. We have several important finds of this period, among which I will specially call your attention to the lake-village of La Tene, in the Lake of Neufchâtel. At this place no flint implements (excepting flakes) have occurred. Only fifteen objects of bronze have been found, and only one of them was an axe. Moreover, this was pierced for a handle, and belonged therefore to a form rarely, if ever, occurring in finds of the Bronze Age. On the other hand, the objects of iron are numerous, and comprise fifty swords, twenty-three lances, and five axes. Coins have also been met with at this station, while they are entirely absent in those of the Bronze Age.

The only other find of the Iron Age to which I will now refer, is that of Nydam, recently described at length by M. Engelhardt, in his excellent work on ' Denmark in the Early Iron Age.' At this place have been found an immense number of the most diverse objects—clothes, brooches, tweezers, beads, helmets, shields, coats of mail, buckles, harness, boats, rakes, brooms, mallets, bows, vessels of wood and pottery, 80 knives, 30 axes, 40 awls, 160 arrow-heads, 180 swords, and nearly 600 lances. All these weapons were of iron, though bronze was freely used for ornaments. That this find, as well as the very similar one at Thorsbjerg in the same neighbourhood, belonged to the Roman period, is clearly proved by the existence of numerous coins, belonging to the first two centuries after Christ, although not one has occurred in any of the Bronze Age lake-villages, or in the great find at Hallstadt.

It is quite clear, therefore, that neither bronze nor stone weapons were in use in Northern Europe at the commencement of our era.

A closer examination would much strengthen this conclusion. For instance, at Thorsbjerg alone there are seven inscriptions, either in Runes or Roman characters; while, as I have already stated, letters are quite unknown, with one exception, on any object of the Bronze Age, or in the great transition find at Hallstadt. Again, the significance of the absence of silver in the Hallstadt find is greatly increased when we see that in the true Iron Age, as in the Nydam and other similar finds, silver was used to ornament shield-bosses, shield-rims, sandals, brooches, breast-plates, sword-hilts, sword-sheaths, girdles, harness, &c. ; and also for clasps, pendants, boxes, and twee-zers, while in one case a helmet was made of this comparatively rare material.

The pottery also shows much improvement, the forms of the weapons are quite different, and the character of the ornamentation is very unlike, and much more advanced than that of the Bronze Age. Moreover, the bronze used in the Iron Age differs from that of the Bronze Age, in that it frequently contains lead and zinc in considerable quantities.

These metals have never been found, excepting as mere impurities, in the bronzes of the true Bronze Age, nor even in those of Hallstadt.

These finds, moreover, clearly show that the inhabitants of Northern and Western Europe were by no means such mere savages as we have been apt to suppose. As far as our own ancestors are concerned, this is rendered even more evident by the discoveries of those ancient British coins which have been so well described and figured by Mr. John Evans.[*]

In conclusion, I would venture to suggest that the Government should be urged to appoint a Royal Conservator of National Antiquities. We cannot put Stonehenge or the Wansdyke into a museum— all the more reason why we should watch over them where they are; and even if the destruction of our ancient monuments should, under any circumstances, become necessary, careful drawings ought first to be made, and their removal should take place under proper superintendence. We are apt to blame the Eastern peasants who use the grand old monuments of Egypt or Assyria as mere stone-quarries, but we forget that even in our own country, Avebury, the most magnificent of Druidical remains, was almost destroyed for the profit of a few pounds; while, recently, the Jockey Club has mutilated the remain-

* *The Coins of the Ancient Britons.*

ing portion of the Devil's Dyke on Newmarket Heath, in order to make a bank for the exclusion of scouts at trial races. In this case also, the saving, if any, must have been very small; and I am sure that no society of English gentlemen would have sanctioned such a proceeding, if they had given the subject a moment's consideration.

In this short Introduction I have purposely avoided all reference to history, all use of historical data, because I have been particularly anxious to show that in Archæology we can arrive at definite and satisfactory conclusions, on independent grounds, without any assistance from history; consequently regarding times before writing was invented, and therefore before written history had commenced.

I have endeavoured to select only those arguments which rest on well-authenticated facts. For my own part, however, I care less about the results than the method. For an infant science, as for a child, it is of small importance to make rapid strides at first: and I care comparatively little how far our present views stand the test of further investigations, if only we are satisfied that our method is one which will eventually lead us to the truth.

JOHN LUBBOCK.

TABLE A.

	STONE					BRONZE								IRON							COINS
	Axes	Arrows	Flakes, &c.	Other Objects	Total	Axes	Knives	Lances	Sickles	Fish-hooks	Ornaments	Sundries	Total	Swords	Axes	Knives	Lances	Ornaments	Sundries	Total	
SWITZERLAND																					
Wangen	1100	...	260	250	1610	...	...	...	...	...	...	...	...	...	...	...	...	...	...	...	0
Moosseedorf	101	...	639	68	808	...	...	...	...	...	...	...	...	...	...	...	...	...	...	...	0
Nussdorf	1000	100	100	30	1230	...	...	...	...	...	...	...	...	...	...	...	...	...	...	...	0
Wauwyl	22	...	237	15	274	...	...	...	...	...	...	...	...	...	...	...	...	...	...	...	0
Nidau	33	...	...	335	368	23	102	27	18	109	1420	305	2004	...	...	...	...	...	...	...	0
Cortaillod	...	...	...	...	...	13	22	4	2	71	515	208	835	...	...	...	...	...	...	...	0
Estavayer	...	...	...	...	...	6	14	...	1	43	403	150	617	...	...	...	...	...	...	...	0
Corcelettes	...	...	...	...	...	1	19	2	7	...	465	16	510	...	...	...	...	...	...	...	0
Morges	...	...	...	...	...	50	20	11	11	10	108	?	210	...	...	...	...	...	1	1	0
Marin	...	...	Flakes	12 Balls	...	1 Pierced	...	...	...	...	1	13	15	50	5	4	23	more than 100	61	250	9
DENMARK																					
Nydam	...	...	...	A few Whet-stones	...	...	...	...	...	...	...	Ornaments very numerous	...	100	30	86	500 at least	?	300 at least	1000 at least	34

TABLE B.

	Nidau	Mœrigen	Estavayer	Cortaillod	Corcelettes	Auvernier	Other places	TOTAL
Celts and fragments . .	23	7	6	13	1	6	11	67
Swords	...	...	...	...	...	...	4	4
Hammers	4	...	1	...	...	...	...	5
Knives and fragments .	102	19	14	22	19	8	9	193
Hair-pins	611	53	239	183	237	22	22	1,367
Small Rings	496	28	115	195	202	14	3	1,053
Earrings	238	42	36	116	...	3	5	440
Bracelets and fragments	55	14	16	21	26	11	2	145
Fishhooks	109	12	43	71	9	2	1	247
Awls	95	3	49	98	17	...	...	262
Spiral wires	...	...	46	50	5	...	...	101
Lance-heads	27	7	...	4	2	5	2	47
Arrow-heads	...	...	5	1	...	...	...	6
Buttons	...	1	28	10	10	...	...	49
Needles	20	2	3	4	1	...	...	30
Various ornaments . .	15	5	7	18	3	1	...	49
Saws	...	...	3	...	...	...	...	3
Daggers	...	...	...	...	...	...	2	2
Sickles	18	12	1	2	7	1	4	45
Double-pointed pins . .	75	...	...	...	...	...	...	75
Small bracelets . . .	20	...	...	11	...	...	...	31
Sundries	96	3	5	16	...	...	4	124
TOTAL	2,004	208	617	835	539	73	69	4,345

TABLE C.

HALLSTADT

GRAVES WITH BODIES BURIED IN THE ORDINARY MANNER

ANTIQUITIES

No. of the Graves	Gold Ornaments	Bronze				Iron		Amber	Glass	Pottery	Stone
		Ornaments	Vessels	Sundries	Weapons	Weapons	Other Objects	Ornaments			
527	6	1471	3	35	18	161	33	165	38	334	57

GRAVES WITH BURNT CORPSES

ANTIQUITIES

No. of the Graves	Gold Ornaments	Bronze				Iron		Amber	Glass	Pottery	Different Objects
		Ornaments	Vessels	Sundries	Weapons	Weapons	Other Objects	Ornaments			
453	58	1744	179	54	91	349	41	105	35	908	100

	No. of the Graves	Gold Ornaments	Bronze				Iron		Amber	Glass	Pottery		Total
Totals	980	64	3215	182	89	109	510	74	270	73	1242		5985

PREFACE.

In placing this essay* before an enlightened Public, I feel it to be incumbent on myself to explain briefly the cause which led to its production, and to the form which it has now assumed.

Besides the study of Zoology, that of Antiquities has from my youth ever been my favourite occupation; and whilst engaged in collecting materials for my 'Scandinavian Fauna,' during frequent visits to almost all parts of the Scandinavian Peninsula, even to within the Polar Circle, I have sought to collect objects illustrative of Scandinavian Archæology.

After having, for a period of twenty-two years, been Professor of Zoology at the University of Lund, I published my first work, 'Essay on the History of Sporting and Hunting in Scandinavia' ('Utkast till Jägtens och Fiskets Historia på Scandinavien,' Lund, 1834),† in which I introduced, from the few

---

* Already in the preface to the first edition in 1838 I have explained that by primitive inhabitants I understand not only the first inhabitants, but all who lived in the country anterior to the period of history—consequently the prehistoric people of Scandinavia, of one or more tribes.

† Shortly before this time, Mr. Thomsen in Copenhagen had inserted in *Nordisk Tidskrift för Oldkyndighet* a treatise, *Om Nordiska Oldsager af Sten*, of which I did not become cognisant until my essay had already been consigned to the printer and put into type.

materials I had then at hand, the comparative method of instruction, which, under the guidance of the
illustrious Baron Cuvier, had been adopted in works
on Zoology.

My first attempt having been favourably received
by several eminent scientific men, I felt it to be my
duty to continue in the path on which I had entered.
But to be able to do this with any hopes of ultimate
success, I found that it would be necessary to visit
those foreign museums in which were preserved a
great number of such implements and weapons as are
still used at the present time by people who live in
so low a degree of civilisation that they are even yet
ignorant of the use of metals, but have for implements and weapons only stone, bone, and other hard
substances, suitable for the purpose.   I therefore
undertook, in 1836, a long journey through Copenhagen and Hamburg to London, Bristol, and Paris,
where were already to be found the richest collections of the kind which I wished to inspect—these
collections being thrown open to me with the
greatest courtesy and liberality.   I also examined
several private collections in various other places.

On my return to Sweden, I arranged the pre-
liminaries for publishing this work, which was
entitled ' Skandinaviska Nordens Urinvånare ' (The
Primitive Inhabitants of the Scandinavian North),
the first number of which was issued in 1838, the
fourth and last in 1843.*

---

* Already in the preface to the first number, I called attention to
the circumstance, that by this title were understood *all the prehistoric inhabitants of Scandinavia.*

Besides the foreign, I had already visited all the collections, both public and private, belonging to the capitals and universities of the peninsula—Stockholm, Upsala, Christiania, Bergen, Lund, &c., with several in the possession of antiquaries in the country; and I had then brought together a very considerable private collection of antiquities.

Even this my first attempt was for the most part favourably received, and, without my knowledge, translated into German by Hr. Masch, who had intended to publish it, had he not been requested by me to postpone its publication, until, as I hoped, a new edition would be ready. Hr. Masch died shortly afterwards, having made a donation of the translation to the library of the Museum at Schwerin, where it was first noticed by Professor Morlot, by whom several extracts from it were published.

Although, as above stated, this first edition was favourably received by most readers, some few voices were raised against my assertion that the inhabitants of the country were from the beginning savages,* and that the very first belonged to the same race as the Laplanders of the present time; my endeavour to interpret from historical sources the origin of the names Dwarfs, Giants (*Jotnar*), Elves, &c., which occur in ancient tales, as being people of different races, also met with considerable opposition.

---

* This occurred already in my first essay in 1834, in which mention was expressly made of *the savages' hunting in Scandinavia*. I then also endeavoured to show that our antiquities of stone, &c., were not exclusively weapons of war, as formerly believed, but principally implements for domestic purposes.

In this work our most ancient antiquities were for the first time compared piece by piece with those of existing savages. Several forms were there described for the first time which here in the North had not previously been noticed, or had been erroneously explained ; for instance, the *angling-plummet*, which was formerly called a sling-stone, whilst at the same time sketches were given of the real sling-stone, which until then was unknown ; harpoons and fishing-forks of various shapes were also sketched; hoes of stone and elk-horn were exhibited; and a long series of tools with which the stone implements were fabricated, and which I have called hammer-stones, or fashioning stones, were likewise for the first time exhibited.

I may here call the reader's attention to the similarity, or rather identity, not only of the simpler implements of stone and bone which occur amongst very distant nations in the Old and New World (see Pl. V. figs. 99–103 ; 109–111 ; 106–108), but also between instruments more or less complicated. I may also remark, that people in the same phase of civilisation are in their natural disposition very much alike ; that the savage hates the colonist, and amongst the rude races themselves, those more favoured by nature pursue and endeavour to extirpate those who are, in a physical and intellectual point of view, their inferiors. This appears to be a universal law of nature.

Certainly no country possesses so many ancient and marvellous tales as Scandinavia. The cause of this may lie in the long winter evenings, when story-telling about past times was the most cherished occupation of the people, who, dwelling in the thick and gloomy forests, filled their minds with mystic images. How marvellous are the tales which originate with rude nations we have endeavoured to show on page 208, and we may thus find the key to those of our own country. In the Eddas, the popular tales being poetised, we do not by them become acquainted with our pagan times; but by the reports of the first Christian missionaries who appeared here, by the cruel proceedings of the corsairs (vikings), and perhaps by the conduct of the Erules.

I have not ventured to divide the productions of the Stone Period into two classes, according to their age, because I have not found any unvaried lines of demarcation (as, for example, in the divisions of plants and animals) which enable me, at the inspection of each object, to determine to which division it ought to belong. I have, on the other hand, divided them according to shape and applicability, because I have found polished, unpolished, and rough-hewn stones together. I will, however, not deny that such articles of flint, which by some antiquaries are called *coast-finds*, and which are also to be seen with us in several places in Scania on the coast of the Baltic, are older than those lying in the tumuli.

Sir John Lubbock, in his 'Prehistoric Times,' pages 1 and 2, has divided prehistoric archæology into four different epochs, of which the first two are reckoned to the Stone Period, and of these the

first to the Palæolitic Period, or, as it is called by
English geologists, the drift, when man in Europe
lived together with the mammoth, the cave-bear, the
woollen-clad rhinoceros, &c.

The second, the Neolithic Period, or the age of
polished stones. To this belong the Megalithic graves,
and to the older part of it the author refers also the
kjökkenmöddings of Denmark (page 96).

I had intended to insert here the 'Bidrag till den
Svenska fornforskningens Historia under de sistför-
flutna några och trettio åren,'* which is inserted in the
preface to the former edition, chiefly as a counterpart to Mr. Hindenburg's 'Bidrag til den Danske
Archæologies Historie,' which is inserted in the
'Dansk Maanadsskrift,' 1859, page 149, and to show
what share the antiquaries on each side of the Sound
have had in bringing the science of northern antiquities to its present state; but want of space com-
pels me to defer doing so for the present; perhaps
until publishing the next volume of the present
work.

I have, on the other hand, taken the liberty to
make a few remarks, more especially intended for
those who are not professed antiquaries. These
remarks contain a few rules, which I, for my part,
will endeavour to follow when commenting on the
works of other ethnographic authors, and which I am
desirous others may follow when commenting on

* *Appendix to the History of Swedish Antiquities during some
Thirty Years past.*

mine; and I am the more anxious that these rules may be adopted, as the main object of every critical work should be that of eliciting truth.

Firstly. When my conviction leads me to reject the opinion expressed by another author on a certain subject, I think it my duty to state the reasons for my rejection, and to explain the view which, on a full consideration of all the circumstances, I consider to be the correct one.

Secondly. When I wish to refute the opinion expressed by another, it is my duty to enumerate *all* the proofs he has adduced to confirm it.

Thirdly. As witnesses throwing light upon ancient times I count not only antiquities, monuments, their different shapes, and the figures engraved upon them, but also *popular tales*, which most frequently originate from traditions, and are therefore remnants of olden times.

Fourthly. When a vicious or evil spirit is mentioned in any tale or popular tradition, I consider it always implies a reminiscence of some being who formerly, during the supremacy of a religion now rejected, was worshipped as a god. He is considered to benefit his worshippers, but to molest those that hold another religious belief. Mankind, when in a rude state, often attribute their own intolerance to their gods. Thus man creates his own god after his own image.

Fifthly. The comparative method ought always to be used; but similarities such as the presence of similar stone arrows in Scania and in Tierra del

Fuego, do not always prove one and the same origin. A sound judgment is required to draw a certain conclusion from the facts, and this can be acquired for each separate science by long experience alone.

Sixthly. Should the enquirer wish to discover whence a certain period of culture is derived, whether it was originally indigenous or introduced, he must make it clear to himself how it appeared in its first state, and what changes it assumed whilst progressing. For instance, if we wish to examine the origin of the Bronze Age, we must first clearly understand which form of bronze sword is the oldest; whether it be the handsomest and best fabricated, with elegant shapes and beautiful ornaments (double spirals), and of which the sword-hilts are invariably short, or those less artistically manufactured, with long hilts, and either plain or with ornaments entirely different from those of the former. I may be allowed to request all who may wish to determine the origin of the Bronze Period in Northern and Western Europe carefully to consider this point. If the former prove to be the oldest, and that culture was at its height when it first made its appearance here amongst a people who, until then, had no other implements and weapons than those of stone, and that it deteriorated by degrees, then it appears sufficiently evident that it was introduced.

With regard to my ethnographical essays, I am certainly desirous that they should be submitted to a just and fair criticism. Whatever, after a strict examination, may be found erroneous, I shall cheerfully abandon; having at any rate the satisfaction of feeling that I have given to men more learned than myself the clue to works of greater research and profundity than my own.

SVEN NILSSON.

Stockholm: *July* 1867.

INTRODUCTION.*

In the present volume I have endeavoured, by a new method, to gain a knowledge of the first inhabitants of the Scandinavian Peninsula, and thus to contribute in some measure to the history of the gradual development of mankind. I feel more and more convinced, that as in nature we are unable rightly to conceive the importance of individual objects without possessing a distinct view of nature, considered as a whole, so are we also unable properly to understand the signification of the antiquities of any individual country without at the same time clearly realising the idea that they are the fragments of a progressive series of civilisation, and that the human race has always been, and still is, steadily advancing in civilisation. To this conviction we are brought by experience, as well as by the analogy of the other natural sciences. *Geology*, namely, teaches us that organic nature on our earth has only progressed gradually, and by a slow development, during successive ages, and that nature's first-born living children were the lowest and most imperfect organisms, gra-

* It is to be remembered that this was written for the first edition, 1843.

dually succeeded by beings more and more cultivated, until we come to the last, which are the most perfect with which we are acquainted. *Physiology* teaches us that every individual organism, including man, continues to develope gradually under our very eyes in the same manner as the whole of organic nature, from the very lowest to the highest condition which nature has destined it to reach.

The development which is here referred to is apparently merely corporeal and material, whereas the development of the human race is spiritual and intellectual; but we ought to remember, that the corporeal is *not* the operative or essential, but the immaterial, concealed under it, whereof the material is merely the veil, visible to our outward senses. All progressive development in nature is, therefore, in reality the development of the immaterial, of the spirit, of the intellect, although its material veil, its shell only, is palpable to our eyes.

If we contemplate the subject from this point of view, we shall doubtless arrive at the conclusion, that, just as the whole of organic nature has unfolded itself from that period in creation of which the earliest productions are preserved in the transition rocks, until the present organic period of the world, and just as every human individual gradually developes both corporeally and psychologically, from his first most imperfect state until his maturity, so is also the whole human race, notwithstanding apparent or partial retrogression, constantly undergoing a gradual and progressive development. Of this even history convinces us, by showing that nations originally rude and barbarous have by degrees progressed to a higher civilisation and more *true* humanity. It is true that history occasionally seems to give evidence of a contrary result, by informing us that nations, which formerly occupied a higher stage of civilisation than others, have since sunk back into a ruder condition. But we may be assured that the degree of civilisation which a nation has *once* reached can never perish, but diffuses itself amongst others and becomes the property of mankind in general, although its first organs have decayed. It is seed sown in another and richer soil, since the first no longer brings forth sound and good fruit. Nations spring into existence, and, in their turn, decline and fall; but civilisation and humanity are steadily progressing, spreading themselves more and more, and will one day be disseminated over every spot inhabited by man.

In this light I have contemplated, and shall endeavour to work out, the subject which I have in view.

I have imagined, in order to investigate the history of the development of the human race, that one ought to search for the earliest traces of man's first appearance in every country; to follow these in order to see whither they lead, and carefully to distinguish from them the more recent footprints which may be found in the same land; thus we shall be able to discover by degrees the migrations of the different races in early times, and the progressive march of civilisation through the world. But I have also imagined that a knowledge of the primeval state of mankind or of its individual races, could not be gained by the general road of history, because the history of each nation does not begin to write its annals until the civilisation of that nation has reached a high point of development. All which lies behind that period is traditional and enveloped in obscurity. But even tradition could not have sprung into life until the first rude wants were satisfied, and until the scattered individuals had long constituted a united nation and had come into hostile collision with others. We cannot, therefore, expect to gain, either from history or even from tradition, any knowledge of the savage race which *originally* and alone appeared in any country.

Still, it may perhaps not be impossible to extend our researches concerning the human race farther back than the time to which either history or tradition throw their light. If natural philosophy has been able to seek out in the earth and to discover the fragments of an animal kingdom, which perished long before man's appearance in the world, and, by comparing the same with existing organisms, to place them before us almost in a living state, then also ought this science to be able, by availing itself of the same comparative method, to collect the remains of human races long since passed away, and of the works which they have left behind, to draw a parallel between them and similar ones, which still exist on earth, and thus cut out a way to the knowledge of circumstances which *have been*, by comparing them with those which still exist. It is by following this method that we shall begin to investigate this subject, during which, however, we have at our command more elements for comparison than the geologist; we have not only skeletons and skulls,* but also implements, weapons, buildings, &c., all of which we shall compare with similar objects still existing and still in use. Farther on in our researches tradition and superstition meet us; the latter a religious tradition, although, like profane tradition, it has often forgotten its *real* signification. We shall avail ourselves of all these elements as means for facilitating our researches in order to reach the goal to which we aspire, namely, to contribute to the history of the intellectual and social development of the human race.

But although we may confidently hope, provided continual researches are instituted in many countries, to penetrate by this road far back into the earliest history of the human race, still we can never obtain any knowledge of the *first origin* of our race. Thus far science can never penetrate. It is in this respect the same with the whole race as with the individual; no mortal knows *how* life was kindled. Nature has thrown a veil over this mystery, which mortal eye cannot pierce. Natural philosophy cannot show us *how* man was created. If any philosopher should attempt to solve this problem, the answer would be mere guesswork, and could not be the result of researches made in the realms of nature. The natural

---

* Hitherto these have unfortunately not been preserved as often as might and ought to have been the case.

philosopher, as such, cannot, as a result of his investigations, even answer this question, whether only *one* couple, man and woman, was created in the beginning, or whether at the Almighty's command thousands sprang into life at one and the same time; whether this took place only ou *one* spot of the earth, and at one and the same moment, or whether the life-giving rays of the Creator's sun fell upon the dust in different places and at different periods of time: concerning all this the philosopher can only tell us what to him appears to be *most probable.* But he can no doubt see, that according to the idea which he generally attaches to the word *species*, the whole human race, from pole to pole, constitutes one and the same species, however much it may be divided into distinct (so-called) races, differing more or less both physically and intellectually, both in outward form, and in natural disposition.

The first origin of the human race cannot therefore become the subject of our investigations. These cannot go farther back than to the period when man was already scattered over the earth, and only from this period can we trace and follow his gradual development up to the present day.

This gradual development of the human race can be perhaps most clearly represented under the image of an individual in his childhood, his youth, his manhood, and his old age. Mankind appears, then, before our imagination first as a *child*, with childhood's lovely innocence, but in its budding development, also with childhood's guileless tricks; * then as a *youth*, with the spirit of liberty, generosity, and frank open honesty of juvenile years, but also with their thoughtless rashness; then as a *man*, with courage to defend his own right and that of others, and to execute with zeal and energy the plans which he has formed for his sphere of activity; and lastly, as the *old man*, more and more regulating his occupations, cautiously weighing and calculating his enterprises,

* Should this view be correct, the natural philosopher may imagine that there existed a period when the whole human race, as well as the individual, possessed no articulate language,[1] and that a language was created only gradually, as in the case of children; in the beginning partly by interjections and partly by imitating the sounds of the animals or objects which they wanted to denote. It may perhaps be advanced, in confirmation of this supposition, that the oldest languages are those poorest in words, employing one and the same word to denote a number of various objects, and languages have evidently arisen in the same manner as when a child begins to form itself a language, by trying to find sounds or words for its feelings and ideas. The child calls the dog *Bow-wow*, the sheep *Baa-baa*, the cow *Boo*, and so on. In Greek, the sheep is called *Bä* (ka), the cow *Bu* (z), and so on. There is in every language a smaller or greater number of words which imitate sounds (so-called *nomina onomatopoietica*), which seem to show how a language has sprung up. That such words constitute only a fraction of the whole stock of words in a language, does not refute this supposition, because the only question there is, how a language has been created, and here, as in every other case, the beginning is the most difficult part.

But be this as it may, at all events it is absurd to suppose that the first language was *poetry*. I must emphatically dispute such fantastic opinions, and shall endeavour in the course of this work to prove their absurdity.

---

[1] I now find the same idea expressed already by Diodorus Siculus, lib. i. cap. 8, 3. 'Voce autem ad huc confusa et nihil significante pedetentim verba articulata pronuntiando, et signis unquamque rem subjectam notando elocutionem tandem rerum omnium sibi notam fecerunt.'

and carefully managing his property. In how far these traits of the various stages of development of the individual can be applied to the whole human race, we shall see in the following disquisition.

The earliest tribes, of which we find traces in every country, show by what they have left behind, as far as we have been able to discover hitherto, that they have belonged to a race of beings standing on the very lowest point of civilisation: mountain grottoes, sub-terranean caves, or stone caverns, their dwellings; rough-hewn stone-flakes, their hunting and fishing implements; no domesticated animals except the dog; no cattle, no agriculture, no written language. Be-tween this, the lowest state in which we can imagine human beings, and the most cultivated state of society which they are able to attain, there are many inter-mediate degrees or stages of development.

Every nation has had, or has, four stages to pass through, before attaining its highest social develop-ment. It shows itself either as *savage*, as *nomad*, as agriculturist, or as possessing a written language and coined money, and labour distributed amongst the various members of society.

1. *The savage* has few other than material wants, and these he endeavours to satisfy only for the moment. To appease hunger for the day; when requi-site, to protect his body against heat or cold; to prepare his lair for the night; to follow the instinct of propagation, and instinctively to guard and tend his offspring—this constitutes all his care, all his enjoy-ment. He thinks and acts only for the day which

is, not for the day which is *coming*. In this state man is necessarily a hunter and fisherman, especially in zones where fruits and berries are scarce, or totally wanting during the greater part of the year. The savage has, therefore, no other alternative; he is compelled to fish and to hunt, or he must perish. In moments of necessity man has ample resources within himself; the savage finds everywhere materials for implements of fishing and the chase, and necessity teaches him how to fabricate and employ them. The earliest hunting implements of stone in every country are synchronous with the first appearance of the savage there, since he required at once the flesh of wild animals for food, their skin for clothing, and water for drinking. Even amongst the savages, also, we find traces of religion. Experience gradually awakens reflection; hunger is a troublesome guest, but is sure to call, when for a day or two the savage has not succeeded in killing any game. The prudent thought then suggests itself to him of saving a portion of the abundance of the day, and still more, that of carrying away the young calf or fawn, whose mother he has perhaps killed in the chase; and collecting several more of them, and forming at last a herd, he becomes

2. A *herdsman* (nomad), subsisting chiefly on the produce of his herds; the flesh of domestic animals his food, milk his beverage, skins his clothes. The chase and fishing, formerly his *chief*, now become his *occasional* occupations. There are various kinds of nomads; some of them have fixed habitations during

all seasons, grazing their herds in the fields and in the neighbouring forests; others have fixed habitations only in the winter, migrating in summer with their tents from place to place; others, again, have no fixed habitations, roving about continually with their herds, living in movable huts or sheds on wheels, *drawn* by cattle, or in tents stretched on poles, and *carried* on the back of their cattle during their wanderings. When the grass-fodder begins to fail in one locality, the nomad breaks up his encampment, and drives his herds to others. There are no boundaries of possession; property is restricted to tents and herds. Distant excursions are undertaken, frequently also forays: the nomad is more ready to attack than to suffer himself to be attacked.* Every family forms itself into a separate horde, in which the oldest member (the father of the family) is the chieftain or head; the government is patriarchal. Then come tradition and legend; the art of poesy springs into life; nomadic life is the element of poetry; the nomad is the *youth* of the human race. The first traces of science appear—leechcraft, botany, astronomy (?);†

* It is evident that the first nomads retained their weapons and implements of stone, because it is not very probable that the smelting and forging of metals can have originated amongst herdsmen. Native copper, however, can be used by the nomad as well as by the savage. But certain it is, that the nomads which are surrounded at a nearer or greater distance by more cultivated tribes procure from them, by barter or by pillage, both weapons and other implements.

† Thus the Chaldæan herdsmen, who in the night tended their flocks on large open plains, invented astronomy by observing the motions of the stars.

but there is as yet no written language,* no coined money; *trade* is nothing but barter.

At last he tires of his wandering life (or, rather, he is obliged to give it up, since the locality has become too small for the increasing population with its flocks); he builds sheds for his cattle, and lays up stores of fodder in barns; he burns a tract of forest-land, and sows corn in the ashes. His first *field* is a place where the trees are *felled*, a clearing in the forest, and his first *plough* a hoe. Thus the nomad gradually becomes

3. An *agriculturist*, and takes a more stable social position. The movable tent gives place to a permanently fixed dwelling; the tilled cornfields yield a richer harvest the more they are cultivated; the forests surrounding his home give him fuel and building-materials; the fields provide him with grass and winter fodder for his cattle, and even the waters yield him their tribute. The owner cultivates and guards his territory; he has devoted all his care and labour to it, it is *his own*, he *will* and he *ought* to

---

* It appears to me probable, nevertheless, that *letters* may have been invented by some tribe in this condition, as the owner's mark upon cattle or upon tents. In the Hebrew alphabet the figure of the first letter is taken from the *ox*, of the second from the *house* (or perhaps the movable tent), of the third from the *camel*, which latter seems to imply nomad life, or perhaps is a Phœnician mercantile caravan custom. But the thorough dissimilarity of the alphabets proves undeniably that they were invented by different tribes, which had no intercommunication whatever. In Scandinavia, where the first letters, no doubt, were runes, they seem to have originated only amongst the agriculturists. Neither in the Stone Age nor in the Bronze Age do we find a written language here in the North.

possess it for himself and for his descendants. Other agriculturists settle in his neighbourhood; each builds his own dwelling-house, tills his own ground, and appropriates to himself the territory which he requires; territories are laid out, *landmarks* between properties are set up; the right of possession becomes more defined, and comprises also the landed territory. The patriarchal life ceases; every landowner becomes a 'man for himself.' In order to mark his property, the owner of every fixed dwelling chooses his own private *mark*, his *bomärke*, which is the beginning of a written language.* Thus, the first written letter (whether we suppose it to have been invented by the nomad, or by the agriculturist) became a sign of right of possession,† and probably the first written line was an agreement between neighbours relating to *mine* and *thine*, consequently a *contract*—the first step towards a future *law* in a more settled state of society.

A man's cornfield and pasture-ground, his forest, his mine, his lakes and rivers, supply *most* of his

---

* At the late Assessor Silfverstråle's, in Stockholm, I saw, ten or twelve years ago, a large folio, in which, during the time when he presided as judge in the courts, if I recollect rightly, of the province of Gestrikland, he had collected *bomärken* belonging to the various farms in the province, which *bomärken*, or marks, the respective farmers or peasants affixed, by way of signature, to public and other documents. Some of these marks had a greater or less resemblance to runes. Researches in this direction might perhaps lead to a more intimate knowledge of the invention of an alphabet in Scandinavia.

† Every letter was in the beginning a hieroglyph, signifying a whole word, in the Hebraic as well as in the Runic alphabet.

wants; not indeed all, but, on the other hand, some in *superfluity*. These superfluous things, then, can be exchanged by barter, and his other needs thereby be supplied; but his personal presence on his property is constantly required; the original trade by barter thus becomes inconvenient, perhaps impossible; some article which finds a demand everywhere, and which within a small compass contains a large value, is made the means of exchanging all kinds of commodities—in other words, it becomes money. At first it derives its value from its weight, but this arrangement has its attendant inconveniences; these are obviated when a piece of this article, of a fixed weight and standard, with its value stamped thereon, becomes *coined money*. With this and with the written language the agriculturist enters upon

4. The fourth stage of civilisation, in a still better organised state of society, where labour is divided amongst its various members. Different professions (sometimes *ranks* so called) arise. Some men occupy themselves in tilling the ground, working the mines, managing the flocks, &c.; others sell superfluities, and procure what is wanting by means of barter or trade with other communities and districts; others, again, defend the property of the community against foreign and domestic foes; and, lastly, others promote intelligence, education, and the cultivation of the mind, and a governor or chief is elected to watch over the whole, and to secure and guarantee the rights of all. Thus the *nation* is enabled, through the organisation of society, to fulfil more and more completely its

allotted mission—to attain the highest degree of culture and the highest stage of civilisation.

I have deemed it incumbent upon me to draw this little sketch, in order to give a short review of the course of development, which I believe mankind in general to have passed through from its first dissemination over the globe up to the present time. Frequently the so-called savage state—the childhood of the human race—is overlooked; one begins with the poetical stage of development—the youthful age of the human race—whereby, according to my opinion, many erroneous ideas have unavoidably been entertained, and the full unravelling of this subject, so important to the history of the development of the human race, has been long delayed.

In the present work I shall, as far as I may be able, endeavour to delineate the first two of the above-mentioned stages.

Whatever errors may be found in this work—and it seems impossible to avoid such in a book of this nature—I hope the courteous reader will mildly judge, and, with his greater knowledge, set right: through such corrections, even my very mistakes will be made to tend to the further development of the subject.

CONTENTS.

CHAPTER VI.

CHAPTER VII.

LIST OF PLATES.

PLATE I.

PLATE II.

PLATE III.

FIG.

41. Harpoon with fixed point, made of bone, with a sharp stone or shell at the point, from the Kurile Islands.
42. Harpoon point. North America.
43. Harpoon point of flint, found in Scania.
44. Flint Spear.
45. Short flint Arrowhead.
46. Harpoon point. North America.
47. Short quartz Arrowhead.
48. Harpoon point of flint, found in Scania.
49. Harpoon with stone point, illustrating the mode of attachment.
50. Bone Harpoon with immovable stone point, found in ancient Esquimaux sepulchre in Greenland.
51. Bone Harpoon, found in a similar sepulchre.
52. Bone Harpoon with movable flint point, from the Kurile Islands.
53. Bone Harpoon with movable

FIG.

flint point, from the Kurile Islands.
54. Flint Spearhead, from Point Barrow, now in the British Museum.
55. Spearhead from Scania.
56. Bone Spear, from the East coast of Greenland, now in the Museum at Bristol.
57. Spearhead from Scania.
58. Bone Spear, found near Högemölla in Scania.
59. Slatestone Spear, from Kolmarden, now in the Museum of the Academy of Antiquities in Stockholm.
60. Flint Knifeblade. North of Europe.
61. Flint Spear. Scania.
62. Ditto ditto.
63. Flint Knife with stone handle. Scania.
64. Ditto ditto.
65. Stone Knife, from New Zealand, now in the British Museum.
66. Flint Knife. Scania.
67. Part of stone Knife. ditto.
68. Bone Spear. Sweden.

PLATE IV.

69. Bone Harpoon. Scania.
70. Bone Harpoon, from Terra del Fuego.
71. Bone Harpoon, found in a Scanian peat bog.
72. Bone Harpoon, from the Périgord caves.
73. Bone Harpoon, from a bog in South Scania.
74. Bone Harpoon, from the island of Seeland.

75. Leister, from the north-west coast of North America.
76. Half of a similar Spear, also from North America.
77. Leister, from North America, now in the Museum at Copenhagen.
78. The same.
79. Half of a similar implement, found in the peat bog of Felsmoose, in Scania.

PLATE V.

PLATE VI.

PLATE VI.—*continued.*

PLATE VII.

PLATE VIII.

PLATE XII.

PLATE XIII.

PLATE XIV.

PLATE XV.

PLATE XVI.

STONE AGE.

CHAPTER I.

COMPARISON BETWEEN THE IMPLEMENTS OF SAVAGE NA-
TIONS AND THE ANTIQUITIES OF STONE AND OF BONE
FOUND IN SCANDINAVIA.

EVERYBODY is aware that in Scandinavia, as well
as in many other countries, objects of stone are
occasionally met with, which have evidently been
fashioned by the hand of man for some special purpose. If we carefully examine a collection of such
antiquities, we shall not fail to recognise amongst
them forms resembling some of those implements
which are still in use, or have been used within the
memory of man, by peasants and fishermen. The implements most frequently met with are the axe, the
hollow adze, the chisel, the harpoon, the arrow, and
others; and it is scarcely possible that their nature can
be misunderstood by anyone who is acquainted with
the form of these implements when made of iron, and
who can imagine what they must be like when formed
of stone. Once convinced of this, it must be easy
to understand that people who employed stone for

implements of daily use must have been ignorant of
the use of metals, and were consequently in so low
a stage of human civilisation, that they resembled those whom we commonly designate as *savages*.* But if this be admitted—and it can with diffi.
culty be contested—then it is evident that the best
means of gaining an accurate and complete knowledge of these implements, of the manner in which
they were helved and used, of the work done with
them, &c., is to enquire whether similar implements
are still in use amongst savage tribes now living, and
to discover how they are employed; since, if we find
amongst them implements exactly similar, both in
shape and substance, we may safely conclude that
they were used in a similar way; nor can we err
if from this we deduce that the mode of life and
the degree of civilisation of the savage races still
living is essentially similar to that of those tribes
who inhabited our Scandinavian North some thousands of years ago, but have long since disappeared.

* This word is here taken in its most general sense, and com-
prehends the different degrees of civilisation, from the homeless
itinerant life in the forests to that in hordes with fixed dwellings
and burial-places. That even the earliest inhabitants of Scandinavia
long remained in one or other of these low grades of civilisation, we
infer from the entire want of metals among the remains of their implements and arms, whereas implements formed of stone are found
in great numbers. In this respect they resembled many tribes still
living, who remain in such a low grade of civilisation as to be ignorant of the fabrication and use of metals, and who therefore employ
implements of stone, bone, shell, or other hard and easily accessible
substances; which, however, they invariably throw aside as soon as
they are able to procure implements of metal.

I shall endeavour to draw such a comparison as far as it is possible to do so. But I encounter at the very outset the great difficulty that, as far as I am aware, not even one of the savage nations now living has yet been studied or described from a truly scientific, that is to say, from a comparative ethnological point of view. All that is hitherto known of them is more or less fragmentary, and the various samples of their implements now found in the museums of Europe consist, for the most part, of scattered specimens which have by chance fallen into the hands of travellers, and of which the proper and principal use is not always known. I have had an opportunity of examining, for this purpose, very extensive ethnological collections in Denmark, Germany, England, France, and elsewhere, which have been thrown open to me with the greatest liberality; but I must confess I have nowhere found *all* that I looked for. I have, moreover, made the acquaintance of many highly intelligent scientific men abroad, who have lived a longer or shorter time amongst savage nations. Through them I have gathered much information of great interest and importance, of which I shall avail myself in this treatise; but none of those I have hitherto met with have been able to enlighten me on all those smaller matters concerning which, for the purpose of comparison, I was anxious to obtain information. Their answer has always been that these subjects had not attracted their attention. In illustration of this, I will mention one instance only; namely, that I have not yet seen in any ethnological collection, nor been able to obtain from any of those who have visited regions where stone implements are used by the natives, any description of the form of the stone implement which the savages evidently made use of in order to shape their flint spears and arrow-heads, and to sharpen them again when they became blunted.*

There are thus, on the one hand, great deficiencies in our knowledge of the implements of those savage tribes which still inhabit Australia and America, and on the other, new forms are constantly discovered amongst the stone implements dug up in Sweden. The materials available for a comparison being then up to the present moment very imperfect on both sides, I cannot hope, in the present case, to produce a complete work—not even in any part of ethnology —but merely an imperfect sketch : enough, however, I hope, to justify my conviction that by the combined exertions of the many, a new field for human know-ledge can be opened through this science, and that if ever we shall succeed in obtaining an exact knowledge of the origin and dissemination of the various na-tions, it must be by these means, namely, by the help of *comparative ethnology.* I cannot coincide in the opi-nion which I have frequently heard maintained, that all endeavours in this direction are as yet premature: the first attempt must always be unsatisfactory, but it induces fresh research, directs our attention to new objects, and leads ultimately, by its very imperfec-tions, to more profound and more complete results.†

* See Note 1.   † This was written in 1838.

I have said before that nobody has been able to
show me the instrument which our savage predecessors
made use of for fashioning their stone axes and spear-
heads. Such weapons, for the most part made of
flint, and chiefly found in the earth or in peat-bogs,
have long been known in Sweden and other parts
of Europe; but it was difficult to understand how it
had been possible to give them their shape, because
they were often made with great skill and sometimes
even with elegance. Strange as were the notions entertained regarding the use to which these flint articles had been turned, they were not more strange than
the extravagant hypothesis which people set up with
regard to the manner in which they had been manufactured. They fancied that in past ages some means
had been discovered for softening the flint, so that it
could be wrought like wood, or any other still softer
material, and that it could thus be easily made to
take any desired form. We find ideas such as these
expressed even in old and learned antiquarian writings. When the absurdity of this had been made
manifest, it was maintained that those who manufactured the beautiful and elegant weapons which
were occasionally exhumed, must, at any rate, have
employed steel instruments for such a purpose; but
as this notion, which has not yet been entirely era-
dicated, throws many difficulties in the way, not
only of the proper classification of antiquities, but also
of a true comprehension of the standard of civilisation in those nations or tribes which have fabricated
and employed these flint articles, I feel justified in

endeavouring to refute the idea. We have in Sweden
many beautiful flint knives, &c., which have been
found in the gallery-graves in West Göthland, and
which, therefore, owe their existence to an age far
anterior to the discovery of metal of any kind. This
seems to be an incontestable proof that the said flint
articles, though elegantly shaped, were made with
stone instruments. We must therefore look for such
instruments amongst the stone antiquities.

When, more than forty years ago, I first began
to collect, I found here and there stones which
had evidently been fashioned by the hand of man
for some special purpose, and which showed distinct traces of strokes or knocks against some other
equally hard, but more brittle stone. Having from
my earliest youth made a practice of chipping flint-
stones, and giving them any shape which I desired, I
was able to recognise in these stone hammers the
instruments by means of which the flint weapons had
in ancient times been made. I hope the reader will
not take it amiss if I refer to my own experience,
gained a great many years ago, more especially since,
so far as I know, I was the first who directed attention
to the instrument by means of which flint implements
were made: and I think it important to have a knowledge of this instrument in order to be able to form a
clear idea of the degree of civilisation of the people
by whom these articles were made. I shall here take
the liberty of stating the means by which I gained
this knowledge. From my earliest youth I have had
an irresistible taste for hunting and sporting, and

during more than twenty years I made use of a fowling-piece with the old-fashioned flint lock.   I never
bought my gun-flints, because, when a boy, I used
a small gun, which no purchased flints would fit.
Besides, the screw of the cock was fixed in such a
manner that I was obliged to knock a semicircular
notch into the back of the flint for the reception of
the screw, in order to hold the flint firmly.   For this
reason I always chipped the flints myself, generally
while on my shooting excursions, which I then made
in the south of the province of Scania, where flint-
stones are abundant.   Whenever in want of a gun-
flint, I first selected a large flint; I then looked
out for a boulder of a suitable size, and of compact
hard granite, or quartz-sandstone; with this I split
the flint into flakes, more or less thin, and of course
with sharp edges.   Having selected one or more
splinters suitable for my purpose, I went to a large-
sized granite-stone, using it as a support for the
splinter, which I held in my left hand, while with my
right, in which I held the hammer-stone, I managed,
by means of some projecting corner or blunt point of
the same, to chip the edges of the splinter into a gun-
flint of the desired form; lastly, I knocked out the
notch for the screw in the back of the flint.   But
it was of the utmost importance that, during the
operation, the point of the splinter on which I was
operating should rest upon the support, as otherwise
the splinter would instantly break.   My habit of
shaping the flint in this way, by means of a piece of
granite or quartz sandstone, enabled me at once to

recognise the stone hammer which the aborigines of Scandinavia made use of to chip out their flint implements. The first which attracted my attention was that drawn on Pl. I. fig. 6. It consists of a hard quartz-sandstone, and, when found in the Kranke Lake, in Scania, bore marks which looked as fresh as if they had only been made a day. It is now preserved in the Museum at Lund, and shows clearly how it was used. Necessity taught *me* this art, and necessity was also the teacher of the first inhabitants of Sweden. All their flint axes were at first shaped, often very tastefully (Pl. VII. fig. 157), by means of a large hammer-stone before they were ground. Every flint implement, indeed, shows the way in which it was made. Take, for instance, the fish-hook (Pl. II. fig. 28), which was first by a single stroke chipped off as a flake from the flint-block; the workman then resting it on a firm support, and chipping out first one flat side and then the other. I presume that he began by knocking or chipping out the concave side, as the most difficult; but if in doing this he had not been exceedingly careful to keep the point upon which he was operating resting upon the supporting stone, the hook would instantly have broken. In the same manner were made the square-edged arrow-heads (Pl. II. figs. 36, 37) from flint-flakes, by first dividing them into lengths and then fashioning the edges of each piece; in the same manner also, the base, or hind part of the arrow-points was chipped into shape. But the edges of the javelin-heads, spears, and knives

(Pl. III. and IV.) were cut out off-hand, and without any support, although, probably, no one would now be able to make so good a flint knife as some of the better ones here drawn. Still, I consider it very probable that if a person had practised such operations from his youth, he might even now attain the same proficiency as the savage of former ages. It would be very interesting to know if those who consider iron and steel to be indispensable in the formation of flint instruments believe that any one provided with the very best steel instruments could form a flint knife—such, for instance, as that represented on Pl. III. figs. 64, 66. I do not believe it. It is not the cutting instrument, but the knack and practice that are wanting. The reason why amongst the flint implements which have been brought away from the savages on the American and South Sea Islands, the instrument with which they cut out their tools has so very rarely been found, is, probably, that the savage, after having used for the purpose a common pebble picked up from the ground, threw it away, since he was always sure of finding another equally fit for the purpose whenever he wanted it. I have, however, found, that amongst many, although perhaps not all, savage tribes, there were individuals who made for themselves special knocking-stones, and it is remarkable that these are everywhere very similar in form. After this short introduction, we will proceed to consider:

DIVISION I.—TOOLS BY MEANS OF WHICH OTHER TOOLS
AND WEAPONS OF STONE WERE MADE.

We have already mentioned that the former must
have been made of stone, because those who made and
employed them were ignorant of the use of metals.
We have likewise pointed out that all stone implements were first rough-hewn before being ground,
and we shall hereafter show that the savage, when his
spears, knives, and other stone implements became
blunted, sharpened their edges, which had previously
not been ground, but merely chipped to an edge; we
shall also show that the sharpened edges, when
blunted, were again sharpened.

The savage must therefore have had two different
kinds of instruments, one used for sharpening the edges
of his implements by chipping. them, and another
for grinding them. For this purpose he must have
been in possession of instruments which were portable, so that he could carry them with him while
hunting. Thus, amongst objects of antiquity, there
will necessarily be found two kinds of instruments; one
intended to chip out or rough-hew the edge, and the
other to sharpen it when blunt. Both kinds invariably
consist of hard stone, mostly of quartz, and occasionally
of pure crystalline quartz, or of quartz-sandstone, but
rarely of flint or gneiss. The former we shall call *hammer-stones*, or *chipping-stones*, and the latter *whetstones*.

§ 1. *Hammer-stones* (Pl. I. figs. 1–14).—There are
antiquaries who would deny that the stone imple-

ments here represented and described were used in
the manner just mentioned; but I have never heard
anyone able even to guess for what other purpose
they were used. As grindstones for iron they do not
answer; and the marks of blows found on them
were, as must be evident to everyone not totally
ignorant of the subject, occasioned by blows on some
hard brittle *stone*; not against any kind of metal
whatsoever. Similar chipping-stones are, besides,
found, from the pole to the equator, among all
nations who use stone implements. The only
objection to my view is, that similar stones have
been found among iron articles. I have hinted
that possibly these were amulets. That they were
grindstones for iron arms is, as above stated, utterly
impossible. It rests with the doubter, therefore, to
specify for what purpose they were used, according
to his opinion. On all these stones, and especially
on the originals of figs. 1, 4, 6, 11, &c., we find
at the edges marks of the purpose to which they
were formerly applied, so unmistakable, that, when
once pointed out, no further doubts can be entertained on the matter. For reasons which I shall
state more explicitly farther on, I am of opinion that
all hammer-stones, without exception, were portable,
and that the savage was in the habit of carrying
them with him while hunting. For this purpose some
of them (figs. 8–10) have a groove or furrow running
along the outline, round which probably a string was
passed, by means of which the stone was tied to the
belt; others are for the same purpose pierced through

(fig. 12), and others again, without either groove or
hole through the centre, were probably carried in a
pouch attached to the belt or otherwise. I have
already mentioned, that this kind of chipping instrument is found in all places inhabited now or formerly by savage people. Pl. I. fig. 2 is a sketch of a
hammer-stone from Greenland, the original of which
is preserved in the Museum at Copenhagen. In
shape it very closely resembles one found in Scania
(fig. 6), and with regard to the indentation on the
flat sides, another (fig. 1), also found in Scania.
Pl. I. fig. 3 is from a plaster cast, received from
Mr. Thomsen in Copenhagen; it is turnip-shaped, an-
nularly compressed, badly hewn, and with a slightly
indentated groove on one side. To this cast a label
was attached, on which was written, ' *Tool for making
Arrow-points.*'   The stone is said to have been found
on the shores of the Delaware River, together with a
great number of wrought flint articles. Hammer-
stones have also been found amongst the flints and
bones discovered by Messrs. Christy and Lartet in the
caves of Perigord, which undoubtedly belong to a
very early age and the first inhabitants of Europe.
Pl. I. fig. 13 is copied from a plaster cast in a large
collection of antiquities which these gentlemen presented to the Academy of Sciences, History, and Antiquities at Stockholm.   It is a simple boulder, on the
rounded edges of which are seen distinct traces of
blows or knocks against some hard object, probably a
flint-stone, indicating the purpose for which it was employed, and showing that it had been used with force.

If I am not mistaken, M. Lartet found a similar stone among the antiquities in the cave at Aurignac. All the others figured in the plate have been found in Sweden, and the majority of them in Scania. I divide the hammer-stones into two classes:—

1. To the first class belong those which have a furrow or notch, more or less distinct, on each of their two flat sides. In all those having a groove round the edge this notch lies with its front end more or less obliquely towards the left, and with the other end obliquely towards the right (figs. 8, 9, 10); this notch has, therefore, just that direction which would have been given to it if the stone had been tied by a strap to the belt, and if the person wearing the belt had held the stone in his left hand, and with the right hand had drawn the edge of his knife or spear across the stone. It is my opinion that this notch was not made by actual grinding, because I do not find the points of arrows, spears, and knives, or other hewn edge-tools, ground; but it may have been produced in this manner: the edges of the tools having been sharpened, by knocking them with the edge of the hammer-stone, they may have been drawn across the flat side of the stone, in order to make their teeth of an equal length. When through a magnifying-glass we examine a flint knife or spear-point, not used after being sharpened, we feel strengthened in this belief: still, it is a mere supposition, a mere probability, and must remain so until something similar can be shown in the stone implements, of which, for instance, even now the North

American Indians make use for fashioning their flint spear and arrow-points, and which, as we shall see, perfectly resemble those found here. Meanwhile, in whatever manner this notch may have been made, it is certain that the stone was used for chipping or shaping flint implements: this is distinctly seen in them all, especially in those which have no groove round the edge, and which, consequently, have not been attached to a string or strap, and with which, therefore, heavier blows could be dealt. The originals of the sketches (Pl. I. figs. 1–7, &c.) have no groove, the narrow sides consisting of a flat-ground even surface, forming an angle, or rounded edge, with flat broader sides. It is on the narrow side, or edge, especially in figs. 1, 4, 6, 9, 11, &c., that we find unmistakable marks of strokes dealt with it upon the flint tools, flint being equally hard, but much more brittle than quartz-stone, of which the hammer-stone consists. These marks we see on both side-edges, and they are particularly evident at the corners, with which the heaviest blows have been dealt. It is, moreover, very remarkable, that while, as mentioned above, the notch invariably lies more or less obliquely upon those stones which are surrounded by a groove, and which have been tied to the belt by a string or strap, it always, on the contrary, lies lengthwise upon those which are without a groove, and which therefore, while they were used, were not attached to any string (Pl. I. figs. 6, 7). Those hammer-stones which have a notch on the side are of various shapes. They are sometimes, as already mentioned, provided with a groove round the edge (figs. 8, 10), and sometimes, but very rarely, the groove is double. Frequently both sides are of equal length; but sometimes one side is longer than the other (fig. 8). All are generally elliptical, and more or less tapering towards both ends ; or they are oval and rounded, as in fig. 10. In some instances they are without a similar groove, being bordered instead by a perfectly flat surface (fig. 7). They are occasionally (as in fig. 7) egg-shaped, and sometimes square (as in fig. 6).

It has been supposed by some that the hammer-stones in this last group belong to the Iron Age, on account of their never having been found in the old Stone Age sepulchres. But it is certain that these *hones*, consisting of a hard kind of stone, most fre·quently of quartz or of quartz-sandstone, could never have been employed for sharpening implements made of iron. Moreover, they always show distinct marks of blows against some hard stone.

2. Amongst the second group of portable hammer-stones we class those which are provided with two or more round indentations, in order that they may be held more securely between the fingers while being used (Pl. I. figs. 1–5). If we examine such a stone more minutely—for instance, the original of fig. 4—it is scarcely possible that we should mistake the purpose for which it was used. We see on its edges the most distinct traces of blows against some other hard stone, while the sides are perfectly smooth and untouched. This is so evident that it cannot escape our notice when we have once perceived it. We find

some hammer-stones which have only one indentation
on each side; these are partly oval (fig. 1).   The indentations go occasionally quite through the stone (fig.
12), partly spherical (fig. 14), partly square (fig. 2).
We also find others provided with several indentations,
and of these some are nearly spherical, or of a round
cubical form, with six indentations (fig. 5); others are
of an oblong cubical form (fig 4).   All these tools are
made of hard and heavy stones, and to all of them
the savage has, by chipping, sharpening, and drilling,
given the form which he considered to be the most
suitable.   We will now endeavour to describe how
he sharpened and drilled them.

On the banks of his fisheries he picked up a flattened silicious stone, rounded by the action of water,
and this he employed as a hammer-stone; sometimes
he drilled an excavation in the sides of it (such a
pebble is in my collection), but at other times he did
not even take this trouble, but used the pebble as a
hammer-stone just as he found it on the bank.   Such
a pebble used as a hammer-stone is the original of
fig. 11.   This pebble, or small boulder, found at the
bottom of a peat-bog in Scania, close to a stone axe
and flint spear, bears unmistakable marks of having
been used for the above-mentioned purpose.   It appears that the hammer-stone found in the caves of
Perigord (fig. 13) was of the same substance.

§ 2. *Whetstones* (Pl. II. figs. 15–22).—These consist, as we have previously stated, of a quartzy kind
of stone, frequently of quartz-sandstone, belonging
to the old transition sandstone, occurring in strata

near Cimbritshamn, Gladsax, Andrarum, and Hardeberga, in Scania, and in many other places. On
the whetstones we always find distinct marks of
sharpening or grinding. They vary considerably in
size and shape. The majority have not been portable,
but have been lying in or beside the huts of the
natives. Some of them, however, are small, flat or
annular; such a stone may have been carried in the
pouch on hunting excursions. Occasionally large hard
sandstone blocks are met with, on which we find indentations which evidently cannot have arisen from the
action of metal, but must have been produced by stone
grinding. A block of this kind is preserved at Barse-
bäck, and belongs to the collection of the late Rev.
Mr. Hofverberg. Such whetstones have, of course, no
definite form, but they are so far interesting, that,
when found in their original position, we can be sure
that a savage who has used flint tools has lived in the
neighbourhood. The largest whetstone which I possess is of the last-mentioned hard sandstone, and was
found near Andrarum. It is an oblong square, about
2 feet long, 11 inches broad, and $7\frac{1}{3}$ inches thick, and
has, on one of its broad sides, a smooth indentation
(the effect of grinding), running lengthwise, almost of
the same length and breadth as the stone itself.

The majority of these whetstones are oblong, polygonal, thin in the middle and thicker at the ends;
some of them are from 14 to 15 inches in length (Pl.
II. fig. 15). The ground surfaces, running lengthwise, are plane, concave, or convex. Lying beside
the whetstones one sometimes finds gouges, which

exactly fit the concave excavations, showing that these are due to the process of sharpening. These whetstones have sometimes the same shape as a thick thigh-bone; and whenever we hear of a very large petrified bone being found in the earth, we may be certain that it is nothing else than such a whetstone.

Whetstones are occasionally short and nearly square, but always thinnest in the middle, the surface lengthwise being sometimes plane, sometimes concave, as in Pl. II. fig. 16, the original of which is 9 inches long. I have another in my possession which is only 4 inches long and 1 inch thick, the four sides being plane, or very little rounded. A large oblong boulder (fig. 17) has sometimes been used by the savages as a whetstone. All those now described are of the above-mentioned hard quartz-sandstone; but I have also one which is of crystalline quartz and $8\frac{1}{2}$ inches long.

It is evident that stone implements have been not only used but also made in those regions where these whetstones have been found. I may, therefore, remark, that these antiquities are found in the earth, at the bottom of fens or bogs, in rivers, lakes, and so on; not only on plains and in the coast districts of Scania, viz., Hardeberga, Flädie, Hög, Ahlstad, Yngsjö, &c., but also in the interior of the country; for instance, at Bleckemåsa, where, however, as far as I am aware, no stone implements have hitherto been found. But such whetstones are not peculiar to Scania. I have one in my possession which was

found in Småland, in the neighbourhood of the town
of Grenna, and of the same kind of sandstone as that
found *in situ* in Visingö. It is 5½ inches long by
about 2 inches in thickness.

We also find granite stones, 3–6 inches thick,
26–28 long, and 12–14 broad, the upper sides of
which have a smooth indentation, more or less distinct, arising from grinding. They are still occasionally found embedded in the earth, and are occasionally employed as troughs for watch-dogs at farms.
That they are antiquities there can be no doubt. It
is believed that the large flint axes (Pl. VII. fig.
158) and the ground wedges (Pl. IX. fig. 183) have
been worked upon them.

To this section belong also, according to my opinion,
those portable stones which have been called, although
erroneously, touchstones (Pl. II. figs. 18–20). That
they have not been used for assaying metals is evident
from their being found in certain graves which are far
older than the use of metals in the North. If gold and
silver had been known to the people who used axes
and chisels of stone, ornaments of amber, and vessels
of clay, these metals would certainly have been found
as well as such implements and ornaments; but this
has hitherto never been the case. It is, moreover,
easy to convince oneself that they were used as whetstones, because one finds now and then some with
engraved ornaments round the edges; and these ornaments have been, more or less, worn away towards the
point, evidently by grinding. It is easy to see, when

we have once been made aware of this circumstance, that they have all been worn away exactly in the same manner. This cannot possibly be owing to the assaying of metals, because, in assaying metals, it is the metal and not the stone which is worn. The stone in question must, therefore, have been a kind of whetstone. There is almost always a drilled conical excavation at the square-hewn end, and one or two such excavations on the sides, all three of which converge towards one point. We see from this that a strap, or some kind of string, was passed through each of these side holes, and was probably fastened to the stone by a knot, and that the stone was in that manner carried at the belt. Occasionally the stone is thinner towards the top end, with a hole right through it. Future discoveries may perhaps show whether these so-called touchstones were not, after all, used by the females as whetstones for their needles, &c., which were probably of bone. But still more satisfactory light will be thrown on this sub-ject when the implements of the North American Indians, and above all those of the Esquimaux, are more carefully examined.

Some very similar stones (Pl. II. figs. 21, 22) have been sent from Greenland to the Antiquarian Museum in Copenhagen. They are numbered 3872, 3925.[*]

---

[*] Since the above was written, Mr. Thomsen has informed me that these stones were used in Greenland by the women as grind-stones for their bone needles. This confirms what has already been said about the signification of similar antiquities found here in the earth.

DIVISION II.—IMPLEMENTS FOR HUNTING AND FISHING.

Having seen with what instruments the savages in Scandinavia made and sharpened their implements, we will now proceed to examine what kind of implements these were, and what were the habits of their owners, as indicated by them.

We will divide and describe specifically the different kinds of implements, to show that they were not chiefly or entirely weapons of war, as was formerly believed. We will begin with those which were evidently used for peaceable and household purposes, and which could not have served as weapons of war, but undoubtedly evince that the ancient savages here in the North lived by fishing and hunting.

§ 1. *Fish-hooks.* — Having seen above that the existing tribes of savages are, or at any rate were lately, using instruments for fashioning their implements similar to those employed by the Scandinavian savages in remote ages, we will begin by describing the fish-hooks, &c., used by the savages of the present day, and then proceed to compare them with those of the savages of former times which have been found here.

1. Pl. II. fig. 26 represents a *fish-hook of shell from Otaheite*, preserved in the British Museum.

2. *Fish-hook of Wood, with Point of Bone* (Pl. II. fig. 27).—This one is from the Kurile Islands. It is easy to understand that in countries situated in the colder zones, where no shells are found so hard and

thick as to be fit for being made into fish-hooks, these must necessarily have been made of some other hard substance, as, for instance, of wood, bone, or stone. Those found in the graves of the Greenland Esqui-maux are generally made of bone. Such fish-hooks are preserved in several ethnological museums; and even within the memory of man the inhabitants of Lapland used to fish for perch with a wooden hook. It is evident, therefore, that the Scandinavian abo-rigines, who did not know the use of metals, must have fabricated their fish-hooks out of such hard substances as were obtainable; but it is clear that those which were made of *wood* must all have de-cayed; those, on the contrary, made of flint—in the art of working which the Scandinavian savage showed great skill—have, even when lying in marshes or in water, been able effectually to resist the influence of time. But as most of the fish-hooks were probably of wood, with a point of bone or stone, we can easily explain the reason why they are so very rarely found among our antiquities.

Meanwhile, in later years, and since archæology has begun to receive attention, at least two fish-hooks of flint have been found in Scania, both on the banks of the water in which they were used.

3. *Fish-hooks of Flint.*—The first of these (Pl. II. fig. 28) was found near Lomma, on the shore of the sound (Öresund). It is in length, from the middle of the end of the shaft to the bend of the hook, about 1 inch 5″, and in breadth, from the outside of the shaft to the outside of the hook, about 1 inch 4″. At

the top it is thick and broken off straight, and below the thick end there is a scarcely noticeable incision, or neck, round which to tie the line. It tapers downwards to the point, and has been *chipped on both sides* towards the front and back; it has, therefore, as we see, been fashioned with some skill to answer its purpose.

Nobody who has seen the fish-hooks of bone, wood, or shell, made by savages, can entertain the least doubt that this one has been used for the same purpose. It is even possible to say, with tolerable accuracy, judging from its size and the place where it was found, what description of fish was principally caught with it. Amongst the fish indigenous to the sound (Öresund), on the shore of which.it was picked up, it would have been too large for the mouth of eels, flounders, or whiting, but it is suitable in every way for the Öresund codfish (*Gadus callarias*, Lin.), and this species of fish is still caught by hooks, here and elsewhere. There is little doubt, therefore, that the said flint fish-hook was used in ancient times for cod-fishing in the sound. The other fish-hook of flint (Pl. II. fig. 29) was found on the bank of the Kranke Lake, near Silfåkra. It is smaller, the length scarcely exceeding 1 inch 1″, and the breadth, from the outside of the shaft to the outside of the hook, not quite 6″. It has likewise been chipped in front and back, and the shaft widens at the top to allow the line to be tied to it. It has been used for catching smaller fish than the former. The Kranke Lake is still stocked with perch and eel, and an experienced angler has assured me that one would still be able to catch these kinds of fish with this very hook.

A fish-hook of bone has also lately been found in one of the old peat-bogs in the·south of Scania (Pl. II. fig. 30).   It is 3 inches long, and about ⅜ inch from the point of the barb to the bar.   The bar and the bend are nearly round, and flattened a little towards the top, which is broad, for the purpose of fastening the line.

It was found in a bog containing fresh water, and has no doubt been used for catching pike, of which enormously large skeletons have been found in the bogs in Scania.   I know no other fresh-water fish in Scania for which such a large sized hook could have been used.   It appears that fish-hooks made of the horns of the ox were used in Homer's time.[*]

§ 2.   *Fishing-plummets.*—Everybody practised in the art of angling is aware that, besides the hook, a *plummet* is used, especially when fishing in the open sea, or in deep waters with a strong current. We have nowadays generally recourse to lead, but before metals were known stones must have supplied its place.[†]   It is worthy of notice, and it seems to me to prove with how little method ethnographical collections have been, generally, got up, that although we find in them hundreds of fish-hooks,

---

[*] *Odyss.* xii. 253.

[†] That plummets of stone were long used here in the North, when fishing with the hook, we learn from an ancient Fœroe song, printed in the *Antiquarisk Tidskrift* for 1852, page 312, where it says of one who was fishing, ' He lost both hook and stone.'

which have belonged to the savages on the islands of the Pacific, yet I have never succeeded in finding amongst them a single plummet.[*] I have seen only one in the British Museum, brought from Otaheite, and used for catching cuttlefish. The fishermen on the coast of Greenland use a so-called *pilk* of bone, provided with iron hooks, and with a stone pierced through it to serve as a plummet. Plummets for proper fish-hooks from Greenland I have not yet seen; but I was some years ago informed by a person who has long resided in Greenland, how the stones were formed which were used by the natives as plummets. He drew a sketch of one, which is still in my possession. Subsequently, a student presented me with a stone (Pl. II. fig. 31) of exactly the same shape as that represented in the sketch just mentioned. This stone was found in the earth in the province of Blekinge. It has very evidently been used as a *plummet*; but it is also easy to understand that this kind of implement must exist under a great variety of forms. But they must all have this in common: either a groove in which the line could be tied, or a hole pierced through for the same purpose; in other respects, their form may be either oblong, or round and short.

Those ancient plummets which occur most commonly are of the form seen in Pl. II. figs. 33, 34,

---

[*] This was written in 1838; possibly these plummets may now be found in the museums. I have, however, since obtained the stone sketched on Pl. XI. fig. 217, which undoubtedly has been a plummet: it was brought from Pennsylvania.

Pl. XI. fig. 216, oval, or ovally rounded, and with a groove round the middle. They have been called *sling-stones*, but this is a mere supposition, especially as nobody has shown, or even endeavoured to show, any similar forms of *sling-stones* found amongst those nations who still use such missiles. I shall prove in the sequel, that amongst our stone antiquities there is in reality a form, hitherto overlooked, which in every point resembles the ancient Greek sling-stones of lead and those of stone used by the Indians in America. But whether these sling-stones belong to the very re-mote age which is here in question, deserves a more careful investigation.

Other *plummets* have a groove along the middle (Pl. II. fig. 32); others have not only one across the middle, but also one or two such grooves, crossing each other lengthwise (Pl. II. fig. 35). These plum-mets are generally large, and have probably been used as weights for trolling-nets, &c. They are still occasionally picked up in islets and reefs on the coast of Bohus-Län (west coast of Sweden).

For *plummets*, as well as for *sling-stones*, no doubt smooth pebbles were chosen; such as were easily and abundantly found. I do not believe that for either of these implements sharp flints could have been used. Every person acquainted with the subject would consider them useless, as they would soon have cut through the fishing-line or the sling.

Next in order to the method of fishing with the hook and plummet, we come to that with the harpoon.

§ 3. *The harpoon* is a common fishing and hunting

implement among those savages who inhabit islands
and the sea-coast.   It can be used only in the water,
where it is thrown in order to fasten in the animal
which is to be caught.   Its purpose is not to kill
the prey, but to check its career in the water, so that
it may be more easily approached and killed with
another weapon, the *spear*, which we shall describe
farther on.

Harpoons occur under a variety of forms, but they
all resemble each other in this respect, that they are
provided with barbs, by which the instrument fastens
in the animal which it has pierced.   Harpoons may be
divided into two kinds: *harpoons with movable* and
harpoons with immovable points.   To the former belong those represented on Pl. III. figs. 52, 53; to
the latter, Pl. III. figs. 41, 50, 51, and Pl. IV. figs.
69–72.   We shall begin with the simplest kind.   These
are :—

1. *Harpoons with immovable Points* (Pl. III. figs.
50, 51, the sketches being half the natural size).—
Both were found in ancient Esquimaux sepulchres in
Greenland.   The one (fig. 51) is entirely of bone, the
other (fig. 50) of bone tipped with a point of stone,
lancet-shaped with sharpened edges ; on the side are
two holes meeting within, through which passes a
strap fastened to the shaft, and several fathoms long,
the other end of the strap being attached to a large
bladder made of an inflated seal-skin.   At the lower
end of the harpoon is a hole into which the top of the
shaft is inserted, fastening the harpoon to it in such a
way that when its point is embedded in the animal,

the shaft is disengaged, and lies floating on the water.
The wounded animal darts off under the water, but
the bladder to which the harpoon-line is fastened
floats on the surface, showing the direction in which
the animal is swimming. It is soon exhausted, when
it rises to the surface to rest or to breathe. The
hunter, in his ' kayak,' or small canoe, then hastens
to approach his prey, and tries to inflict the death-
blow by means of the *spear* (Pl. III. fig. 54), fastened to the top of a long pole.

Pl. III. fig. 41 represents a harpoon from the
Kurile Islands; it is of bone, with two barbs on one
side, and with a sharp stone or shell inserted in a
groove at the point; below is the strap by which it is
fastened to the shaft, which fits on to its lower end.
Harpoon-points of flint, exactly like this one from the
Kurile Islands, are also found here in Scania (Pl. III.
figs. 43, 48).

Similar harpoons of many varieties, both of bone
and of wood, are found amongst savages. They are
always provided with a smaller or greater number
of barbs at the side. The stone points vary also in
shape; sometimes they are as in Pl. III. figs. 45, 47.
Such are likewise found in Scania, especially in the
sand upon the shore between Ystad and Ahus. The
broad head seems to indicate that they have been
harpoons rather than arrow-heads. On Pl. V. fig.
100, I have sketched such an antique harpoon-point
from the north of Ireland; and on the same Plate,
fig. 99, is a similar one from America.

It appears to me certain that Pl. X. fig. 203 has

been the stone point of a harpoon, similarly constructed.   A person who had long resided in Greenland recognised it at once as such; and in order
to show me the way in which the stone point had
been fastened to the harpoon, and the harpoon to the
shaft, he provided it with a piece of wood as represented in the sketch, Pl. III. fig. 49.   At the lower
end of this piece of wood is an indentation into which
the shaft of the harpoon enters.   Below is the loop
by which the harpoon is attached to the shaft as well
as the strap, to the end of which a bladder is tied.
This harpoon-point of flint (Pl. X. fig. 203) was
found in the earth near the sea-shore of the sound of
Lomma, in Scania.   Pl. III. figs. 42, 46, appear to me
to be also harpoon-points.   I received the originals
from His (then) Royal Highness Prince Christian
of Denmark (afterwards King Christian VIII.), in
whose exceedingly rich museum was also preserved
a collection of stone antiquities, found in North
America, and which, according to the information
received therefrom, belonged to a tribe which was
extirpated ninety or a hundred years ago.*

Harpoons of bone, sharp pointed, with barbs on one
side, are occasionally found in our ancient peat-bogs
in Scania.   Such a one is seen on Pl. IV. fig. 71.
This harpoon-point appears, like those from Greenland, to have been fastened to its long shaft in such

---

* It is very remarkable that all these antiquities, as has been
mentioned before, are exactly like those which are found here in
Europe.   An antiquarian research in those parts of America where
they are found would be of the greatest interest to ethnology.

a manner as to be disengaged therefrom when it stuck
fast in the harpooned animal, because above the
point of attachment is a projection over which the
strap or line seems to have been tied.   It was found
in Scania in a bog near the sea-coast.   It may have
been used for hunting seals, or small whales, or other
similar animals.   Meanwhile, it is very remarkable
that amongst the objects which Messrs. Christy and
Lartet have found in the caves of Perigord, and
which may be considered as being among the most
ancient traces of man in Europe, are harpoons of
bone, which seem to have been helved in the same
manner (Pl. IV. fig. 72).   Other harpoons of bone
(Pl. IV. fig. 69) are likewise found in Scanian bogs,
like the former, fig. 71, but showing traces of having
been helved in a somewhat different manner, namely,
by the point of bone being fastened to the handle.
A great number of bone harpoons, more or less like
this one, are to be seen in the British Museum (Pl. IV.
fig. 70), all from Tierra del Fuego, labelled, ' *Heads
of Fishing-spears used by the Natives of Tierra del
Fuego.*' *   We thus see that these bone points are
really fishing-harpoons.   The length of those from
Tierra del Fuego is $9\frac{3}{8}$ to $15\frac{3}{8}$ inches.   Those from
Scania are from $9\frac{4}{8}$ to $12\frac{4}{8}$ inches in length.   They
are thus alike both in length and shape, and there is
therefore every reason to assume that they were
destined for nearly the same purpose.   But we are
not aware how they were used in Tierra del Fuego,

* See also *Prehistoric Times*, fig. 156, page 436.

whether they were shot from a bow, thrown by the
hand, or used for striking, because we have not seen
in the British Museum,* or elsewhere, any specimen
having a shaft.† We ought also to reckon amongst the
harpoons of bone sketched on Pl. IV., figs. 73 and 74,
both found in bogs; the former in the south of Scania,
the latter in the island of Seeland; one rather like
the latter was also found in Scania, in the parish of
Tryde, and is preserved in my late collection in Lund.

2. *Harpoons with movable Points* (Pl. III. figs. 52,
53).—These are of a more complicated construction
than the former. The flint point, lancet-shaped, is
fixed in a round bone shaft, ending in two points,
between which points is a hole, into which the end
of the central piece projects. Through the side holes
goes a strong strap, made of sinews, which connects
the two pieces of bone together. Round them and
the strap is twisted a strong thread, in order to
keep them in a straight position, and a cross-peg is
inserted between the two pieces of bone. The lower
end of the central piece is fastened to the harpoon-

* Captain Werngren informs us that the savages in the islands of the
Pacific are in the habit of fishing sometimes with hooks and at other
times with well-made nets, and that they occasionally *shoot the fish*
with arrows from their canoes; when the fish rise, they pierce them
with their javelins, then jump overboard and secure their prey. It
seems that the harpoons of this kind found in Scania may also have
been used by fishermen, while sitting in their boat, to shoot or
transfix the fish, especially as these harpoons have been discovered
at the bottom of bogs which have formerly been small lakes, where
the skeletons of gigantic pike are occasionally found, which may
have been proper objects of such fishing with harpoons.

† See also Note 2.

shaft, and the strap already mentioned is joined to the long cord, at the end of which the bladder is attached. When the harpoon has entered the animal (it is principally used in catching blubber animals, such as seals and whales), the terminal piece buries itself completely in the wound, and then separates itself from the shaft, when, owing to the mode in which the strap is attached, it comes to lie across the wound inside the hide of the animal, and operates, of course, as a strong barb. The originals of these figures are preserved in my late collection, and are from the Kurile Islands. The Esquimaux in Greenland also use harpoons of the same construction.*

There are undoubtedly as many harpoons of wood as of bone, and when made of wood they are always provided with a barb of stone. This was the case not only with those made by the savages of Scandinavia, but also with those of other savages. It is easy to understand that the part of the harpoon made of wood must have decayed, leaving only the stone point; it is therefore worth enquiring if, among the stone points found in our antiquities, there are any like those with which the harpoons of existing savages are provided, as in that case they have probably been handled in the same manner. We have already seen that such articles of flint as those from Mexico and the Kurile Islands are also found in the south of Sweden. It

* It is worthy of remark, that iron harpoons, of nearly the same construction and with movable points, are used on the west coast of Norway for catching sharks (*Squalus maximus*). I saw some during my first visit to Norway in 1816.

ought, however, to be observed that it is difficult to draw a line of demarcation between the stone points which have been *harpoons*, and those which have belonged to *arrows*, because the same stone point could have been adapted either to a *harpoon* or to an *arrow*.

§ 4. Next in order to the harpoon I shall speak of the *leister* (or *fish-spear*), and begin with the one which I saw and sketched in 1836, in the Museum at Bristol (Pl. IV. fig. 75), and which, according to the label attached to it, is from the north-west coast of North America. Beside it I have sketched one half of a similar spear (fig. 76), also from North America. We see by the sketch how this instrument was constructed. On the top of a long pole are fastened two tolerably long sharp-pointed bones, the points bent a little outwards, and the inner side provided with teeth pointing backwards, to hold the fish securely when struck. These bones are fastened to the shaft in such a manner that each, independently of the other, is in some way movable inwards and outwards; their sides are therefore flat at the other end, and the inner edge provided with one or more teeth, pointing forwards in order to be tied fast, so that they cannot be torn away by the fish; and, in order to prevent their being bent too much apart, they are tied together by means of a strap at a short distance from the handle.

A nearly similar leister, from the north part of North America, north of Hudson's Bay (Pl. IV. figs. 77, 78), is preserved in the ethnological department of the Museum at Copenhagen. Its entire length is 38 inches, of which the wooden shaft measures 31¾ inches; the bone points, in all 11 inches long, are, to a length of 5 inches, fastened to the shaft, and consequently protrude 6 inches beyond it. The shaft is round, about ½ inch in diameter, somewhat compressed in front of the lower end, the end itself cut off diagonally with an incised broad round notch, showing that a thick bow-string has been resting thereon; at the end three feathers are fastened lengthwise. It appears, however, that this implement was made rather for shooting birds on the wing than for spearing fish in the water.

But be this how it may, it is nevertheless very remarkable that the half of an implement, evidently similar to this last-mentioned one, has been found in the peat-bog of Felsmosse, about three English miles from Lund, in the province of Scania. I have sketched this on Plate IV. fig. 79. This bone dart is 7 inches long, round, and compressed; the back a little thicker, pointed towards the top end, round and bent outwards a little; the inner side somewhat compressed, with five broad incisions forming teeth, bent backwards; the lower end broader and also compressed, the inner edge provided with oblique notches forming teeth, pointing forwards, which thus prevent the dart from being drawn forward. But what still more shows the perfect likeness between the North American and the Scanian instrument is, that if we carefully examine the latter we shall find it scratched transversely in two places, the one at the place where the strings on the American one attach the points to the shaft, and the other a little way higher up, where the shaft ends in the American implement, and where the points are tied round; the Scanian dart is in other respects entirely even and smooth.

Thus we see that the Scanian implement was constructed exactly in the same manner as the American, and it is difficult for us to understand how implements so complicated could have been constructed so completely alike by the Esquimaux of the present day, living in the most northern part of North America, and by the aborigines in the most southern part of Scandinavia, between which two races, so very dissimilar in origin, and so widely separated as to locality, we cannot suppose any relationship to have existed. That implements so simple in construction as the flint arrow should be alike in most countries, even in Scania and Tierra del Fuego, can be explained by a kind of instinct in man, *as man*, everywhere, as long as he stands at the very lowest point of civilisation; but the perfect similarity between implements so complicated as those now in question, I look upon as one of the great, still unsolved, enigmas of ethnological science.

§ 5. *The Spear.*—This implement of the chase can also be used for killing marine animals which have been secured with the harpoon. The spear which I have sketched (Pl. III. fig. 54) is of flint, and is preserved in the British Museum, and labelled '*Flint-headed Spear.*' It is from Point Barrow. There is

also one from Kotzebue Sound. Both are fastened to
a long, somewhat slender and light wooden shaft, of
some kind of pine-wood, and measuring 5 to $5\frac{1}{2}$ feet in
length, tapering towards both ends, especially towards
the lower end. The flint point is deeply inserted
in the top end of the shaft, and wound round with
thread.

Flint spear-points like these are not unfrequently
met with here. I possess a number of them of various
sizes, found in different parts of Scania. Compare
Pl. III. figs. 61, 62, and others.

We also often find here spear-heads of a more
slender shape and greater length ; they are generally
thin ; compare Pl. III. figs. 55, 57. Sometimes they
are extremely long, broad, and thin. In the Museum
of the Academy of Antiquities, in Stockholm, there is
one measuring $14\frac{5}{8}$ inches in length, and $2\frac{2}{8}$ inches in
breadth, and very thin. The largest which I have
seen was 15 inches long by $2\frac{1}{2}$ inches broad, and not
more than $\frac{3}{8}$ths of an inch thick. The ordinary length
is 7 to 8 inches, by $1\frac{1}{2}$ inch in breadth. That these
spears, as well as the former ones, must have been
provided with long wooden shafts, is more than probable. They must in that case have made most excellent
hunting implements for killing the larger mammalia,
such as the urus, bison, elk, stag, reindeer, wild boar,
and others, which, at the time when these spears
were in use, were abundant in the south of Scandinavia. They were, however, unsuitable as weapons of
war against an armed enemy, being too brittle. Even
amongst these there is no other difference between

the blade and the shaft-handle, than that the edges
of the latter are more blunt. Such a bone spear is
preserved in the Museum at Bristol (Pl. III. fig. 56),
and is labelled: '*Head of an Esquimaux Spear, East
Coast of Greenland, Lat. 74° 32′ N.*'

We have also found here in Sweden some *spears
of bone* (Pl. III. fig. 58; Pl. IV. fig. 68) made of
thigh-bones, so that the shaft was inserted in the
lance-head, not the head in the shaft. They were,
moreover, secured by a wooden peg passing through
both the shaft and the handle. These bone spears
are no doubt synchronous with the flint spears, having
been found near Högsmölla, and in other places in
Scania, in a deep peat-bog, in which also stone implements were discovered.

In the British Museum a spear is preserved *from
the interior of Chili*; it is of iron, but of the same
shape as the flint spear which I have sketched on
Pl. III. fig. 44. The shaft is of bamboo, and about
four fathoms in length.

There is no doubt that the similar flint spears
found in Sweden were also mounted on long wooden
shafts, and would have been excellent implements
for killing the larger mammalia. Spears of this
form occur of various sizes, from 3 to 8 inches in
length (compare Pl. III. fig. 62). One variety
has the haft shorter and broader (see Pl. III. fig.
61), and resembles Pl. III. fig. 54. Others have no
shaft, but they have been attached to the handle
by means of a notch, at the sides near the lower
end, as in Pl. VI. fig. 120, found in the earth in

Ohio, north of Cincinnati.   Pl. VI. fig. 121 is a spear, the point of attachment of which has been broken off; the sides near the broken end have afterwards been provided with notches, in order to allow of its being tied to the shaft.   It was found in the south of Scania.

The spear which is sketched on Pl. III. fig. 59 is a peculiarly shaped one.   None similar to it has been found as yet, either in the south of Sweden or in Denmark; but it is met with in the northern and central parts of this country.   This specimen is from Kolmarden, and in the Museum of the Academy of Antiquities, in Stockholm.   A similar one is preserved from Norrland, measuring $7\frac{2}{8}$ inches in length, and $1\frac{5}{8}$ inch in breadth.   This form of spear is never of flint, but of a hard slatestone.[*]

§ 6. *Knives*:—

1. *The Hunting-knife.*—This ranks next to the spear; and, indeed, a spear is, properly speaking, nothing but such a knife fastened to a long shaft.   It is, therefore, often impossible to judge from the blade whether it has been a *spear* or a *knife*.

I will begin by mentioning a stone knife from New Zealand, preserved in the British Museum, in London (Pl. III. fig. 65).   The blade, consisting of a kind

---

[*] It is probably not so ancient as the flint spears.   Those parts of the country in which it is found with us were, according to some opinions, to which I shall refer by and by, not yet inhabited when stone implements were first used in the south of Sweden and Denmark.   One similar, of bronze, and of about the same length, 10–11 inches, was found in England, and copied in the *Primeval Antiquities of Denmark*, page 30.

of jasper-like stone, is, exclusive of the handle, $3\frac{1}{2}$ inches long, $1\frac{6}{8}$ inch broad, lancet-shaped, pointed, and with chipped edges. It is fastened by means of some black gum, or cement, to a wooden handle, which has been tightly wound round with some strongly twined thread,* at the lower part of the blade. The handle is about 5 inches long, roundly compressed, a little widened at the back, split at the end, and provided with a small round hole, in which a strong cord is inserted, forming a loop 14 inches long, probably for carrying the knife.

Similar knife-blades made of flint are often found in Northern Europe. It is clear that in those cases where the handles were made of wood, these latter have decayed, so that only the blade remains. To these belong, without doubt, Pl. V. fig. 80, Pl. III. fig. 60, and perhaps also Pl. V. fig. 83. This last-mentioned flint blade has evidently had a broad handle.

Other *flint knives*, which are not common with us, have the handles also of stone (Pl. III. figs. 63, 64, 66, 67 ; also Pl. V. figs. 81, 22). These handles are frequently nearly of the same shape as the wooden handle which is sketched here, namely, roundly compressed, widened at the back, and even a little indented, as, for instance, Pl. III. fig. 67.

It is scarcely to be doubted that the modern New Zealand, and the ancient Scandinavian, stone knife, which in all essentials are perfectly alike, have been used for the same purpose. Of these ancient Scandi-

* Probably of *Phormium tenax.*

navian *stone knives*, with handles widened towards the back, there are four varieties:—

1. Those with the handle roundly compressed, widened towards the back, but not very elaborately finished (Pl. V. fig. 82).

2. Those with a similar handle, but with the sides, which form a continuation of the edge, carved (fig. 81).

3. Those with one of the broad sides carved along the middle, the other flat (Pl. III. fig. 67).

4. Those in which both the long sides, as well as the edges, are carved (fig. 66). These latter especially are frequently worked with great skill.

Besides these *knives with handles widened towards the back*, there is a form of knife frequently met with here, with square handles of stone of uniform breadth, and cut off straight at the back. It is shown amongst those already sketched (Pl. III. figs. 63, 64). These also are frequently more or less tastefully carved along the edges ; we have two varieties of them :—

1. With the blade longer than the handle, lancet-shaped, and pointed (fig. 64).

2. With the blade shorter than the handle, less pointed, and more oval (fig. 63). In the former, the handle forms an acute angle with the edge, and in the latter, with the flat side of the blade.*

2. *Cutting-knife.*—Under this name I propose to denote a variety of flint knife which is more rarely found amongst our antiquities. It has a sharp edge along one side, and a broad chipped curved back

* See Note 2.

along the other (Pl. V. figs. 84, 85); it resemble
consequently, very much what is called a 'Dutchman
knife,' or kitchen-knife, and is generally from 5 to
inches long, by $1\frac{4}{8}$ to $1\frac{6}{8}$ inch broad.   The edge
always chipped, never ground or notched, except th
back, which is notched across.   That it has been pro
vided with a wooden handle cannot be doubted.   Th
edge is always sharpened on the right side, whic
shows that it has been made for cutting *away from*
not towards, the person using it (fig. 85), provide
with a broad hewn notch to bind it to the handle
both the specimens figured were found in Scania.

3. *Semilunar Knife.*—This shape I have not hithe
to found amongst the implements belonging to an
other tribes than those living in the Polar regior
of North America; but amongst the Esquimaux
appears to be common.   There is one preserved i
the Museum at Bristol (Pl. V. fig. 86), which
entered in the Catalogue as '*Knife obtained fro:
the Esquimaux Indians, East Coast of Greenlan
Lat. 74° 40′ N.*'   It is made of iron, and has bot
ends broken off; but both Sir John Ross, and D:
Richardson, who happened to be in Bristol at th
time of my visit there in 1836, and who, as is we
known, have long resided amongst the Esquimaux i
North America, agreed with me that the Esquimau
knife in question is of an unusual shape, dependin
on that of the piece of iron from which it was mad
Dr. Richardson assured me that he had often see
knives of stone amongst the Esquimaux of Nort
America, of the same shape as those semilunar kniv

of which I shall speak farther on ; and Sir John Ross
told me that he had seen similar ones of bone amongst
the Esquimaux in Boothia.

The handle is of wood, frequently like the one
sketched here, but sometimes of a somewhat different
shape.   This one is of some kind of fir-wood, badly
cut, and wound round with a strap of seal-skin, in
order to hold fast the blade in the slit of the handle
in which it has been inserted.   The Esquimaux call
these knives *olomik*, or *ulomik*, which, I believe, is the
plural of *olo* or *ulo*.

Such flint forms are frequently found here in
Sweden; they occur in a great variety of shape and
size (see Pl. V. figs. 87, 91).   Some are shorter,
broader, with one side bent, the other straight (fig.
88); length from 4 to $4\frac{1}{2}$ inches, breadth $1\frac{7}{8}$ to 2
inches.   The edges of these are merely roughly
sharpened.   Others are narrower and longer, from 6
to $7\frac{1}{2}$ inches long.   Amongst these the most bent
side is almost always sharpened ; the other side
is occasionally a little bent inwards (fig. 87), sometimes straight or bent outwards a little, and toothed
(fig. 91).   This implement seems, in that case, to
have been used both as a *knife* and as a *saw*.
Lastly, we find occasionally specimens of the latter
shape, roughly toothed on both edges (fig. 90).
These appear to have been used as *saws*.   There is
reason to believe that in some specimens the handle
has enclosed one edge, the edge having been inserted in a groove running lengthwise.   It is probable that the curved knife formed as a saw (Pl. V.

fig. 91) has had such a handle. These so-called semi
lunar knives occasionally, as in fig. 89, have one ed
chipped up, so that it may fit into a handle.

§ 7. *Arrows.*—Everybody knows how the arrow
shot from a bow, provided with a string. For th
purpose it has a round, slender, wooden shaft, mo
or less long. Arrows, headed with stone, are st
used by many savages. We may divide arrow-hea
into such as have, and such as have not, a tang
projection for insertion into the shaft. Of the form
we have *two* forms, both amongst the ancient ones, ai
also amongst those still used; the *long* and the *sho*
An arrow of this description (Pl. V. fig. 102) is pr
served in the British Museum. The shaft is slende
light, 2 feet 8 inches long, and at the lower end,
usual, provided with feathers. Of the latter for
Pl. V. fig. 107 represents one from Scania; fig. 1
another from Tierra del Fuego. Those provided wi
shafts, which I have had, were from California (Pl.
figs. 104, 105). The shafts are about 2 feet lor
and the heads tied on by means of strings of g
which have dried on round the shaft.

Long stone arrow-heads with a shaft-tongue (pi
are not unfrequently found in the ground in Swede
These have been chipped out of flint-flakes, mc
or less thin; sometimes they consist only of fli
splinters with a chipped tongue (Pl. II. fig. 38); son
times they are chipped along the edges (fig. 39
sometimes toothed (Pl. V. fig. 92), when they a
proach more nearly the triangular form. Lastly,
find those which are triangular, with the sides a

angles equal, and with chipped edges, occasionally more or less distinctly toothed (Pl. II. fig. 40). Such a flint arrow-head resembles a small bayonet.

There is a kind of arrow-head made of an oblong, three-cornered piece of bone, pointed at both ends; and on both sides provided with a narrow groove, running lengthwise (Pl. XIII. fig. 241). As far as I know, arrow-heads of this kind have hitherto been found only in the island of Öland, and it is uncertain whether they belong to the Stone Age.

The short arrow-head, with a pin or tang, is more slender and flat. To this form belong Pl. III. figs. 45, 47, and others. The larger ones of this form cannot be distinguished from harpoons; fig. 47 is of quartz; fig. 45 of flint; fig. 103, Pl. V., is of obsidian, from Tierra del Fuego, and was used, I am informed, as a knife.

Arrow-points without a Tang.—These are always tolerably thin and broad, both side edges chipped, and more or less excavated at the base (Pl. V. figs. 94–98, 113, 114); sometimes they are provided on both the flat sides with a notch, in order to be tied to the shaft (Pl. V. fig. 104). This form comes near the harpoon-head (Pl. X. fig. 203), and can be distinguished from it only by the size. They are often without any side grooves, in which case they are fastened in a slit at the end of the shaft (Pl. V. figs. 94–98). I saw, in London, in 1836, at Mr. Stokes's, arrows from California, headed with a triangular piece of metal of exactly the same shape as the flint arrow-head found in Scania (Pl. V. fig. 113); and in the

collection of the late King Christian VIII. we
similar ones of flint from North America.*

§ 8. Next in order to *spears* and *arrows* stands
peculiar group of stone implements, all known fro
their being two-edged, more or less sharp-pointe
broadest at the lower end, which is chipped thinn
in order to allow of its being inserted in a slit at t
end of a wooden shaft. To this class belongs t
stone spear (Pl. VI. fig. 119). It is round, co
pressed, with sharpened side edges, pointed in fro
at the back thin and sharpened, so that it can
inserted in a shaft. Length up to 10 or 12 inche
breadth from 1 inch 3″ to 1 inch 5″. We oft
find some shorter, broader, and thinner; the low
end sometimes straight, sometimes cut out roun
but always sharpened, and the front part alwa
pointed (Pl. VI. fig. 118). Length $7\frac{1}{2}$ inches, bread
2 inches; or length 6 inches, breadth 1–5 inche
or length 7 inches, breadth $1\frac{3}{8}$ inch. These form tl
transition to *harpoons* and *arrows*.

§ 9. *Javelins.*—This hunting implement we find st
in use amongst the inhabitants of the Kurile Islan
and in Greenland. The one sketched here (Pl. V
fig. 122) is from the former place. They are of bo
or wood, 6 to 10 inches long, round, but along o
side usually provided with an edge, and that ed
notched so as to form two or three points or bar
directed backwards, the top sometimes armed wi

* In the collection made by Sir George Simpson in the Huds
Bay territory, are similar arrows, some tipped with stone, oth
with metal.

a small sharp stone-flake, but sometimes merely sharpened; the lower end pointed so as to be inserted in a wooden shaft about 5 feet long. This implement is now, in Greenland, made of iron, and provided with one or two barbs (Pl. VI. fig. 123) (see also Crantz, 'History of Greenland,' Pl. V. figs. 6, 7); formerly it was made of bone (as we may see by those found in ancient Esquimaux graves). H. Egede says of them, in 'Grönland's Perlustration,' page 56:—' On the water they (the Greenlanders) do not shoot birds by means of a bow and arrows, as on land, but kill them with the javelin, which, at the point, is provided with a sharp bone or iron.' This proves that even as late as the time of Egede, the javelin was in Greenland sometimes made of bone.

We find now and then in our peat-mosses implements (Pl. VI. figs. 124, 125, 126) which have evidently been used in the same manner as the javelin from the Kurile Islands, above described. These implements are of bone, 6 to 10 inches long, $2\frac{1}{4}$ to 3 or 4 lines broad, occasionally round, but generally rather compressed, tapering to a point towards both ends, and either provided along both sides with a deeply indented groove (figs. 125, 126), into which thin sharp flakes of flint are inserted, and fastened by means of black putty resembling pitch,*

* This burns with a strong flame, and is a resin exactly like that which forms the chief ingredient in the 'pigmy-bread,' or 'incense-loaves,' which are here found in the earth or in bogs, and which Hühnefeld quite seriously considered to be petrified Scanian bread. See *Isis*, 1836, page 718.

or the groove with the flint-flakes is found only alon
one side (fig. 124).*   The front end is pointed, an
behind, the point is occasionally widened, in shap
like a spear-point, so that the whole bone represent
a spear in miniature, with its long shaft; the groov
holding the flint-splinters does not reach quite to th
point.   Such is the implement in its *original* form, bu
by degrees, as it wears out and is again sharpened t
a point, the spear-shaped expansion disappears an
the point is worn down to the grooves.   The hinde
end is likewise sharp-pointed, and has evidently bee
inserted in a wooden shaft.   Generally this end i
to a certain distance less smooth than the remainde
of the bone, and sometimes the resin, by means c
which it has been cemented in the shaft, remains u
to a little more than 1 inch (fig. 126).   This imple
ment is principally found in bogs in the south c
Scania, also in the province of Bohusland on Tjör
(west coast of Sweden); it is said to have been als
found in the island of Öland.   In the Museum of th
Academy of Antiquities, in Stockholm, there is
specimen, the longest which I have seen (10 inche
in length), found during the digging of the Goth
Canal, between Påfvelstorp and Tåtorp, in peat
earth, under a bed of clay, and 8 feet under ground
But where there is peat-earth there must hav
been water; consequently, everything that is foun
on, and especially under, peat-earth, has sunk t
the bottom in some water.   It is probable, therefore

---

* The point is said to have been occasionally armed with a flin
splinter, as in the Kurile Islands.

that the implements in question, while being used on the water, have dropped therein and gone to the bottom. In order to form a correct idea of the manner in which these implements were used by the Scandinavian aborigines, we ought to enquire how they are employed amongst the nations where they are still in use.

The Greenlander uses this weapon *only* on the water, in the pursuit of aquatic birds. It is provided with a shaft five feet in length, ending at the back with some ornament, generally a reindeer foot or something of that kind, and is thrown by hand at birds while they are resting on the water. It strikes usually at the distance of from fifty to sixty paces, and Egede relates that the Greenlander can hit his prey at a tolerably long distance, as surely as a good shot could do it with a fowling-piece. From his early childhood the Greenlander begins to practise throwing the bird-javelin. It is thrown by means of a *throwing-stick* or *board*, with such force that it flies whizzing through the air, and with such wonderful skill that it generally pierces the head of the duck.

There is scarcely any doubt that the darts here sketched have been the same kind of hunting implements, and that they have been employed in the same way. That they have been, and were intended to be, thrown by hand, we can easily see, because they could have been used only on the water; for if thrown on land they must infallibly have been broken to pieces and destroyed. They are, therefore, found only in peat-bogs, which in former times were open waters, sometimes of considerable extent. They occur not unfrequently in the south of Sweden. Our museums contain a great number of them; but in Denmark they are rare.

After the *javelin*, we shall here speak of another kind of weapon, also intended to be thrown, namely, the *sling-stone*.

That *slings* and *sling-stones* are used both as weapons of war and implements of the chase amongst many savage nations now living, we know from accounts received from travellers, and by the slings and sling-stones brought home by them, and preserved in several of the European ethnographical museums. We see, from accounts of the ancients relating to their battles, that, even as late as the Iron Age, the inhabitants of Scandinavia, as well as the Greeks, in their wars with the savage hordes of Asia, used the sling and sling-stone amongst their weapons. The practice of throwing with the sling dates, probably, amongst ourselves, as far back as the time of the pure Stone Age.

From the remotest times two kinds of slings have been in use: *wooden slings* * and *ribbon-slings*. Since this was written, I have seen Ed. Vischer's ' Antike Schleudergeschosse.' Basil, 1866. The author does not seem aware that any other than ribbon-slings have been found; but besides having myself, as a

---

* It appears that it was with such a sling that David flung the stone at Goliath's forehead, because Goliath said to him, ' Am I a dog, that thou comest to me with staves?' i. e. the shepherd's staff and sling-handle. 1 Sam. xvii. 43.

boy, used the wooden sling, and frequently seen it used by other boys, I can refer to one described in Lepsius's work. The wooden sling consists of a stick, in the upper part or near the end of which is a slit or *hole*, in which the stone is put; such a sling with a hole is sketched in Lepsius's great work on Egypt, where a man is represented, at whose feet lies a heap of small stones, and who holds in his hand a wooden sling of this description, which he appears to be using very actively in the fight.

The other kind, the *ribbon-sling*, consists of a string or strap, of the breadth of about one to two inches, and is about three feet long. One end is twisted round the forefinger of the right hand, the other held between that finger and the thumb; the sling-stone is placed in the loop formed by the ribbon, and the sling then swung round the head until the stone has obtained a sufficiently swift motion, when one end of the ribbon is let go, and the stone flies forward with immense speed through the air. Those who have long practised the use of this weapon are able to take a good aim with it. We see by this that the sling-stones must be smooth, and, in preference, *oval*; but they need not be so carefully fashioned as was formerly thought necessary. All round articles of antiquity were, until lately, considered to be sling-stones, as, for instance, those which are seen on Pl. I. figs. 1, 9, 12, 14, and others, Pl. XI. fig. 216, and almost all *plummet-stones* as well. But a little reflection will convince us of the absurdity of supposing that a man would give himself all this trouble

to fashion sling-stones, which were to be thrown
away the next moment, when he could find many
natural pebbles quite as suitable.   The stones called
by the Danish antiquaries *flinte-knuder* have also been
regarded as sling-stones; * but they are too irregular
and too sharp-cornered, so that they would soon wear
out the sling, even if it were made of leather.   I presume that these sharp-cornered stone balls were the
first hand-missile weapons of the earliest and rudest
savages, and used by them to throw at wild animals
or enemies.   I have since had many proofs that the
stone (Pl. V. fig. 115) which was sketched in the first
edition of this work, twenty-eight years ago, actually
was a sling-stone as I then conjectured.   During
my visit to England and France, I saw, in the British
Museum, and in the Louvre, many such sling-stones,
both from New Caledonia and from New Zealand,
made of a greyish-white, sometimes bluish, very
heavy kind of stone, which I took to be a kind of
spar.   On Pl. V. two such (figs. 116, 117) are sketched
by the side of the Swedish one.   The one from New
Caledonia, which I measured, was 2 inches long and
1 inch in diameter; another from New Zealand was
1⅝ inch long, and also 1 inch in diameter.   They are
all somewhat smaller than those found here, of which
three are preserved in the Museum at Lund and
two at Stockholm, being of a heavier kind of stone.
Not only the *sling-stones*, but also the *slings*, are
preserved in the said museums.   They are made
of bast, artistically plaited into long strong ribbons,

* See *Prehistoric Times*, Pl. I. fig. 12, page 60.

and widened in the middle so as to form a kind of cushion woven of bast threads, on which the stone rests when it is to be thrown. M. De Longperier, conservator of the Museum at the Louvre, informed me that one occasionally sees ribbon-slings drawn on Greek monuments and Etruscan vases.* There are also at the above-named museums, sling-stones of lead with Greek inscriptions; they are generally a little smaller than those of stone, on account of their greater weight; the usual length is $1\frac{3}{8}$ inch, only one as much as $1\frac{6}{8}$ inch in length, but they are all nearly of the same shape as the stones, though not round like them, but somewhat compressed. The Romans called them acorns (*glandes*), from their shape, and cast them of lead (*glandes liventis plumbi*, Virg. 'Æneid,' vii. 687). Compare ' Æneid,' ix. 586–589, where the poet describes how the lead acorn is slung and kills. There is no doubt that such slings, probably made of a leathern strap cut out of the hide of some animal, were used by the northern savages both in war and in hunting; and this weapon, in their expert hands, was a never-failing one. The reason why such carefully prepared sling-stones are so very rarely found, appears to be that the savage, like David when he slew Goliath, *chose smooth* stones out of the brook, which he could pick up on the banks of the rivers and lakes beside which he dwelt, and carry with him on his hunting excursions. These smooth and round stones, fashioned by Nature's hand, were

---

* It is probably this kind of sling to which Homer alludes in the *Iliad*, xiii. 599-600.

probably used by warriors even at a comparatively late period.

How far the dexterity in throwing stones by the hand, or by a sling, can be carried, we see by what Strabo (lib. v. c. 17–18) relates about the inhabitants of the Balearic Islands, which islands have derived their name from the Greek word βάλλειν, to throw. He says, 'with slings they throw large stones better than other people. They attain this dexterity by constant practice from their youth up, for the mothers fix a loaf of bread on the top of a high pole, and the boys must starve until they have hit and knocked down the bread.' *

DIVISION III.—CARPENTER'S OR MECHANIC'S TOOLS, WITH THEIR EDGES LYING ACROSS ONE END.

The edge-tools, of which we have spoken hitherto, are all provided with a point, and they all have chipped, but never ground, edges along one or both sides. We come now to tools which are distinguished by the end opposite to the shaft being broad, rough-sharpened, and frequently having a ground edge. To this series belong the chisel, the axe, and others. We divide them into two classes, those *with* and *without* a hole for the handle.

Class I.—*Implements without a Hole for the Handle.*

§ 1. *Chisels.*—These well-known implements occur in the ancient graves in Scandinavia, sometimes of

* See Appendix, Note 3.

stone, sometimes of *bone*, but exactly alike in form, as amongst the inhabitants of Otaheite and New Zealand. We divide the chisels into *narrow* and *broad* chisels, and we subdivide these again into *square chisels* and *hollow chisels* (or gouges). We shall speak of each separately.

1. *The narrow square Chisel.*—A chisel of nephrite (a green serpentine stone), from New Zealand, is preserved in the British Museum. It was used by the natives as a chisel, as lately as within the last fifty years. In order to show the manner in which this kind of stone implement is handled, and how it has been used, I have given two sketches of it (Pl. VI. figs. 129, 130). The stone chisel itself is about $4\frac{1}{2}$ inches long, square, and somewhat rounded, especially on the two sides; the edge is straight, and sharpened from both sides. The handle, which is of wood, has on one side a deep notch, against which the heel of the chisel rests, and on the other side is a small indentation for a string, by which the chisel is tied to the handle. This string is of a coarsely twined thread of the *Phormium tenax*. It is easy to see by the crushed end of the handle that this implement has been used exactly in the same way as our own modern *iron chisels*, namely, it has been driven into the wood by means of a wooden mallet, in order to produce therein square holes or indentations.

Stone chisels, exactly similar to the New Zealand one, are frequently found here in the ground. They are mostly of flint, but occasionally of other kinds of stone. I have seen one made of quartz, and there is one

of diorite preserved in my collection. The majority,
and the most beautiful ones are, however, as before
mentioned, of flint. These occur of various dimensions, from 4 and 5 to 10 inches in length, and from
$\frac{1}{2}$ to $1\frac{1}{8}$ inch in breadth (Pl. VI. fig. 127). Sometimes
they are entirely square with flat sides; sometimes
more cylindrical, with the sides a little convex, and
with rounded edges. Like all flint instruments with
ground edges, they have been rough-hewn before
being ground. We find also some which are only
rough-hewn and which there has been no time to
grind: these have never been used. The upper part,
which has been covered by the wooden handle, is
generally rough; the lower, uncovered part is usually
more even and smoothly ground; the edge straight
and equally ground from both sides. We see by
the foregoing how this implement has been handled
and used (Pl. VI. figs. 129, 130).

Similar implements made of bone are also found in
our ancient funeral vaults. The one represented in
Pl. VI. fig. 128, was found in Denmark, and is preserved in the Museum of Antiquities in Copenhagen.
Pl. VI. fig. 131 represents another similar one, but
round, found in Scania, and preserved in the Museum
of Antiquities in Stockholm. That these have been
handled in the same manner as the *stone chisels* and
used in the same way, namely, driven into soft wood
by blows from a mallet, will be evident when we examine the *bone chisel* from Otaheite, of which we shall
speak presently.

2. *The narrow hollow Chisel, or Gouge.*—This is

distinguished from the square chisel merely by its having one side of the lower end scooped out, the other rounded, so that the edge is curvilinear. It is of about the same size as the square chisel, but generally somewhat rounded, and the edges quite so. As far as I am aware, all those hitherto found in Sweden were made of flint (Pl. VI. fig. 134). There can be no doubt that they were handled and worked by means of blows from a mallet, in the same manner as the former.

I have certainly not yet met with this implement amongst those which have belonged to any tribe now extant in the islands of the Pacific ; but it is evident that it must occur there also, especially as we have several similar implements made of bone from those regions. In the British Museum is a narrow gouge of bone from Otaheite (Pl. VI. figs. 132, 133). It is provided with a wooden handle, twisted round with a cord. But what deserves the greatest attention is, that this wooden handle also shows unmistakable marks of blows from some mallet. Thus the *bone*, as well as the *stone chisels*, have been used for working in wood.

3. *Chisels with Handles.*—In the British Museum is preserved a *stone chisel*, *with a handle* also of stone, from Nootka, which is sketched on Pl. VI. fig. 135. This implement is not of flint, but of a species of dioritic stone. The handle there evidently supplies the place of a wooden handle, while blows from a wooden mallet are applied to the widened knob. I have no doubt that this implement has been used in

the same manner as the stone chisel with a wooden
handle from New Zealand.

An implement which, both as to general shape and
material, resembles the one from Nootka, occurs also
amongst our articles of antiquity here in the North
(Pl. VI. fig. 136). It has repeatedly been found in
Denmark, and several specimens of it are preserved in
the Museum of Antiquities in Copenhagen. (Compare
Mr. Thomsen's treatise, ' Nordiske Oldsager af Steen,'
inserted in ' Nordisk Tidskr. för Oldkyndighet,' 1 vol.,
page 27 (Pl. III. fig. 17)). Owing to this implement
being made of a talcose or dioritic species of stone,
which very easily decays, the surface has become soft
and the edge blunt, and it was supposed to be unfit for
being used as an instrument for working in wood; it
was therefore inferred ' that it was used at sacrificial
festivals for flaying the animals or victims about to be
immolated, the hide or skin having previously been
ripped open by means of some more cutting instrument.
But having seen that even *chisels of bone* have been
used as cutting instruments, there is no further room
for this supposition. The implement in question has
probably been used in the same way as the similar
one from Nootka, and as the stone chisels previously
mentioned.

Next to the *narrow chisels* there occurs a sort of
tool which differs from it merely in size. I shall call
these the *broad chisels*, and divide them in the same
way as the narrow chisels, namely, into broad chisels
with *straight* and with *curved* edge. To the former
belong:

A. The broad square Chisel (Pl. VI. figs. 137, 138). It is square, thick (never thin), and its section forms a square, cut short off. The edge is ground convexly from both sides, but generally more from one than the other.

Like all flint implements, these chisels have been rough-hewn before being ground. We find, therefore, specimens which have been only rough-hewn, others which have been ground on the two broad sides, and others again which have been ground on all sides.

a. With those sides straight which lie at right angles with the edge (fig. 137), and *b*, with the same sides bent inwards (fig. 138). The former are the most numerous and the largest. Through intermediate forms they merge into the *narrow chisel*; and I have two in my possession which, from equally valid reasons, can be classed either amongst *broad chisels* or amongst *narrow chisels*. The last-mentioned form (fig. 138) is not actually *rare*, but is less frequently met with than the former, and is generally of smaller size.

There can be no doubt that this implement was provided with a wooden handle, attached to it in the same manner as in the New Zealand stone chisel (Pl. VI. figs. 129, 130); and that it was driven into the wood by blows from a mallet. The upper part is consequently square and thick, to prevent its penetrating into the handle while being used.

B. The broad Gouge (Pl. VI. figs. 139, 140).— Amongst the stone implements brought home to the museums in Europe from existing savage nations, I have certainly not met with this form of chisel; but

some flint implements exactly similar are preserved
in the collection lately belonging to King Christian
at Copenhagen, which were sent here from North
America, where, together with several other stone
implements, *all exactly like our Scanian ones*, they
have been discovered in ancient burial-mounds, and
are said to have belonged to a tribe expelled 80 or
100 years ago.   Meanwhile, it is easy to see how this
tool has been used.   It is rounded, more or less
smooth, and often chopped off short at the upper
end.   It has therefore evidently been made to grasp
with the left hand, and to be driven by blows from
a mallet, held in the right hand, into the wood which
it was intended to scoop out.   The marks left by the
mallet are almost always seen on the upper end.
But this implement is sometimes short, sometimes
more or less pointed; in these cases it seems to have
been provided with a wooden handle, on which the
blows from the mallet have been inflicted.

To this division belongs, no doubt, the implement which has been sketched on Pl. VII. fig. 146.
It is of an oblong conical shape, pointed at the top,
convex at the bottom, and with a flat-ground surface
on one side, sloping towards the lower end, by which
a somewhat rounded edge is formed.   This kind of
implement, which is never made of flint, but generally of basalt, is frequently found in Scania and
West Göthland, especially in and near former or still
existing water.   While digging the West Gotha canal,
a great number of them were found in Billströmen.
Probably, the implement now in question has been

helved as a chisel, and been used for scooping out trunks of trees for canoes, or some similar purpose.

A stone implement of exactly the same description is in the British Museum amongst the ethnographical collections from the north-west coast of North America. It is not on record in what manner it was helved, nor for what purpose it was used; but it would perhaps not be impossible to obtain information on this subject.

§ 2. *Hatchets or Axes.*—Next in order to chisels stand *axes*. It is, indeed, often difficult to distinguish between them; in both the cutting part is broad, square, and provided with an edge. But in the chisels the handle has the same direction as the blade, being in fact merely a prolongation thereof; in the axe, on the contrary, the haft forms either a right or an acute angle with the blade. The upper part in the chisel is square; in the axe it is compressed.

We divide the axes, according to the direction of the edge in reference to the haft, into *straight axes* and *cross-axes.* In the former the edge lies parallel with the haft; in the latter its direction is across the handle.

1. *The Cross-axe.*—Next to the *broad chisels*, of which we have already spoken, stands the *cross-axe,* or *adze,* which varies greatly in substance, shape, and size. Of all tools, indeed, the *cross-axe* offers the greatest variety of forms, whether we examine the modern ones preserved in ethnological museums or the ancient ones which are found with us in the earth.

a. The Cross-axe, with a flat chipped Edge only on

one Side (Pl. VII. fig. 147).—This axe is from California, where it is used by the natives, we do not
know exactly for what purpose. It is made of a hard
and thick shell; its form is oblong with two narrow
sides, the broad front side somewhat convex, the other
flat, and on the lower part of the latter is a flat surface,
which forms a very open obtuse angle with the broad
side of the back part, and an edge with the front
convex broad side — the edge is therefore a little
curvilinear.

We see from this how these cross-axes are generally
handled, another illustration of which is Pl. VII. fig.
150. I have a stone axe, in shape exactly like fig. 147,
from the parish of Willand, in Scania, where it was
found in the ground with other antiquities of stone
(Pl. VII. fig. 148). It consists of black basaltic
stone. Its length about 6 inches, greatest breadth 2
inches, and thickness $\frac{7}{8}$ inch. It has no doubt been
helved like the former, and used in the same manner.

A *cross-axe* of *clay-slate*, belonging to the same
class (Pl. VII. fig. 149), is distinguished by having
both its broad sides flat. That it is short is probably
owing to its having lost more or less of its original
length by frequent grinding. It was found near Böke,
in Scania. One often finds, in ethnological collections
from North America, small axes of the same shape
as this.

It is very remarkable that the savage in Sweden,
thousands of years ago, and the savage in America in
the last century, used both hard and soft substances
for edge-tools, such as hard and soft stone, and bone,

and that he made them of the same shape in both places.

To this same group of cross-axes belongs also the one sketched in Pl. VII. fig. 150, being one-sixth of the actual size. The original is in the British Museum; it is from Nootka. The blade is of black basaltic stone. How it is fastened to the shaft and how the axe is used is easily seen by the sketch.

b. Cross-axe with edge ground on both sides, but more on one than the other. — I possess an axe-blade of stone from Pitcairn's Island, in the Pacific (Pl. VI. fig. 142), which, both with respect to the species of stone, the size, and shape, resembles some of those which are found in our ancient tombs, on the coast between Åhus and Cimbrishamn (Pl. VI. fig. 143). It seems to me that there can be no doubt that they have both been cross-axes.

Hereto belongs also Pl. VI. fig. 145. Axes of this form are always of trap, and are also found in the above-mentioned coast district in Scania. They are small, compressed on both the broad sides, slightly rounded, without narrow sides, tapering upwards, sometimes pointed, the edge sharpened on both sides. They are not unfrequently found with handles in ethnographical collections.

A nearly similar form is that sketched on Pl. VII. fig. 161; but the broad sides are flat and the narrow sides rough-hewn. It is found in sepulchral barrows and in peat-bogs, especially in the south and west of Scania. Next to this comes the form of an axe represented in Pl. VI. fig. 141, which has provisionally been called *ice-chisel*. (See the paragraph about it among undetermined antiquities.)

2. *Straight Axes.*—That is to say, those of which the haft has the same direction as the edge. The blade is wedged into the handle. They are, therefore, known by their being thinned off towards the top, and having no plane or square surface. The edge, which is straight, and equally, or nearly equally, sharpened from both sides, wears out, for very obvious reasons, more in front than at the back, which causes it, if looked at sideways, to appear crooked. (Compare Pl. VII. figs. 159, 160.)

In the British Museum there is an axe from 'Tierra del Fuego, which I have sketched here (Pl. VII. fig. 155), one-sixth of the actual size, in order to show how such axe-blades were fastened to the handle.* The handle of this axe is club-like, of a hard ponderous wood, badly shaped, evidently by means of a cross-axe of stone, which has had a somewhat curved edge, because the marks left by it are a little concave. The blade of iron appears to have been flattened and fashioned between stones, is inserted deeply in the shaft, and is a little broadened towards the cutting end. The edge is blunt, with sides somewhat convex.

Axes of copper, of precisely a similar form, are occasionally found here in the earth in Scania. (See Pl. VII. figs. 154, 156.) Like the former, they have two broad and two narrow sides, all flat, and the former widened towards the edge; towards the top

* See Note 4.

they are thinner, evidently in order to be inserted in a wooden handle like the former. There cannot, therefore, be any doubt about the manner in which this axe has been helved, and that it has been used in the same way as our wood-cutter's and carpenter's axes are still.*

We also find here in Sweden *axes made of flint*, precisely like the aforesaid metal axes. I have sketched such an one on Pl. VII. fig. 153. This form of flint axe is not rare here. Its breadth is three or four times its thickness. There is no doubt that it has been helved in the same way as the former, namely, in such a manner that the upper thinner end, which was made thinner on purpose, has been inserted in the side of a thick wooden shaft; it is also easy to see how it has been used.

Another form of flint axe which is commonly found here, is the one sketched on Pl. VII. fig. 158. It resembles the former one in this respect, that it has been thinned in the upper part and sharpened (though without an edge) in order to be inserted in a wooden handle, in the same manner as the axe from Tierra del Fuego; but it differs therefrom in this,

* I have seen three such copper axes, all found in the earth in Scania, but there was no account whether they were discovered lying alone or amongst other antiquities. Although they are of copper, I still think it most likely that they belong to the same early times as the sharpened stone axes, and that they are older than the bronze swords; because, although evidently made as edge-tools, they are nevertheless composed only of copper, without any admixture of tin, which shows that they have belonged to a people so rude that they have not understood how to temper the edge by smelting and adding tin.

that the broad sides, which in the former are flat, are
here a little convex, and the narrow sides, which in
the former are bent outwards in the lower part, here
are straight.   Besides, this axe is thicker and larger
than the former.   Its length is sometimes $12\frac{1}{2}$ inches
and more, the breadth across the middle $3\frac{1}{4}$ inches, and
thickness $1\frac{1}{2}$ inch.   The usual length is 9–10 inches.

The flint axe here sketched has not been worn or
its edge re-ground; but I possess several of exactly
the same breadth and thickness, which from constant
use have become more or less worn and shorter.
Fig. 159 shows the remaining part of such an axe,
which from constant use and repeated grinding is
nearly worn out.   The piece resembles exactly the
upper part of the axe, fig. 158, and we cannot doubt
that it was at first of the same length.

If we more closely examine the shape of the edge
of these worn and frequently re-ground axes, we
can see how they have been helved and used.   The
edge, namely, of such axes is never straight, but,
seen sideways, obliquely bow-shaped; it has the
same shape as a rod, a little bent, and which is
thinner and more flexible at one end than at the
other.   (See the edge in fig. 160.)   The edge of
our common wood-cutter's axe with a long shaft has
just the same shape when it has been used a long
time, and been re-ground.   The reason is this, that
the blow dealt by it affects more especially that part
of the edge which lies farthest from the hand holding
the shaft.

We therefore learn herefrom, first, that these axes

have been provided with shafts like our wood-cutter's axes; and secondly, that they have been employed in every-day use, during which they have become blunted, have been re-ground and worn, until they were entirely worn out. This is evident. It is probable, at least, that the handle has originally been fixed over the middle of the axe (fig. 158), and that the latter has been more firmly fastened in the cleft of the handle by straps tied crosswise, and that by degrees, as it became more worn, it has been moved lower down.

Plate VII. fig. 157 is a flint axe exactly like the one at fig. 158, but it has not yet been ground, only rough-hewn. I have already observed, that all ground stone implements have been chipped out before being ground. In almost all flint implements, however well the grinding may have been performed, we see distinctly some few traces of rough-hewing. I have examined a great number of implements either wholly ground or only chipped, or ground on two and chipped on two sides (this difference is therefore not at all material), but I have not met with one upon which I have not found marks of preliminary rough-hewing. This last-mentioned form is sometimes thin and broad, resembling Pl. VII. fig. 153, except that the broad sides are always a little convex.

Straight axes of other stone than flint, usually of basalt, occur not unfrequently, especially in those districts where flint is wanting. The edge is sharpened equally on both sides. In shape they resemble most frequently Pl. VII. fig. 158; namely, they have

the broad sides a little convex, and the narrow sides
flat, sometimes concave. The narrow sides are even
occasionally convex, and the whole axe has then a
compressed round appearance; at other times they
are tolerably thin and broad, and at others again this
form is even more flatly convex than fig. 151, and
instead of narrow sides, there is a rounded edge.
(See Pl. VII. fig. 152.) Occasionally also it is less
tapering. These axes occur also both ground and
rough-hewn, especially in the north-east part of Scania,
where, however, they mostly are of diorite. Occasionally this form of axe is quite round (Pl. VII.
fig. 162); it resembles the former in so far that it
tapers towards the upper part, sometimes almost
into a point, both sides at the lower part being equal
and roundly sharpened. An axe of this form is said
to have been once found in a bog in Scania, still
fixed in its rude shaft.

Straight axes of the same general form as fig. 158,
but always smaller and with a hole in the broad side
near the upper part (Pl. VIII. fig. 165), though
rather scarce, are occasionally found in the south of
Sweden and in Denmark. They are never of flint,
but always of a talcose material or of greenstone. As
I have previously mentioned, there are never any
drilled holes in flint tools. These axes have been
mounted as fig. 158, and through the hole a strap or
a wooden peg has been passed, in order to fasten it
more firmly to the handle. (Compare ' Nord. Tidskr.
för Oldkyndighet,' vol. i. page 425, Tab. II. fig. 11.)
I have seen such an axe found here in Scania, with a

projection a little above the middle, as also one with a projection, but without any hole. (Pl. VIII. fig. 164.)

To this division belong, probably, the edge-tools round which runs a transverse furrow (Pl. VIII. figs. 166, 167), unless, indeed, they have not rather been wedges with which to split wood. The haft has rested in the furrow, and may have consisted of some round flexible withe (a willow-shoot, for instance), which has been twisted round the blade, forming a handle to steady the wedge while it was driven into the wood by means of a club. This form is never of flint. Fig. 167 is of hornblende, and was found in a bog near Lund; fig. 166 is of diorite, and was found in the ground near Gaddaröd, in the parish of Hörröd, also in Scania.

Class II.—*Implements provided with a Hole for the Handle.*

These are never of flint, but generally of basalt or of diorite, occasionally of gneiss, potstone, or of horn. Implements of this kind are not so numerous as those above mentioned, in the ethnographical collections which I have had an opportunity of examining. This may be owing either to their being rarely found amongst existing savages, or perhaps more to their not having been preserved by travellers, because, generally, it is the war weapons of the savages rather than the implements used in daily life which have been brought to our museums. But that these articles of antiquity, pierced for handles, have belonged to the aborigines of Scandinavia, is proved by their being found together with the implements described above, even in the gallery-tombs, which belong exclusively to the Stone Age.

They may be divided into:—

A. *Those in which the Edge, or sharpened Part, has the same Direction as the Handle.*

To this belong:—

§ 1. *Hammers* (Plate VIII. fig. 172) of stone, and (fig. 171) of stag-antlers, found amongst stone implements in a peat-bog. They have a shaft-hole close under the centre, and they end in a straight or flatly convex square bottom, the top being sharpened like a wedge. They are of a variety of shapes. The first, fig. 172, is of diorite, and of a very convenient shape. It was found in a bog in Scania, and fell into the hands of a carpenter, who provided it with a handle and used it a long time in his workshop as a hammer. Fig. 171 is made of a stag's antler, and has an oblong square hole for the handle, formed, no doubt, with a small straight chisel.

Hammer-axes.—In these, as in the former variety, the hole for the handle is near the middle; but they are distinguished by a different form. Among them I reckon Pl. VIII. fig. 179; it is nearly boat-shaped, roundly compressed, broadest in the middle, with the side edge either sharp or rounded off, or cut straight off into a flat surface; it ends below in a more or less distinctly marked knob, and the haft-hole in its back is surrounded with a raised edge. Hammer-axes of this form are often made of a grey diorite, and sometimes of black basalt. The haft-hole is small in comparison to the weight of the hammer itself, which seems to prove that the handle must have been short.

That this form belongs to the pure Stone Age we may infer from the circumstance, that one of them was found together with other things made of stone, namely, an axe of flint, one of greenstone, a narrow gouge, and a polygonal grindstone (Pl. II. fig. 15). They were in a bank of gravel at Arendala, near Lund.

A hammer-axe of this description was found, in 1842, at Katslösa, together with three broad gouges of flint. They were lying in a stone cist 12 feet long, 4 feet broad, and 4 feet high, constructed of boulders cemented together, each of which was a heavy load for a man. In another similar grave were lying a broad chisel and several flint-flakes.

Hammer-axes of this shape are sometimes very beautifully wrought; as Pl. VIII. fig. 178, the original of which is made of basalt, well polished, and was found in a heap of stones at Hurfva. A similar one was found in the so-called King Roe's Cairn.

The specimen figured in Pl. VIII. fig. 169 is distinguished by having a keel ridge along the side, and by the haft-hole, which is not surrounded by a projecting edge; the top consists of a large convex knob. It is made of diorite.

Specimens resembling Pl. VIII. fig. 163 I also take to be hammer-axes. It is remarkable that they are, in most instances, made of porphyry, which does not occur in Scania, where, however, this form of hammer-axe is frequently met with. Pl. VIII. figs.

176, 177, which also have the shaft-hole near the centre, appear to me to have been *battle-axes* used during the actual Stone Age, as well as during a later period, even so recently, indeed, as the *Iron Age*. The former is proved by their being found in the *gallery-graves*; the latter, by their being found sketched amongst the war weapons from the Iron Age, on the incised rocks in the province of Bohusland. (Compare Nilsson, 'Bronsåldern,' page 56.)

§ 2. *Amazon Axe* (fig. 173).—Stone weapons of this kind are rather variable, and the central part is often much shorter than the figure here referred to, resembling that shown in fig. 174. The original of this sketch is from the south of Scania, and is preserved in my collection, but is not finished, there being no hole for the handle; but this weapon is always known by both ends being much expanded and more or less sharpened. It is exactly like the axes with which the Amazons are armed, wherever we see them represented. On a marble sarcophagus in the Museum of the Louvre, at Paris, bearing the inscription, '*Sarcophage trouvé à Salonique en Macédoine*,' the warriors wield axes with one edge and a pointed sharp back; but all the Amazons have such two-edged axes as the one here sketched. The Amazons are represented with such axes even in other places also; for instance, on some antique friezes in the British Museum. In a treatise on 'The Sword of Tiberius' (in German, 4to., with coloured engravings), an Amazon is also represented with a similar axe. It is called '*Amazon axe*.'

Xenophon mentions it in the 'Anabasis,' iv. 4; and Horace speaks of '*Amazonia securis*' in the Odes, iv. 4, 20.*

§ 3. *Helved Wedges* (Pl. IX. figs. 183, 184).—These are commonly very large, thick, and square, made of a heavy kind of stone, and have one end sharpened, the other forming either a rounded or a square flat surface. The shaft-hole lies nearer the butt than the cutting end.

These have been called axes for throwing; it has been thought that in battle they were thrown at the enemy, and various accounts have been referred to in confirmation of this opinion. It has been alleged that Thor's hammer, *Mjolner*, was thrown from the hand, but it has been overlooked that Mjolner had the peculiar property of returning of its own accord to the hand of its owner. Reference has also been made to a sentence in Wilh. von Poitier's ' Historia Guilhelmi Conquestris,' in which he says : '*Jactant Angli cuspides*

---

* This form of axe occurs with us during the Stone Age, not only of the full size of stone (Pl. VIII. figs. 173, 174), but also in the shape of small ornaments of amber for women (Pl. VIII. fig. 175), found also in gallery-graves in West Göthland amongst other ornaments of amber. But what appears to me to be very remarkable, in an ethnological point of view, is that exactly the same form of axe which was worn as an *amber ornament* by the women in the North during the Stone Age, was worn by Grecian women, being, however, in that country made of gold. In the comedy of 'Rudens' (the Shipwreck), by Plautus, Act iv. Scene 4, vv. 112–116, it is said that the girl *Palæstra,* from Athens, amongst the ornaments given to her as a child by her parents, had also received such an axe, in miniature, of gold (' securicula anceps'), inscribed with her mother's name. This coincidence is very difficult to account for. It appears to me to be one of those circumstances which deserve the attention of the comparative ethnographer.

et diversorum generum tela, sævissimasque secures et lignis imposita saxa;' but one ought to remember that the word *jactare* does not always signify *to throw from the hand,* but that it often signifies *to brandish, or swing backwards and forwards;* for instance, *jactare cæstus,* to brandish the battle-axe. Liv., '*jactare brachia,*' to throw one's arms about. Virg., ' Æneid,' v. 376:

> . . . . . alternaque jactat
> Brachia protendens, et verberat ictibus auras.

That these stone implements now in question could not have been used with a long handle is evident from their being too heavy and unwieldy, and the shaft-hole being too small. The shaft which was fastened in this little hole must therefore have been too slender to allow such a heavy axe being brandished as a weapon, or applied in daily use to wood-cutting or any similar purpose. These wedges appear to me to be most suitable for being held in the left hand by a short handle, and driven into wood by blows from a club held in the right hand. I have therefore called this form *handled wedges*; that is to say, a wedge intended for a handle or shaft. I also class among the shafted wedges, Pl. VIII. fig. 170, made of a stag's antler.

B. *Those in which the Edge, or sharpened Part, lies across the Shaft.*

Hoes.—It is certainly possible that there may also be found axes of this form, but they must then have been cross-axes, or cooper's adzes. But I have never yet seen any of this kind with shaft-holes. The only implements of this shape which I have met with have evidently been *hoes*. I have two (Pl. VIII. figs. 1*0, 1*1), which resemble each other in this, that the sharpening in both is more rounded on the front part, otherwise thick and convex, and that the hole is nearest to that part which is not sharpened. One of them (fig. 180), which is of basalt, has the shaft-hole lying upwards in an oblique direction, so that the person using the hoe may be able to avoid stooping while at work. In the other (fig. 181), made of the horn of an elk, the shaft-hole is straight and oval ; it has not been drilled, but scooped out with some sharp instrument, probably a flint. We see distinctly how this hoe has, by constant use, been worn quite smooth up to, and even above, the shaft-hole. Both these hoes were found in peat-bogs in Scania ; the one of stone in the Öja bog, near Ystad, and the other, of elk-horn, in a bog at Sjörup. A hoe made of a stag's antler is sketched on Pl. XV. figs. 256, 257, a third of its natural size. It was found in the south of the province of Scania, and probably in a peat-moss. It is not certain that these implements have belonged to the same time and to the same people as those who built the *gallery-graves*, nor is it quite certain that these hoes have been used in actual agriculture. It must, nevertheless, be acknowledged, that if agriculture, as seems most probable, consisted originally in burning tracts of forest, and then sowing among the ashes, these rude hoes must have been very suitable for such operations. Future discoveries will, no doubt, in time, solve this as well as other questions.

Pl. IX. fig. 186 shows us the form of an implement, of basaltic material, not unlike a hoe, but without a shaft-hole. It is possible that it may have been fastened by means of a strap, or by bast, to a shaft bent at the end, something like the cross-axes of the savages (for instance, Pl. VII. fig. 150), and that it actually has been a hoe, notwithstanding the want of a shaft-hole.

DIVISION IV. — SOME FORMS OF STONE IMPLEMENTS WHICH CANNOT SATISFACTORILY BE CLASSED AMONGST ANY OF THE FOREGOING DIVISIONS.

To these belong, first, the *Battle-axe* (Pl. IX. fig. 189).—This implement is provided with a shaft-hole, and has four pointed arms projecting in different directions. It was found in the province of Bohusland, and is preserved in the Antiquarian Museum of Lund. It was formerly regarded as the anchor of a boat—an opinion which I also shared; but it seems to me now more probable that it has been a battle-axe. This is, however, by no means certain. A nearly similar instrument, on which are engraved several zigzag lines, has been copied and described by Mr. G. Brusewitz, in his beautiful work, ‘Elfsyssels Historiska Minnen,’ page 271. This specimen was also found in Bohusland, and is preserved in the Museum at Gothenburg. It seems also to have been a *battle-axe*, provided with a handle. I have not, however, yet found this form among weapons used by modern savages.

2. *Flint-flakes* (Pl. II. fig. 24).—These are long, thin, occasionally somewhat bent inwards towards the point; sharp on both sides; on the inner side flat, on the outer provided with one, two, or even several longitudinal ridges. They were obtained by a single blow on the upper end from a hard stone, as though peeled off from a flint-core or nucleus. These nuclei are not rare: one is represented in Pl. II. fig. 23. For evident reasons, no two are exactly alike. They are sometimes found of considerable length. Flint-flakes are the simplest and oldest among the flint implements known. They were used as knives, and also for various other purposes.

Of these flint-flakes, for instance, different weapons have been formed. The arrow-point (Pl. II. fig. 38) is merely such a flake, at one end of which a shaft-point for attachment has been chipped. Fig. 39 represents another, the edges of which have also been chipped. The *square-edged arrows* (Pl. II. figs. 36, 37) are made of such flakes, which have been chipped *crosswise*, after which the edges of the flakes have been formed.

3. *Scrapers* (Pl. IX. fig. 188).—This implement of flint occurs of various forms, though the one end is always rounded, the other elongated sometimes to a slender handle; on one side convex, on the other flat, or even concave, being a flake struck right off by a single blow. Similar stones have been met with in use amongst the Greenlanders, for scraping the hair off skins or hides. There is, in the Museum at Copenhagen, a similar scraper, from the most northern

parts of North America, provided with a handle of wood, with indentations for the fingers of the person using it.

4. *The stretching Implement*, represented in Pl. IX. fig. 185, ought, I think, to stand next in order. The widened part, representing the edge, has been rounded off by *constant wear*, probably from being rubbed against leather or something of that kind. A person who has lived many years as a mechanic in Greenland, thinks that he has discovered a great resemblance between this stone implement and the bone implement, provided with a handle, which is there used for stretching the skins in order to give them the requisite softness. A somewhat similar stretching implement of iron is still used in those parts of Scania where the winter dress of the peasantry consists of sheep-skin coats.

5. *The Ice-chisel* (Pl. VI. fig. 141).—The implement here sketched very closely resembles the ice-chisel of the Greenlanders, and I have therefore given it the same name. They occur chiefly near the coast, and are found in greatest number at Lindormabacken, on the coast of the Baltic, and below the Widsköfte estate. It may possibly have been intended for an axe; but the greater number are so rude, and of such forms, that it is impossible to guess for what purpose they were intended.

6. *The rough-edged Arrow* (Pl. II. figs. 36, 37).— These small hewn flint articles are found in abundance on Lindormabacken, among the above-named; they are of the same form, though less in size, and

like them, but are rarely found in other localities.
Their purpose has long been a matter of doubt, but
in a bog in Denmark a similar flint-stone has been
found attached to a slender shaft, which proves it to
have been an arrow. Regarding this, it may be remarked that in the Egyptian department in the
British Museum there are a great number of arrows,
which are provided in front or at the point of attachment with a metal pin, and end in an expanded
transverse edge. The shafts are of wood, very long,
and have in the back end an indentation for the bow-
string. One of these arrows was provided with a
flint-flake lying crosswise.

In Rosellini's 'Monumenti,' Pl. XV., is the figure of
a man shooting an arrow from a bow just like those in
the British Museum. On Pl. CXVII. many warriors
are sketched with bows and rough-edged arrows.

7. *Gimlet or Auger?* (Pl. II. fig. 25).—Amongst our
antiquities we find some with drilled holes, even from
the pure Stone Age. The savage of that age understood the art of drilling holes. Implements with
bored holes are, however, never of flint, generally of
basalt and trap, sometimes of gneiss and potstone,
even of horn. The savage did not understand boring
holes in flint. We sometimes find among collections
of antiquities, flint axes with shaft-holes; but if we
observe them more carefully, we shall find that these
holes have not been made by the hand of man, but
are the traces of some natural hole in the flint. The
savage did not drill the hole, but sometimes chipped
the edge of it more or less, so as to be enabled to use

it as a shaft-hole. I have seen several such flint axes, both in the Museum at Copenhagen and elsewhere.

Though we have only been able to guess hitherto how the savage bored the shaft-hole in his axes, yet we seem near the truth, as we are even able to call experience to our help. During a visit to Orö pilot-station, on the coast, in the province of Ostro-Gotha, I saw a fisherman engaged in drilling holes in flat slate boulders, to use as plummets for his fishing-line. He worked his gimlet, or auger, with a drill-bow (*spärrborr*), and the gimlet itself was of iron, not pointed, as one would suppose, but of the above-mentioned form and with a rough edge, like a small chisel, or screwdriver. The hole made in the stone with it was not rough in the bottom, but scooped out, just such as is found in those stone implements where the bored hole is more or less deeply indented from the surface, or like the indentations on hammer-stones, to place the fingers upon during use. I conclude from this, that the savage used a similar gimlet, or drill, and that his flint gimlet had the same form as that of the Orö fisherman, namely, that of a small chisel. If, as I suppose, the stone (Pl. II. fig. 25) has been a gimlet, then the pointed end has, probably, been fastened in a handle, and the rough end used for boring. We meet with stone axes now and then, made of basalt or diorite, and bored with a centre-bit; and when they have not been quite bored through, a plug is always present in the intended hole. These stone implements, which are never found in gallery-graves or in our oldest bogs, I consider as belonging to the age when metals were in use, and most likely to the Iron Age. I have heard it said that such bored holes were made with a wooden pin and wet sand, but this I consider as an impossibility. I have before me now an axe of diorite, on which there is the commencement of such a hole. It consists of a circular ring, very small, and evidently made with a metal instrument.

8. *Anvil.*—The instrument sketched on Pl. IX. fig. 187 is rough, and made of a hard quartzy sandstone. The lower half of this instrument is narrower than the other, nearly square, with two broad and two narrower sides; the upper part is thicker, somewhat rounded, and finishes with a flat even surface. It is considered to have been a smith's anvil, but this is somewhat doubtful. The age even to which it belonged is uncertain.

9. Pl. XI. fig. 214 seems to have been a *hunting-whistle.* It is made of an antler, and is found at the bottom of one of the bogs in Scania. It is evident that it has been a *whistle*, and it does not seem improbable that it was used on hunting excursions, particularly as we know that even during the pure Stone Age dogs existed, and were probably used in the chase.

10. Pl. X. fig. 204. A punch, made of an antler.

11. *The Saw* (Pl. V. fig. 93).—This instrument, which has already been mentioned, is very like a lance-point, sharpened and thin at the base, where it was fastened to the haft; but from the many teeth at regular distances from each other, I am disposed to think that it has probably been a saw.

12. Pl. X. fig. 205 is an implement of flint, the use of which I cannot guess. It is oblong square, very thin, chipped on both sides, and with all four edges sharpened. It is not a common type.

13. *Stone Beads.*—Generally of a porous kind of fine sandstone, and provided with a round hole in the centre. They are of various forms and sizes; from 1 to $1\frac{6}{8}$ inch in diameter, either flat on both sides, in which case they are generally smooth (Pl. IX. fig. 199), or tapering upwards, and in that case usually fluted horizontally, or also rounded on both sides with a raised border round the hole (Pl. IX. fig. 192).

The former are the rudest, and appear to be the most ancient. They are found in the earth and in peat-bogs, and where they are met with at all they generally occur in great numbers. I suppose that they were used as plummets for *drag-nets,* and consequently for the same purpose for which leaden balls are now employed. Some of these stone plummets are considerably larger, and appear to me to have been used as flies in a spinning-wheel.

14. (Pl. X. fig. 208.) This is an instrument made of hard sandstone, oblong, and with six grooves running lengthwise, between which are rounded elevations. Possibly this was used to keep the threads separate while bast-rope was twisted. It is out of a peat-moss in the south of Scania.

15. (Pl. XV. fig. 260.) An oblong round pebble of flint. Along the one side it is evenly ground, flat convex, and seems to have been used as a rubbing-

stone, for pressing down smooth seams. This form is not uncommon.

DIVISION V.—ORNAMENTS.

To these belong all wrought and pierced articles of amber, whether large or small. They vary in shape; sometimes they resemble stone plummets, but are more frequently smaller in size (Pl. IX. figs. 194, 197), occasionally, however, as large (Pl. IX. fig. 198; compare 199 of stone and 197 of amber); sometimes they have other forms, resembling stone implements in miniature. Thus we have those which in shape resemble axes, hammers, wedges, hammer-axes, and so on. The form shown on Pl. IX. fig. 195 is no doubt intended to represent on a small scale some kind of stone implement not yet discovered. That these amber ornaments have been worn round the neck is quite certain, as they have actually been found surrounding the neck of skeletons in gallery-graves.*

Together with stone implements and the amber beads just described, *glass beads* (Pl. IX. figs. 201, 202) of a very rude manufacture are sometimes found in the old Scanian bogs, and in gallery-graves. The hole in them is not drilled, but has been either blown, or made by passing some hard instrument of metal or burnt clay through the molten mass; and there is no other trace of grinding than that the edge, projecting round the hole on one side, has been ground

---

* *Gotheborgs Handl.*, 1806, page 93. Monuments on Axevalla Plain.

away.   They thus show us the infancy of the art of
glass-blowing ; but yet it is scarcely to be supposed
that they could have been fabricated by the same
people who made use of axes and chisels of stone.
They must be referred, undoubtedly, to some foreign
nations who had commercial intercourse with the
savage aborigines of Scandinavia, and who bartered
their glass beads and similar wares for amber, furs,
and other produce, in the same manner as in our own
days goods are exchanged between Europeans and the
savages in North America and in the islands of the
Pacific.   The teeth of wild animals, pierced through
and used as ornaments, have also been found in
gallery-graves.

To this series belong also some objects made of
stone.   Such an ornament, consisting of fine sandstone, is shown on Pl. IX. fig. 196 ; they are but
rarely met with.   With these are probably to be
classed the articles shown on Pl. IX. figs. 192, 193,
which are sometimes made of stone, sometimes of
burnt clay.   I am also of opinion that the ornamented
object of bone represented on Pl. IX. fig. 200, has
belonged to this class.   It was found in the earth
at Bjellerup, in Scania.   There is another in the
Copenhagen Museum, made of amber, and ornamented
with the same figures.

§ 3. *Buttons of Amber* (Pl. IX. figs. 190, 191).—It
is not difficult to see how these have been used;
a strap, provided with a knot at one end, has been
passed through the hole, and has been attached with
the other end to one side of the dress (the skin

with which the savage was clothed); to the other side of the dress was attached a strap, forming a loop by way of button-hole. A great number of such buttons are often found lying together. It is possible that the stone objects shown on Pl. IX. figs. 192, 193, may have been buttons, and that they may have been used in the same way.

DIVISION VI.—VESSELS OF BURNT CLAY OR STONE.

The vessels of burnt clay, which are found together with stone implements and skeletons in the most ancient graves, cannot have been placed there to hold the ashes of the dead, as in those times dead bodies were not burnt. They were evidently deposited in the grave from the same motive as other household furniture belonging to the departed; it may therefore be assumed that they were in daily use by the aborigines : we do not know for what particular purposes, but these may have been manifold. The larger vessels have no doubt been used as kitchen utensils for boiling meat, because those who know how to burn clay for pots would also understand how to boil meat for food. Most of the existing savages understand this mode of cooking, although they more frequently broil or roast their meat, fish, and other food. The natives of the Brazils also possess burnt clay vessels, which are made by hand. After having first formed the bottom of the vessel, they roll the clay into a long thin cylinder, lay it in a circle on the bottom, and form the border out of it; on the top of this they place another similar cylinder, then paste the two together with water, and polish the vessel inside and outside with a shell. Continuing their work in this manner, they give the vessel any shape and form they please. When completed, they impress some kind of ornament on the surface. When the vessel has been finished, they burn it in fire, in the open air, as verbally described to me by Dr. Natterer. The clay vessel here represented on Pl. X. fig. 209, and which was found by the Rev. M. Bruzelius in the above-mentioned tomb, in the Åsahögen, near Quistofta (see 'Iduna,' vol. ix. p. 2?5), has evidently been made by hand, without a potter's wheel, and in the same manner as the clay vessels of the South American savages, and the ornaments on the surface seem to have been made with a wooden peg, or something of that kind. The vessel has no ears, but the edge, which runs round the middle, is on both sides provided with two holes, and there are two smaller similar holes just below the border round the top. It is evident that a strap has passed through these holes, forming a kind of handle, and that it has been fastened in the border at the top by means of another thinner strap, which has passed through the two smaller holes. The vessel not being more than $4\frac{2}{3}$ inches deep, and of about the same width at the widest part, it cannot well have been used for cooking; but it has most probably been employed for raising and carrying water for drinking.

Burnt clay vessels are found among most of the existing nations, savage as well as civilised, and they are likewise found in all sepulchral mounds, from the earliest period up to the close of paganism. Fragments of vessels from North America, exactly like ours from the earliest ages, and ornamented in the same manner, are found together with stone implements also resembling ours.

I have, however, not had an opportunity of carefully examining a sufficient number of clay vessels, out of graves from different ages. This subject, therefore, I must leave to the more careful researches of others.

Plate X. fig. 210 represents a vessel rudely formed and scooped out of a compact limestone belonging to the chalk formation. It has been tolerably round, not deep, and provided with a thick round border. On one side is a small scooped-out ear: whether a corresponding one was found on the opposite side, where the border has been knocked off, cannot now be seen. It was discovered in a gravel-pit; it is therefore doubtful to what period it belongs.

DIVISION VII.—IMPLEMENTS WHICH HAVE BECOME WORN OUT OR BROKEN THROUGH USE.

By carefully enquiring into the manner in which implements have become worn, we can frequently ascertain the way in which they have been used. We have already directed the reader's attention to the sloping edge of the worn and re-ground square axe, and inferred therefrom that this axe must have been provided with a long handle or haft, somewhat like that of our wood-cutter's axe.

We have further shown that in a great number of the implements which are provided with a haft-hole, this has been very small in comparison to the size of the implement itself; and we have from this circumstance drawn the conclusion that the handle could not have been long. It must have been tolerably short in the hammers (Pl. VIII. figs. 169, 172, 178, 179), in the hammer-axes (Pl. VIII. figs. 176, 177), very short in the helved wedges (Pl. IX. figs. 183, 184); but it may have been tolerably long in the Amazon axe (Pl. VIII. fig. 173), and very long in the hoes (Pl. VIII. figs. 180, 181, and Pl. XV. figs. 256, 257). We find, further, in the hammers, distinct traces of much wear on the knob and on the sides, as well as on the sides of the wedge. If they had been used merely as weapons of war, they could not have been worn in the same manner. We find, moreover, amongst the helved wedges some so much worn down that only a small part of them still remains (Pl. IX. fig. 184). We draw from hence the conclusion that they must have been used in every-day life, and that they could not have been worn in such a manner as they are, if they had merely been battle-axes; still less if they had been lying in pagan temples as symbols: whereas this would have been the result if they had been used for wood-splitting or some such work.

This remark applies also to some of the carpenter's axes (Pl. VII. figs. 158–160, as well as figs. 151, 152). We can easily see by the sloping edge of the much-worn and frequently re-ground axes (figs. 159, 160), that they have been employed for working in wood. Sometimes implements with shaft-holes have been broken right across while being used at work; after which they have been provided with a new hole (Pl. X. figs. 206, 207). Equally illustrative of our subject is the manner in which the spear (Pl. XIII. fig. 225) has been worn while being used. This spear has evidently been of the same length, size, and shape as Pl. III. fig. 55. It has been inserted in the shaft to about $1\frac{1}{2}$ inch of its length; but has, while being used, been broken straight off near the shaft (the pin having previously been broken off), and has then with its broader end been wedged into the shaft to a depth of about $1\frac{1}{2}$ inch. Afterwards, having become blunted by frequent use, it has been repeatedly sharpened on both edges, almost down to the shaft, by means of a hammer-stone, in shape like Pl. I. figs. 6, 10, or Pl. I. figs. 1, 5. The broad part fixed in the shaft could, of course, not be worn, for which reason the spear-point, when inserted in the shaft, has got a marked indentation in both edges. I have in my collection several such worn-down and broken-off spear-heads.

This wear and tear shows that the savage was in the habit of always sharpening his pointed hunting weapons by means of a hammer-stone; and there is no doubt that he carried with him on his hunting excursions a portable instrument for this purpose. The spear-head (Pl. XIII. fig. 226) has evidently also been sharpened by means of such a tool, so that its blade, which originally resembled the spear-head (Pl. III. fig. 44), has ultimately become almost as sharp

s an awl. Spear-points worn in the same manner
re not uncommon in collections.

All this coincides perfectly with the explanation
which I have given already (at p. 10) of the articles
of antiquity (Pl. I.) which I have called hammer-
stones, i.e., chipping-stones or hones, and to which explanation I have been led by the unmistakable traces
which they show of blows against some hard stone.

In several of the antiquarian museums in Europe
there are knives and harpoons of flint obtained from
modern savages, worn and sharpened in a similar manner; and we know now that in such cases hammer-
stones have been used very much like those of ancient
times.

On the upper end of *broad gouges*, such as Pl. VI.
figs. 139, 140, we often see distinct marks of blows
dealt upon them by clubs while scooping out wood.

DIVISION VIII.—IMPLEMENTS WHICH HAVE BEEN TRANSFORMED INTO IMPLEMENTS OF ANOTHER KIND.

We meet not unfrequently with stone implements
which have evidently been formed out of a broken
fragment of a tool belonging to a totally different
class. I will mention a few which are preserved in
my former collection, now in the Academy at Lund;
but as it would be very difficult to make any intelli-
gible sketches of them, I do not attempt to do so.

1. Square narrow chisels made out of a spear-shaft,
as is perfectly evident at a glance.

2. Axe made out of a large broken knife-blade.

3. Axe, narrow and rounded at top, formed out of a worn-out broad axe.

4. Spear-head, somewhat like Pl. III. fig. 44, made out of a large knife-blade.

5. Arrow-head, like Pl. III. fig. 48, made out of the point of a knife-blade.

6. Semilunar knife, transformed into a saw or toothed spear-head, Pl. V. fig. 90.

These facts show (what, however, now scarcely needs a proof) that the above-mentioned stone objects have been employed as tools in every-day use; and that they have, while being so used, become worn, resharpened, and broken, and that the fragments have been made into other kinds of tools.

I ought, finally, to remark that sometimes, though very rarely, we find that even the aborigines of this country, who possessed weapons and implements only of stone, bone, and similar materials, endeavoured to sketch outlines of their animals. I have figured two such sketches (Pl. XV. figs. 258, 259) on a hoe made of a stag's antler (Pl. XV. figs. 256, 257), found in a bog in the south of Scania. These are evidently first attempts in the art of drawing, and can in no wise be compared with the masterly sketches of the savages in Perigord, who have so well figured their reindeer and other animals.

APPENDIX.

Pl. XVI. figs. 263–265 are of bone, and seem to have been a kind of awl for boring holes in skin, and so on. That they could not have been used as needles is proved by the projecting knob on the upper end: the hole at the end and sides shows that these, like the small whetstones (Pl. II. figs. 18–20) were carried in a strap attached to the belt. These forms, so far as I know, were not known before their recent simultaneous discovery in Sweden and Denmark.* They belong to the Stone Age, and have been found in Sweden in a gallery-grave at Luttra, in West Göthland, and in Denmark, in a similar tomb on the island of Seeland;† formed of a bear's and wolf's tusks pierced through, and having served doubtless as ornaments worn round the neck. Figs. 266, 268, belong to the variety already described on page 77, and sketched in Pl. II. figs. 36, 37. They are again brought forward here to show how much this form varies. Fig. 269 is a piece of a ground axe, very roughly hewn into a chisel. Fig. 270 represents a stone disc, ornamented with circular concavities, and was probably used as a button. Figs. 271, 273, we will describe in Chapter III.

* See the *Antiquarisk Tidskrift för Sverige*, vol. i. page 262, fig. 17; *Aarböger för Nordisk Oldkundighet*, vol. iii. page 213, Pl. III. figs. 7, 9.

† *Antiquarisk Tidskrift*, vol. i. page 264, figs. 261, 262.

CHAPTER II.

RETROSPECT OF THE WHOLE COLLECTION, AND AN ATTEMPT TO DRAW FROM IT A POSITIVE RESULT.

I WILL commence this chapter by citing a few opinions which have been expressed about these antiquities, but which I cannot consider correct.

As long as it was taken for granted, without any proof, that all these implements had belonged to one and the same tribe, namely, to the warlike, man-sacrificing Goths, from whom we ourselves descend, so long these antiquities were pronounced to be weapons of war and instruments of sacrifice, or symbols of worship of the Gothic heathen god, Thor. But it appears to have been forgotten that the most ancient records of this very people unmistakably indicate the then existence of still ruder tribes, whom they had found in the country on their arrival, and with whom they had bloody feuds; nor does it appear to have been remembered that these more ancient, and still ruder people, in order to subsist, must necessarily have had implements, which were doubtless rude, like themselves. We must either suppose that no other race than the present ever lived in the country, or else we must admit that many of our ancient implements may have belonged to this more ancient people. We shall enquire in the fol-

owing chapter whether several separate tribes did
ive here; in this, we will enumerate the usual modes
)f explaining these antiquities, and state why we
;annot consider them to be satisfactory.*

Thus, first, respecting the supposition that they
.vere merely weapons of war. Let us glance over
:hem, from the first to the last, to decide which of
;hem were exclusively made use of for that purpose.

No one can suppose the fish-hooks (Pl. II. figs.
28, 29, and 30) to have been offensive or defensive
weapons. Fishing-weights (Pl. II. figs. 31–35), if
they were fixed at the end of a string, might certainly
be used as weapons of war in case of need; but that
they were not intended for this purpose may be
inferred, partly because similar sinkers are still used
by savage people, and partly from the fact that
they have nowhere been met with, so employed,
amongst savages, although it is to their weapons of
war that the attention of Europeans has been especially directed.

Plate III. figs. 43, 45, 47, 48, represent harpoons,
which are so similar to those still used by savage
people, that their purpose cannot be questioned. The
small flint arrows (Pl. V. figs. 94–98) resemble those
which are still used in some places for shooting game;
that they have, however, in case of need, sometimes
been used as weapons of war, we have also evidence.
As to the curved knives (Pl. V. figs. 87–90), the

* The reader will please remember that this was written for the
first edition, upwards of twenty years ago. Now, perhaps, some of it
may be considered superfluous.

chisel, the convex axe, the cross-axe, &c., no one, I think, can suppose that any of these instruments were manufactured expressly to be used in war. The remaining forms are, the spear, the knife, the flint-pointed pike-shaped arrow, the straight axe, the hammer, and the hafted wedge.

1. With regard to the spear (Pl. III. figs. 55, 57), it appears at first sight as if it may have been a formidable weapon of war; but if we look into the matter a little more closely, we shall probably come to a different opinion. A man who goes to war does not go like an assassin against a defenceless victim, but in open battle against an armed foe. Thus it is evident that a warrior armed with such a thin brittle flint spear would get it broken at the first onset, and become disarmed. This long and thin flint spear could not therefore be fit for a weapon of war. It has been asserted that it would be the more fatal if it were broken in the wound; but here again the thought is of murder, not of war. I will not deny that the lance may possibly, on some occasions, have been used as a weapon of murder; various things have been used for the same purpose. But that it was chiefly used as a hunting weapon we may learn from the savages of North America, who still use similar flint spears for the chase (Pl. III. fig. 54, page 39).

2. The axe is so necessary an instrument of daily use, even amongst the rudest savages, that we cannot suppose it to have been exclusively a weapon of war. The savage here in the North required wood for warmth, timber for building his hut, a boat for

ishing, &c. For all this the axe would necessarily
ɔe required. How this was worn down by use, was
sharpened and again worn, so that the edge became
hacked like that of our own wood-axes, we have
already shown (Pl. VII. figs. 159, 160).

It is quite impossible that an axe, which was only
used for war, could be thus worn out to the stump,
and get a hacked edge: this could arise only from
daily use.

3. The hafted wedge (Pl. VI. figs. 129, 130). This
has been called the mace of war, and the hammer
(Pl. VIII. figs. 172, 179, &c.), the hammer of war;
as if in those remote times mankind did not require
anything to subsist on, but only to fight with; they
are not allowed to have had any implements, but
only weapons. But, it is manifest, by the manner in
which these antiquities were worn by daily use (in
particular the hafted wedge), that they were employed as wedges to be driven into wood by a mallet.
We do not, however, mean to deny that the savage,
in case of emergency, may have seized upon it, to
defend himself against an attack.

4. The knife exactly resembles the New Zealand
stone knife on Pl. III. fig. 65, which certainly was
used for domestic purposes.

5. The sharpened arrow (Pl. II. figs. 39, 40) may
no doubt have been used in war; but it is likewise a
suitable hunting weapon, and well adapted for killing
the larger mammalia.*

* That such *sharpened arrows* as Pl. II. figs. 39, 40, have been
found in tumuli on the plain of Marathon, where the Persian army

From this we can perceive that all the stone implements which have been described and sketched here are perfectly suitable implements for a rude tribe, which subsisted here in the North principally by hunting and fishing; that most of them could not even have been used for weapons of war, and that almost all the rest while in use were worn in such a manner as to show that they were employed for peaceable and domestic purposes.*

It has likewise been asserted that all spears and knives were used as sacrificial knives in the worship of Odin. It is perhaps possible that a few may have been used for that purpose, and that the worshippers of Odin, who, however, evidently already had metal for implements and weapons, used flint for sacrificial knives.†

was beaten by the Athenians, under the command of Miltiades, a countryman of mine, who has visited the battle-field, told me a few years since. But this kind of arrow was likewise used for hunting larger animals, and it is probable that it was with such an arrow that the *Urus*, the skeleton of which is now in the Zoological Museum at Lund, was wounded (though not killed).

* I do not, however, mean to deny that some of them were used in war. We have reason to suppose that every tribe, when they still remained in the lowest degree of civilisation, would use both implements and weapons of war made of flint, when this kind of stone was to be found. Even the Egyptians appear, during the most ancient times, to have made use of flint points for arrows and spears as weapons of war. Such were found by Mr. Brugsch on Mount Sinai, where, in olden times, according to tradition, an Egyptian garrison had been quartered.—*Wanderungen nach den Turkis-Minen und der Sinai-Halbinsel.* Leipzig, 1866. (Page 71.)

† It is quite possible that flint knives were occasionally used at these divine services, but neither history nor even tradition, as far as I have hitherto been able to ascertain, relate anything of the sort.

Such was, we know, the case with several ancient ations, and many instances of it occur in history. Vhen the Jews journeyed out of Egypt, they were lready well acquainted with iron, and yet Zipporah, he wife of Moses, circumcised her son with a sharp tone;[*] and when Joshua again introduced the sacraient of circumcision, which had been forgotten during he wandering in the desert, he used the same instruient that had formerly been used for that purpose, amely, the stone knife.[†] As far as we know, circumciion was practised by the Egyptian priests—it belonged o the ceremonies of reception in their order; and ccording to Herodotus,[‡] the Egyptians used a sharp thiopian stone at the embalming of their corpses. This last-named statement corresponds also perfectly vith the fact that there are in the Egyptian antiquarian ollections which I have seen at Berlin, and at Paris, n the Louvre, besides arrows and other weapons nade of metal, some sharp-edged implements of flint, vhich probably, therefore, were used at the embalmng.

The Phœnicians, likewise, after they had become cquainted with the use of metals, took sacred oaths

n Sturlöger's Saga (chap. xviii.) we are told of a house of offering ı Bjarmaland with the images of Thor and Odin. The priestess ·aved in her hand a short two-edged sword—perhaps a sacrificial nife—the two edges of which appeared to sparkle. Therefore it ·as bright, and consequently of metal. Nowhere in our records is ıention made of a sacrificial knife of flint; such were, however, robably in existence nevertheless.

* Ex. iv. 25.

† Josh. v. 2.

‡ Herod., book ii. chap. lxxxvi.

at the altar in this manner.   The person about to be
sworn held a lamb in the left hand and a flint knife in
the right, vowing by gods and man that if he broke the
promise given, the god might slay him the same way
that he killed the lamb.*   When the Horatii and the
Curiatii were to decide the fate of Rome and Alba
by single combat, the Romans were no doubt well
acquainted with weapons of metal, and yet Livy relates ('Histor.,' chap. i. 24) that the priest, at the
sacrifice, killed the victim with a flint knife; and other
instances might be mentioned.   In the same manner
it is possible that the worshippers of Odin (who evidently, until the introduction of Christianity, offered
human sacrifices,† in accordance with a barbarous
custom, which, no doubt, had its origin far back in
ancient times) used flint knives at their sacrifices;
although, if such had been the case, it appears strange
that it is nowhere mentioned.   But even if the practice of human sacrifice be admitted, independently of
historical testimony, there is no connection between
it and the flint knives and flint spears which lie in
the gallery-tombs; at the most it may serve to explain
those which, with metal weapons and burnt bone-
splinters, are occasionally to be found in more recent

---

* Corn. Nep. *Hannib.*, edit. Kuchen.

† It is singular, however, that human sacrifices are nowhere
spoken of in the Eddas. (Comp. Finn Magnusen, *Edda Sæm.*) This
is nevertheless a proof, amongst many others, that the Eddas are not
much to be depended on for historical knowledge as to the worshippers of Odin and their devotional customs.   More trustworthy
information is obtained from the first missionaries and from the
proceedings of the worshippers of Odin in foreign countries.

heathen tombs.   The former have, as already shown, no doubt been used chiefly for hunting.

It is well known that some antiquaries have thought themselves justified in pronouncing these stone weapons to be symbols of a primeval fire-worship.   It has been asserted, e.g., that the flint axe was a religious symbol, which in its substance (the flint) contained the holy fire, and in its shape (the wedge) betokened the quality of lightning ; namely, to cleave. Such explanations may possibly be considered ingenious, but they want every trace of historical as well as ethnological proof.   They betray, moreover, a paucity of information which alone ought to have prevented any such rash suggestions.   Any one who will but glance over an extensive collection of these antiquities, may easily convince himself that objects of exactly the same shapes occur, not only of flint, but likewise of greenstone (aphanite, diorite), basalt, slate, &c., even of bone, deer's horn, and other substances, which certainly do not contain any ' holy fire ; ' and yet they had undoubtedly the same signification and object, and answered the same purpose as the articles of flint, together with which they are found.   By this simple observation, the hypothesis is thus thoroughly refuted.   The very small specimens which are sometimes to be met with, resembling the large ones in everything but their size, and which have likewise been regarded as symbols, if they were not ornaments, were perhaps made for boys, to give them an early training in the use of arms.   Thus the Greenlanders are said to provide their boys with

suitable small 'kajaks' and darts.   Such, on the other
hand, as are made of amber in the shape of axes, &c.,
were ornaments like those of the Greeks, which were
made of gold.   (See page 72.)

Having, in the preceding part, described and
sketched, one by one, our most ancient antiquities of
stone and bone, and having, as far as possible, compared them with those instruments of the same materials which are still made use of in some countries, let
us again throw a glance over the whole collection,
that we may, as it were, bring together into one
single view the scattered ideas which it has given us
respecting the degree of civilisation and mode of living
of the people who used them.

In the first place, we find similar implements
among all people who still remain at a very low stage
of human civilisation ; and amongst them only.   We
have seen that similar implements, as late as the last
century, were used by the savages of New Zealand,
Taheite, Easter Island, Nootka, California, Boothia,
Greenland, Australia, and parts of North America ;
but wherever civilisation has diffused her light they
have been thrown aside.   Hence we may safely come
to the conclusion, that the people who, in Scandinavia,
made use of similar implements, stood in the same
low degree of civilisation as these savages.

Secondly, we have seen the very same kind of
chisels, both of stone and of bone, from New Zealand
(Pl. VI. figs. 129, 130, 132, 133), and from Scania
and Möen (Pl. VI. figs. 127, 128, 131) ; similar chisels
with hafts, from Nootka (Pl. VI. fig. 135), and from

Denmark (fig. 136); spears of flint and bone from
Scania (Pl. III. figs. 55, 57, 58), and from the most
northerly parts of North America (Pl. III. figs. 54,
56); fish-hooks of flint and bone from Scania (Pl. II.
figs. 28–30), and of the same kind of bone and shell
from Taheite (Pl. II. figs. 26, 27); straight axes from
Tierra del Fuego (Pl. VII. fig. 155), both of flint
(Pl. VII. fig. 153) and copper (Pl. VII. fig. 148),
and one perfectly similar of shell, from California
(Pl. VII. fig. 147); hammers from Scania made of
diorite (Pl. VIII. figs. 169, 172) and of stag's horn
(Pl. VIII. fig. 171), &c. From all this, we come to
the conclusion that in Scandinavia, as in the South
Sea Islands and in America, the savage did not con-
fine himself to one single material for his implements, but had resort to any suitable substance that
he could obtain.

Thirdly, we may infer the mode of living of the
people who made use of them. That these people
practised angling, both in the sea and the lakes, is
apparent by the fish-hooks and the places where
these have been found; that they practised hunting
on the water with harpoons and spears, like the
savages of North America, we can tell by their perfectly similar implements. They also, like the
latter, made use of the dart or the fowling-arrow
(Pl. VI. figs. 124–126), which could not be used
except on the water. The savages of Scandinavia
consequently had boats. These seem to have been
excavated trunks of trees, for the broad gouge (Pl. VI.
figs. 139, 140) has evidently been used for excavating

wood.* They knew the use of fire, for they understood how to burn clay into vessels, very much like those made by the savages both of South and North America. They also had, no doubt, like these latter, huts in which to live. These huts were probably of the same shape as the sepulchral huts (Pl. XIV. figs. 243–246, or figs. 249, 250), in which latter the aborigines were deposited after their death, doubled up in their graves in the same posture as that in which they had during their lifetime been accustomed to sit in their huts. (See Chapter III.) In order to build their huts, they must have used various kinds of tools: the felling-axe (Pl. VII. figs. 158–160, 153) for felling the trees and chopping the logs; the chisel (Pl. VI. figs. 127, 134) to cut holes in them, etc. For splitting wood, they probably used the hafted wedge (Pl. IX. figs. 183, 184), which they drove in with a mallet, for traces of blows are to be seen both on the plane of the mallet and on the wedge.

They used buttons (Pl. IX. fig. 191); consequently, they did not merely wrap themselves up in whole hides, but had clothes which were cut out. These clothes were probably made from the skins of those animals which they killed in the chase.† For

---

* It is remarkable that the denomination *ika*, which is still the name for such excavated boats, both in Scania, where they also are called *eka*, as well as in Norway, is derived from a Lapland word (*Urda*, i. 3, page 276). Christie has found a number of Lapland words in the Norwegian dialects, and a great many of those which he cites are to be found as well in the Scanian dialect.

† If we carefully examine the earth round the skeletons in our gallery-tombs, or tumuli, we may possibly find in them hair from the skins in which the corpses were wrapped when they were deposited

cutting these clothes they must have used a knife;
perhaps chiefly the curved knife (Pl. V. figs. 87, 88,
91): possibly also such an instrument as Pl. VII.
figs. 151, 152. They possessed the dog, like almost all
other savage nations; but, like them, they had hardly
any other tame animals, at least we have no satisfactory evidence that any bones of other animals have
been found in their tombs, while there are many of
the dog and various wild animals, such as the wild
boar, the hedgehog, the wild cat (?), the stag, the
elk, etc. No images are found amongst them, and
they had evidently no knowledge of written language;
neither letters nor hieroglyphics; for on their monuments, tombs, urns, or implements, we never meet
with any sign of letters. Neither do we find amongst
them any evidence of the use of metals, either ham-
mered or cast.

A remarkable fact in this branch of ethnography is
the great resemblance that exists amongst the stone
implements of nations of different tribes, during very
different periods and in the most distant countries
of the earth. If the question were asked, whether
we could infer from the resemblance of the implements that they had belonged to one and the same
tribe, we must, after a strict examination, answer *No*;
they only indicate the same degree of civilisation. To
give a few decisive proofs of this thesis, I have here,
on Pl. V. figs. 99–103, 106–111, sketched similar stone
arrow-heads, with a tongue for the shaft, from various

in the tomb; and in that case we can infer whether these skins
were of deer, seal, etc.

distant parts of the world; also (fig. 113) a triangular arrow-head from Scania, and (fig. 114) a similar one from Pennsylvania. But above all, the small heart-shaped arrow-heads (fig. 106) of flint, from Scania, and (fig. 107) of obsidian, from Tierra del Fuego, both of which are, with regard to shape and mode of construction, even in the most minute details and when closely viewed with a microscope, surprisingly similar, as if they had been made by the same hand and on the same day.* And yet there is between their places of origin such a vast distance as the space between Sweden and Tierra del Fuego; and such a gulf of time, that the one was made about twenty years ago, and the other is at least from 2,000 to 3,000 years old.

Indeed, it is hardly possible to explain the close resemblance between the fishing-tools and hunting weapons of the most distinct savage nations, as to time, place, and origin, without assuming that all of them, in one and the same low degree of civilisation, contrived these hunting weapons † instinctively, and in consequence of a sort of natural necessity. We are urged to this supposition, as we find even very complicated fishing and hunting implements of exactly

---

* The resemblance is even greater than is here shown on the Plate.

† If any one objects that the difference of the implements as to materials (see page 78) proves that they were made at will, and refutes the theory of instinct, I will only remind the reader that although the beaver builds its houses, and the birds their nests, by instinct, every zoologist knows that they are modified, more or less, even in one and the same species, according to access to different materials and local circumstances.

he same kind with all savage people from pole to ᵖole. Thus, for instance, the bow and arrow, though ι very ingenious contrivance, is found amongst almost *ill*, even the rudest savages; and, as already shown, ᵥery different races of men have instruments which ιre, not only similar, but even, so to say, identical. I ιave in another place enlarged on this subject.* I ᵢee here the evidence of a higher Wisdom, which has ᵢistributed to man natural weapons, with, however, ᵗhe power of discarding them as he improved in civiliᵢation. The lion received from nature his sharp ᵢlaws, the bear his muscular arms, and the wolf his powerful teeth; but they received them as parts of, and inseparable from, the individual. They cannot be improved.† Every lion is still, with regard to disposition and action, exactly such as lions were thousands ᵒf years ago. Man alone can make progress; he alone ᵢan throw aside his first rude weapons and alter them ᵃccording to his improved cultivation and more refined activity. I may here add, that man, in order that he might become the most powerful, was made at first the weakest. Through that alone he was induced to develope his higher talents; for it was not by bodily strength, but by the power of the mind that he was to be the king and lord of the earth.

* Public discourse at the meeting of the Scandinavian Naturalists at Stockholm, 1842.

† See Note 5.

CHAPTER III.

A COMPARISON BETWEEN THE ANCIENT CRANIA FOUND IN SCANDINAVIA AND THOSE BELONGING TO THE RACES NOW LIVING THERE.

WITH the stone implements, which were described in the first Chapter, there are not unfrequently found in our ancient tumuli, skeletons of the people who used these ancient weapons in life, and were buried with them after death. In our oldest peat-bogs we likewise occasionally discover ancient crania associated with implements of stone.

I have in another place expressed an opinion that it would be easy to decide to what particular race and tribe those people belonged who in Sweden employed implements of stone and of bones of animals, etc., if we would only carefully examine the skeletons, and more especially the crania, found beside the implements in ancient sepulchres.

I now propose to undertake such an investigation, in as far as it is feasible with the assistance of the materials which I have at my command. I propose to compare the fossil crania with those of the races now living amongst us.

But before proceeding to my task, I ought to premise that this subject (craniology), so highly important to ethnography, was in a very unsatisfactory condition until our illustrious countryman, Professor Anders Retzius, published his system of classification of human skulls. He first enunciated this system in his remarkable discourse at the Meeting of Naturalists at Stockholm in 1842, ' On the Form of the Crania of the Inhabitants of the North,'* when the races of man were for the first time classified, according to the shape of the skull, into *gentes dolichocephalæ* (long-headed) and *brachycephalæ* (short-headed), and each of these again were subdivided into *orthognathæ* and *prognathæ*. Since then the learned professor has completed his system, with indefatigable diligence and sagacity, by unceasingly working upon the foundation which he then laid down, so that craniology has at last grown into a science resting upon a firm and solid foundation.† Before the publication of this system, which made an epoch in the craniological department of ethnology, it was generally supposed that the Laplanders and the Esquimaux, for instance, belonged to one and the same race.‡ Professor Retzius has proved that they belong to entirely different

* Report of the Third Meeting of the Scandinavian Naturalists at Stockholm, 1842, page 157.

† After the lamented death of Professor Anders Retzius, his son, Dr. Gustaf Retzius, collected his father's lectures on this subject, and published them in the German language, in a very well illustrated edition, under the title of *Ethnographische Schriften von Anders Retzius, nach dem Tode des Verfassers gesammelt.* Stockholm, 1864. Filial love has thus raised an imperishable monument to an illustrious father.

‡ Cuvier also adopted this view in *Le Règne Animal.* Paris, 1829. Vol. i. page 84.

races: that the Laplanders are *brachycephalæ orthognathæ*; and the Esquimaux, on the other hand, *dolichocephalæ prognathæ*.

The two most essentially heterogeneous races, now inhabiting the Scandinavian peninsula, belong to the *gentes orthognathæ*; but one, the Laplanders, are, as already mentioned, *brachycephalic*, while all the others are *dolichocephalic*. These latter being comparatively the most numerous, we shall begin by examining them.

I consider the sketches given here of a cranium of a Swede (Pl. XII. figs. 227–229) to represent the true type of the so-called Germano-Gothic race, now the most general in Sweden, and the more so as Professor A. Retzius himself has acknowledged it to be such in his paper at page 166 (page 6 of the German translation). The sketch given by Professor Retzius in 'Ethnologische Schriften' (Pl. I. fig. 1) also agrees with this. In my first edition, 1838, I have described in the following manner the same cranium, of which I here reproduce the figure on a somewhat reduced scale.

Seen from above (fig. 228), the skull presents an oval, or rather, an elongated oval figure, a little broader at the back than in front, but rounded in both parts. The greatest length, measured from the most prominent part of the forehead to the most prominent part of the occiput, is, in proportion to the greatest breadth, measured across the crown of the head, as 4 to 3, or as 9 to 7; the line of contour at the sides of the frontal bone is directed forward, not obliquely inwards. The coronal suture, formed by he frontal and parietal bones, divides the cranium into two parts, of which the one situated behind the suture is much longer than that in front of it.

Seen sideways (fig. 227), the upper contour of the head forms an evenly curved arch, descending in front at the forehead almost perpendicularly, and a little more sloping behind the vertex, with a slight depression over the projecting occiput. If a line be drawn parallel with the upper edge of the jugal arch, the highest part of the arch formed by the contour of the vertex will generally be at, or in front of, the coronal suture. The height from the external auditory aperture to the crown is equal to two-thirds of the distance from the arch of the eye-brows (arcus supraciliares) to the most projecting part of the occiput.

Seen in front (fig. 229), the forehead is high and roundly arched, the jugal arches passing obliquely backward: the face appears to have been rather oval than round, which form is chiefly the effect of the high forehead and the more elongated upper jaw-bones.

More or less projecting brow-ridges; a more or less deep depression beneath them, above the root of the nose; a longer or shorter, a straight or more aquiline nose, with a more or less projecting bridge, and a larger or smaller nasal aperture, etc., are only individual and casual varieties. The same is the case with the greater or less unevenness of the facial bones in those places where the muscles have their attachments; the former indicates strong, and the latter weak facial muscles, and in this respect we meet with great individual varieties in the existing race to which we ourselves belong.

As I think that the method adopted by Professor Retzius in describing human crania is undoubtedly the right one, and as, moreover, it is the one now most generally followed, I shall here give an extract from his description of a cranium, such as I have described above.   He says:*—

'The shape of the skull, seen from above, is oval; the greatest length is in proportion to the greatest breadth as 1,000 to 773, or nearly as 9 to 7.   On an average, the greatest length from the glabella to the most projecting part of the tuber occipitale is 0·190 m.; the breadth in front (between the anterior part of the temporal fossæ) 0·107 m.; the greatest breadth posteriorly (immediately behind the temples), 0·147 m.; the greatest circumference of the skull over the glabella and the tuber occipitale, 0·540 m.; the height of the cranium, from the anterior edge of the foramen magnum to the highest part of the crown, 0·135 m.

'The contour of most skulls is somewhat straight in the front part of the forehead; the superciliary ridges are in general strongly developed, and the skull behind its line of greatest breadth becomes narrower towards the occiput, and is produced into a strongly projecting, rounded prominence.

'The greatest breadth of the cranium falls most frequently below, and a little in front of the parietal

* Report of the Meeting of the Naturalists at Stockholm, 1842, page 162.

minences which lie in front of the commencement of
he occiput and more at the side of the skull; these
minences are, however, often wanting, or they are
ounded off and project but slightly.

'The hinder part of the parietal bones and the
agittal suture between them slope backwards. The
ipper angle of the occipital bone is situated low
lown; the lambdoidal suture is visible on the lateral
urfaces of the cranium. The margins of the attach-
nents of the cervical muscles (lineæ semicirculares
najores) meet together at nearly a right angle, lying
)elow and in front of the very projecting occipital
spine, which generally projects, forming in adult males
ι considerable eminence.

'When the skull is viewed sideways, the occipital
protuberance also appears very large, as a prominence
bounded superiorly by an indentation above the angle
of the lambdoidal suture, or at the spot where the
large fontanelle was situated, which constitutes an
essential characteristic of crania of this type.

'In consequence of this considerable elongation of
the occiput, the outer auditory opening comes to lie
farther forward than in the skulls with short occiputs.
If, for example, one imagines a plane, passing through
the two outer auditory openings, intersecting the
cranium at right angles, this plane will intersect
the longitudinal diameter very near its middle; frequently it intersects it exactly in the middle, more
rarely in front, but occasionally a few millimeters
behind the middle. Another consequence of the
lengthened occiput is, that the temporal lines do not

extend so far back as in the skulls with short occiputs, but are situated, like the inferior and posterior angle of the parietal bone, entirely upon the side of the cranium and do not encroach at all upon the occipital aspect. It should be remarked that these lines diverge posteriorly from the borders of the attachments of the temporal muscles, which pass nearer the squamous suture of the skull directly across to the zygomatic process.

'Seen from underneath also, the Swedish crania are characterised by an elongation of the occiput, which causes the outline to be elliptic. In order to define this elongation, we may imagine a straight line drawn through both the outer auditory orifices. If on this line, as a chord, an arc be drawn round the most convex part of the occiput, the height of the arc will be nearly equal to the chord. It is to be observed that the line referred to will intersect the anterior border of the foramen magnum, and that the arc at first coincides with the borders of the mastoid processes. The distance between these points, therefore, easily defines the length of the chord, whilst the distance between the front edge of the occipital foramen and the most projecting part of the occiput represents the height of the arc. The surface to which the cervical muscles are attached, and which is bounded by the superior curved lines, falls entirely within this segment. This surface, corresponding to the cerebellar fossæ, in which the cerebellum rests, is in the Swedes nearly horizontal, and does not ascend on the hinder part of the head, but lies in the base

of the cranium, and is very slightly convex. The
occipital protuberance corresponding to the cerebral
fossæ, in which are lodged the posterior lobes of the
brain, projects considerably behind the cerebellar portion. The shape of the occipital foramen is oval; its
average length is 0·036 m., and breadth 0·029 m.: in
some crania it is pointed, both towards the front and
towards the back; in others either only towards the
front, or only towards the back. The mastoid processes are in most cases large and strong, and are
divided on the inner side lengthwise by a deep narrow
digastric fossa. The pterygoid processes are almost
perpendicular.

'If we now direct our attention to the framework
of the bones of the face, we shall find that, looked at
from above, it projects very little beyond the circumference of the brain-case; thus the external angular
processes of the frontal bone are small, and the lower
orbital edge nearly vertically below the upper one.
The malar prominences (the tubera zygomatica) lie
immediately below the external angular processes.
This formation is consequent upon the slight prolongation or prominence of the jaws. The jugal arches in
some individuals pass backwards almost in a straight
line, and widen only near the insertion at the temporal
bones; in others they form nearly a regular arch, the
longest convexity of which is in the middle. The distance between the greatest convexity of the zygomatic
arches is generally from 0·130 to 0·135 m. The
zygomatic bone is flattened externally, occasionally
rounded and large, and has a malar prominence pro-

jecting perpendicularly, whereby the whole of the lower edge of the zygomatic arch becomes strongly S-shaped, and an indentation arises frequently below the adjoining malar process of the superior maxillary.

'The circumference of the orbits varies in shape; in some people it forms a rhomb inclining obliquely outwards and downwards, with rounded angles; in others a parallelogram, also with rounded angles: sometimes this circumference is oval, sometimes nearly circular; but generally it inclines obliquely outwards, so that the corner of the malar bone is, as it were, drawn downwards.

' The distance between the orbits, which is occupied by the root of the nose and the ethmoid, is in general broad, as in the other northern races.

'The palate is generally highly arched; but in many instances it is also seen flattened in front.

'The alveolar process (processus alveolaris) of the upper jaw is high; the distance from the spina nasalis externa to the alveolar edge varies from 0·020 to 0·025 m. A line drawn and produced backwards in the direction of the lower edge of the alveolar process, falls a little below the point of the mastoid process, and on the centre of the ascending branch of the lower jaw. The face becomes, for the same reason, long. The average length in men, from the junction of the bones of the nose with the frontal bone to the alveolar edge of the front teeth, is 0·077 m. The canine fossa is, in the majority of skulls, tolerably deep.'

With the exception of the Laplanders, who belong to the short-headed people (*gentes brachycephalæ*), all the inhabitants of Scandinavia have, from time immemorial until the present day, belonged to the class *dolichocephalæ*. These have, ever since pagan times, chiefly consisted of Swedes (Svear) and Goths (Göter), of which the latter are by far the oldest inhabitants of the country, and their arrival here dates far anterior to the commencement of history, when they were spread over the southern and western districts of the country. The Swedish colonists have immigrated at a much later period, and were at first settled in the country surrounding the Mälar Lake, whence they have gradually spread themselves over the rest of the country.

In dialect, as well as in idiosyncrasy, the difference between the two is still very noticeable ; but I must confess that, with respect to the shape of the skulls, they do not appear to me to offer any distinct features by which they can be certainly distinguished from one another. We find also in Gotha (Göta rike), in different districts, a marked dissimilarity in dialect and features; for instance, in the neighbourhood of . Cimbrishamn, in Scania, in certain districts of Små-land, and elsewhere; all which seems to me to imply, that in ancient times settlers arrived from different parts and fixed their habitations in various places. Whether, by assiduously studying the peculiar expres-sions and words in the dialect of each, we shall be able to throw any light upon this subject, time must prove. I have in another place* endeavoured to show

* *Bronzåldern*, by S. Nilsson.

that colonies of Semitic people, employing implements and weapons of bronze, have settled in various places in the southern and western parts of the country; but their crania do not belong to the period now in question.

I cannot omit mentioning here a skull of widely different shape, especially on account of the place where it was found.

At the meeting of the Scandinavian Naturalists in Christiania, in 1844 (see 'Reports,' 1847, page 101), I referred to some human skeletons which were discovered in the shell-beds, in the province of Bohusland. They were situated high above the level of the sea; their position, and the undisturbed layers of shells resting upon them, seem to prove that they were not buried there, but that they accidentally perished at the time when these shell-beds were still the bottom of the sea. In the year 1843, two human skeletons were found in a shell-bed at Stångenäs, in the parish of Bro. They were discovered lying about three feet below the surface of the bed, and the shells in the bed as well as those above the skeletons were found in horizontal layers in a perfectly undisturbed state. The skulls of the skeletons were lying about two feet distant from each other, but the skeletons themselves were lying in different directions; the legs of one were spread out, the other one was lying straight. Everything seems to indicate that they had perished by some accident, and that part of the beds had afterwards been formed over them. This bed is now at least 100 feet above the level of the sea.

)nly the two crania were preserved, and they were n a fragmentary condition; they are now in the Museum at Lund. I have here (Pl. XV. figs. 253, 254, 255) sketched the larger. But it is not ascertained whether it belongs to the *Stone Period*. It is unusually large, and appears to me to resemble most nearly, though not perfectly, a plaster cast of a cranium sent by Sir W. R. Wilde, of Dublin, to Professor Retzius, and said to have belonged to O'Connor, who is called the last King of Ireland, and of whose skull a plaster cast is preserved both in the Museum of the Caroline Institute at Stockholm, and in the Zoological Museum at Lund. This cranium is oblong, and almost of equal breadth and length, with both sides convex and even, above the temporal fossa, so that the outlines of the sides form uninterruptedly a rather arched line. In other crania a depression above the temporal fossæ, more or less perceptible, will be observed; the upper outline is slightly convex; the forehead low. The same form of cranium is occasionally met with even in persons now living.

Another cranium which was found many years since in a niche of one of the catacombs at Malta, and is now preserved in the Zoological Museum at Lund, has a strong resemblance to this form. It was much decayed, and fell altogether to pieces while being transported, but it has been skilfully restored.

I have, for the sake of comparison, given a photograph of it on Pl. XVI. figs. 271–273, and will now briefly describe this cranium, notwithstanding that it does not belong to the Stone Age.   The fore-head is high and prominent, sloping above and between the eye-brows, which protrude but little, and there is only a slight indentation at the root of the nose.   The upper outline is rather straight across the crown of the head, more arched in front, with a small concavity above the eye-brows (glabella), but sloping backwards still more towards the protube-rance of the occiput; the *pars basilaris* of the occi-pital bone almost horizontal.   The teeth in the upper jaw appear rather protruding.

Another form of cranium, which undoubtedly be-longs to the stone age in Scandinavia, is that which occurs in the gallery-graves in West Göthland, and of which I have given sketches on Pl. XIII. figs. 236, 237, 238.

Some of those found in 1863, while searching a gallery-grave near Lock-Gården, in the parish of Luttra, Professor Baron G. von Düben has measured and described in the following manner:—

Length	19·00 centimeters
Height	14·20 ,,
Breadth across forehead . . .	9·70 ,,
,, ,, crown . .	13·80 ,,
Zygomatic arch . . .	12·70 ,,
Circumference . .	52·60 ,,
Height of face	6·90 ,,
,, jaw	3·20 ,,

With regard to the shape, Baron von Düben says, in the 'Antiquarisk Tidskrift för Sverige,' vol. i. p. 279: 'The crania are, with *one* exception, *dolichocephalic*.

n the present Swedish race, the length in propor-
ion to the breadth is as 1000·00 to 771·87.   In
welve of those exhumed in these tumuli, and in
vhich the proportions could be measured with great
ιccuracy, the length in proportion to the breadth was
ιs 1000·00 to 731·45.   Most of them also were rela-
ively narrow across the forehead, but they presented
n other respects the usual curvature and breadth
ιcross the parietal protuberances, zygomatic arches,
&c., and projecting occiput of the Swedish cranium.
But by the size of the superciliary ridges and the
proportions of the face, they are easily distinguished
from the existing race.   The superciliary arches pro-
ect enormously in most of them, and are high and
thick.   In several of them the face is nearly pro-
gnathous; the alveolar edge of the upper jaw projects
strongly.   If we can in any way judge of the shape
of the nose by the bones, it must have been a very
prominent one.   The vertical diameter of the orbits
was smaller than in the crania of the existing race;
the horizontal diameter of the usual size.   The palatal
arch is very high.   The teeth, in which caries occurs
rather frequently, were for the most part so much
worn at the crown, that the edges had become sharp
and cutting; the masticating surfaces sloping inwards.'

I have quoted from Baron Düben this accurate
and minute description of the skulls found in the
gallery-graves in West Göthland, in order that we
may be able in future to discover by comparison
whether the gallery-graves found in other parts of

Western Europe, in Asia, and in Africa, have also been constructed by the same ancient race which constructed those found in the south and west of Sweden.

We now come to the second essential shape of cranium, viz., the *brachycephalous*. It belongs to the European polar race, which we call Laplanders, and to many other races in various parts of the world.

A skull of a Laplander, from Stensele parish, is figured on Pl. XII. figs. 233, 234, and on Pl. XIII. fig. 235. If we compare these figures with figs. 227–229, we see at once how much they differ from one another. Seen from above, the head of the Laplander presents a much shorter and broader oval shape, which, therefore, much more approaches to the spherical form. This form is not only broader at the back, but also much more square and less protuberant. The greatest length, from the most projecting part of the forehead to the most prominent part of the occiput, is, in proportion to the greatest breadth across the vertex, about as 8 to 7, and to the breadth across the zygomatic arch about as 5 to 4. The contour lines at the sides of the frontal bone slope obliquely inwards. The coronal suture divides the calvaria into two parts, of which the hinder is much broader, but not longer than the one in front.

Seen sideways (fig. 233), the upper contour of the head forms an arch rather sloping in front and descending rather perpendicularly at the back, therefore just the reverse of what is the case in the cranium of the Goth. If a line be drawn parallel with the upper

:dge of the jugal arch, the highest part of the curve above it will be found to lie behind the coronal suture, or nearly in the centre between it and the lambdoidal. The height from the external auditory orifice to the summit of the crown is more than three-fourths of the entire length of the head.

Seen in front (fig. 235), the forehead is rather flat, low, and sloping backwards; the jaw-bones somewhat prominent. The face appears to have been much shorter, in comparison with its breadth, than in the Goths, and this chiefly proceeds from the low forehead, the protuberant check-bones, and the short upper jaw-bones.

Sometimes, but very rarely, a cranium of this kind has been found in Stone Age tumuli amongst the crania of dolichocephalous shape, which is the common type in such tombs; the one which I have sketched here (Pl. XII. figs. 230–232) of this description was found many years ago in a gallery-grave on Möen. It resembles very much that of a Laplander. (Compare figs. 233, 234, and 235.)

The skull figured on Pl. XIII. fig. 239 is that of a Lapland woman from Lyksele, preserved in the Museum at Lund; the one given on the same Plate, fig. 240, is copied from a plaster cast, the original of which was found in a gallery-chamber at Möen, and described by Professor Eschricht in ' Dansk Folkblad,' Sept. 15, 1837, page 111.

Some isolated brachycephalous crania have therefore been occasionally found in our stone sepulchres; but it may be taken for granted that the people who constructed these sepulchres belonged to one of the dolichocephalous races which still inhabit the greater part of the country. We may, however, infer that the Laplanders have been more disseminated in former times than now, partly from the fact that we occasionally find crania in our bogs which appear to have belonged to that race, and partly from sundry local names, said to be of Lapland origin, of which we shall treat further in another chapter. There is still much wanting to complete our investigations concerning the skulls of all the different races which have inhabited the Scandinavian peninsula; but we trust that this department of ethnological science may also reach its full development, since a desire to open and examine scientifically our numerous sepulchral monuments of different kinds has been more generally awakened. We will, in conclusion, here give a synoptical table of the dimensions of the various crania to which we have referred.

Synoptical View of the Dimensions of the Crania here described.

	Swedes	West Gothians	O'Connor	From a Shell-bed	Malta	Laplander
Length from the forehead to the most projecting part of the occiput	188—185	189—187	209	196	187	179—160
Greatest breadth of cranium	148—146	138—136	153	147	147	150—140
Breadth across forehead	˙98— 97	98— 90	118	117	118	100— 91
Breadth across the jugal arches	142—134	126—127	—	—	122	136—120
Breadth between the points of the mastoid processes	112—102	107—105	—	—	110	110— 95
Length from the nasal spine to alveolar border	24— 19	21— 19	22	24	24	17— 17
Length from the orbit to the lower edge of the malar bone	44— 40	47— 40	—	—	—	—
Circumference	542—535	530—525	575	556	538	530—480

* The measures are millimeters. When two different ones occur in the same column, the former is probably that of a man, and the latter that of a woman.

CHAPTER IV.

SEPULCHRAL MONUMENTS BELONGING TO THE STONE AGE
—COMPARISON BETWEEN THESE AND THE DWELLING-
HOUSES OF THE ESQUIMAUX.

WE know scarcely more of the tombs of the primitive
inhabitants of Sweden than of their dwellings. It
is probable that they wandered about scattered in the
woods, without any fixed dwellings or burial-places.
The sepulchres which we shall here describe were
erected of large stones, collected together by main
force.   They are of two kinds, which in different languages have different names.   The one kind we call
passage-graves, or gallery-graves (*gång-grifter*); the
other *dösar* (dolmens). We shall first describe the
former. Every such tomb has evidently been erected
for a whole horde, or for the family of their chief, and
was intended to last a long time. These sepulchral
monuments do not therefore betray the first stage of a
savage state, and we observe that the people who built
them had already established a certain social order,
although they belonged to the proper Stone period,
which preceded all use of metals. They had probably
their dwellings in the vicinity of their burial-places.
But as regards this distant period, when stone implements only were as yet used in Scandinavia, we cannot
with certainty find any traces of dwelling-houses, inas-

much as these were built more or less below ground, and probably of small stones, or of earth and wood, and would therefore, by the influence of time, have been reduced long ago to dust.

But if we do not meet with houses for the living, we do meet with sepulchral chambers, in which the corpses of the dead were successively deposited; and these having, as above mentioned, evidently been burial-places for whole families and generations, it is more than probable that they were built after the same model as the common family-huts, although of more solid materials, and far greater durability.

These primeval burial-houses, in which we find stone implements, and skeletons with crania like those already described, and sketched on Pl. XIII. figs. 236–238, and on Pl. XIV. figs. 243, 244, 245, 249, and 250, present a peculiar style of architecture, which cannot be confounded with that of any existing European nation. Nevertheless it is far from being incidental or only of occasional occurrence. On the contrary, a whole class of ancient tumuli are of this form, and in them are found, as above stated, implements and weapons of stone only, never of metal. They have special denominations, and are called in North Germany, *Hünenbetten*; in Denmark, *Jettestuer*; and with us, *Gång-grifter*. And with respect to the people who constructed and occupied them, the skulls found show that with few, perhaps incidental, exceptions, they belong to the dolicho-cephalous race.

In order to give at once a diagnosis by which they

may easily be distinguished from others, I will observe that they have the following appearance and construction.

They form, generally, an oblong square (sometimes a circle), with flat roof and a long narrow gallery, pointing either to the south or to the east, which, in the square ones, proceeds from the centre of one of the longest sides, and is lower than the sepulchral chamber itself.

These tumuli vary in size, but they are all constructed to contain a number of corpses, occasionally up to twenty or more, of different ages and of both sexes, according as the individuals of the family or horde by degrees expired.

One of the tumuli of this kind which has been most completely described and most skilfully sketched, is that which was opened in 1805 on the plain of Axevalla, in West Göthland (Gotheb. Wett. o. Witt. Sam. Hand., 1806, page 82, with Plate; Id., 1808, page 87, with Plate, and also the annexed Pl. XIV. figs. 243–5). Two tumuli of an exactly similar form as the one now mentioned were opened by Mr. Hage, in 1836, near Stege, on the island of Möen, and these I had an opportunity of examining while on a journey there the same year.

The walls of such tombs always consist of large, erect, and, at least on the inner side, flat slabs of granite, joined together as closely as possible; the crevices between them are carefully filled up with fragments of stone, to prevent animals of prey from penetrating, and attacking the corpses; the wall inside is tolerably smooth, although we have never observed that the stones were hewn or ground.* The floor of the chamber is sometimes paved with flat stones, sometimes covered only with sand, and the roof consists of massive oblong and broad granite-stones, which lie with the flat side downwards across the tomb (fig. 245), the height of which, from floor to ceiling, is from 5 to nearly 6 feet. In the centre of one of the long side walls is an opening from which proceeds towards the east or south (i.e. towards the sunny side, and never in any other direction) a long narrow gallery of upright granite-stones, but lower than those which form the walls of the chamber. This gallery is also covered with smaller granite-slabs, and is commonly 16 to 20 feet long, $2\frac{1}{3}$ to 3 feet wide, and 3 feet high, having the farther end closed up with a flat stone, by way of door. We find here a remarkable resemblance to the grotto at Aurignac (Haute-Garonne), discovered by Lartet.† In this grotto the corpses had also been buried one by one, together with their weapons or ornaments and whatever else

---

* The coarse wall-stones, of which these tombs are constructed, are never hewn. If they were split by the hand of man, which seems to have been the case occasionally, it must have been done by placing on the rock burning piles of wood to heat it, and then suddenly cooling it by pouring cold water on it, when it would split. Some of the inhabitants of our forest districts still have recourse to this mode of splitting rocks.

† See Lyell, *Antiquity of Man*, page 182. Lubbock, *Prehistoric Times*, page 262.

was considered to be of use for the life which they were thought to continue after death. The chamber itself is usually 24 to 32 feet long and from 7 to 9 feet broad, the breadth generally being about one-fourth of the length.

In these burial-vaults the corpses are placed along the sides of the walls in a sitting or lying position; they are less frequently placed in the centre of the chamber. The corpses, often very numerous, being those of men, women, and children, have evidently been buried at different times, and probably during a long series of years. The vault was consequently finished and covered over before any burials took place therein; and the corpses were carried into the tomb through the entrance-door, and this was again closed after each funeral.

The chamber appears to have been frequently divided round the walls into cells or stalls, and in each stall a corpse was deposited. The partitions between the stalls were sometimes, when circumstances permitted, made of flat stone slabs-(as in the tumulus at Axevalla), and where this was the case the corpses are in such good preservation that they were found sitting in their original position, with the legs bent double under the trunk and the fore part of the arm raised against the chin. For the most part, however, the walls of the cells were of wood, in which case, when these became rotten and decayed, the skeletons fell to the ground. But that the bodies had originally been sitting in an upright position, we can see by the bones of each skeleton lying crosswise in a heap, on the top of which the skull was lying. All the skeletons found in the above-mentioned tumulus at Stege, on Möen, were in this position. I will not, however, deny that skeletons may also have been found buried in an extended position; children at least seem to have been buried in that way. With regard to this, it is also possible that the same tribe, in different districts and at different times, may have had a somewhat different way of burying their dead. With each skeleton we find generally one or two, sometimes several, stone implements or wrought pieces of amber; the former are found amongst the male, and the latter most frequently amongst the female skeletons. Amongst some skeletons which were discovered sitting in a cell filled with sand, were amber beads still lying round the neck; these had, therefore, evidently been worn as ornaments. ('Gotheb. Handl.,' page 93.)

These tumuli are, as far as I know, never bare, but always covered, both at the top and round the sides, so that the roof or top-stones are never seen above, and at the sides scarcely ever the outermost gallery-stones. I have since seen such quite bare, and of a gigantic size, on the heath Ekorrewallen, in West Göthland. But the covering material is different in different districts; in the isle of Möen the tombs were covered with earth forming mould-hills, but in West Göthland they were mostly covered with larger or smaller boulders, and have outwardly the appearance of large cairns. (See 'Gotheb. Handl.,' 1806, page 84; Id. 1808, page 87, and 'Iduna,' Part VIII.

page 110, Pl. II. fig. 1.)　All cairns or tumuli, however, do not contain such stone huts as are here described.　It is impossible to judge from the outer form of a tumulus, or cairn, what kind of tomb may be contained therein, or whether such a monument belongs to the Stone, Bronze, or Iron Age. It is only by seeing the tomb itself that we can tell with certainty to which period it belongs ; and if a side gallery be found, we may be perfectly sure that no metal will be found in the tomb.

Such half-cross graves, or gallery-tombs, as those described, are mentioned and sketched in many works ('Antiquar. Annaler,' vol. iii. Pl. II.), and fig. 3 on the same Plate, which represents one found in the isle of Möen ('Antiquar. Annaler,' vol. ii. Pl. II.). This latter presents this peculiarity, that the gallery is a double one, and that there is a partition-wall in the vault between the two wings.

To this ancient time, and to this same people, belongs also the tumulus which was opened in 1819 on the Åsa-hög, near Quistofta, as described and sketched in 'Iduna,' Part IX. page 285, Pl. I. figs. A, B, by the Rev. Magnus Bruzelius. This ancient sepulchre is especially remarkable in two respects. That it belongs to the same class of ancient monuments as those sketched here, on Pl. XIV. figs. 243–245, will at once be seen by the long gallery pointing to the south (see 'Iduna,' Pl. I. fig. B), and we are still more fully convinced thereof by the description, which informs us that a number of flint implements and ornaments of amber were found in it, but not a trace of any metal.

The sepulchral chamber itself is not, like the former
ones, an oblong square, but round (see sketch in
' Iduna,' and Pl. XIV. fig. 250).   This form is unusual and highly remarkable, as we shall show presently. The vault seems, besides, to have been divided
by a partition-wall. Another remarkable circumstance
which we notice in the description of this sepulchre is that an older series of corpses were interred
therein, without any regard to order or regularity,
forming a layer, which was covered by a bed of sand,
forming a floor, upon which other corpses had in their
turn been deposited. This mode of interring the
dead has also been noticed in the tumuli in West
Göthland. This proves also that the same sepulchral chamber had been used as a sepulchre for a
long period.

We occasionally meet with tumuli, especially in
cultivated districts, containing square stone graves
without a side gallery, in which stone implements
have been found; but if we examine them more
closely, we shall see that they are mutilated, and that
they constitute a wing only of the original gallery-
grave; in such cases we always notice more or less
distinct traces of the destroyed side gallery.

The tumuli here described do not often lie singly,
but there are generally several in the same district,
frequently placed close together. Most of them lie
on high ground, not far from where water was formerly or is still found, on the banks of which the
inmates of the tumuli appear to have dwelt. Whether
any of these tumuli were actually dwelling-houses,

it is impossible either to prove or to deny. It is worth noticing, that in one of the stone huts opened at Stege, on the isle of Möen, no trace of any skeletons was found, but instead, a great number of stone implements, clay vessels, and amber ornaments. This was also the case with one of the gallery-graves, which was examined on the Glanslöfs hills.

From what has hitherto been stated concerning the ancient tumuli, it appears to me to follow, that the gallery-graves which were constructed by one of the ancient nations here, during the Stone Age, are distinguished from all other ancient monuments by a narrow side gallery, running south or east, and by the chamber itself being sometimes an oblong square, sometimes round. This form, whether of the graves or of the dwellings for the living, we look for in vain amongst any of the German nations.*

Neither amongst them, indeed, nor amongst any people of the so-called Caucasian race, so far as I know, have any counterparts to these tumuli been found; but if we turn to the Esquimaux in Greenland and in North America, we shall find in their winter huts a most surprising similarity to our tumuli. We shall not here enlarge upon this; but so much we may venture to say without being considered as

---

* 'The grave of Harold Hårfager, described by Sturlesson, has quite a different form and construction.' (Sturlesson's *Kunga Sagor*, translated by Jacob Aal, vol. i. page 83.) Such tombs, surrounded by stone columns and with a higher stone at the head and feet, were still a few years since to be seen in the old churchyard at Dahlby, near Lund. The same is the case with the grave of Thyre Danebod and others.

advocating any hypotheses, since there must be, to every intelligent reader, a great difference between a similarity founded upon comparison and a hypothesis. And whether the similarity here alluded to does in reality exist, the reader can easily determine by a glance at Pl. XIV., wherein fig. 243 represents a tumulus on Axevalla plain, in West Göthland, and fig. 246, an Esquimaux winter hut in Greenland.

It is, however, not only the outer contours which are identical, but also the construction, the dimensions, and the interior arrangement. In order to show this, we shall first describe an Esquimaux winter hut in Greenland, partly according to the information which Captain Graah gives us in his ' Journey,' page 49,* in which also the sketch of a Greenland hut is given, which is copied on Pl. XIV. fig. 246, and partly to the verbal statements of persons who have long resided in that country.

The hut forms an oblong square. The size varies according to the number of families who agree to inhabit it together. The largest huts are about 60 feet long by 14 to 16 feet in breadth, which therefore is about one-fourth of its length. The walls are 6 to 8 feet high, constructed of stone, and the crevices between them filled up with turf.† The floor is

---

* *Undersögelse-Reise till Östkysten af M. A. Graah.* Kjöbenh., 1822. In the sketch I have made the side gallery a little larger than in Captain Graah's sketch, because it is so in reality, both according to the verbal account of those who have seen Greenland winter huts and according to Captain Graah's own description thereof.

† There are also dwellings in Greenland, the walls of which consist of stones alone.

usually paved with flags. The roof is flat, and constructed of drift-timber, stretching across from one wall to the other. Upon this, smaller timber, or balks, are piled crosswise, and on the top of these rafters are thrown sweet-broom and juniper-twigs, then turf and a thick layer of earth. In the centre of the longest wall, towards the sunny side, is the passage or entrance, also covered; this is from 20 to 30 feet long, sometimes a little curved, about $2\frac{1}{2}$ to 3 feet broad, and so low that one must rather crawl than walk to get in. In most cases, indeed, it is necessary to crawl on hands and knees. (Pl. XIV. fig. 251.) The interior of the hut is loftier, but still not more than 5 or 6 feet high from floor to ceiling. With regard to the interior arrangements, it is only along the walls that the inmates of the house can sit or lie. Benches are placed there for that purpose, and the room is occasionally partitioned off, along the inside of the wall, by means of hides, into separate cells, like the stalls in a stable. Each family occupies one stall, but the unmarried women have one to themselves.

The reader will please to compare this description of an Esquimaux winter hut in Greenland with the description (page 110) of our ancient tombs in the south of Scandinavia. They are, in fact, identical in all essentials—the form, proportions, height, size, and direction of the long narrow side gallery, the division of the vault into stalls along the walls, etc.

I have previously mentioned that Esquimaux huts have been found in Greenland, the walls of which were constructed, like those of our tumuli, altogether

of stone. In the ' Tidskrift för Nordisk Oldkyndighet,'
vol. ii. pages 332, 333, there is a very interesting description of such ancient huts in a mountain district in
Greenland. The walls of these huts were not, as in the
Greenland Esquimaux huts in general, constructed
of stone and turf, but only of stone; in their form,
however, they resembled the Greenlanders' ordinary
winter dwellings. The stones in most of them were
of moderate size, but in others the walls were constructed of large flat stones, partly square, placed
upright, and so accurately fitting one with the other,
that they hardly required smaller stones to fill up the
crevices. In one of the sides there was an opening
leading to a gallery, consisting of a row of stones at
each side of the opening. Having been abandoned
long ago, these huts are now without roof, and open
at the top. The place where they were situated in
considerable numbers, was on three sides surrounded
by a large lake. One cannot but be astonished, when
reading the description of our Scandinavian gallery-
graves, to find it applicable, almost word for word, to
the Greenland huts. It is not difficult to see the
reason why these Greenland stone huts were not
roofed in with stone, like our tumuli. They were
disposed in groups like ours, and, like them, in the
vicinity of water.*

* It is true that the Greenland guide of the traveller who has
described these huts endeavoured to make him believe that they
were monuments of the colonies of the ancient Norsemen in
Greenland. This is easily accounted for, because, as he was bound
on a voyage for discovering such monuments, his followers probably
expected some reward for every such discovery which they assisted

But it is not in Greenland only that we meet with dwellings constructed as here described; we find them amongst all Esquimaux tribes, wherever they are domiciled. They are invariably and everywhere characterised by the long, narrow, straight, or curved covered side gallery, pointing to the south or east, and by the chamber about 5 feet high. The latter, however, varies in circumference and building materials.

The Esquimaux huts, sketched in Pl. XIV. figs. 247, 248, were found by Scoresby the younger on Jameson's Land, in lat. 71° N., on the east coast of Greenland. They were nine or ten in number, deserted by the inmates, and lay close to each other, near the declivity of the shore. The roofs had either fallen in or been removed. What remained of each hut was an excavation in the ground about 4 feet deep, 15 feet long, and 6 to 9 feet broad. The side walls consisted of unhewn stones, and the floor of sand and clay. The entrance, as usual in all Esquimaux huts, was a horizontal covered gallery,

him to make. They were therefore so zealous, that they tried to make out even Esquimaux pitfalls for foxes, and natural cavities in rocks, to be monuments left by the Norsemen. We might, perhaps, be induced to credit the statement, that the said stone huts with their long narrow side gallery were of foreign origin, and that they had served as models for the Greenland winter huts, did we not know that huts constructed after this same model are met with not only amongst the Greenlanders in those districts where foreign colonists have dwelt, but everywhere throughout the whole of Greenland and North America inhabited by the Esquimaux race. This form of hut belongs, therefore, originally to this race, as we shall presently show by further evidence.

which led from the hut to the south or south-east,
under ground, a distance of about 15 feet, having an
egress to the open air lower down and nearer the
shore. This gallery was so low that an entrance to
the hut could be gained only by crawling on hands
and feet; the top was covered with flags, and this again
with turf. The roof of such huts is very little elevated
above the ground, and being covered with turf and
overgrown with moss or grass, it so much resembles
the surrounding ground as scarcely to be distinguish-
able therefrom.* Who does not fancy he sees in this
description our gallery-graves hid under an earthen
mound? What Scoresby mentions afterwards deserves
likewise our attention in the highest degree. He tells
us that two or three huts, to all appearance of older
date than the others, seemed to have been used as
sepulchres, because in them were found graves containing human skeletons. Several graves contained,
besides human bones, fragments of such implements
as are used by the Esquimaux, when fishing or
hunting, and which had been deposited amongst
the corpses, to be employed by the dead in another
world (page 236).

Another proof that the Greenlanders' winter huts
were occasionally used as sepulchres, is afforded by
the following circumstance. A credible person, who
had been domiciled a long time in Greenland, has
informed me that there existed, about 1830, at Kan-
garsak-Tange, two miles from Godhavn, an ancient

---

* See *Tagebuch einer Reise auf den Wallfischfang*, by W.
Scoresby, Jun., page 234, Pl. VIII. See also Note 6.

Greenlander's hut, in which were found a number of corpses provided with implements and ornaments. They were placed in a sitting posture along the walls, consequently exactly in the same manner as in the tumulus on Axevalla plain. Several similar cases are mentioned by Sir John Lubbock in the 'Annual Report of the Smithsonian Institution for the Year 1863,' pages 326, 327, in an article reprinted from the 'Natural History Review.' The Baschkiers, for instance, bury their dead also in a sitting posture. (See Erman's 'Reise,' vol. i. page 436.)[*]

We have seen that the sepulchral hut in the Åsahögen, near Quistofta, was quite circular, but had, as usual, its long narrow gallery towards the south. It is worth noticing that, in the most northerly parts of North America, the winter huts of the Esquimaux are, according to Sir John Ross, of a similar shape (Pl. XIV. fig. 251). They are there built entirely of frozen snow, with windows of ice. These have likewise a long gallery, occasionally curved, leading to the interior of the chamber, which forms a circle of about 10 feet in diameter, when intended for only *one* family, but when for two[†] it forms an oval of about 15 feet by 10. These winter huts are constructed very rapidly; in about half an hour's time the edifice is completed. When the Esquimaux, on their travels in dog-sledges, are over-taken by a snow-storm, which stops their progress,

---

[*] See also Lubbock's *Prehistoric Times*, page 409.

[†] Captain Sir John Ross, *Zweite Entdeckungs-Reise nach den Gegenden des Nordpols*, 1829–1833, vol. i. pages 322–324.

they immediately erect such a snow-hut. The manner of constructing it we learn from Sir John's narrative, page 390. They never forget, even when building such temporary dwellings of snow, to construct the long gallery. This gallery constitutes, therefore, an essential part of the Esquimaux dwellings, whether round or square, and whether the walls are constructed of stones, of turf, or of snow. The same is the case with our earliest tumuli, in which stone implements are found; they also have the long narrow side gallery, whether they are round or square, large or small.

What, therefore, the Esquimaux huts and the tumuli have in common with each other is that they all have flat roofs, that they contain a chamber about 5 feet high, and are provided with a long, covered side gallery, 2 or 3 feet broad and 3 feet high, always pointing to the east or south. They resemble each other also in their form, which varies, being sometimes round and sometimes an oblong square. Their interior arrangement also is in the main the same. In both the centre of the floor is unoccupied, but the chamber is divided along the walls into cells or stalls, and in these stalls the inmates—of the sepulchres as well as of the dwellings—sit in the same stooping position which all polar people affect. It seems scarcely possible to assume that all these various important and minute similarities should be only accidental. And yet it appears impossible, with the knowledge which we *now* possess of the essential dissimilarity of the tribes, to suppose that there should be anything in common, or any connection between them. There must be some other reason, for which we cannot as yet account.

We have already seen that the Esquimaux, like the aborigines of Sweden, place the implements of the dead beside them in the grave. The missionary Cranz relates, in his ' History of Greenland,' page 301, that they place the boat (kajak) of the departed, his arrows, and every-day utensils beside his grave, 'in order that he may use them in the next world for his support.' Even in this circumstance we find a similarity between them.

This same missionary, Cranz, relates in another place, that a great many Greenlanders, even in his time, used to lay the head of a dog beside the grave of a child, ' in order that the soul of the dog, which can always find its way home, may show the helpless child the road to the country of souls.' Whether this beautiful idea belongs to the Esquimaux or to the missionary, has not been ascertained; but it is at all events certain that the skulls of dogs have been found in Esquimaux graves also in other places. Thus Scoresby informs us, on page 230, that he had found in Jameson's Land the skull of a dog 'in a small grave, which probably was that of a child.'

But be this as it may, it is nevertheless a fact, that there have also occasionally been found in Sweden a few skulls of dogs amongst human skeletons in our tumuli. Continued researches will decide whether these skulls of dogs, when found thus, usually indicate the skeletons of children.

The result of the researches communicated in this chapter is this: that the remains of the architecture of the aborigines which are found in Sweden do not in the least resemble the architecture of the Gothic, or of any other known tribe of the German race; but that, on the contrary, they present an unmistakeable resemblance to the architecture of the people of the polar race—the Esquimaux, who have, even to the present day, retained their ancient manners and customs.

This applies equally to the custom of our aborigines of interring their dead, and apparently to other religious ceremonies in connection therewith; and yet these did not belong to the same race of people. There is not the least sign of Scandinavia having been inhabited by people of the Esquimaux race. The similarity must be ascribed to the fact that they were in the same grade of civilisation and in similar circumstances.* During the years which have elapsed since I first discovered and pointed out this resemblance between our ancient graves and the houses of the Esquimaux, I have carefully examined many of the former, and found my former statement more and more confirmed. But what I now consider myself entitled to assume, if I cannot fully prove, is that some of these gallery-graves are ruins, or actual dwelling-houses, although most of them have, I admit, been sepulchres for the dead. It is evident from what I have quoted on page 116, from Scoresby's Travels and from verbal narratives, that even amongst the Esquimaux,

* See Note 7.

at all events in some districts, the custom of burying
the dead in tombs exactly resembling their dwelling-
houses has prevailed up to recent times. And, in truth,
if we compare dwelling-houses more closely with sepulchres, we shall find that they resemble each other
amongst all rude nations; and if we enquire into the
cause of this curious ethnological fact, we feel convinced that it must be so, and cannot be otherwise.
The rude child of nature has a kind of presentiment, although dim and confused, of a continuation
of life after death. But unable to soar to a purer
and nobler conception thereof, he believes that the
departed are destined to continue after death the
same activity which marked their life in this world.
Therefore he builds the same kind of dwellings for
the dead as for the living; therefore he places them
in the grave in the same position which they were
wont to take while alive in their hut, and therefore he
hangs upon, or places beside them their implements
of daily use. I shall show farther on that this is in
perfect harmony with the oldest traditional history of
most nations. What I have now adduced may be
enough to prove that if any ruins of dwelling-houses
from the period now in question and the people
belonging to it are found amongst us, they must be,
in respect to form and construction, exactly like the
sepulchres of that period and of that rude tribe. The
truth of this assertion must be obvious to everybody
who is inclined to enquire more closely into the same.
We may therefore rest assured, that before the savage of the forest plains of Scania and West Göthland

began to build gallery-chambers for the dead, he had already constructed similar ones for the living. Such ruins of ancient dwelling-houses have indeed already been observed in Sweden. They are distinguished from the sepulchral chambers by never containing any skeletons, and, as far as I have been able to ascertain, by their having rarely, if ever, any stone blocks as covering stones; but they stand open, which implies that they had the same kind of roof of rafter-work as the Greenland and North American Esquimaux houses, which they completely resemble in size, form, and construction. I will here describe the ruins of a couple of such supposed ancient chambers, of which one lies to the right, close to the turnpike-road from Skifvarp to Ystad, west of the Bay of Skar, not far from the shore. It is called Hölingen, lies on a low eminence, and is in shape rather an oblong square than an oblong oval, stretching from west to east. It is constructed of coarse upright granite-stones, placed with their corners side by side; of these a few have tumbled down, but the others are still standing erect. From the centre of the long south side goes a gallery in an ESE. direction, consisting of smaller and lower stones than those of the chamber itself. This was 20 feet long by $8\frac{1}{2}$. The coarse wall-stones were placed upon a pavement of small stones, in order that they might not settle down, and were about $5\frac{1}{2}$ feet high. The gallery, which was 15 feet long, had a breadth at the opening of 2, and at the entrance of the chamber of $2\frac{1}{2}$ feet. The stones of the gallery, which were lower than those of the walls, were not measured. This

open hut ruin stood about half, or a little more, above
the surrounding ground. Beneath the greensward,
inside the ruin, the soil was found to consist of a quantity of small stone-splinters, mingled with earth, and
when these had been removed, and the floor, which
consisted of clay mixed with sand, had been reached,
we discovered several fragments of flint-flakes (Pl. II.
fig. 24), which no doubt were the most ancient and
rudest knives, and a few pots of burnt clay of various shapes, with graven ornaments on the outside.
They were all broken, and of some of them we could
find only one or two fragments—a proof that they
were broken already when the hut was erected; they
were all empty, and no trace was seen of burnt bone-
splinters, but there were a few amber beads, scarcely
recognisable from decay (see Pl. IX. figs. 191–195),
and a few pieces of bone, which certainly were not
human.   In the northern wing were found charcoal
and ashes—a proof that the fireplace had stood there,
and near these were lying two or three broken clay
vessels: nothing was discovered in the southern wing.
If we now imagine (and it must at any rate be ima-
ginable to everybody) that we have here before us
the ruins of a hut, which two or three thousand
years ago was inhabited by savages, and that it had
been covered in the same way as the Greenland Esquimaux huts described at page 134, namely, with a
flat roof, consisting of timber and trees lying crosswise on the wall-stones, on which, probably, small
stones, brushwood, heather, juniper, and, lastly, earth
was lying; then, when the wood-work had decayed

in the course of time, it would of course fall in and become dust, so that the ruin would have come to the exact condition in which we found it. I am of opinion that the stone fragments which are always found in great quantities in and about such ruins were placed in the chinks between the wall-stones, in order to make the wall air-tight. This is the more certain as such fragments are always found remaining in the chinks between the wall-stones of those gallery-huts which are covered by a heap of earth, and of which the walls have consequently been protected and preserved in their original condition.

In the month of May, 1842, I examined two gallery-huts which are situated upon an eminence running past the village of Glumslöf, and called Glumslöf Hills; the most northern of these huts is sketched on Pl. XIV. fig. 249. In the same district, in Glumslöf, Quistofta, Barslöf, and other neighbouring parishes, ruins of this kind, more or less demolished, are frequently met with; and, owing to there being still a good supply of stone, they have not been disturbed. In other districts, however, where stone is more scarce, they have been demolished, in order to make use of the stones for houses, bridges, and field enclosures.

The hut here sketched is nearly oval, 15 to 16 feet in length and 8 broad, and the wall-stones nearly $5\frac{1}{8}$ feet high from the floor. The gallery, which runs south, with a slight inclination towards east (ESE.), is about 16 feet long and 2 feet broad. Here also the surface of the earth inside the chamber, as well as round the outside, was mingled with a great quantity of stone fragments. Amongst these, near the surface, a broken flint spear or spear-point (Pl. III. fig. 57) was found. Nearer the floor—which was of sand—or on it, but in the earth, mingled with stone fragments, were found other effects of the dead, consisting of several vessels of clay, all broken, of various shapes, some of which were very shallow, and widening towards the top, like small basins. Some were ornamented with graven figures on the outside, others plain. A great number of fragments were discovered, and many ornaments more or less decayed; viz., beads and buttons of amber; a flint knife with a handle, like that on Pl. III. fig. 64, and several spears, axes, and flakes, all of flint. Amongst the amber articles was lying a needle whetstone, sketched on Pl. VIII. fig. 182, and described on page 81. Here also were found in the chamber ashes and charcoal, more especially on one spot, where the fireplace probably had stood.

Here likewise the ruins were uncovered to more than half their height; but inside, as well as around them, the earth was a little raised above the surrounding ground, and was more than usually mixed with angular stone fragments, which, as it seems to me, must have served to fill up the chinks in the walls. I found here likewise a few broken bones, which certainly were not human. Neither here, nor in any other half-cross building, have any traces of burnt human bones ever been discovered.

I repeat here what I stated above, that supposing these ruins to have been, two or three thousand years ago, dwelling-houses, provided with roofs of the same materials and construction as those Greenland huts, which they exactly resemble in shape, they must now, after the lapse of thousands of years, and since the decay of the wood-work which fell down into and round the house, present themselves to us exactly in the same condition as the ruins which I have here described.

It appears to me that the objection raised against my view, that the ruins in question are those of dwelling-houses and not of sepulchres, has been refuted by the fact, that traces of human skeletons have never been found in them, but always a greater or less quantity of the household furniture of their former inmates, and invariably also a place which seems to have been the fireplace.

Since this has been shown, we ought to observe, before proceeding farther in our investigations, that the name *half-cross tombs*, by which these monuments of past ages were formerly designated, is, in more than one respect, a misnomer, and gives rise to erroneous ideas; partly because, as it now appears, they were not all sepulchres, and partly because the chamber only forms a half-cross with its gallery when the former is an oblong square; whereas this is not the case when it is round (see Pl. VIII. fig. 250). The form of the chamber is either an oblong square, an oval, or a circle; the form is therefore indeterminate; but what is never wanting in this kind of ancient dwelling is the more or less long gallery, consisting of two rows of stone running east or south. This is the most characteristic feature of these monuments of antiquity, and one which at the first glance distinguishes them from all others. In order to get a clear conception of the subjects of our investigation, we ought to designate them by their peculiar and essential feature, viz., the more or less long gallery, and as they all consist of stones raised on end, and, consequently, were built, we shall call them

GALLERY-HOUSES.

And these being, as we suppose, of two kinds, namely, houses for the dead, or *tombs*, and houses for the living, or *dwellings*, we shall class them accordingly, and call them (1.) Gallery-huts and (2.) Gal-. lery-tombs. We have already mentioned, that these ancient buildings vary in shape, and may therefore be divided into—

1. *Round Buildings.*—To this class belongs the gallery-tomb on the Äsahögen, near Quistofta (page 112), here represented (Pl. XIV. fig. 250) in the condition in which it was before some portion of the side stones had tumbled down, but without the imposts, or roof-stones, with which it was formerly provided.* It derives its name from its site upon an 'ås,' i.e. upon the top of a ridge of hills. Between this and another chain of hills, on which lies a tumulus, called Stenshögen,† is a watercourse reaching down to the river, which formerly was more considerable than now. These gallery-houses with round chambers are less common, but are nevertheless

---

* See the periodical *Runa*, Plate III. fig. 9.

† *Runa*, Plate, fig. 6.

occasionally found, in Sweden, as well as in Denmark and in other places, even down to France. In 'L'Institut, Chronique Scientifique,' for February 24, 1839, it is related that some labourers at Saumur found an ancient tomb, in which human skeletons and stone implements were discovered. The wall-stones forming the tomb in which these antiquities were discovered stood in a circle; upon them was lying a large block of stone 6 to 7 metres in length, about the same in breadth and 1 metre in thickness. In this tomb a large quantity of human bones were lying in such a manner that thigh and arm-bones, etc., were all lying crosswise in a heap, and on the top of it the skull, which shows that here also the corpses had been interred in a sitting posture. It is indeed worth observing that here, as in the Åsahögen tumulus (page 113), was discovered, underneath the first layer of bones, another similar one in which the bones were found in the same position as the upper ones. Amongst the bones were found flint axes, flint arrows with very sharp heads and toothed edges, besides others of a ruder shape, but also of flint. There were, moreover, found two dirks, the handles of which consisted of an oblong piece of bone, in one end of which was fixed the tusk of a wild boar by way of blade. The whole were buried under a layer of earth, 50 centimetres in thickness.

This description presents an astonishing resemblance to the one given in 'Iduna' of the Åsahögen. In this were also found two or more layers of bones, as was observed in the West Göthland tombs;

the side stones in the tomb were standing upright in a circle, and above them were lying large top-stones, or imposts. In the Åsa tomb were also found, besides axes and arrows of flint, etc., a wild boar's tusk, probably used as a dagger, the handle of which, having perhaps been of wood, was decayed. It is not recorded whether at Saumur the chamber had a gallery of two rows of stones issuing from the round chamber. Yet such a one must evidently have existed.

In the periodical 'Das Ausland' for May 1840, page 579, there is also mentioned a very similar sepulchral hut lately discovered in France. A gallery led to a large grotto or chamber, consisting of nine stones, standing upright, on the top of which a flagstone of 26′ 3″ was resting. The interior was filled with skeletons in a sitting posture, with their heads leaning against the wall; behind and beside them stood vessels containing victuals for the dead. Nuts and acorns, contained in them, were in perfect preservation.[*] There were also found two axes and two knives of stone; several small sharp implements, the use of which was not known; two necklaces, one of shell and the other of burnt clay;[†] several boar-tusks, the bones of a dog, and a stone slab upon which traces of a rude sketch were discernible. We see at once that this was a gallery-tomb.

[*] Nothing similar has ever been found here with us, as far as I am aware. The savage here probably for the most part subsisted on meat, as now in higher latitudes.

[†] We often find here similar ones of burnt clay, and especially in Öland.

2. *Oval Chambers.*—This shape is more common than the former, and is that of most of the gallery-huts which I have had an opportunity of examining closely.   Many of them, however, approximate to the following.   One of these, lying on the Glumslöf Hills, is sketched in Pl. VIII. fig. 249.

3. *The Oblong Square.*—This is also a very common shape, both with us and in Denmark.

Houses of this kind, covered with earth, and at a distance resembling tumuli, are still used by the Esquimaux in Greenland, and were formerly found in far more southerly districts in America than now. In the ' Antiquitates Americanæ,'* we are told, on page 43, that when the Icelander Thorwald and his followers arrived in Winland (east coast of the United States of North America, about 40°–42° lat. North), they saw some mounds on the shore in a bay, and they took them to be habitations, which proved to be the case, because the Icelanders were soon afterwards attacked by a number of Skrälingar—the name given by them to the Greenland and American Esquimaux.   Our oldest legends tell us that the houses were of old built after the same model, which indeed is indicated by our ancient ruins, so that these houses must have resembled earthen mounds.

From what has been already remarked, it follows that gallery-houses may be considered either as monuments belonging to ancient times, or as dwellings still used in various parts of the world, far separated

* *Antiquitates Americanæ, sive Scriptores septentrionales rerum ante-Columbianarum in America.*   Hafniæ, 1837.

from each other; in Boothia (the most northern part of North America), in Greenland, in the ancient Winland, in Sweden, in Denmark, in the north of Germany, even down to France; and it is highly probable that they occurred formerly in various districts where now no perceptible trace of them is left.

The remarkable fact that these dwellings and tombs are so similar in countries so widely separated, and inhabited by such different races, cannot perhaps be explained in more than *one* way: that, namely, in which we have in Chapter I. endeavoured to account for the phenomenon that we find everywhere, all over the earth, implements and weapons of stone so exactly alike.   All savages which inhabit nearly the same climates,* and stand upon an equally low point of civilisation, must resemble each other in all outward essentials: they clothe themselves in fur skins, they fish, they hunt, and finally, their dwellings must be alike, namely, caves, into which they crawl, like the animals, through a low narrow entrance. (See Pl. VIII. fig. 251.)   But with regard to the gallery-huts in question, it is easy to understand that the first habitations of man were not of this character.

Let us picture to ourselves a race of savages arriving, from some cause or other, in a climate which,

---

* Did the same climate prevail in France as in Greenland, at the period when these buildings were constructed? This question seems to be naturally prompted by the figure of the mammoth found in Perigord with skeletons of other arctic animals. It appears to me, however, that the gallery-graves belonged to a period comparatively much more recent.

though milder on the whole, was characterised by occasional periods of great cold. If even the nights only were cold and the days hot, still this would force the inhabitants to seek some shelter. This they would find in mountain-caverns, which would protect them against the cold of the night and the heat of the day.* The mountain-cavern was therefore man's first dwelling. All the oldest traditions refer to this fact. The earliest inhabitants of Greece dwelt in mountain-caverns. People in Siberia, anterior to the Samoyedes, lived in subterranean caves.† The Cyclopes of Homer, dwelling on the coast of the Black Sea, although endowed by the fancy of the poet with many extravagant attributes, are to sober prose nothing but nomads, living in mountain-caverns.‡ The country between the Black and the Caspian Sea has generally, and with every reason, been looked upon as the region of the world from which a race of human beings, endowed with great susceptibility of civilisation, has emanated, and most of the earliest traditions of existing European nations point to that region. There man dwelt in mountain-caverns, and thence the nations were disseminated over far distant lands, carrying with them their earliest memories, their native customs and manners. But a great many remained behind, and their numbers increased more and more; so much so that the

---

* The same idea is expressed by Diodorus Siculus, lib. i. chap. viii. : ' hieme in speluncas refugere,' &c.

† Erman's *Reise*, page 710.

‡ *Odyss.*, b. i. vv. 113–115 ; 182, 399, 400.

caverns formed by nature could not shelter them all any longer; they then dug out caves for themselves in the softer rocks; the number of these increased, and thus by degrees whole villages or towns of caves * sprang into existence. The nations of the South and East also buried their dead in the same kind of habitations in which they themselves had originally dwelt (see page 119). The Hittites, a tribe in Canaan in the time of Abraham, buried their dead in mountain-caves. Abraham bought from them a double cave, in which to bury his deceased wife,† and this custom of burying the dead in that manner was kept up afterwards amongst the Jews in Jerusalem; hence the crypts, etc., found there. We may ascribe to the same origin—namely, a copy of the primitive dwellings (the mountain-caves), and afterwards of the tombs — all catacombs, crypts, temple-grottoes, etc.

But when the people who dug out and dwelt in the crypts of the Caucasus were expelled by more powerful hordes, and forced to retreat to countries where either no mountains existed, or none of such soft material that they could dig out habitations in them, they found themselves compelled to build such dwellings by means of heaped-up stones or timber. I imagine that the art of architecture arose out

---

* We find sketches of these artificial mountain-caves in the works of several travellers. I will only mention Dubois de Montpereux's *Voyage autour du Caucase*, Atlas, sér. iv. Pl. I., II., and III. In Ainsworth's *Voyage* whole villages of artificial caves are mentioned. Compare *Das Ausland*, 1842, No. 170.

† Genesis xxiii.

of this circumstance, and was gradually developed;
it emanated from the mountain-cave man's earliest
dwelling, thence developing itself in two different
ways, as dwellings for the living, and tombs for
the dead: in the former it grew into palaces, in the
latter into temples. We should here observe that
as long as a people continues to dwell in mountain-
caves, it will also bury its dead in such caves; and
this custom, like all religious customs (less subject to change than profane ones), survived long
after people had commenced to inhabit proper houses.
Thus it was with the Jews in Jerusalem, and so with
many other nations. This proves that religion with
them is ancient—almost as ancient as their own
race. But if a nation changes its religion, or re-
ceives it long after having possessed regular dwelling-
houses, it frequently gives to its tombs the shape
and appearance of its dwellings. The tombs of the
Tartars in Kasan resemble exactly, but on a small
scale, their dwelling-houses, and are built in the
same manner of balks attached one to the other.* A
Circassian tomb resembles a Circassian house.† The
tombs of the Karaite Jews in the Valley of Jehosh-
aphat resemble houses and churches.‡ The tombs of
the modern Greeks in the Crimea resemble churches.

But in the hotter zones of the South, the savage
sought out the mountain-cave, not so much for a
shelter against the cold as for a cool retreat from the
heat of the sun.

* Erman's *Reise*, vol. i. page 248.
† Dubois, *Atlas*, sér. iv. Pl. XXX. f. 1.   ‡ Ibid. ff. 7, 9.

On the other hand, if we direct our looks towards the more frigid zones of the earth, we shall find that the case is somewhat different. Let us picture to ourselves savages appearing, for some reason or other, on the shores of waters in these zones and in those wild forests, where the soil during the greater part of the year is covered with ice and snow; we shall find that their first care is to hunt and to kill wild animals, in order to procure from them flesh for food and skins for clothing, and their next to find protection in deep mountain-caves from the terrible cold of the winter. Caves were in this instance not sought out in order to afford cool retreats in summer, but for peace and protection against snow-storms, tempests, and bitter cold. This being the object which the savage had in view, it naturally follows that he should seek out and prepare for himself mountain-caves with a long gallery pointing towards the sun;* and where such an entrance was wanting, it was constructed. We have ample proofs that such was the case, and that savage nations, even in the cold and temperate climate of Europe, lived in mountain-caves. I have already, in Chapter IV., stated that the Laplanders formerly lived in such caves. In several of the bone-caves in Germany and France, filled with bones of now extinct animals, human remains have been found, together with axes and implements of the chase, made of flint; and the most plausible explanation which has been given of this circumstance is probably this—that those

* Animals have the same instinct. See *Scandinavian Fauna*, vol. i. page 217.

mountain-caves, in which the bones of animals occur in such large numbers (occasionally also of animals which had served for food) were inhabited by savages, who died in them, and there left behind their weapons and sometimes their bones. Jordanes had heard of people in Sweden (Scania) which, like the wild animals, lived in caves cut out in the rocks.*

But the savage could find such dwellings only where there were mountains with caves. If he wandered out of such a district into the plains, and wanted to fix his habitation there, he was compelled to collect blocks of stone, and to form with them caves, resembling as much as possible the mountain-caves. In this manner the gallery-houses arose, where the long narrow gallery corresponds with the narrow entrance to the mountain-cave, and the chamber with the cave itself. This may, therefore, vary in shape, but the gallery is never wanting.

By this definition of the gallery-buildings, that they are with several distinct nations originally an imitation of the mountain-cavern, I believe we may explain the remarkable phenomenon, that those of the same shape are to be met with in countries so widely separated, and where they were undoubtedly erected and inhabited by different nations.

But if this explanation be correct, which I think we must admit, it follows also that gallery-houses constructed of stones collected for this purpose can

---

* Jordanes, *de Reb. Geticis*, cap. iii. I believe that I must thus interpret ‘Hi (populi) exesis rupibus quasi castellis inhabitant, ritu belluino.’ Jordanes’ accounts of Sweden are, however, very confused.

never occur in mountainous or rocky districts, where such caves are formed by nature. And this agrees exactly with real facts. Here in Sweden they occur only in the large plains of Scania, West Göthland, etc.; nay, even in Scania, where in some parts of the plains they are very numerous, and where, consequently, a great number of the people who erected them must have lived, especially on hilly grounds near or between waters now dried up; they are, on the other hand, completely wanting in all districts where there are mountains and rocks, containing caves and crevices. This is the general view, and, as far as I know, without exceptions. It is very remarkable also that in such mountain districts there are crevices to which tradition attaches similar stories or legends, as to certain hillocks on the plains, namely, of giants, goblins, pigmies, etc., which were said formerly to have inhabited them. Certain gallery-houses in the plains are called *giants' caves*, *giants' tombs*, *goblin caves*, *pigmies' hillocks*; and exactly similar names are given to certain mountain-grottoes in the mountainous districts. Thus there is in the single district of Scania a *goblin-cave*, in Björnekulla Crag, and one with the same name in Billeshall; two giant-caves on Skärali, one in Klöfvahallar and one in Röstånga village, etc. These exactly similar designations of the mountain-cave and the gallery-house, handed down to us from former ages, intimate that according to tradition they were applied to the same purpose in ancient times. This appears to me to be a ground for explaining the real fact, that gallery-houses occur only in plains.

I have already expressed my conviction that several tribes in Scandinavia have employed stone implements; that is to say, the earliest savages, who certainly had no fixed habitations, as well as the later settlers, who built the gallery-graves; and it appears to me more than probable that several kinds of stone implements continued to be used even long after the time when the people had ceased to build gallery-graves. Such implements are found scattered everywhere also in Central and Northern Sweden, sometimes in greater quantities, and consisting sometimes of large heavy articles, which could not have been amulets, as was once supposed. Sometimes also tools are discovered with which stone implements were manufactured (hammer-stones, Pl. I.). The stone implements found in Central and Northern Sweden are, besides, frequently made of those species of stone which are indigenous to the district in which they are found, which clearly proves that they have not been brought there from other parts of the country.*

The other kind of sepulchral monument belonging to the Stone Age also occurs with us. They are called in Scania *dös*, in Denmark *dyss*, in England *cromlech*, and in France *dolmen*. They consist of three to five stones, raised in the shape of a ring, with a large block on the top of them. (Pl. X. fig. 211.) They were erected in order to contain *one* corpse, which was always

---

* This is most easily explained by assuming that stone implements were used also by people who had neither gallery-houses nor gallery-tombs, the more as these are not always to be seen in the districts where stone implements are to be met with.

placed in a sitting posture, and beside it implements and weapons, which are always of flint. Whether these *dosar* and the giants' huts before described were coeval, and built by the same people, does not appear to me to be fully proved, although it is probable. They are to be seen here and there, both in Scania and West Göthland, in the same districts as the former. Sometimes we meet with several lying in a row, surrounded by a circle of raised stones.

Whether the so-called *dolmens*, which have been found in Africa, near Constantine, and are sketched in the 'Magasin Pittoresque,' 1864, page 80, belong to this category, or should be counted to the trilithic class, and consequently, to the Bronze Age, I do not venture to decide. A glance at the previous page 79 will show a striking resemblance with the construction of Stonehenge. To this may be added, that in them have been found objects both of bronze and iron.

It cannot be supposed that the interment of the dead was the original purpose to which the gallery-tombs were applied. Some naturalists think that they were *charnel vaults*, in which human bones were deposited after having been stripped of the flesh in some way or other. It has been ascertained, for instance, that human bones of people of all ages and of both sexes were deposited in these tombs, and they remain there in separate layers, in such a number and so closely packed, without order or arrangement, that one has been led to suppose that the flesh must have been by some means removed from them before they were thrown into the grave.

As far as I am aware, the Rev. M. Bruzelius was the first person in this country who (see page 130) made any observations bearing on this circumstance, while examining the Åsagrafven in Scania, which he described in his periodical 'Iduna' for 1822, No. IX. page 285. Besides stone implements, clay urns, and a number of amber ornaments, he found therein a vast quantity of human bones, divided into two layers by a bed of sand of about six inches in thickness. It was the opinion of the Rev. M. Bruzelius that the bones had been stripped off the flesh before being deposited in the vault, from the circumstance that he found in one place only the bones of the extremities and no vertebræ (page 290); in another a quantity of skulls (page 293; compare page 328 and others); and he relates on page 312, that the natives of Otaheite and Siam have a similar manner of burying the dead.

The Danish antiquary, Mr. V. Boÿe, who in the year 1863 examined a gallery-tomb at Hammer, in the south-east part of the island of Zeeland (Denmark), has given a detailed description thereof, and, like the Rev. M. Bruzelius, has given us sketches of the articles of antiquity found therein.* In this gallery-tomb, the

* This treatise of Mr. Boÿe's is interesting and instructive, because it shows that in one and the same gallery-tomb (Pl. I.) there were found not only the rudest pieces of flint, figs. 11–19, but also some exceedingly well made, and even drilled, stone implements, on account of which fact a doubt arises as to the proposed division of the Stone Age into two series, in proportion as the antiquities are in a rude state or ground, which has been adopted by several antiquaries. We see from this and various other facts, that they may be coeval. (See Note 8.)

M

bones were likewise found lying in several layers, without any order or arrangement, and as they had evidently been thrown in after being divested of the flesh.   In explanation of this, Mr. Boÿe refers to Mr. Schoolcraft's statement in his 'Historical and Statistical Information respecting the History, etc., of the Indian Tribes,' vol. i. pages ⁊0, 102, that when a person died, the corpse was rolled up in hides and deposited in some high place in a cave, to protect it from the voracity of wild animals.   There it remained until the flesh, through the influence of atmospheric air, had fallen off from the bones.   When several corpses had in this manner been changed into skeletons, the bones were collected at certain times of the year and deposited in large common vaults together with sundry weapons, implements, and ornaments.   Many such bone-graves (ossuaries) of large size have been discovered there.   Mr. Boÿe supposes that the gallery-tomb at Hammer was an ossuary of this character.

In the summer of 18⁊3, about the time when Mr. Boÿe opened the grave at Hammer, two gallery-tombs were opened and examined in West Göthland by Prof. Hildebrand, Baron G. von Düben, and Mr. Retzius, M.D., the first of whom has inserted in the 'Antiquarisk Tidskrift för Sverige,' vol. i. page 255, descriptions of these tombs and of the articles of antiquity found in them.   In page 256 he describes a gallery-tomb near Luttra.   It was filled with closely-packed black loam, with which a few boulders were mingled.   After removing this layer to the depth of about 4 feet, a great quantity of human bones were

found, packed together indiscriminately in the loam
and between the boulders, part of them, especially the
skulls, more or less crushed and broken. All the
bones were lying in the greatest confusion. Only a
few implements of flint and bone were found. The
greatest number were discovered in the lower part
of the bone-layer and upon the lowest layer of closely
packed mould. The descriptions are given in much
detail, as well of the graves as of the discoveries
made in them; besides which, the work contains
woodcuts of some of the most remarkable articles of
antiquity found in the tombs.

Mr. Hildebrand says, finally, page 271:—'As a
general result of our researches, I believe I may assume that the two gallery-tombs which we have opened
may be considered as a kind of ossuaries, rather than as
tombs in the usual acceptation of the word; because
it is not possible that the bones could have been in so
confused a position, packed between mould and stones,
as here described, if the corpses had been carried into
the grave whole, and deposited therein either in a
straight or in a sitting posture. Besides, in the latter
case we should, on the strength of our experience from
the Axevalla tomb and some other similar gallery-
tombs, have expected to find the grave divided by
slabs or fragments into several smaller compartments,
each enclosing one or more corpses, etc.'

I will not dispute the opinion given by several
scientific men, ' that the gallery-tombs were ossuaries;'
but I must candidly confess that I cannot coincide
with them; and having said thus much, I consider

myself bound to state my reasons for entertaining a different view.

None of the authors who consider our gallery-tombs to have been ossuaries have informed us by what process the corpses were divested of their flesh before being thrown into the tomb as skeletons. Was it done by depositing the corpse in some other place until the flesh had rotted and fallen off? But why should it be so, when they had the large and costly granite mausoleums, in which the dead might have been placed? Or perhaps they suppose that the flesh was cut away from the bones by means of sharp flint-knives? Those who know how much the ignorant classes of the people, even at the present time, dread laying their hands upon a corpse, and that very few could be induced, even by a promise of a considerable reward, to cut off a hand or a foot from a dead body, cannot suppose that anybody could be prevailed upon to cut away the flesh from the bones, least of all during the Stone Age here in the North, when the inhabitants were in the highest degree rude and superstitious. We know, besides, that the people here who built the gallery-tombs had the same customs as the Greenlanders in pagan times (compare page 130), and that they placed at the side of the deceased men the weapons and implements which they were wont to use while alive, and at the side of the women their ornaments—all evidently for the purpose (of which also, as regards Greenland, the Christian missionaries were aware) that the deceased, who were supposed to carry on in the tomb the same occupation as when on earth, might avail themselves thereof. That the pagans, who built the gallery-graves in West Göthland, had the same religious belief, we may conclude from their depositing the corpses in the same sitting position as they had in their houses when alive, and placing beside them their weapons and ornaments, as, for instance, in the gallery-tomb on Axevalla plain. And it follows, therefore, that they had evidently some dim presentiment of immortality. The belief in the immortality of the soul our Creator has deeply implanted in the human race from its very first appearance upon earth; it is only since speculation has gained some ascendency over the still voice of conscience, that doubts have arisen here and there. But no one who had this religious belief could have been induced to lay hands upon the dead, in order to remove the flesh from the bones, either by means of fire or sharp cutting instruments. We have seen that some of the corpses in the Axevalla tombs were ornamented with necklaces. The flesh had certainly not been removed from them before they were interred. We must therefore suppose that at least some corpses were placed intact in the grave. We might at first suppose, however, that others were transformed into skeletons before the bones were laid into the tomb; but on more mature reflection, it is easy to see that this could not have been the case, and that all must have been buried in exactly the same manner.

For my part, I must assume that all the bones found in a gallery-tomb were formerly deposited there as whole corpses, and we shall see whether this my conviction is not confirmed by the facts which the investigation of the West Göthland tombs brings to light. We should here remember that the tomb must have been in reality completed, and that the roof-stones must have been in their place, before a corpse or any bones could be deposited in it; otherwise foxes and wolves would have run away with the bones. How anxious the aborigines were to protect the remains of their dead in the tomb we can see by their having, as before mentioned, closed up the chinks between the larger stones with fragments of stone. We ought likewise to remember that every tomb had its side gallery, through which the access to the vault itself was opened whenever the owners chose, and that it was closed by an end-stone against any attempt of ravenous animals to penetrate into the grave.

After these observations we shall now enquire what has been the result of the researches of Baron von Düben in the so-called Luttra tomb. On page 279 the Baron says: ' When the intervening mould and larger or smaller stones had been carefully removed, we saw the broken bones lying in regular order and arrangement; for instance, leg-bones, vertebræ, and so on, and amongst them a skull was lying.'* Here, certainly, there can be no question of anything but a complete connected skeleton, which, as a corpse, had been buried in a lying posture on the floor. ' Occasionally

---

* This observation could hardly have been made by anybody but an anatomist. I beg, therefore, to mention that Baron von Düben is professor of anatomy, and perhaps the first anatomist *ex professo* who has investigated any gallery-tomb in our country.

we could see the bones of the trunk and of the extremities crossing each other in all directions, and on the top of the heap a skull.' It is evident that these skeletons were placed in the grave as corpses, and in a sitting, not a lying posture. The Baron says, farther on:—'The mould in which the bones were embedded was very fat and unctuous, more so than the mould which was lying farther off.' Everybody must see, when this is pointed out, that the 'fat unctuous' mould about the bones was the decayed flesh which had surrounded the bones, and consequently, that the bones had not been deposited in the tombs as skeletons, but as whole corpses, provided with flesh and blood. 'But,' says the Baron, 'the bones in most cases adhered so firmly to one another, that it was impossible to say which belonged to one and the same individual.'

How are we now to account, on the one hand, for the large quantity of bones which occur in the separate layers, and on the other for the utter disorder in which they were lying—sometimes closely packed together? The answer does not to me appear difficult, if we only from the beginning picture to ourselves the case as it most probably was. There can, it appears to me, be no doubt that these burial-vaults, constructed of colossal stones, collected from a greater or smaller distance, and then raised on end, were built in order to last for a long time, perhaps for centuries, as sepulchres for a whole tribe, or perhaps only for the chief of the tribe and for his relatives.* After such a vault had been finished, and

* Aristocracy is strongly developed amongst all savage nations.

the floor made level by means of earth, sand, or clay, the corpses were deposited in it by degrees, as some member of the tribe, or of the chief's family, died.   For this purpose the gallery was constructed. When, in course of time, the whole floor had been covered with corpses, sitting or lying, the owner of the vault, in order to prepare the necessary room for a fresh series of corpses, ordered those which had already become skeletons to be levelled with the floor, and those last placed in the vault, whose bodies had not had time to become skeletons, were at the same time flattened down on the floor, and on the top of this crushed layer of bones was thrown a layer of earth or sand, and in some instances of stones, like a pavement, by which contrivance another solid floor was obtained for a new series of corpses.   When this second floor, after many years, had also been filled up, the same process was renewed, as often as required.   In this way we can account for the fact of the bones lying in the confused and partly broken state in which they were found by the excavators.

The hypothesis that the corpses were reduced to skeletons before they were deposited in the grave, is refuted by the following considerations:—1stly, that no one is likely to deposit implements and ornaments with skeletons; and 2ndly, that the graves being family graves, into which *one* corpse at a time was deposited only every tenth, fifteenth, or twentieth year, the previous one would certainly have been changed into a skeleton before a new one would be deposited there.

CHAPTER V.

OF THE MANNER IN WHICH THE ABORIGINES MADE USE OF THEIR WEAPONS IN THE CHASE AND IN WAR.

HAVING, in the previous part, shown in what manner and by what means the savages of Scandinavia prepared their implements and flint and bone weapons, and the shape of them, we will now give a few examples of how these weapons were used—partly in the chase and partly in war. The following account may serve as a specimen of the former.

§ 1. *Evidence of the Manner in which Missile Weapons are used in the Chase by Savages.*

During the summer of 1840, there was exhumed, in my presence, out of the bottom of a deep bog in the south of Scania, a complete skeleton of the gigantic *wild bull with flat forehead* (*Bos Urus*, 'Scandinavian Fauna,' vol. i. page 537).* This ox had, some few years previous to its death, been hit in the

---

* I have in my *Fauna* endeavoured to prove that this is the real *Urus* of Cæsar, Gesner, and others, which the ancient Germans called *Ure*. It has in much later times been called *Bos primigenius* by Bojanus, which denomination seems to have originated through ignorance of the fact that the former denomination (Urus) belongs to the present fossil species.

back by a javelin, fitted, to all appearance, with a flint point, like some of those which have been sketched on Pl. III. figs. 55, 57, or 60.

The javelin, which must have been thrown at the animal from in front, probably while rushing upon the hunter, struck the processus spinosus of the first vertebra lumbaris (Pl. XI. figs. 220–222) at an angle so acute with the surface of the bone, that it appears almost incredible that the spear could have penetrated ; and this would have been impossible, had it not been exceedingly sharp-pointed and propelled with great speed by some means which I shall explain hereafter. It passed, as I have already said, through the processus spinosus of the first vertebra lumbaris from front to back, and penetrated into the second, where it stuck fast (figs. 221, 222). The hole which it had made (fig. 220) became rounded in consequence of suppuration, but on the other side, where the javelin had passed out (fig. 222) we see, by the shape of the wound, that the weapon was compressed like a flint spear; and the scar left where it passed into the second processus spinosus shows that it must have been sharp-pointed. The animal, according to the opinion of Mr. Nordling, a veterinary surgeon, who saw the skeleton, was not above five years old when it was killed, probably by falling through a hole in the ice on the bog, where it was found lying with the horns embedded in the clay; and by the bone formation (callus), where the javelin had passed out, we see that it must have lived for some time after it was wounded. It must, therefore, have been a very young animal when it was struck by the javelin.*

Professor Japetus Steenstrup has given me other proofs of flint arrows having been used in the chase, by showing me fossil skulls of stags, in which small arrow-heads were embedded; and in the Hunters' Hall in the castle at Schwerin, several flint arrows are preserved which have been found in bogs together with skeletons of stags.

§ 2. *The Mode of using Missile Weapons in War.*

These small flint arrows have likewise been used as weapons against man. Mr. Strunk, at Copenhagen, has shown me a human skull in which a flint arrow was embedded, which had penetrated through one of the eye-holes.

But, in one respect, the most remarkable of all the antiquities with which I am acquainted is the following, by which we learn that the savages of our country used to attack the first settlers when they commenced to clear the woods. When, about thirty years ago, a level piece of ground near the village of Tygelsjö, in the south of Scania, was to be cultivated, there were found, close under the surface of the earth, a number of skeletons of human beings who had been interred there, and round each skeleton was a row of stones forming an elongated square 7 feet by 3 (Pl. XIV. fig. 252). This manner of interring the

---

* I have presented this skeleton to the Zoological Museum at Lund, where it is preserved amongst other bones from the peat-bogs of Scania.

dead occurs only amongst those nations who used weapons of bronze, and probably only amongst the poor, never amongst people who use only stone weapons. As a further proof that these skeletons belonged to a tribe which, when settling in the south of Sweden, were in possession of bronze, I may mention that one of the skeletons, probably that of a woman, had round one of the arm-bones a spiral ring made of semicircular bronze wire, such as was worn by the people of the Bronze Age.

The skull of one of the skeletons was pierced with a javelin of bone (Pl. XI. fig. 213, half-size) made from the point of the antler of an elk, which, when it came into my hands, was mutilated (fig. 213), but, when found, had been quite perfect; about 7 inches long, round, having the smaller end pointed, the thicker cut off straight, and about an inch in diameter. The surface was scraped lengthwise, and made smooth with some sharpened instrument, probably of flint, which had had a hacked edge, and caused the scratches along the surface.

In order to show how this missile was fixed to the shaft, I have sketched it on a reduced scale on Pl. XI. fig. 212. The string or strap, which no doubt was tied more closely, I have represented loose in the sketch, to show how well the savage understood the construction of his weapons in the most approved manner. An even straight surface of the spear, resting against an even straight surface of the haft, gives the greatest possible strength to the latter to impel forward the former. In the same way the stone chisels of modern savages are helved (Pl. VI. fig. 129), and so were also evidently the ancient chisels (Pl. VI. figs. 127, 134) in old times. The spear-shaft now mentioned must have been both long and heavy, probably of oak, whereby great speed was given to the weapon thrown with the whole force of the arm.

This missile, which had pierced the left parietal close to the angle between the sagittal suture and coronal suture (Pl. XI. fig. 219), had penetrated about five inches into the skull, and was so firm that it could not be wrenched out without force, having made a round hole such as would have been caused by a musket-ball. The circumstance that the bone of the skull was not cracked or splintered proves that the javelin had been *thrown* with extraordinary force, and not *thrust* in by the hand at a short distance, because in the latter case the bone would inevitably have been splintered. It must astonish everybody that the point of one bone could penetrate another like a rifle-ball, and force a round hole in it without even cracking the bone pierced through. We may therefore infer that the savage of ancient times understood the art of which the savages of the present day avail themselves to impart the requisite speed to their missiles. The Esquimaux in Greenland employ a narrow *throwing-board*, provided with a groove running lengthwise, in the middle of which is a pointed wooden peg, bent forward, and in about the middle of the spear-shaft is a hole running in the same direction, into which the peg fits. When he wants to throw his spear, he lays the throwing-board along the under part of his arm, which he bends till it lies horizontally, throws forward the arm instantaneously, retains the throwing-board in the hand, and allows the spear to fly out with an astonishing speed, causing it to whiz in the air. This was related to me by eye-witnesses.* By the manner in which this spear-head, made from the antler of an elk, had no doubt been fastened to the shaft (Pl. XI. fig. 212), we can easily explain how it could remain unbroken in the head; namely, the shaft must, in consequence of the sudden jerk which the flying weapon received when its point pierced the hard skull, have snapped in its weakest part, or just where it was tied at a thin part to the bone point.

If the savages of Scandinavia had any implements with which they could increase the velocity of their missiles, they must have been made of a substance which has been destroyed by time, and we can there-

* The New-Hollander uses for the same purpose a nearly similar throwing-board ; at its lower end is a peg, bent forward, and in the lower end of the long javelin is a hole into which the peg is passed. When the spear is thrown it is therefore impelled forward with an incredible velocity.

In New Caledonia, New Zealand, and other neighbouring islands, no throwing-board is used, but the savage throws his javelin by means of an implement which he calls ' sipp,' a short thong or plaited ribbon, which at one end has a loop through which he puts his forefinger ; he then lays the thong round the middle of the spear-shaft, to which he imparts a vibratory motion before throwing it out, when it flies off with an immense speed and hits the mark.

It is remarkable that the Romans had also such an implement, with which they imparted great speed to their javelins, namely, a *throwing-strap*, which in their language was called *amentum*. (Virg., *Æneid*, ix. 665.)

fore scarcely expect to meet with any such. But from the effect produced by their missiles we can, with the greatest probability, conjecture that they also possessed some such implement.

It is worthy of remark that we find javelins of the same kind as that described above amongst another half-savage tribe, belonging, moreover, to another part of the world than Scandinavia.

Herodotus, in the seventh book of his ‘ History,’ describing the arms and accoutrements of the various nations composing the army led by Xerxes against Hellas, mentions in the sixty-ninth chapter also the Ethiopians, who were so uncivilised that their weapons, like those of the savages in Scandinavia, were made only of stone and bone. They were clothed in the skins of wild animals ; they had long bows made of the stem of the leaves of the palm-tree, and arrows made of reeds with sharp-pointed flint heads. They had, further, javelins to which they had fixed the pointed horn of the gazelle, in the same manner as a spear. We observe that our savages were armed exactly in the same way, with the difference only which different latitudes required.

On the same occasion, when the savages at Tygelsjö used the bone-point now spoken of as a javelin, they used also the flint point for the same purpose, because several spear-points made of flint, partly in good preservation and partly broken, were found amongst the skeletons where this skull, pierced by the bone point, was exhumed.

I have said that the bone point had hit and penetrated the skull near the angle formed by the sutura sagittalis and the sutura coronalis, consequently on the top of the head, which seems to indicate that the person who was killed with it was in a reclining position when attacked. The assault on the colonists was probably made at night-time by a horde of the savages. That they were many in number is apparently proved by the circumstance that several spear-heads of flint, partly whole and partly broken, were found amongst the skeletons, and had probably been used in the combat.

After the assault the savages withdrew, and allowed the surviving colonists to inter their dead according to their own custom. Similar scenes of murder to this between the savage aborigines of the country and the first settlers in Scandinavia still occur between the savages of America and the European colonists who destroy their hunting-grounds. But it was formerly even more fierce here, though the passion of extirpation in the stronger race against the weaker one is by no means extinct. We will here cite an instance which may illustrate certain passages of our legends. It will likewise prove that the savage of America attacks his victims when they are asleep, as was apparently the case at Tygelsjö.

For this purpose we shall here insert some extracts from Hearne's ' Journey in North America,'* in which the tribe-hatred of the savages is depicted by an eye-witness in all its ghastly colours.

* *A Journey from Prince of Wales's Fort to the Northern Ocean.* By Samuel Hearne. 4to. London, 1795.

In order to examine the Copper-mine River down to its mouth, Hearne had joined a tribe of Copper Indians, and commenced his march along the bank of the river. The Copper Indians are savages of the American, or copper-coloured race, and are generally tall powerful men. Although in language, as well as in appearance, religion, etc., they are divided into different tribes, frequently waging war, pillaging, and murdering each other's women, etc., still they intermarry, and look upon each other as human beings. But their conduct towards the Esquimaux is quite different; these they consider scarcely human, or at least far inferior to themselves. They have, without the least cause, and from mere wantonness, an insatiable desire to murder these poor defenceless people.

Hearne continues his narrative as follows:—

'During our stay at Clowey, a great number of Indians entered into a combination with those of my party to accompany us to the Copper-mine River; with no other intent than to murder the Esquimaux, who are understood by the Copper Indians to frequent that river in considerable numbers. This scheme, notwithstanding the trouble and fatigue, as well as danger, with which it must obviously be attended, was nevertheless so universally approved by these people, that for some time almost every man who joined us proposed to be of the party. Accordingly, each volunteer, as well as those who were properly of my party, prepared a target, or shield, before we left the woods of Clowey. These targets were composed of thin boards, about three-quarters of an inch thick, two feet broad, and three feet long, and were intended to ward off the arrows of the Esquimaux.*

'Soon after our arrival at the river-side, three Indians were sent off as spies, in order to see if any Esquimaux were inhabiting the river-side between us and the sea.   On their return, it being about noon (July 16, 1771), they informed my companions that five tents of Esquimaux were on the west side of the river.   The situation, they said, was very convenient for surprising them; and, according to the account, I judged it to be about twelve miles † from the place we met the spies.   When the Indians received this intelligence, no further attendance or attention was paid to my survey; but their whole thoughts were immediately engaged in planning the best method of attack, and how they might steal on the poor Esquimaux the ensuing night, and kill them all while asleep.   To accomplish this bloody design more effectually, the Indians thought it necessary to cross the river as soon as possible; and by the account of the spies, it appeared that no part was more convenient for the purpose than that where we had met them, it being there very smooth, and at a considerable distance from any fall.   Accordingly, after the

---

* In one place (page 166), Hearne tells us that the arrows of the Esquimaux were pointed either with a triangular black stone (consequently like ours on Pl. V. fig. 98), resembling slate, or with a bit of copper, but the former were the most common.

† About 1¾ Swedish mile.

Indians had put all their guns, spears, targets, etc., in good order, we crossed the river, which took up some time.

'When we arrived on the west side of the river, each painted the front of his target, or shield; some with the figure of the sun, others with that of the moon, several with different kinds of birds and beasts of prey, and many with the images of imaginary beings, which, according to their silly notions, are the inhabitants of the different elements, earth, sea, air, etc.

'On enquiring the reason of their doing so, I learned that each man painted his shield with the image of that being on which he relied most for success in the intended engagement. Some were contented with a single representation; while others, doubtful, as I suppose, of the quality and power of any single being, had their shields covered to the very margin with a group of hieroglyphics quite unintelligible to every one except the painter. Indeed, from the hurry in which this business was necessarily done, the want of every colour but red and black, and the deficiency of skill in the artist, most of those paintings had more the appearance of a number of accidental blotches than " of anything that is on the earth, or in the water under the earth;" and though some few of them conveyed a tolerable idea of the thing intended, yet even these were many degrees worse than our country sign-paintings in England.

'When this piece of superstition was completed, we began to advance toward the Esquimaux tents; but

were very careful to avoid crossing any hills, or talk‧
ing loud, for fear of being seen or overheard by the
inhabitants, by which means the distance was not only
much greater than it otherwise would have been, but,
for the sake of keeping in the lowest grounds, we
were obliged to walk through entire swamps of stiff
marly clay, sometimes up to the knees.

'It is perhaps worth remarking, that my crew,
though an undisciplined rabble, and by no means ac‧
customed to war or command, seemingly acted on this
horrid occasion with the utmost uniformity of senti‧
ment. There was not among them the least altercation
or separate opinion; all were united in the general
cause, and as ready to follow where Matonabbee led,
as he appeared to be ready to lead, according to the
advice of an old Copper Indian, who had joined us on
our first arrival at the river where this bloody busi‧
ness was first proposed.

' Never was reciprocity of interest more generally
regarded among a number of people than it was on
the present occasion by my crew, for not one was a
moment in want of anything that another could spare;
and if ever the spirit of disinterested friendship ex‧
panded the heart of a northern Indian, it was here
exhibited in the most extensive meaning of the word.
Property of every kind that could be of general use
now ceased to be private, and every one who had
anything which came under that description, seemed
proud of an opportunity of giving it, or lending it to
those who had none, or were most in want of it.

' The number of my crew was so much greater than

that which five tents could contain, and the warlike manner in which they were equipped so greatly superior to what could be expected of the poor Esquimaux, that no less than a total massacre of every one of them was likely to be the case, unless Providence should work a miracle for their deliverance.*

'The land was so situated that we walked under cover of the rocks and hills till we were within two hundred yards of the tents. There we lay in ambush for some time, watching the motions of the Esquimaux. While we lay there, the Indians performed the last ceremonies which were thought necessary before the engagement. These chiefly consisted in painting their faces ; some all black, some all red, and others with a mixture of the two; and to prevent their hair from blowing into their eyes, it was either tied before and behind, and on both sides, or else cut short all round. The next thing they considered was to make themselves as light as possible for running; which they did by pulling off their stockings, and either cutting off the sleeves of their jackets, or rolling them up close to their armpits ; and though the mosquitoes at that time were so numerous as to surpass all credibility, yet some of the Indians actually pulled off their jackets and entered the lists quite naked, except their breech-cloths and shoes.

* It makes our blood freeze with horror when we see that an enlightened Christian could be prevailed upon to witness such a horribly preconcerted massacre of defenceless innocent fellow-creatures, instead of doing all in his power to prevent this crime. But see Note 9.

' By the time the Indians had made themselves thus completely frightful, it was near one o'clock in the morning (July 17), when, finding all the Esquimaux quiet in their tents, they rushed forth from their ambuscade, and fell on the poor unsuspecting creatures, unperceived till close at the very eaves of their tents, when they soon began the bloody massacre. It was shocking beyond description; the poor unhappy victims were surprised in the midst of their sleep, and had neither time nor power to make any resistance; men, women, and children, in all upwards of twenty, ran out of their tents stark naked, and endeavoured to make their escape; but the Indians having possession of all the land side, to no side could they fly for shelter. One alternative only remained, that of jumping into the river; but as none of them attempted it, they all fell a sacrifice to Indian barbarity!

' The shrieks and groans of the poor expiring wretches were truly dreadful; and my horror was much increased at seeing a young girl, seemingly about eighteen years of age, killed so near me that when the first spear was stuck into her side she fell down at my feet, and twisted round my legs so that it was with difficulty that I could disengage myself from her dying grasps. As two Indian men pursued this unfortunate victim, I solicited very hard for her life; but the murderers made no reply till they had stuck both their spears through her body, and transfixed her to the ground. They then looked me sternly in the face, and began to ridicule me by asking if I wanted an Esquimaux wife; and paid not the smallest regard to the shrieks and agony of the poor wretch, who was twining round their spears like an eel. Indeed, after receiving much abusive language from them on the occasion, I was at length obliged to desire that they would be more expeditious in dispatching their victim out of her misery, otherwise I should be obliged, out of pity, to assist in the friendly office of putting an end to the existence of a fellow-creature who was so cruelly wounded. On this request being made, one of the Indians hastily drew his spear from the place where it was first lodged, and pierced it through her breast near the heart. The love of life, however, even in this most miserable state, was so predominant, that, though this might justly be called the most merciful act that could be done for the poor creature, it seemed to be unwelcome, for, though much exhausted by pain and loss of blood, she made several efforts to ward off the friendly blow.

'The brutish manner in which these savages used the bodies they had so cruelly bereaved of life was so shocking that it would be indecent to describe it.

'When the Indians had completed the murder of the poor Esquimaux, seven other tents on the east side the river immediately engaged their attention: very luckily, however, our canoes and baggage had been left at a little distance up the river, so that they had no way of crossing to get at them. The river at this part being little more than eighty yards wide, they began firing at them from the west side. The poor Esquimaux on the opposite shore, though all up in arms, did not attempt to abandon their tents; and they were so unacquainted with the nature of fire-arms, that when the bullets struck the ground, they ran in crowds to see what was sent them, and seemed anxious to examine all the pieces of lead which they found flattened against the rocks.*   At length one of the Esquimaux men was shot in the calf of his leg, which put them in great confusion.   They all immediately embarked in their little canoes, and paddled to a shoal in the middle of the river, which, being somewhat more than a gun-shot from any part of the shore, put them out of the reach of our barbarians.

'When the savages discovered that the surviving Esquimaux had gained the shore above mentioned, the northern Indians began to plunder the tents of the deceased of all the copper utensils they could find, such as hatchets, bayonets, knives, etc.; † after which they assembled on the top of an adjacent high hill, and standing all in a cluster, so as to form a solid circle, with their spears erect in the air, gave many shouts of victory, constantly clashing their spears against each other, and frequently calling out *Tima!* *tima!* ‡ by way of derision to the poor surviving Esquimaux, who were standing in the shoal almost knee-deep in water.   After parading the hill for

* They behaved exactly like children.   Compare Introduction.

† There occurred lumps of pure copper in the neighbourhood, which the Esquimaux beat between stones into axes, knives, etc.

‡ This word is, in the Esquimaux language, meant to be a friendly acclamation, signifying How are you?   It was here used as a cruel derision.

some time, it was agreed to return up the river to the place where we had left our canoes and baggage, which was about half a mile distant, and then to cross the river again and plunder the seven tents on the east side. This resolution was immediately put in force; and as ferrying across with only three or four canoes took a considerable time, and as we were, from the crookedness of the river and the form of the land, entirely under cover, several of the poor surviving Esquimaux, thinking, probably, that we were gone about our business, and meant to trouble them no more, had returned from the shoal to their habitations. When we approached their tents, which we did under cover of the rocks, we found them busily employed tying up bundles. These the Indians seized with their usual ferocity; on which, the Esquimaux having their canoes lying ready in the water, immediately embarked, and all of them got safe to the former shoal, except one old man, who was so intent on collecting his things, that, the Indians coming upon him before he could reach his canoe, he fell a sacrifice to their fury: 1 verily believe not less than twenty had a hand in his death, as his whole body was like a cullender.

'I ought to have mentioned in its proper place, that in making our retreat up the river, after killing the Esquimaux on the west side, we saw an old woman sitting by the side of the water, killing salmon, which lay at the foot of the fall as thick as a shoal of herrings.* Whether from the noise of the fall or a

* She was fishing with a leister armed with a few points. The fish were so abundant, that when the leister was thrust into the water

natural defect in the old woman's hearing, it is hard to determine, but certain it is she had no knowledge of the tragical scene which had been so lately transacted at the tents, though she was not more than two hundred yards from the place. When we first perceived her, she seemed perfectly at ease, and was entirely surrounded with the produce of her labour. From her manner of behaviour and the appearance of her eyes, which were as red as blood, it is more than probable that her sight was not very good; for she scarcely discerned that the Indians were enemies till they were within twice the length of their spears of her. It was in vain that she attempted to fly, for the wretches of my crew transfixed her to the ground in a few seconds, and butchered her in the most savage manner. There was scarcely a man among them who had not a thrust at her with his spear; and many in doing this aimed at torture rather than immediate death, as they not only poked out her eyes, but stabbed her in many parts very remote from those which are vital.

' When the Indians had plundered the seven tents of all the copper utensils, which seemed the only thing worth their notice, they threw all the tents and tent-poles into the river, destroyed a vast quantity of dried salmon, much oxen-flesh, and other provisions, broke all the stone kettles, and, in fact, did all the mischief they possibly could to distress the poor creatures they could not murder, and who were standing on the shoal

and drawn up, it rarely failed to transfix two or three fish. (Compare chap. i. page 70.)

before mentioned, obliged to be woful spectators of their great or perhaps irreparable loss.'

The author then goes on to describe the ceremonies which the Indians performed after the massacre, which show that they considered themselves unclean from having touched such despised and detested beings as the Esquimaux. In another passage (page 333), the author informs us that the main cause of these persecutions is that the Esquimaux are looked upon as sorcerers; and that when any Indian chief dies, it is said generally that the Esquimaux have killed him by witchcraft. In the summer of 1756, upwards of forty Esquimaux were treacherously assailed and murdered by Indians, from no other motive than that two of their chiefs had died the preceding winter.

We shall now more closely contemplate the relation here described between savage people of different races and tribes. It is evident that religious fanaticism had a share in this tiger-like ire of the Indians against the Esquimaux; they looked upon them as goblins. That each of them painted their god, or gods, on their shields before the combat, proves that they hoped for victory from him; and to him it was also afterwards ascribed. This is likewise proved by the ceremony on the hill.*

It is clear as daylight, that after such deeds and victories as now described, stories must arise in which the god of the Indians, whatever his name may be,

* The religious ceremony after the battle reminds us of the purification of the Jews after slaying the Midianites. Num. xxxi. 19.

is represented as the killer of goblins, as the destroyer and extirpator of the cave-dwelling people,[*] and so on; and that these stories, when handed down from father to son, became more and more intermixed with marvellous additions. Let us imagine that European civilisation, or a written language, had never been introduced in America, but that the Indians themselves had transmitted these stories by word of mouth to their posterity. What prose could not achieve, the Skalds would do, for even half-savage nomads have their bards; and, therefore, the recital of these occurrences would, after thousands of years, or perhaps even sooner, after the introduction of some civilisation amongst the Indians, and when tales and lays of ancient times were written down, appear no less extravagant and marvellous than the most improbable of our own Sagas and lays of antiquity.[†]

Everybody who reflects upon this, and impartially studies our ancient Sagas, in which it is related how imps, dwarfs, goblins, and other enemies of the saga-telling nations were either slain *en masse* and extir-, pated by their gods, or hunted down by them and pursued into the depths of their caverns, mangled by blows from axes, and pierced with red-hot arrows, and so on, must undoubtedly recognise in these our ancient Sagas the same hostile relation between

---

[*] The winter habitations of the Esquimaux are earth-caverns, see page 133.

[†] And in the same way some historian might also, in the course of time, assure his contemporaries and posterity that all these tales and lays from ancient times were mere creations of fancy, mere myths and allegories, which had no foundation in reality.

the earliest savage and semi-savage tribes of Scandinavia as that existing between the savage tribes of America of our own day, as related by Hearne and other travellers.

But although this hereditary hatred is more or less intense between all savage nations, and consequently also amongst the different Indian tribes (page 164), still it manifests itself nowhere perhaps with so much bitterness and with so little apparent cause, as when the more powerful races, gifted with more susceptibility and capable of a high civilisation, come into contact with the now so-called polar race in America and Europe.* It is evident that this race, so weak in a physical and intellectual point of view, was formerly spread more widely over both the hemispheres; but, probably in consequence of this hereditary hatred between the races, has been extirpated in many regions.

We have here already seen with what fury the Copper Indians, without any provocation, murder the poor Esquimaux. We find the same contemptuous hatred against this defenceless people amongst the Icelanders, who discovered Winland (the east coast of North America, under lat. 40°–42°). We are told (in ‘ Antiq. Americ.’ page 42) that ‘ when Thorwald and his followers had landed there, having seen on the beach of a small headland three mounds, they went there, and discovered three boats, made of the skins of wild animals, and three human beings (Skrälingar †) under each boat. They then divided and

* The same has probably been the case also in Asia.
† That is to say, Esquimaux.

pursued the natives, seizing all excepting one, who escaped in his boat. They slew the remaining eight, and then returned to the headland, whence they saw at a distance in the bay several other mounds, which they supposed were houses,' etc.

We see thus, that in the tenth century the Gothic tribes of the Caucasian race were animated by the same desire as the Indian tribes of the American race, to steal upon the helpless Esquimaux and to murder them without any provocation whatever. The same deadly hatred of the dwarf people in Europe, as of the Skrälingar in America, is expressed in strong and unmistakable features in our ancient Sagas. To what end has this murderous propensity been implanted, as it appears, by Nature herself? The paragraph in the code of Creation which ordains that everything meaner, when it has fulfilled its mission here on earth, shall perish and make room for something better, does it also refer to the different races of man? This subject may deserve to be more fully considered and reflected upon by the philosopher.

CHAPTER VI.

THE STONE AGE OF DIFFERENT NATIONS.—THE SOURCE OF
TRADITION.—DWARFS, GIANTS, GOBLINS, ETC., WERE ORI-
GINALLY PEOPLE OF DIFFERENT TRIBES AND RELIGION.

EVERY nation, even those most anciently civilised, has
had its Stone Age, * and where this has disappeared
before the commencement of history, traces of it have
still often been preserved in religious observances and
ceremonies, as already mentioned in Chapter II. of
this work.

Of all the different phases of civilisation through
which a nation must pass before it attains the highest
grade of development, the first rude state is the most
enduring and the most difficult to get over.   An important ethnological discovery was made by Erman
during his travels, namely, that the Argippæans of
Herodotus are the now existing Baschkirs of the Ural
mountain-districts, and that their present mode of
life is exactly like that described by Herodotus more
than 2,300 years ago; † and this people had no doubt
lived in the same wild state long before Herodotus
described them.

* As regards the Egyptians, see Chapter II. page 7, *note.*
Besides this, during a visit to the British Museum in 1847, I saw,
among the Egyptian rough-edged arrows, *one* tipped with a rough
flint-flake.

† Erman's *Travels in Siberia,* vol. i. p. 297.

That this first period of cultivation, the Stone Age, was of long duration, even with our forefathers, a people of the Indo-Germanic race here in the North, we may conclude from the occurrence of many facts, of which several will be mentioned in the following chapter; we would only notice here, that this first period of civilisation with us is so remote that neither our history nor our traditions mention the use of any other weapons than those of iron. The Bronze era is not even mentioned,* and in all cases when *arrows of stone* are mentioned, reference is invariably made to the most ancient time of the Sagas, and to an entirely different race. Certain, however, it is, that I have been unable to find, either in history or in the ancient Sagas, a single passage where any other weapons of war than those of iron are mentioned as being used by our ancestors (the people of the Gothic race).

This is certainly only a negative proof, and may therefore be looked upon as indecisive, but it gains strength from the circumstance, that our ancestors, especially the more wealthy and enlightened amongst them—those, therefore, who have left records to posterity—were a warlike people, and occupied themselves almost exclusively with the manufacture and management of their weapons. Ancient laws contain

---

* Nor, indeed, is it mentioned with any other European people in the North or West. With the Romans it was only known by tradition that the Bronze era had preceded that of iron ('prior æris erat quam ferri cognitus usus,' Lucret.). Hesiod regretted that he lived during the Iron Age. Homer's heroes belonged to the so-called heroic age. The iron weapons of the Romans can be traced as far back at least as Tarquinius Priscus.

strict rules regarding the kind of weapons which were to be furnished and employed.   In hundreds of Sagas, various weapons are described and extolled, but every epithet there found proves that reference is made to *iron weapons* only, and not to weapons of bronze or of stone.   Swords inlaid with gold and silver, gilt helmets, and harness 'shining *like ice*,' are mentioned in our Sagas from the earliest historical period.*

I have visited several places in Norway which the national traditions indicate as having been battle-fields in ancient times, but the weapons which have been dug up there have all, without exception, been of iron.   The weapons used in the battle of Sticklerstad, in 1030, were of iron and steel.   Rusty pieces of such weapons found on that battle-field have been figured in several works.   It may be supposed that the iron weapons found there belonged to the fallen Norsemen, and that the pagan army of peasants used stone arrows.   But this is not the case, at least not generally.   It is, moreover, an indubitable fact that one arrow at least shot from the hostile ranks was of iron.   Thormodr Kolbrunnarskald, who, on the morning previous to the commencement of the battle, and at the king's request, sang the beautiful song:

> Dagr er uppkominn, dynia hana fjadrir;
> Mäl er vilmögum at vinna erfithi,† etc.,

received during the engagement an arrow in his chest.   The arrow broke off in the wound, and the

* John, *Om Krigsväsendet*, page 192.
† *Iduna Tidskrift*, vol. i. page 58.

surgeon, who, according to the custom of those times, was a woman, endeavoured to extract it by means of a pair of pincers, but in vain, the wound having begun to swell. Thormodr therefore desired her to cut into the flesh until the iron could be reached, and she having done so, he himself pulled out the arrow-point, which had become bent.* That the skald died from the operation is irrelevant, but not so the fact, that the murderous arrow, *which had become bent*, must have been of iron, and not of stone.

In the battle on Bråvalla plain, which was fought at a much more remote date, viz. about the year 700†, and in the records of which many weapons and various kinds of armour are described, nothing is stated which will in any way justify the inference that stone weapons had been used by any of the various hordes which took a part in the battle.‡ As those, however, by whom records of these events have been left to posterity belonged to the more wealthy and distinguished class, who used iron weapons, they no

---

* *Fostbrœdra-sagan*, page 215.

† The time is differently stated by different authors; namely, from the year 680 to 735.

‡ All this, however, does not prove that the use of stone weapons was entirely abolished. We cannot suppose it possible that iron came into general use *all at once*, but rather gradually and by degrees, until it came down to the soldiery, and that the latter used their weapons of stone for a long time, while the chiefs and richer men had weapons of iron. We also see them together on *sculptured stones*. (*Urinvånarne*, vol. i. page 56.) The Bronze era did not succeed in rooting out the use of stone weapons (even then stone only was employed here for missile weapons); it was during the Iron Age that the use of stone was at first gradually, and at last altogether abolished.

doubt considered the weapons of stone employed only by the soldiers as too insignificant to be mentioned.

In the same way it may be explained that our Eddas and ancient Sagas, which, as regards this subject, go back to the most remote antiquity, do not in any single passage speak of war weapons of *stone* as having been used by the people of the historical race, whereas their war weapons of *iron* are frequently mentioned, and extolled in the most exaggerated terms. Their swords would cut stone as well as cloth, and in order to test the sharpness of the edges, a lock of wool was thrown into slowly running water; the sword was held in it with the edge towards the current while the wool was drifting down upon it. If it cut the wool through, the weapon was considered to be sufficiently sharp.*

It is also remarkable that stone weapons were, as far back as we are acquainted with their history, used neither by the Gothic race in Germany nor in Scandinavia. Tacitus relates ('Germ.' vii.) that the Germans had war weapons of iron, and states that the reason why few of them used swords or large spears, like the Romans, but lances, which in their language were called *framea* (*ohrime*, awl, a kind of pike armed with a narrow and short piece of *iron*) was, that iron was not abundant with them.† The only people

---

* Didr. of Bern's Saga, chap. xxi.

† It appears to me incomprehensible that notwithstanding Tacitus relates this as a fact in plain words, there are antiquaries who in later times declare that the *framea* of Tacitus were of bronze, and resembled the so-called *paalstav* of the Danes; which is certainly neither narrow nor pointed, but broad at the edge, and like a chisel.

known by Tacitus who were so poor and rude that they were not even acquainted with iron, were the Fenni. These Fenni were the same people who at a later period were throughout the North called Finns, i.e. Laplanders. For want of iron, they armed their arrows with a sharp-pointed bone, as was the custom of the Laplanders even as late as a century ago.

We see by all this, that the people who have transmitted to us some account of their history from ancient times, as far back as history relates and the Sagas recount their adventures, have not, either in Scandinavia or in Germany, spoken of weapons of any other kind of material than of iron, but that, on the other hand, the Laplanders had, at any rate, their arrows tipped with *bone*. We also find that all nations who are unacquainted with the use of metals, and who employ arrows and other implements made of *bone*, have also others of *stone*, and we know that the Laplanders employed them even at a much later period. From this circumstance alone, we come to the conclusion that the *dwarf people* of the Saga, who clearly belonged to the race of Laplanders, must have had implements of *stone* and of *bones of animals*, but not of metal. But we have a still more positive proof in favour of this opinion. There is, at all events, *one* passage in the Sagas in which it is distinctly shown that the arrows of the dwarfs were of *stone*. This remarkable passage occurs in ‘ Örvar Odd’s Saga,’

(See *Lisch Jahrbücher*, vol. ix. page 335, fig. 6, page 376.) I can see no reason why *ferrum* should be translated *bronze*.

which, as some of our readers are perhaps aware, is a
very interesting romance, and which has this in common with our modern so-called historical novels, that
real facts are mingled with imaginary adventures. It
is there related that the Viking Örvar Odd, having
in several battles lost his bravest and most faithful
followers, wandered about alone and restless, from
one country to another, seeking adventures. Finally,
he came to Huneland, where, in a forest, he met an
old man cutting wood near a small cottage. The
old man was of short stature, and his name was Jolf.
Örvar, wishing to conceal his real name, called himself
Vidförul, passed the night in the old man's cottage,
and in the morning, on leaving, presented him with a
knife. As a return present, the old man wished to
give him *three stone arrows*, when Örvar observed:
'It is a good present, old man, but I am not aware
that I need carry stone arrows about with me.' 'It
may happen, Odd,' said the old man, 'that these stone
arrows may help thee, where the Guse arrows cannot
avail.' 'Knowest thou then that my name is Odd?'
'Yes,' replied the old man. 'Then,' said Odd, 'it
may be that thou knowest also why thou didst now say
that I shall have occasion to use thy stone arrows; I
shall therefore accept them, and I thank thee much
for them;' and he put them into his quiver.

An explanation of this passage stands in immediate
connection with our subject. It is indeed not distinctly mentioned here that the little old man Jolf
was a dwarf (i.e. Laplander); but from many parallel
passages in the Sagas, and from his demeanour, his

cunning, his skill in witchcraft, and his prognosti-
cations, we clearly infer that he belonged to the
dwarf race.   I must further remind the reader that
the *Guse arrows* which Odd carried in his quiver, and
of which circumstance Jolf was aware, were three
magic arrows taken from the Lapland chief Guse,
which arrows had the property of hitting everything
at which they were aimed, after which they returned
of their own accord to the bow-string.   Odd's answer,
which in a romance would of course be considered as
expressing the general opinion at that period, has
therefore the following meaning: The present is in
itself valuable, but I am not aware that I shall need
these magic stone arrows, as I already carry in my
quiver the Guse arrows, which have a certain magical
power.   But the old man, who was a sorcerer, and
who could read the future, gave Odd to understand
that he should one day be exposed to sorcery, against
which only his own magic arrows, and not the Guse
arrows, would be able to protect him.   The old
man's prediction was soon verified, for ·Odd became
the leader in a battle, in which an invisible witch,
Gyda, caused him great loss of men.   Odd aimed
at her first with the Guse arrows.   'When Gyda
heard them whistling through the air, she held
up the palm of her hand to receive them, but they
made no more impression thereon than upon a stone.
Odd shot off all the Guse arrows, but they all fell
amongst the grass.   " Now," said Odd, " what Jolf
predicted has come to pass : the Guse arrows are lost;
it remains now to try his stone arrows."   Thereupon

Odd took one of the stone arrows and aimed at Gyda;
she heard it whistling through the air, and held up her
wrist; the arrow pierced her hand, entered her eye,
and came out at the neck. Odd shot off the second
arrow, which flew the same way. Then he let off
the third arrow, and it hit Gyda in the forehead, and
immediately she fell down dead.'

This ancient romance shows very clearly that at
the time when it was composed, neither arrows, nor
other weapons of stone, were in common use as
weapons, but that even then the opinion was generally
current that these stone weapons, which owed their
existence to the dwarf race, skilled in sorcery, were
endowed with a magic power against witches and
witchcraft, which no other weapons possessed.

We still find, here and there, traces amongst
the peasantry of the superstition that stone implements possess inherent magic power. Some of the
peasantry even now believe that stone wedges are a
protection against lightning, and they have therefore
always a few of them in their possession, which they
cannot easily be prevailed upon to part with. In
some districts they were formerly placed in the bed
beside women near their confinement, in order to
lighten the pains of labour. They are still occasionally used by the peasantry against a cutaneous disease
in children called the 'white fire.' With the aid of
a piece of steel, sparks are emitted from them which
are made to fall upon the head of the child.

Superstitious notions of the same kind appear to
be entertained also by the peasantry in Ireland and

land. Mr. E. Lloyd relates, in his 'Observations
Vales,' that during his journey in Scotland, he
particularly amused with the many different kinds
mulets preserved by the inhabitants. Amongst
e he mentions *stone arrows*, which were believed
hem to have belonged to the elves. In 'Nenia
annica,' London, 1793, page 154, is the figure of
ne arrow from Ireland (like that given on Pl. V.
96), mounted in silver ; and the author states
the peasants call these flint arrows 'elf-arrows,'
they mount them in silver, and wear them round
throat as amulets against ' elf-shots.'* We must
remember that the elves of the Eddas and
is were of two kinds, and that one of them, the
k elves, were identical with the dwarf people,
aplanders ('Snorr Edda,' pages 119, 123). Thus
' elf-shots' of the Irish peasantry are identical
the 'Lap-shots' of the Swedish peasantry, and
cquently, this is a further proof that the magical
e implements belonged to the dwarf people. Some
le may think it strange that a person should carry
.t with him ' Lap-arrows' as a protection against
)-shots,' but this is in perfect accordance with an
)opular superstition, and is not more strange than
icreditary conviction of the same people that stone

These accounts are very instructive. They prove that it was
ie Celts themselves, but a people considered by them to be
l in magic, who fabricated and used these stone arrows.
erly stones shaped like a heart were set in the same way in
and worn round the throat as amulets, probably as a pre-
ive against ' Lap-shots' and other sorceries carried on in the
I have never seen them made of flint, but only of amber.

bolts, which have fallen during thunder-storms, are a protection against lightning. This accords with an old popular belief already mentioned in the Edda, namely, that the same matter which has hurt can also cure: thus the flesh of the snake, or hair of the dog, which has bitten a person, is laid as a salve upon the wounds.

We have already seen by the description, as well as the sketches of skulls in Chapter III. (both short-headed, *brachycephalic*, and long-headed, *dolichocephalic*, the former resembling those of the Laplanders, the latter those of the other inhabitants), that people of different tribes inhabited this country even during the Stone Age. It may be assumed, for several reasons, that the race of people of which the Laplanders form the remnants was spread over Sweden, Denmark, and other places; since, on the one hand, crania, which evidently belong to this race, have been found in many places in the earth, and in bogs in the south of Sweden; and, on the other hand, because many words in the Swedish and Danish languages have a great similarity to synonymous words in the Lapland tongue. Profound investigators, as Rask, Petersen, Christie, and others, have already proved this. Those who doubt it may perhaps reply, that at any rate some of them might just as well have originally been adopted from the Swedish into the Lapland tongue, as *vice versâ*, and though this mixture of languages certainly proves an intercourse between both races, it does not prove that the Laplanders necessarily inhabited those places where, in the language, one

with Lapland words, and therefore it has
een proved that the Laplanders formerly inha-
the central and south part of Sweden. But
es the Lapland skulls found in ancient tombs,
resence of Lapland local names strongly sup-
the above-mentioned opinion. Those who are
acquainted with the Lapland tongue have re-
sed several such names, not only in the central
outhern parts of Sweden and Norway, but also
untries south of Sweden. The distinguished
ist, Mr. Rask, assumes, in consequence of this,
the Laplanders in ancient times inhabited the
e of Denmark.* According to his interpretation,
ame Samsö is from the Lapland language. The
ds of Hvidn, anciently Hoidn, owe their name to
pland word, apparently derived from *voudn* (bay,
ith). A great number of other names in the
h, which cannot be traced to Gothic roots, seem
to have been derived from the Lapland language;
nstance, *Falstr*, *Fjön*, *Hledra*, *Thotn*, in Norway,
others. *Trollhättan* is said to be derived from the
name *troll* (goblin) and the Lapland word *haüte*,
ids). On the Dovrefield, the people assert that
local name *Jerkin* was of Lapland origin, and
ace of the residence of the Laplanders in that
; the lake Jerkin, in the province of Upland,
the same name. The *Allvar* of Oland may
asily traced to the Lapland words *all* (high) and
(hill). There is a similar locality in Scania, the
ent name of which, *Allvar*, seems to have been

* *Om det Nordisk Sprogs Oprindelse*, page 114.

retained for a farm in that province, Allvarstorp,
pronounced *Alfvastorp* by the peasantry. The word
all has been retained in a great number of names of
hills and eminences in Scania. Thus, the Lapland
words *stock* (sound, inlet) and *garn* (lake) seem to
enter into many Swedish local names.

If we now consider, that besides Lapland local names
peculiar to the south of Sweden there are a great
many ancient Sagas, which have evidently been handed
down from generation to generation, relating to
dwarfs, cavern-people, or *goblins,* who formerly lived
in such or such a mountain-cave, and in such or such
a crag—and many such places are still shown by the
country people, especially in those districts where
crags are found, but sometimes also in districts
where only larger earth-mounds are met with; and if,
moreover, we remember that to these places are attached detailed Sagas of occurrences which are said to
have happened there, and *in which Sagas the student
easily recognises ethnological features which cannot possibly have been invented*—then we are compelled to
admit that these stories, still current amongst the
people, must have some historical basis, and that it is
impossible they can be merely creations of fancy;
we are forced to assume that individuals of the Lapland people have lived at all events near or about
those places which the national Sagas indicate as
their dwellings.

Thus, this smaller and weaker tribe have been expelled, even here in the North of Europe, by a
stronger and larger race of people; as is also the case

North America, where the Esquimaux, the polar
e of the New World, were the first settlers, but
e by degrees expelled by a larger and stronger
, namely, the copper-coloured Indians.
ery nearly the same thing happened long ago
e in Europe, as is now taking place in America.
can thus trace a similarity between the two
lds, inasmuch as in both the conquering and
re powerful tribes believed the polar race to be
led in sorcery, and for that reason expelled and
secuted them. I have alluded to our Sagas and
ditions. It appears to me evident, that during the
g period extending, probably, over thousands of
rs, when the aborigines of the country were unable
er to read or write, verbal traditions began, and
e handed down from generation to generation; it
appears evident, that when the more civilised
ple arrived in the country, where they gradually
ame settlers, and fell in with a ruder people of
ther race, with different features, and of different
from their own, with dress, language, manner of
ng, and religious ceremonies also different from
irs, whom they then conquered, expelled, or extir-
ed, just as is the case now with savage and half-
age nations, the memory of these occurrences,
highly important to them, must have taken deep
t in their minds, and have been transmitted from
ents to children through succeeding generations:
torted, probably, by numerous additions, in conse-
nce of their religious views changing with time, but
l preserving so much of its original characteristics,
t, if treated without prejudice, these may easily be

recognised. The national traditions and Sagas, of
which Scandinavia possesses so rich a store, having
been here alluded to, I must beg the reader to remember that they are of two kinds, *secular* and *religious*,
both resting upon historical ground. In favour of the
former, we have no other evidence than that they are
related by the people, but exactly alike in districts
very remote from one another: this was, at least, still
the case sixty or seventy years ago. He who does not
remember that time, and still more, he who has been
brought up in a large town, cannot easily form an idea
of the veneration with which they were told and list-
ened to by the country people. Other times have succeeded to these, and the enlightened man of the world,
or the town-resident, if occasionally he has an opportunity of listening to these Sagas, looks upon them
as mere foolish prattle, unworthy the attention of an
educated man. The religious Sagas seem to have a
little more foundation than the others, because they
continue to live in certain religious customs and rites
among the people. By the enlightened they are called
superstition. Every remnant of a religious worship
subverted in the course of time through changed
ideas, becomes *superstition*. No superstition can have
arisen isolated and of itself. When it arose, and
for a long time afterwards, it was a *faith*, and formed
part of a distinct religious worship; but when this
worship was destroyed, the external forms, which were
still continued by the people, became mere *superstition*. Superstition is, therefore, nothing else than
the spectre of a formerly living faith; it is the ruin
of an ancient temple long overthrown.

Such remnants of pagan worship are still found
ongst the people here, and the impartial enquirer
l be able, without much difficulty, to distin-
sh which of them have belonged to the worship of
or, Baal, or Odin. Every religious *change* in a
ple is in fact only an intermixture of religions;
ause the new religion, whether received by means
convincing arguments, or enforced by the eloquence
ire and sword, cannot *at once* tear up all the wide-
eading roots by which its forerunner has grown in
heart of the people: this must be the work of
ny years, perhaps of many generations.
Looked upon in this light, enquiries into national
ditions and superstitions are of great interest to
ethnologist, as they enable him to trace the ear-
t history of the race to which they belong. In my
acity of ethnographer I must contemplate the na-
ial Sagas from an historical, not from an æsthetic,
nt of view, although I am well aware that there are
ny who consider the latter as the only right one.
n my researches relating to this subject, I intend
owing the method hitherto adopted; namely, to
it the same as *comparative ethnology*. And in
er to prove that our national traditions rest upon
orical foundation, I may be permitted, first, to
iind the reader of what has previously been said—
v savage tribes in America conquer and expel
iker ones, even in our own days; and we shall
n endeavour to discover, in the earliest tra-
ons of our own native land, the traces of similar
urrences.

We shall begin by enquiring whether the names in the ancient traditions, *dwarfs*, *giants*, *goblins*, and *elves*, really refer to human beings, or whether they denote mythical and allegorical beings, which have had no historical existence.

Proofs that the Dwarfs and Pigmies of the Sagas were Human Beings, that they belonged to the same Race as the Laplanders of the present Day, and that our Ancestors considered them to be skilled in Witchcraft.

It has often been asserted that the dwarfs mentioned in the ancient Sagas were not real men, but mythical and allegorical beings, meant to typify certain powers and conditions of nature. This mode of explanation is a very convenient one for fancy; since if we can only succeed in transferring any given object to the realms of fiction, we can then treat it according to our own fancy, and play with it as a child with its doll.

But in the description of dwarfs as given by the Sagas we find too many and too distinct ethnological characters to admit of any such theory. The reason for supposing that the dwarfs have no historical reality is, probably, in the first instance, that they are said to have performed several supernatural and impossible feats, or, in other words, that they practised sorcery.*

* Poets and inventors of Sagas in olden times were always in the habit of embellishing their stories with extravagancies, and yet these were always founded upon real events. Thus Homer describes the giant Polyphemus and the Princess Circe as sorcerers; and yet

t this does not fully entitle us to deny their
orical existence.   In that case not only the Lap-
lers in Europe, but also the whole Esquimaux
e in America, ought for the same reason to be re-
ded as mythical and allegorical, because it is not
g since that people living in their neighbourhood
.eved (and possibly still believe) the former to
 sorcerers ; and the Indian tribes in America
ik, even to this day, that the latter are still ac-
inted with the black art.   This is the chief reason
y they wish to extirpate the Esquimaux race.
Neither is it reasonable to consider the dwarfs as
gorical beings, merely because a great many ex-
vagant things have been told about them in the
as; for we ought to remember, that rude nations
ays relate the most exaggerated stories of people
onging to a strange race.   I will endeavour to elu-
ite this by an example.   When Mr. Mackenzie was
velling in North America, the Esquimaux described

ois de Montpéreux, who visited the localities where the adven-
s described by Homer are said to have happened 3,000 years
has, in our own days, shown, by local and ethnological evidence,
these fictions had an historical foundation ; that the Black Sea
its shores were the scene of the wanderings of Ulysses ; that
Greeks were rovers, like the Vikings of the North; and that the
ns whom they visited during their expeditions were more
ised than they were themselves. (Compare Dubois, *Voyage
ir du Caucase*, vol. i. pages 60–61, and also a subsequent
ne.) This fact is very remarkable in an ethnological point
iew. What was the nation that 1,200 years before Christ was
vilised ? Without doubt a people of Semitic race, which spread
isation to many regions of the earth and was also the teacher
ie Greeks, although these in the course of time far surpassed

to him certain white people (the English), who were
said to have a citadel on the banks of a river near
the west coast—in terms quite as extravagant as any
that are to be met with in the Sagas.   The Esquimaux, for instance, believed firmly that the white men
were giants; that they had wings; that they could
kill with a glance of their eye, and swallow a whole
beaver at a mouthful.

If the dwarfs mentioned in the Sagas are to be
regarded as mythical beings, the English and other
Europeans might just as reasonably be so described;
and the whole white population of America might,
in the course of ages, come to be looked on as a
mere myth and allegory.

We find a counterpart to the Esquimaux description of the whites in the Saga of Olof Trygvadson,
relating to a couple of Finns (Laplanders), with
whom the fair Gunhild was staying in order to learn
the science of sorcery.   They also could kill with
a glance, because when anything living encountered
their eye, it fell down dead at once, and when they
were angry, the earth recoiled at a look.   They missed
nothing at which they aimed; they could follow
the trail like dogs, on frozen as well as on damp
ground, and they could run in snow-shoes so swiftly
that neither man nor beast could overtake them.

Yet this description is not in reality more extravagant, neither does it deserve more to be looked
upon as a myth or allegory, than the description
which the Esquimaux gave of the Englishmen with
their gigantic stature, etc.

P

Scarcely anything of an uncommon character ha
escaped exaggeration and distortion by ignorance
It would be wrong to believe that nothing whicl
becomes thus changed, while going from mouth t(
mouth, ever existed in reality; but no sensible perso1
will believe that it has existed or occurred exactly a
it is described in our ancient tales.

In many passages of our early Sagas we are tol(
that the dwarfs *were* corporeal and human beings
and *considered as such* by the narrators theinselves
although of another race. The dwarf Sindre, wh(
dwelt in a mountain-cavern on the small island o
Brännön (in the province of Bohusland), had tw(
children, a boy and a girl, whom Thorstein Vikingsor
found playing together near a brook in the island
In order to procure an interview with their father
he made some presents to the children, by whicl
the father, who was very fond of his children, wa:
won over to give Thorstein the advice and assist:
ance which he required. Thus it is told, that when i1
single combat, one of Eigil's hands had been choppec
off, he met near a brook in the forest *a dwarf's child*
coming with a bowl to fetch water. Eigil dropped :
gold ring into the child's bowl, for which the fathe:
(the dwarf), in order to prove his gratitude, in
vited Eigil into his mountain-cave, where he cure(
his wound ('Eig. Saga,' page 46). In the vicinity o
Odin's castle (which in the Saga of Hedin and Högn(
is transferred to Asia), there lived some men skille(
in the art of fabricating all sorts of things. 'Sucl
men are called *dwarfs.*' 'They dwelt in caverns, bu

at that time they had more intercourse with "men" than now.'

I must remark in passing, that all rude nations apply the designation 'men' to themselves only, *all* others being differently designated. To the Greenlanders, Greenlanders alone, and to the Samoyedes, Samoyedes alone are *men*. When, therefore, in any Saga, dwarfs and *Jotnar* (giants) are mentioned in contradistinction to *men*, it proves only that they did not belong to the same race as those who narrated the Saga. So it is in Didrik of Bern's Saga (chap. xx.), etc. In Sturleson's 'Ynglinga Saga,' it is said: 'In Sweden (Suithiod) there exist several nations, and sundry languages; there are *giants* and there are *dwarfs*.' We cannot doubt that by dwarfs is here meant a certain race of people.

In Thorstein Bejarmagn's Saga we are told that Thorstein came once with his ship to Jemtland, where he went ashore. On an open plain he saw a large stone, and beside it a dreadfully savage-looking *dwarf* wailing aloud. It appeared to Thorstein as if the dwarf's mouth was open from ear to ear. 'Wherefore dost thou weep?' enquired Thorstein. ' Dost thou not see,' answered the dwarf, 'the large eagle flying yonder? He has carried off my son, and I believe that the brute has been sent by Odin. I shall die if I lose my child.' The dwarf, therefore, was no Odin worshipper, which indeed the Laplanders never were. Thorstein shot the eagle, and brought the dwarf-child unscathed to the father, who, in his joy, made Thorstein a present of some magical implements, which afterwards became very useful to him.

From what I have now stated, we see that the dwarfs lived in mountain-caves. The Laplanders likewise dwelt in similar caves during later times. Mr. Högström saw caverns in which they had formerly lived, in order to escape the persecutions of the Karels. In the Piteå Lapland district it is said that traces are still to be found of such caverns in several places. The Lapland families took shelter in them, 'in order to conceal themselves from their enemies, while they were ravaging the country.' P. Læstadius* narrates as follows:—

'There is a Saga which tells us how some hostile people once discovered such an earth-cavern by hearing a woman from within calling out to somebody who was in an inner room to fetch the cooking-ladle. This was overheard by the enemy outside, who forthwith broke in upon them, and slew those who were in the cavern.' †

The Laplanders, however, now live almost generally in huts, called *gammar*, and there is no other people

* *Forstättning af Missionsresor*, page 486.

† This narrative recalls very vividly to my mind a great many Sagas in the south of Sweden, in which we are told of people who happened to pass some mountain-crag or earth-mounds, or who had laid down to rest and who overheard the cavern-people speaking in the mound, or heard their children cry, or had peeped through a chink to see what they were doing, or had seen smoke issue out of a hole in the mound. In Scania there are several crags of which similar things are reported by tradition. Amongst others, there is the Saga of Finn, who built the cathedral at Lund.

in the world, except the Laplanders, who live in such dwellings. It is therefore very elucidative of our subject that at least in *one* of our ancient Sagas it is expressly mentioned that a *dwarf* was living in a *gamm*. In Didrik of Bern's Saga (chap. xvi.) we are told how one day Didrik was out hunting on horseback in a forest, and that while chasing a stag, he saw a *dwarf* running at some distance from him. He hastened after him, and seized hold of him ' before he had time to reach his *gamm*.' The name of this dwarf was Alfrik; he was a famous thief and a great artificer. He had forged the sword *Nagelring*, which was owned by Grim, whom he (the dwarf) advised Didrik to challenge.

That the dwarfs, in their scattered dwellings, still used stone implements, even after more civilised people had settled in the country, the following story (told in Scania) leads us to infer:—A peasant who had gone out to look for his horses, wandered about nearly the whole day without finding them. Towards evening, when he came into a previously unfrequented tract, he met with a dwarf who was working in the forest. The dwarf, on perceiving the peasant close beside him, became so alarmed that he immediately threw down his tools, and ran away as fast as he could. The peasant then approached the place where the dwarf had been, and found there an axe, a chisel, and some other *tools*; but he could not make any use of them, ' because the dwarf, before running away, had transformed them all into stone.'

This Saga contains too much genuine truth not to

be a fact.   It shows the opinions held by the Gothic
people of the scattered dwarf race; namely, 1stly, tha
the dwarfs worked like other people, and had humar
wants to satisfy; 2ndly, that they were shy, anc
would run away as soon as a person of another rac
appeared to them; and, 3rdly, that they could deceive
one's visual organs, and change themselves, or any
other object, into what they pleased; or, in othe:
words, they were sorcerers.   To those who do no
believe in sorcery, this Saga only proves that the
dwarf tools were not *transformed* into stone, but tha
they *were really* of stone.

We have mentioned above, that stone amulets are
still worn by the peasantry in Scandinavia, Scotland
and Ireland.   It is clear that the Christian religion
during the thousand years it has been preached
amongst us, has swept away most of the pagan super
stitions, and that, therefore, such stone amulets were
formerly much more generally worn than now.*   Tha

* Some remnants of paganism may still be traced in severa
customs of the common people; but being perfectly harmless, anc
containing nothing which is offensive to the Christian mind, they
neither cast reproach on the popular teachers, nor do they neec
contradiction.   They are, however, interesting to the historica
enquirer, as the ruins of a religious edifice, crumbled into dust ter
centuries ago, and they tell him, perhaps, much upon which histor
is silent.   It would be an interesting undertaking, and one at the
same time of considerable importance in its results, to collect all the
remnants of popular customs which have their root in paganism
I shall here state one instance.

Those who have travelled in the south of Sweden, and perhaps ii
other countries, have no doubt often observed a mound of stone
piled up, and near it a wooden cross, bearing an inscription informin
the traveller that such or such a person has perished by som

such is the case we are told in our ancient Sagas.   In them are mentioned *life-stones, victory-stones,* etc., which the Gothic warriors carried about with them in battle, in order to secure victory.   In Didrik of Bern's Saga, chapter xxv., it is related that King Nidung gathered a large warlike host, with which he marched against his enemies.   He was only one day's march distant from the hostile army, expecting to do battle on the following day, when he discovered that he had forgotten his *victory-stone,* which he had left at home.   ' This stone was an heir-loom in his family, having passed from father to son during many generations, and it possessed the virtue of ensuring victory

accident near the spot.   This heap of stones is the pagan cairn, beside which Christianity has planted its cross.

I remember well how astonished I was in my childhood when I saw old men amongst the peasantry never daring to walk or to ride past such places until they had found a stone to throw upon the heap.   If no stone could be found, they took pieces of wood, branches of trees, or twigs of bushes, or such like, to throw upon it, since it was held to be a sacred duty that the cairn should be in some way increased.   But why?   This they could not themselves explain. The only answer that I could obtain from them was, that some mischance would befall them if they neglected this duty.   This ancient custom is, however, now less conscientiously observed.

May we not reasonably conclude that this practice, which has fallen very much into disuse during the last fifty or sixty years, was held more sacred one or more centuries ago, and that it was honoured most particularly during pagan times?   And may we not be certain, that the large cairns, which date from that period, and which are found lying for the most part near the more public roads, were not raised at *once,* but were built up by degrees by the passers-by? I remember having read somewhere, that it was considered as honouring the dead to increase his cairn with one or more stones. See Note 10.

to him who carried it in the fight.' The king, dreadin
to lose the battle if he had not his victory-stone abou
him, especially as his army was weaker in numerica
force than his adversary's, promised the hand of h
daughter, together with a third of his kingdom, t
him who should bring him this valuable stone befor
the commencement of the battle. Valent, the a
mourer, rode back to fetch the stone; he gave it t
the king, who thereupon attacked the enemy and wo
the battle.

In the ninety-sixth chapter of this Saga there is
still more elucidative narrative concerning such
victory-stone. Ditlew, a youthful champion from Tu
matorp, in Scania,* encountered an old warrior, Sigur
by name, in single combat. Towards evening, Sigur
became fatigued, and observed that he had left h
victory-stone at home. He therefore invited Ditle
home with him to spend the night in his house, a
that they might continue the fight on the followin
day. Here Ditlew made the acquaintance of Sigurd
brave daughter Gunhild, and they forthwith fell i
love with each other. Old Sigurd, as soon as h
entered his house, *hung his victory-stone round h
neck*; but having drunk deeply during the night, h
fell into a heavy sleep. Gunhild then stole the stor
from her father, and gave it to her sweetheart. Whe
the combat was renewed on the following day, Sigur
received three wounds, whereupon he owned himse
vanquished.

---

* Now Tomerup, or Tomarp, a hamlet of Gladsax, formerly
town of some importance.

It follows from this, first, that the amulets which the warriors carried about with them in order that they might be victorious were of stone; secondly, *that they were worn on a string, or strap, round the neck.*

We find in collections several other stones, which appear to have been worn as victory-stones; e.g. a hammer-stone with an iron hoop and loop.*

Among other qualities, the dwarfs were supposed to have the power of rendering themselves invisible.   In the Swedish, as well as in the Danish *folk-sagas*, there are often narratives of how the *goblins* (as the dwarfs are sometimes called †) attended a wedding, but invisibly, and ate all the food of the guests.

In the vicinity of Romeleklint, in Scania, where formerly many tales were told about pigmies who dwelt in the *klint* (crag), it is also narrated, that whenever the dinner-bell was rung in Heckeberga Hall, the goblins ran thither from the crag and carried off all the eatables prepared for the inmates.   As this was of constant occurrence, the family was ultimately reduced to great poverty.

An exactly similar story is related by Sturleson in his 'King's Sagas' (vol. i. page 79).   We are there told that King Halfdan Svarte (the Black) one day was a Yule guest in Hadeland, and that on Christmas-eve, while at supper, and a great many guests being assembled, all the eatables and drinkables suddenly

---

* *Urinvånarne*, first edition, Pl. XII. fig. 154.

† *Goblin* is an appellation which seems generally to be applied to those who did not belong to the Svea (Åsa) or Gothic race.   They might thus belong as well to the Jotna as the dwarf race, though mostly to the latter.

disappeared from the banquet-tables.   The king sa
sorrowfully in his seat, whilst all the guests returne(
to their respective homes.

In order to learn who had played him this unplea
sant trick, the king ordered a Finn (Laplander), wh(
was much skilled in witchcraft, to be seized, and h(
had him tortured in sundry ways to compel him t(
reveal the truth; but he revealed nothing.   The Finr
then made his escape, and with him fled the king's
son, Harold, then ten years old.   On their flight they
came to the dwelling of a chieftain (without doubt ε
Finn chieftain), by whom they were well received.
and with whom they remained until the following
spring.   One day the chieftain said to Harold: 'Thy
father was very wroth that I took some victuals from
him last winter; but I will now make amends by
telling thee some good news.   Thy father is dead,
and now thou shalt return home and take the kingdom which was his; and I will give to thee besides
the whole of Norway to reign over.'

It was therefore, as we see, the Finn chief who,
with the assistance of the Laplanders, had enchanted
away the viands from the Yule-board.   This Saga
and its solution thus explain also how the sorcery
at Romelcklint was managed.   Nearly similar witch-
eries, now generally called thefts, are said to be still
practised amongst those Norwegians who live in the
neighbourhood of the mountain-ridges, along which
the Laplanders wander with their reindeer herds.
The Laplanders—at least, many of them—are still
believed to be as thievish, cunning, and skilled in

witchcraft as formerly. Everybody who wishes to do so, can easily convince himself that stories similar to those which are told in the old Sagas about Finns, dwarfs, and goblins, and which are still told by the country people in the south of Sweden, of pigmies and goblins who formerly dwelt in such and such a mountain-district, are related even to this day by the peasants in the northern parts of Norway of the Finn Laplanders. The locality has been changed, but the scene is the same, with the difference only which a different degree of civilisation must create.

It is possible that against a comparison between the Laplanders of the present day and the dwarfs of ancient times, the objection may be raised that the Laplanders from time immemorial have been a nomad race, leading a roving life with their reindeer herds; but that it is never related in the Sagas that the dwarfs owned any reindeer. This objection would only betray very little acquaintance with the real facts, which are these, that the Laplanders, from being originally only hunters and fishermen, did not become nomads and owners of reindeer herds until some centuries after the Christian era. Procopius describes the migratory Finns, which evidently are Laplanders, not as nomads, but as roving hunters. Paulus Varnefredi, who lived in the eighth century, speaks of them also as being only a tribe of hunters, and Tacitus, who wrote his ' Germania ' towards the close of the first century, knew also that *Fenni* (evidently the Finns of the Saga) were wild huntsmen, and the most savage of all the tribes which had come

under his notice. The picture which he draws
them is classical but exaggerated, and it is easy to s(
that the materials were supplied to him by some tril
hostile to the Fenni.   IIe says: ' Amongst the Fen:
great barbarism exists, and a disgusting poverty; the
possess neither arms, horses, nor dwellings.   The
food is herbs, their clothing skins, their bed tl
ground.   Their only dependence is on their arrow
which, for want of iron, they arm with a bone poin
The chase is the support of the women as well as (
the men; for they hunt in common, and divide tl
spoil between them.   Their children have no oth(
protection against wild beasts and storms than a hov(
made of the branches of trees.   This is the resort (
youth, this is the receptacle of old age; yet the
consider this manner of living happier than groanin
over the plough, toiling in the erection of houses, (
subjecting their own fortunes and those of others t
the agitations of alternate hope and fear.   Havin
nothing to fear from man, nothing to hope from tl
gods, they have attained that, which is most difficu
to gain, namely, that they have not even a wish.'*

We see thus, that the *Fenni* were even at that tin
a tribe despised and detested by the Germanic rac
holding about the same relation to the Germans (
that which the Esquimaux of the present day hold (
the Indian tribes of North America.† (See Chap. V
We see, further, that they had no reindeer, th:
they were not nomads, but subsisted solely t
their arrows (' *sola in sagittis spes* ').   So it was al:

* Tacitus, *Germ.* xlvi.   † See Note 11.

in Scandinavia previous to the immigrations of more
cultivated tribes. Consequently, the dwarfs, driven
out from amongst the people and leading an isolated
life, could not have had any reindeer. It is not
known with certainty in what century the Laplanders
here in Scandinavia first began their nomad life. We
find, however, from many passages in the earliest
history, and in the Sagas, that this people, even after
having been expelled from the southern and also from
the central part of Sweden by more powerful tribes,
enjoyed for a considerable period a much higher reputation (for instance, in central Norway) than now.
They had their own chiefs and their own popular assem-
blies. The daughters of their chiefs were occasionally married to men of the Gothic race. The mother
of Örvar Odd's father was a Lapland woman, for
Örvar was a son of Grim Lodikin, and he was a son
of the niece of the Finn chief Guse by Kettil Häng.
Kettil Häng seems also to have descended from the
same race, because he was the son of Halbjörn, sur-
named Halftroll (Half-goblin), which shows that his
mother was descended from a goblin (*troll*) race.
Harold Hårfager was, according to Sturleson, married
to Snäfrid,* the daughter of the Finn (Laplander?)
Svase.

* In the title of the Saga, Svase is called *Jotun*, but in the Saga
itself *Finne*. That this last was the right name, we are led to infer
from his daughter Snäfrid being expressly called ' the Finn-woman.'
The king, when he became aware of her witchcraft, was roused to such
violent anger, that he drove away her sons from him. We see by
her being able to practise ' Seid,' that she was a Lapland woman, and
we also find by Thiodolfer's words to the king (that he ought not to

In addition to what I have already adduced in proof
of the dwarfs of the Saga being people, and of the
same race as the Laplanders, I will here add the
following. The dwarfs, or, as they are commonly
called in the Sagas, mountain-pigmies, or goblins, are
always represented as having formerly dwelt in mountain-caverns, crags, or hillocks, i.e. earthen mounds,
mostly in solitary tracts, and generally in the vicinity of water. They were little and ugly, and were
of both sexes. They had children, and sometimes ser-
vants. They were believed to possess large trea-
sures, mostly silver and copper ('as rich as a *goblin*'
is still a proverb among the peasantry). They were
very thievish, and frequently visited the farm-houses
and country seats in order to steal, especially victuals,
ale, and such like. Sometimes they wanted to borrow
some things, and they then approached the houses of
the country-people, in the evening, to ask for them;
they never dared to pass the threshold, but stood
outside the house, calling in a loud voice for what
they wanted. They generally sent one or two of
their children on such an errand. If what they asked

despise his sons by Snäfrid, ' because they would willingly have had
a better and nobler lineage by the mother's side, if thou hadst let them')
that Snäfrid belonged to a despised race. But the Jotna race was
not despised; Odin himself married Skade, the daughter of a Jotne,
and through many of his chief warriors he endeavoured to befriend
this powerful race. It may, however, seem strange, that if Snäfrid
was of the ugly Laplander race, she could so captivate or enchant
the powerful Harold Harfager by her beauty, as is related in his
Saga. I may, however, observe, that the Lapland girls are not always
ugly; on the contrary, even at the present time we occasionally
meet with some who are very pretty.

for was given to them, it was always found lying early
in the morning, a few days after, in the same place,
and beside it, as a gratuity for the loan, a silver coin,
or something else of value. They held no social
intercourse with 'human beings,' but only with each
other. They frequently gave feasts, celebrated weddings, etc., to which the goblins from other moun-
tain-crags were invited. They were cowardly; they
shunned man and daylight.

Although, at first sight, all this may be regarded as
mere superstition, it has, nevertheless, its root far
down in the most remote antiquity, which can easily be
shown by ancient Sagas. The ancient original hatred
to the dwarfs (mountain-goblins), which manifests
itself in the oldest Sagas, telling how they were per-
secuted, shot through with red-hot arrows, cut to
pieces with axes, etc., has died away in the later
national Sagas. In them they figure mostly as a
degraded race, often thievish and dangerous, often
generous and beneficent, but with whom, nevertheless,
nobody wished to become legally more closely united.
I infer from all this, that when the Indo-Germanic
people, now inhabiting the greatest part of the country,
settled here, there remained of the Lapland race in
the south of Sweden a few households, living isolated
in remote districts. It was only in Norway, and
especially in its more northern parts, that they still
formed a united people, having their chiefs and holding their popular meetings.

In order to complete the evidence, that the dwarfs
of the Saga and the *pigmies* of popular tradition

belonged to the same race as the Laplanders of the present day, I will here sketch the outlines of a parallel between them :—*

1. The Laplanders are ugly and short, just as the dwarfs of the Sagas are represented to be.

2. The Laplanders are clothed in a grey reindeer-kirtle, and they wear a blue or red cap. The pigmies are also so described in the Sagas. (Compare Thiele's 'Danske Folkesagn,' vol. i. page 122; vol. ii. page 3.)

3. The Laplanders, for instance, in Norway, speak the language of the country very badly. When the Norwegians imitate the Laplanders, it is done nearly in the same way as when the Danish peasant imitates the pigmy. (Thiele, vol. i. page 114.)

4. The Laplanders are cowardly, they are unfit to be soldiers. The dwarfs of the Sagas are represented as exceedingly cowardly. When they see a human being, they try to steal away. A child can vanquish them. An, a child twelve years old, compelled the dwarf Lit to forge arrows for him.

5. The Laplanders are considered to be cunning and deceitful. In Norway it was a saying, that if a merchant wished to keep the custom of a Laplander, he must cheat him a little, and let him know it at parting. In order to be revenged, the Laplander would return again; but if he had succeeded in

---

* I need scarcely observe, that the question here is less what the Laplanders *are*, than what they are *considered to be*, and how they are represented by their neighbours. Whether they, in reality, have all the faults which national hatred attributes to them, is not the subject of this disquisition.

cheating the merchant, he would return no more. This characteristic feature we find also in the dwarfs of the Sagas. They are cunning, sly, deceitful, and thievish.

6. The Laplanders are skilful; they are even able to manufacture their own rifles. The skill of the dwarfs as craftsmen is spoken of in many Sagas.

7. The Laplanders delight in collecting glittering metals, especially silver. They do not willingly receive any other than silver coin. Many an old avaricious Laplander is thought to have concealed his silver in some out-of-the-way place amongst the mountains, known only to himself, where he pays now and then a visit. The dwarfs are also spoken of in the Saga as being rich in silver.

8. It was thought that the dwarfs were skilled in sorcery; the same was believed of the Laplanders. They were aware of this, and threatened to ' *sätta gan i*' (bewitch) those who did not give them what they asked for. We hear also occasionally, in the south of Sweden, *Lappskott*, etc., spoken of. The Laplanders were, and are still, considered by many to be a weird race of sorcerers.

9. The Lapland race is considered inferior to, and is despised by, the Goths living in their neighbourhood. In consequence of this hereditary hatred between the tribes, a Swede or a Norwegian rarely marries a Lapland woman. Mr. P. Læstadius, although a great friend of the Laplanders, says: 'The races appear to be so distinctly divided from each other, that it seems to be repugnant even to physical nature to unite them.'

10. The Laplanders therefore marry and hold feasts only amongst themselves, as was the case with the mountain-pigmies.

This comparison might be carried much farther, and even into the smallest details; but what I have already adduced may suffice to prove that the dwarfs of ancient times and the Laplanders of our own day are identical.

Having proved that the dwarfs of the ancient Saga were men, we will now endeavour to show the same of the *Jotnar*, or giants, of the ancient Saga, though they belonged to a different race.

All nations make their own stature the scale by which they measure the stature of others. Certain, therefore, as it is, that it must have been a race of low stature which gave the epithet of giants (*Jotnar*) to another race, it is equally certain that it must have been a tall race which gave to another the epithet of dwarfs. Consequently, the giants need not have been taller than people in general of Celtic, Germanic, or Gothic races, in order to have been called giants by a dwarf race such as the Laplanders or Esquimaux. We can prove this by examples. In Ikaresarsuk, in the district of Fredrikshaabs, in Greenland, an ancient Saga still exists amongst the Greenlanders, which evidently has some connection with the fall and ruin of the ancient Norwegian colony there. Thus, it is related that a Greenlander, by name Poviak, had once upon a time come up amongst the mountains, and there met accidentally with two

women of supernatural stature, who lived in the
interior of the country. They seized hold of him
and carried him along with them. After having
lived with them for some time, it happened one day
that they all three came down to the seashore together, at the moment when several travelling Greenlanders had landed. Poviak called out to his countrymen, who hastened to his assistance. The women
tried to escape, but only one of them succeeded in
getting away; the other was taken, and carried off
by the Greenlanders. They took her on board one of
their women's boats, but she was so tall and strong,
that every one of her movements threatened to upset
the boat. She thenceforth resided amongst the Greenlanders, until she gave birth to a child, which cost
her her life.*

This national Saga amongst the Greenlanders, in
connection with the tale of the Esquimaux, referred
to before (page 208), about the 'gigantic' Englishmen in North America, proves, beyond a doubt, that
the Sagas of giants have originated amongst a race of
short stature. And as we know that there never
has been found in Europe any other dwarfish race
of people than the Laplanders, it follows that the
notions about, and the epithet of, *Jotnar* (giants)
have emanated from them; and since we know, besides, that there never has existed in Europe a race
of larger stature than the Goths, Svear, and those
whom we in Sweden call Finns (*alias* Quanes), it follows that these races (either one or all of them) were

* *Nordisk Tidskrift för Oldkyndighet,* vol. ii. page 324.

the *Jotnar* of the polar race; and hence follows one circumstance which seems not to have been noticed hitherto, namely, *that all our ancient Sagas about ' Jotnar' have originally emanated from the dwarf race —the Laplanders.* But if such be the case, then there must still exist amongst the Laplanders Sagas about *Jotnar* in which the dwarf peoples have expressed their opinion of their gigantic conquerors, just as the notions of these latter about the Laplanders are illustrated by their Sagas about the dwarfs. According to the accounts of Mr. Læstadius* there are still a great many giant Sagas current amongst the Laplanders. The fundamental features are the same in them all; the *jotna* (giant) is there described as being unwieldy, large and strong, but awkward and stupid when compared with the cunning Laplander, who, of course, arrogates the epithet, the honour, and the dignity of ' human being ' (man), and who always cheats the simple giant into whose hands he happens to fall.† It does not follow, that because the giant in the Lapland Sagas is represented as being a cannibal, he was one in reality, but merely that the childishly timid Laplander had a panic terror of him.‡ The giant in the Lapland Saga is called *stallo*, or *jatton*, and he who dupes him is called ' man.' This latter is frequently a cunning boy, who is called ' Askovis'-- an epithet which,

---

* *Fortsättning af Journ.*, page 460.

† The Greenlander also ridicules the European on the sly, and considers his manners awkward and simple. What the opinion of the Laplander is now upon this subject I am not aware.

‡ Compare, however, *Nord. forny. Saga*, vol. ii. page 107.

according to Læstadius, has been imported by settlers. Such an Askovis, whom we will call simply a Laplander, had once fallen into the hands of a giant. One day, when they were abroad together, the Laplander pretended that he saw a great many things happening at a great distance, of which he informed the giant. The giant, who of course could see nothing of all this, wondered what made the Laplander so clear-sighted. The Laplander made him believe that one became so by pouring melted lead in one's eyes. The stupid giant believes it. After becoming blind from the cure, he endeavours to catch the Laplander, who, however, deceives him, and gets away from him in the same manner as Ulysses from the cave of Polyphemus.*

It is the same in all our giant Sagas; inferior weakness vanquishing superior physical force by cunning. This fundamental idea pervades all giant Sagas, amongst what people soever they may be current; and if we consider the matter more closely, we shall find this trait of character psychologically true, founded upon human nature, and therefore common to all.

The reason why such giant and dwarf Sagas, so very similar, should have been invented amongst so many races differing so materially one from the other, is no doubt this, that each of these races has occasionally, in the course of time, while in a state of barbarism, come into hostile contact with some other

* The story will be found in Læstadius, *Fortsättning af Journ.*, page 463.

race, either larger or smaller than itself. We may safely conclude that this must have been the case, not only in Europe, but in all quarters of the world, because races of diverse statures are found in them all, and these races were of course formerly far less mixed than they are now. And we may be sure, that where such hostile meetings did take place, Sagas more or less resembling ours must also have arisen.

I have shown, on page 217, § 1, how dwarf Sagas have been invented, and on page 208 I have shown, by historical facts, how the English in North America have given rise to giant Sagas amongst the Esquimaux dwarf people there. Something similar has occurred in the Old World.

How easily an excited imagination can create exaggerated forms, is proved by the following historical fact. When Moses was wandering through the desert with the Israelites, who went out of Egypt after having lived there in a state of bondage, and when arrived in the desert of Paran, he sent spies into Canaan, in order to procure information of the fertility of the country, the number of its inhabitants, the strength of its towns, etc. The spies returned, after the lapse of forty days, with the report that, amongst others, there were also living ‘ Anakims’ (the children of Anak), ‘ and,’ added the messengers, ‘ we were in our own sight as grasshoppers, and so we were in their sight.’

Hearing this report, ‘ all the congregation lifted up their voice, and cried; and the people wept that night.

And all the children of Israel murmured against Moses and against Aaron;'* and they were so frightened, that they wished to return to Egyptian bondage rather than face these formidable giants.

Thus much Holy Writ tells us; but what it does not say, and what, nevertheless, we may take for granted, is that in a rude and timorous people, where such a foolish panic is created by the mere mention of a tall race, imagination must also create exaggerated and ludicrous images, and these, being handed down from generation to generation, became ultimately the giant-Sagas of ancient times. Several passages in the Bible show that the Anakims were looked upon as giants. 'And the land of the children of Ammon also was accounted *a land of giants*; giants dwelt therein in old times.' They were 'a people great, and many, and tall, as the Anakims.'† In the desert of the Moabites 'the Emims dwelt in times past, a people great, and many, and tall, as the Anakims.'‡

These giants, the Anakims, were the same people as the Philistines, and of Phœnician origin. Joshua vanquished them several times, and destroyed them in the interior mountain districts of Hebron, Debir, and Anab (Josh. xi. 21), and they remained only in the coast districts, in Gaza, Gath, and Ashdod.§ Thus, then, Joshua extirpated the giants of Canaan, as Asa Thor did those of Scandinavia.

---

* Num. xiii. 33; xiv. 1, 2.   † Deut. ii. 20, 21.
‡ Deut. ii. 10.   § Philistine cities.

The same scene which took place amongst the Israelites on the borders of Canaan, out of fear of the Anakim giants, was enacted in the Roman camp, when Cæsar marched against the giant people, the Germans, under Ariovistus. When Cæsar had arrived at Besançon, a report was spread by Gauls * and merchants throughout the Roman army of the gigantic size of the Germans. This caused such a panic amongst the officers and soldiers, that many of the former returned home, under one pretence or another, and those who did not dare to ask for furlough, ' wept and groaned in their tents.' They all made their wills; terror seized even veteran soldiers and chiefs.† It is scarcely possible to read the historical account of these events without feeling convinced that they would give rise, amongst the lower classes of people, to all kinds of exaggerated Sagas; and, knowing this, it is also impossible to read Sagas about giants without seeing that they are founded upon some such occurrence.

From what has now been said, it is evident that the Sagas about giants and dwarfs (which epithets are relative, because the one could not exist without the other) are not a mere play of fancy, but have an historical foundation, although a frightened imagination has exaggerated and clothed them in the garb of fiction.

* This does not prove that the Gauls were a very large people, at least not like the Germans, although taller than the Romans. (Cæs. *de Bell. Gall.* ii. 30.)

† Cæs. *de Bell. Gall.* i. 39.

And consequently :—

1. The Philistines were the giants of the Israelites, and these were the dwarfs of the former.

2. The Cimbrians were the giants of the Greek adventurers, and these were the dwarfs of the former.*

3. The Germans and the Celts were the giants of the Romans, and these were their dwarfs.

4. Icelanders, Normans, Englishmen, and others, were the giants of the Greenland and North American Esquimaux, and these latter were their *skrälingar*, i.e. dwarfs, etc.

We can easily see in every giant and dwarf Saga whether it has emanated from the dwarf or from the tall race; because the race amongst which it originated always styles itself ' man' (human being), and considers itself only to be of the proper size; the strange race is always described, when the Saga has been invented by the large size, as being wretchedly small and weak, and when by the small people, as being enormously bulky and strong. The stronger race boasts of its strength, and treats the weaker one with insolent contempt: thus Thor kicked the dwarfs into Balder's funeral pile; the Anakims of Canaan despised the Israelites as grasshoppers; and the Gaul looked down with contempt upon the smaller-sized Roman.†

---

* *Odyss.* ix. 105–230; 231–566. Dubois de Montpéreux has shown that the Cyclopes, on the coast of the Bosphorus, pointed out by Homer as frightful giants, hurling huge pieces of rock at the Grecian ships, were a gigantic nomad race of Cimbrians, and the Greeks adventurers comparable to the Vikings of the North.

† Cæs. *de Bell. Gall.* ii. 30.

Those, on the other hand, who in physical strength are inferior to their gigantic oppressors, avenge themselves by calling them awkward and stupid, and arrogate to themselves greater intellect and cunning: thus, Ulysses in the cave of Polyphemus ; thus, the Roman smiling at the simplicity of the Gaul, when he makes it the subject of a proverb;[*] thus, the Greenlander, who, behind his back, smiles at the awkward and simple European;[†] thus, 'Askovis,' and, indeed, everybody who, under the name of 'man,' appears in a giant Saga.

With regard to the giants (*Jutnar*) of the Scandinavian Saga, they belonged to a gigantic tribe who worshipped the god Thor.

We know that the statues of the gods in the heathen temples were painted wooden images, clothed in their costumes, and provided with their attributes. Thor's figure was very large,[‡] and he had a red beard; he was frequently called the *Red-bearded One*, or *Red Beard*, by friend as well as by foe. As we may assume with certainty that the god was a representative of the people amongst whom his worship first arose (because every people creates its god after its own image), we have, then, here two ethnological marks of recognition for ascertaining the origin of Thor. Thor's people were of large stature, and had red hair and beard, and consequently blue eyes.

---

[*] Camd. *Brit.*, page 2.

[†] According to the verbal statement of a Dane who has resided a considerable time in Greenland.

[‡] *Olof the Holy's Saga*, chap. cxviii. and others.

According to authentic accounts, there are still many Finnish tribes dwelling in the interior of Russia, and these are divided into two main branches, of which one has red hair and blue eyes, and much resembles Finns (Quänes) and Esthonians,* namely, the Björmer (Permians), Siräns, the Obi Ostiaks,† Votiaks, and Tschuwaschers;‡ and what, in connection herewith, deserves our attention, is that, at any rate amongst some of these tribes, God is even to this day called Thor. Pallas informs us, in ' Zoographia Rosso-Asiatica,' vol. i. page 529, that the swallow is called by the Beresow Ostiaks *Torom sischki*, which signifies God's bird, and at Irtis it is called *Toromvoi*, God's animal. Erman relates, in his ' Reise um die Welt,' vol. i. page 700, that the Ostiaks, which are a tall, well-built, handsome people, call God *Torium* (page 677) or *Torum* (page 699), which means with them the Supreme Being. Also the Votiaks are tall, broad-shouldered, and powerful men, with hair and beard red (page 253). The Tschuwaschers call God *Tora*, and the god of thunder and weather of the Esthonian Finns was *Tara*.§

Hence we may be induced to suppose that the name of Thor, and his worship, were introduced into Scandinavia, and spread amongst the inhabitants, by some

---

* Portraits of Esthonians are given by Kruse in his *Necrolivonica*.

† Ostiaks and Vuguls, who dwell on both sides of the Ural mountain-chain, are of the same original race, but the one is dark and the other red-haired. (Prichard, vol. iii. page 214.)

‡ Rask, *Om den nordiske Sprogs oprindelse*, pages 96, 97, after Dobrowsky.

§ *Geij. Sv. Rik. Häfd.*, vol. i. page 290, note 3.

Finnish tribe; but we may likewise remember that
Thor was also worshipped by the Goths, and that the
national tales relate that he had conflicts with the
diminutive aborigines anterior to the time of Odin.
To this class of prehistoric Sagas belong also all Sagas
of Thor, still living on the lips of the common people
in the south of Sweden, and all relating to the
period preceding the introduction of the Walhalla
worship in Scandinavia.

In all our national Sagas about Thor, his conflicts
with goblins and pigmies are therefore related, and as
a remembrance thereof, thunder and lightning are still
called *Thordön* in the whole of the south of Sweden.
When a child, I often heard old people say, when
there was a thunderstorm, that Thor was driving his
carriage through the clouds, striking the goblins with
his lightning.*   When the thunder was rolling con-
tinuously, they said: 'Now he † is in a hurry to chase
the goblins;' and the goblins were always imagined to
be pigmies dwelling in mountains, in hollow trees,
earthen mounds, etc.   Formerly, it was proverbial
that 'if there were to be no thunderstorms, the world
would be destroyed by goblins.'   When I was a child,
I often heard old people say: 'It thunders much less
now than formerly, because most of the goblins are
now killed.'   How small the goblins, which Thor was
chasing, were sometimes represented to be, we can
infer from the following.   When a violent thunder-

---

* I have never heard it said that he slew *giants*.

† Without mentioning Thor's name, the people merely said 'he,'
or 'he, the old one.'

storm was. raging, and the harvest-labourers were
overtaken by showers of rain, the peasant-women did
not venture to cover their heads with the skirts of
their gowns (as they always did in rain), for fear that
the goblins should hide themselves therein. This
did occasionally happen, but the woman had then
been warned by some strange voice, and had dropped
the skirt of her gown, when the goblin, falling out,
rolled like a ball of thread along the field, and was
instantly killed by lightning.

When the Walhalla worship was introduced into
Scandinavia, the Thor worship was the one most generally spread, although not the only religion.* But it
was politically important and prudent on the part of
the Asar,† a princely priest-caste, who settled here on
the borders of the Mälar Lake, and who had brought
with them Odin's Walhalla worship, to unite in
themselves all the gods of the country, in order to be
enabled to rule all the different tribes.‡ The more
ancient gods of the country were therefore adopted as
Odin's sons. And as the Goths, who were worshippers of Thor,§ were a numerous, probably the most

---

* There was also a Baal-Balder worship.

† Under this name I comprehend those priests who introduced
the Walhalla worship of Odin, and of whom I shall say more in
the treatise on the *Iron Age*.

‡ The Romans did the same; the gods of the conquered nations
were received amongst their own gods.

§ Demonstrable by the historically true traditions. (See below.)
That the Thor worship is very ancient, and arose amongst a people
who were in a low stage of civilisation, we can infer from Thor's
war weapon, which was a hammer (' *malleus sax.*') or club (*clava*

numerous people,[*] Thor was pronounced to be the first-born of Odin;[†] and in order to flatter the powerful tribe whose god he was, his image was placed in the chief seat in Odin's principal temple in Upsala, where Odin[‡] (the principal god of the race which had last immigrated) stood on one side, and the Vendian god Fricco, or Freyr, on the other.[§]

Many passages in the ancient Sagas seem to intimate that the Åsa race, immediately on its arrival in the valley of the Mälar, allied itself with the powerful Jotna families. *Niord, Odin, Frey*, and others, were married to Jotna maidens. The Jotna women were

sax.); because the club (the hammer is but a different kind of club) is older than the sword, and even older than the axe. It is the *patoo-patoo* of the savage; it is a war weapon made of a log of a tree, thicker at one end than at the other. Hercules is thus represented exactly like a savage—naked, with the root of a tree as a weapon, and a wild animal's skin thrown over his shoulder.

[*] Procopius, *de Bello Got.* ii. 15.

[†] According to the Edda.

[‡] Odin was the god of the Indo-Germanic race, whose name, with various pronunciations, appears amongst many ancient people of this race. The priests of the Odin worship were called *Asir, Osser, Asar*, etc., and the most ancient known place of that worship was called *Asgård*, or *Ashof.* Tacitus mentions an Asburg (Aschiburgium), in the south of Germany, dating from such a remote period, that by some it was thought to have been founded by Ulysses, who lived more than twelve hundred years before Tacitus (*Germ.* iii.). It is scarcely possible to refer this Asburg with any degree of probability to the Odin described by Sturleson. It may rather be assumed that the Odin worship existed, and was spread in the south of Germany, many centuries earlier than it was reformed into Walhalla worship and introduced into Scandinavia by the Herulean invasion of settlers there in the sixth century after Christ. I shall treat of this in my work on the *Iron Age.*

[§] Adamus Bremens, vol. i. page 25.

beauties of a fair complexion, with golden (light-red) hair and blue eyes, as, for instance, Gerda, the daughter of the Jotun Gymer, and Skade, the daughter of the Jotun Thjasse, and others.

Several Norwegian princes, aware, from authentic family traditions,* that they derived their descent, through father and mother, from the Jotun race, remained, therefore, always faithful to the Jotna god *Thor*, and sacrificed to him, although, as princes, they did not disdain the delights and glories of Walhalla.

The Norwegian Hlade-Jarls, who, from their mother's side, traced their descent to Skade, daughter to 'the pomp-loving Jotne Thjasse,' sacrificed therefore mostly to Thor. The powerful Hakon Jarl, who was chiefly devoted to the Jotun worship,† had a temple in which, with other Jotna gods and goddesses (amongst which the statues of the witch-sisters Thorgerdr Haurgabruds and Yrpas),‡ stood

---

* Before the art of writing was known in this country, tradition must have been far more lively, determinate, and clear than afterwards. The art of writing is the death of tradition, and we see proof of this amongst our own country-people.

† When it is said of Hakon Jarl that the goblins made a boast of his friendship, it is evident that by goblins are meant the same as the descendants of the Jotnar, who remained in the country. The name *troll* (goblin) is never given to any man or woman of the Saga relating to the Åsa race; it was given only to the foreign tribes who were looked upon as conquered, for *troll*, or *tröll*, seems to be the same as *thrall*, and signifies *serf*, because prisoners of war were made slaves. Thus the name of Slavonians, Slavians, signifies in most European languages *serf* or *thrall*.

‡ Her temple in Norway. See *Urda*, vol. iii. page 7. It was to this, his guardian-goddess, to whom Hakon Jarl offered up his

also the statue of Thor, ornamented with golden rings and placed on a chariot,* consequently the ancient *Öku Thorr*.

Nor could the Odin doctrine gain ground amongst the bulk of the people; because this doctrine, with its princely Walhalla, was not qualified ever to become a popular religion.† The Walhalla doctrine of Odin was therefore adopted chiefly in Svealand, and, as it appears, also by some royal courts, related to the so-called *Asar*, in other provinces of Sweden, Denmark, and Norway. For these traced their descent up to 'the high gods;' but the bulk of the people, and a few princes in Norway and Göthland, continued to remain worshippers of Thor.

Therefore the *Thor worship* was at the introduction of the Christian religion more widely disseminated amongst the common people, and consequently more difficult to exterminate; and thence it also follows, that the traces of paganism which are still to be found in Göthland and Norway are principally the remnants of Thor worship.

Thurs-day (in Swedish *the day of Thor*) was still, about a hundred years ago, considered in certain parts of the country as a kind of holiday,‡ on which no serious or heavy work was to be done. When a

---

son Erling, then seven years old, in order to obtain a victory over the Joms-Vikings (Olof Tryggva's Sagn, *Schöning Norg Hist.* vol. iii. page 269. Compare *Urda*, page 8.)

* Compare *Geijer*, pages 282–283.

† It was more properly an aristocratic military religion, and the life in their heavenly kingdom (Walhalla) was that of a barrack.

‡ This I was told by old people in my childhood.

child, I remember having occasionally seen, in the south of Sweden, some old woman who would never churn butter or spin on a Thursday.

Many ancient Sagas of warnings given by *the old one with the beard* not to desecrate Thursday-eve by any kind of work, are told. This was evidently a remnant of Thor worship. On the other hand, all kinds of pagan superstitions and sorceries were to be practised on the Thursday, in order to make them efficient. On a Thursday, people were to go to the necromancer, in order to see in a pail of water the face of the thief who had robbed them; on a Thursday (Maundy-Thursday), all witches rode to 'Blå-kulla' on a broomstick; on a Thursday morning, he who suffered from toothache had to walk silently into the forest, carrying with him a nail with which he had to pick his teeth, after which the nail was to be stuck into a tree, when the toothache would be cured; he who was born on a Thursday could see spectres, and so on. All this was evidently a remnant of *Thor-ism*, and such was the case in Göthland. It seems to have been much the same in Norway. Finn Magnusen relates* that the peasants in certain mountain districts in Norway, even as late as the close of last century, used to preserve stones of a round form, and reverence them in the same manner as their pagan ancestors used to worship their idols. They washed them every Thursday evening, smeared them before the fire with butter, or some other grease, then

* *Annaler för Nordisk Oldkyndighet*, 1838–1839, page 133.

dried them and laid them in the seat of honour upon fresh straw; at certain times of the year, they were steeped in ale, and all this under the supposition that they would bring luck and comfort to the house.[*] Such a remnant of Thor worship in Norway, in those more modern times, I consider to be very remarkable and illustrative.

Even in the ceremonies of our Christian Church there are still, here and there, traces which seem to imply that the Thursday has long been looked upon as a pagan day, on which no Christian religious ceremonies of any importance ought to be performed. This is still the case, at all events in the rural districts in the south of Sweden. On a Thursday no Christian funerals are held, no weddings, no baptisms celebrated, and so on, because nobody would ever think of requesting the performance of these ceremonies; but if asked the reason why they do not wish them to be performed, they are at a loss for an answer: they merely say that it is not customary,

---

[*] Finn Magnusen, who is perfectly correct in believing that the pagan ceremonies of the peasantry were Thor worship, is also of opinion that the Thor worship must have consisted in stone worship, because these amulets were of stone. This conclusion is evidently too hasty; they were not worshipped because they were of stone, but because they were heathen amulets. Had they been of wood, or metal, or of bone, the peasants would have reverenced them equally. It was only accidentally that they were of stone. The Sagas mention no stone images of Thor, but of wood when of a large size, and of bone when small. Halfred Vandrada-Skald was accused by Rolf before Olof Trygvardson of having, after being christened, made offerings in secret, and of having *Thor's image of bone* in his possession. Müller, *Saga*, vol. iii. page 276.

and nobody cares to find out the origin of this ancient prejudice.

I have mentioned this to show that our Sagas are founded on history. Most of the Sagas belong, however, to a less ancient period, or to that part of the subject which relates to the Iron Age, which I purpose to describe in a future work.

CHAPTER VII.

ON THE PROBABLE CONDITION OF SCANDINAVIA AT THE ARRIVAL OF THE FIRST PEOPLE.

To form a clear idea on this subject, let us cast a retrospective glance on the far more ancient state of this part of the earth after the glacial period, when it had been entirely covered by ice, and was in about the same condition as Greenland and Spitzbergen are at present. We meet with unmistakable traces of such a state in innumerable places in our peninsula. They consist in the granite rocks being smooth, polished, and often furrowed, the ground being in many places bestrewn with more or less colossal blocks, which usually have their origin in far distant places, and which are themselves sometimes smoothly polished and grooved, and here and there lying in heaps, so that we plainly recognise in them the remains of moraines.

We may assume that this fearful destruction has occurred during the present organic period of creation; but we cannot with the least probability even guess at the immeasurable space of time which has since elapsed, nor do we know whether, previous to this period of destruction, there were human beings in the north of Europe. It is certain that similar changes have likewise taken place in other countries, and indeed, apparently, all over the northern hemisphere; but we think we have reason to suppose that they have happened in different places at different times, and that no new creation was required to refurnish a part of the earth, thus depopulated, with animals and plants.

The causes of the beginning, continuation, decline, and end of this period of destruction may have been manifold, and have by some been sought for in astronomical circumstances: for our part, we think it sufficiently accounted for by a phenomenon, which is still continued in our days, namely, *the oscillation of the earth's crust.* For if we consider it possible for the motion which is now going on (and which consists in the rising of the northern parts and the sinking of the southern of our Scandinavian peninsula) to be continued without interruption during a sufficiently long time, the same period of destruction would again indisputably return; the whole country would be changed into an ice-field, where everything that has life would perish.

To prove this, we have only to call to mind that the atmosphere around our earth is cold, and that the heat which is given off from the earth diminishes as we ascend, until, at an inconsiderable distance above its surface, we arrive at what is called *the snow-line,* above which is perpetual snow and ice. This line has been imagined to be in the shape of a parabola round the earth, from the one pole to the other, so that its position is highest above the equator, and sinks to the surface of the sea towards the poles.

From this it is evident that if the rising of the country, which is now going on, were to continue constantly until a sufficiently large portion of the surface of the earth would lie *above* the snow-line; and if not only *that* portion, but likewise surrounding parts, were thus changed into ice-fields; a state of things would arise resembling that of which we find the above-named traces belonging to an age long past. But before the motion can reach to this height it may cease, and become a return in an opposite direction, as has evidently been the case once before. For, during the latter part of the ice-period, the northern regions, which were high up, had sunk down deep below the surface of the sea, and we consider ourselves likewise authorised to suppose that, after this motion had reached to a certain extent, the opposite, which still continues, again commenced; so that when the northern parts, which then were sunk in the deep, had again risen nearly to the surface of the sea, those shell-fish which live in shallow water collected on them. Moreover, inasmuch as the water after the ice-period must still have had a very low degree of temperature, these mollusca were of those varieties and species which now *live* only in the waters on the icy shores of Spitzbergen and Greenland.

By degrees, after the ice on the surface of the sea had melted and the temperature of the water had become milder, other mollusca which required water less cold made their way into our seas; at the same time the land rose more and more, until at length the water of the sea had the same temperature as it has now, and in it were produced the same mollusca that are now living in the sea round our shores.

That the circumstance here described has taken place, we shall find if we examine those shell-banks which are met with in various places of the north-western part of Sweden and Norway, frequently to a height of several hundred feet. We shall then discover that those species which are in the highest shell-banks belong to an icy climate, and that their fellow-species now live in the cold zone of Spitzbergen; but if we descend the sides of the mountain to shell-banks lower down, we shall find that these are composed of species which belong to a more temperate water; and finally, we meet with those that still live on our coasts.*

That a gulf had passed from the Arctic Ocean across Finland, which was then the bottom of the ocean, down to Göthland, or farther, we think we may conclude from the fact, that Professor Erman has met with fossil shells in the boulder-clay of the coasts of the Baltic, in the central part of Sweden, which are now seen alive only at Spitzbergen; amongst others, for instance, *Yolida pygmæa*.†

* This circumstance has been observed both in Scandinavia and Scotland. Professor Sven Lovén reported it to the Academy of Sciences at Stockholm in 1839, and more fully in the *Review* of the same Academy, 1846, page 254. Mr. Smith has observed the same in Scotland. See *Memoirs of the Wernerian Society*, vol. viii. chap. i. page 49.

† In the shell-banks at Uddevalla the following species have been found: *Pecten islandicus, Arca glacialis, Terebratula Spitzbergensis, Yolida arctica, Margareta undata,* &c., defined by S. Lovén and O. Forell.

Moreover, Arctic crustacea are still to be met with alive at the bottom of the deep lakes Wenner and Wetter, which proves that these lakes were once connected with the gulf that formerly passed down from the Arctic Ocean.*

After the northern part of the peninsula had by degrees risen a little, but was still uninhabitable, and the southern part was higher than now, this latter appears then first to have become qualified to receive plants, animals, and finally mankind, from the southern parts which had not *simultaneously* been visited by a glacial period.   And it is not difficult to determine with a high degree of probability in what order these immigrations took place.

Plants must have first appeared, beginning with those which need for their support the least amount of black humus, and afterwards the others in proportion as they required more of it. Of animals, the phytivorous first presented themselves when vegetation had so far increased as to afford them the necessary subsistence; then came the carnivorous, in order to subsist on the former; and at last, man, who at first could subsist as well on the roots and fruits as on the flesh of animals, while clothing himself with the skins of the latter.

Then, and long after man had settled in the south of Sweden, the southern part of that country was connected by land with the continent of North Ger-

---

* S. Lovén, *Review Ac. Sc.*, 1861, page 285. These crustacea are *Mysis relicta, Gammarus loricatus, Idothea entomon, Pontopereia affinis.*

many, and those animals whose migratory habits lead them to wander from place to place, roved at large during certain seasons from the one country to the other. In this manner the reindeer, the Ure-ox, the bison, etc., wandered from Germany into Scania, and back again at will.

(If we now take a retrospective view of the state of the south of Sweden during this period, it will appear to have been as follows. The ground was as yet uncultivated, the whole country covered with forests, lakes, and marshes (bogs). In the forests wandered stately elks and stags, gigantic Ure-oxen and bisons, while each of these restricted its wanderings to its own district.*   In swampy places roved herds of wild boars of large size, and from the mountain districts of the southerly continent immigrated from time to time flocks of wild reindeer.†   In the rivers beavers

---

* I have never yet seen skeletons of Ure-oxen and bisons found in the same peat-bogs; they were deadly enemies, and there is still an unconquerable enmity between the tame cattle and the bison of Lithuania. As yet, it has not been possible to make a bison-bull breed with a tame cow. The former will immediately gore the latter to death.

† The reindeer annually makes extensive peregrinations. (See Blasius, *Reise in Russland*, vol. i. page 265.) The reindeer, skeletons of which are met with in the peat-bogs of Scania, belong to quite a different race from those of Lapland. They had no doubt immigrated to Scania from some more southerly part, and may possibly belong to the same race as the reindeer, which during Cæsar's time still lived in the Hercynian forest. No zoologist who reads what Cæsar states in the twenty-sixth chapter of *De Bello Gallico*, lib. vi., of that animal which has ' *cervi figura*,' with horns that were longer than those of any other animal that he had seen, and from the upper end of which, as if from the palm of a hand, branches (points) extended,

built their ingenious houses, and in the lakes, which abounded with fish, were river-turtles (*Emys lutaria*) and enormously large pike, skeletons of which are occasionally found.

The first people that came to the country seem to have had their haunts in the thick forests and along the shores of lakes and water-courses, in which they practised fishing and hunting, then their only means of subsistence; here, therefore, we find the implements they have left behind.

That this first migration of people to the southern parts of Scandinavia took place at a period far removed from us, we find from the fact that human productions and bones of the cave-bear (*Ursus spelæus*, Pl. XI. figs. 223, 224) are met with together, in our oldest peat-bogs, even in those that lie under the Jära-Wall, of which we shall speak farther on, and consequently previous to the phenomenon that threw up this ridge.*)

and the female of which had horns like the male, etc., can indeed doubt that Cæsar had seen at least *one* horn of a reindeer, and by misunderstanding the language, believed that the animal had but one, as likewise that from the same cause he had obtained but a confused idea of the animal itself. That the reindeer had not by degrees proceeded from Scania up towards Lapland, is also proved by there never having been found a skeleton nor even a bone of a reindeer in any of the provinces that are situated between Scania and Lapland. The Lapland reindeer have, in a comparatively much more recent period, crossed over Finland to the Norwegian mountain-ridge, where they are now mostly to be found.

* That the time when man first made his appearance here in the North was far distant from the present, we can conclude from the following reasons :—Firstly. Human implements have been found with bones of the cave-bear (*Ursus spelæus*), and yet this was by no means the first mammal that came to this country, it having been

But we do not know what space of time has since elapsed, and as yet we have found no means of ascertaining it, even within thousands of years.) We have certainly found, about one hundred feet above the present surface of the sea, a couple of human skeletons in a shell-bank which lay *under* the surface of the sea at the time when it was formed, and when the two persons were drowned; but we do not know what time was required to raise the shell-bank and the mountain on which it lies to their present height. For although the motion of the earth's crust is now taking place uninterruptedly, we must not take it for granted that it has always been so; on the contrary, we have reason to think that the motion, at the commencement of the rising, took place suddenly, and at long intervals; and that during these long intervals it may have continued uniformly and slowly. As a reason for this supposition, I may mention that on the sides of the mountains in the district of Bohus, we meet with unmistakable marks of beaches lying horizontally one above the other, at long distances, and that barnacles and other productions of the sea remain even to the present day entire on the stones

preceded by *ruminants*, with which came man. For he probably made his appearance before the large beasts of prey. Secondly. Human works occur in the submarine peat-bogs, and are therefore older than the great phenomenon which separated Scania from Pomerania. Thirdly. Some arrows and spears have been altogether reduced to a soft white substance. I have seen several such. Compare Pl. XIII. fig. 242. See also *Revue des Deux Mondes*, avril 1867, page 645 : ' Ces silex dont la patine blanchâtre dénote l'excessive antiquité ; ' therefore still more those which are entirely reduced to a chalky substance. See Note 12.

of these beaches, which would not have been the case
had not the shore, on which they grew, been, with
them, quickly raised to a height where the dashing of
the waves could not reach them; otherwise they
would have been crushed by the stones of the shore.
These considerations caused me to believe that the
elevations which have occurred in other places have
also been sudden.   Hence I am led to explain the
following phenomenon.

Along the coast of the Baltic, from Ystad to the
part between Trelleborg and Falsterbo, there lies a
ridge, in many places more or less imperfect, consisting of gravel and stones, called the Jära-Wall; in
some places it is high and broad, in others, several
such walls seem to lie behind and above each other,
which proves that the cause which raised them has
been several times repeated.   Under the ridge there
are in several places peat-bogs, which lie below the
surface of the sea.

How these ridges have been produced may perhaps
long remain undecided.   For my part, and taking
into consideration several well-ascertained facts relating to this subject, I can only conceive these ridges
to have originated in one way, namely, by a violent
momentary motion in the waters of the Baltic, caused
by a simultaneous sinking of the southern and rising
of the northern part of the surface of the earth under
this sea.*

* It will be remembered that geology, as well as history, records
several sudden risings and sinkings of the earth's crust.   Amongst
other instances of rising is the following :—On November 19, 1822,

It can be made manifest, both by geological and zoological proofs, that, during a very ancient period, a broad gulf passed from the Arctic Ocean at Archangel over Finland, which then was the bottom of the sea, down to about Göthland, or Öland, and that Sweden south of this gulf was, as above mentioned, connected with the German continent. At the time of such a sudden rising in the north and sinking in the south, I imagine that a mighty mass of water must have been brought into violent motion and thrown itself impetuously over the land then existing between Pomerania and Scania, changing them into a sea, breaking out through the Sound and the Belts, raising walls on the Scanian coast and the so-called '*havstokkar*' on the Danish islands; in a word, modelling the shores to their present configuration, and

it was found, after a violent earthquake, that a long range of the coast of Chili had been lifted from three to four feet, so that oysters, limpets, etc., became fixed on stones above the surface of the sea. In 1819 a long range of land in the delta of the Indus was raised to the height of ten feet, etc.

Proofs of a sudden sinking are given in Holland. In 1530 an inundation occurred which carried away seventeen villages, and in 1569 another occurred which deluged the Dutch coast and submerged a great portion of Friesland. By this inundation of the sea 20,000 people lost their lives. It is plain that this overflow was caused by a sinking of the land, and that a corresponding rising had taken place simultaneously in some other place.

During the time of Cæsar, Flevus was a lake; in 1225 a large portion of the country sank, and now it is the broad bay called the Zuyder Zee. The statue of Hercules which Tacitus speaks of as standing on the coast has long been sunk in the sea. The Dutch antiquaries ought not, therefore, to conclude from the absence of Phœnician monuments that such did not formerly exist there.

lowering numerous peat-bogs to the bottom of the
sea in the southern part of the Baltic, where they now
lie at a depth of from ten to fourteen feet beneath the
surface of the sea.* Likewise a peat-bog under the
Jära-Wall, having a thickness of 10 feet, 2 feet 5 inches
of which lay above, and 7 feet 7 inches below the surface of the sea. The turf under this stone wall is so
compressed, that when dry it is almost as hard as
brown coal; the trees are also, like the layers of
coal, pressed together, and when a fir-chip is broken it
is found to be black and shining in the cross section,
all the results of great pressure and of age. The turf
has here, as in the *submarine* peat-bogs which lie outside Falsterbo, been formed in fresh water, of which
the bottom, when the turf was formed, lay above the
surface of the sea; inasmuch as in it were found the
same species of shrubs as those that are found in the
other Scanian peat-bogs, situated farther in the interior of the country. But on the bottom of this peat-
bog, on the fine blue clay itself, there have frequently,
during the cutting of the turf, been found *arrows,
knives*, etc., of flint, which proves that human beings

---

* The vegetable products which are met with in these submarine
peat-bogs are—stems of the fir, birch, alder, oak, etc., but never
the *beech*; numerous moorland plants—*Equisetum palustre* and
*fluviatile, Arundo phragmites, Polygonium amphibium, Calamagrostis,
Hypnum fluitans*, etc.; the insects also belong to fresh water—
Dytiscus marginalis, a *Gyrinus*; insects attached to moorland plants—
two species of *Donacia*, etc., which all prove that the bog was
formed in fresh water, and consequently surrounded by land. Indeed, I do not doubt that traces of human workmanship may likewise
be found here.

already existed in these districts at the time when
the bog was an open water, and peat began to grow
in it.

Consequently, there were people here even before
the great phenomenon which raised the ridge in
question, and threw a wide sea between the south
of Scandinavia and the north of Germany.   How
many thousands of years have passed since this event,
and from the end of the glacial period until now, we
do not know, but that it did happen during a very ancient period we may safely conclude from there being
found under the same ridge, in more than one place,
bones of the cave-bear; and as such have likewise been
found on the bottom of other peat-bogs with bones of
the *reindeer*, for instance, in the peat-bog on Kulla-
berg (in which flint-flakes, Pl. II. fig. 24, have also
been found in great numbers), we may suppose that
these peat-bogs are coeval with the one under the
Jära-Wall, and consequently *they* also are more ancient
than this remarkable ridge.   Moreover, it should be
remarked, that in these ancient peat-bogs there has
never been found a vestige of metal, and therefore
we can likewise conclude that the above-mentioned
cataclysm took place during the Stone period, before
bronze had yet been introduced into the North, and
during an early part of the Stone Age, inasmuch as
not a single stone axe or any other ground stone instrument was found there, but only flint-flakes, arrows,
and knives.

The tribe which had then migrated to the south
of Sweden came, no doubt, from more southerly coun-

tries, and it appears that the northern districts of the country had not yet risen sufficiently from the condition of the glacial epoch, but were in such a state that they could not be inhabited by man or beast.

(But we do not positively know what tribe came first, for we have not yet found any human skeleton which can with certainty be said to have belonged to this ancient period; that is to say, we have not found any such, under the Jära-Wall or elsewhere, with bones of the cave-bear. They belonged, however, probably, to a brachycephalic race; for skulls of this race have been found in the old peat-bogs of Scania, and of this race the Laplanders are the last remnants on our peninsula. They were wild hunters long before they became nomads. They were by degrees exterminated and gradually driven up to the most northerly parts of the peninsula, by the stronger people belonging to a dolichocephalic race.

The *reindeer* appears to have become extinct in Scania very soon after the separation of Scandinavia from North Germany.* The people who left behind them the celebrated *Kjökkenmöddings*, or shell-mounds, most likely lived somewhat after this period, and hence we can explain why it is that bones of the *reindeer* have not been found in these mounds, though they occur in the peat-bogs both in Denmark and Scania. But if the reindeer, which necessarily made extensive migrations annually, died when such migrations were

---

* It is not even certain that at the time when this catastrophe happened there were as yet any reindeer in Scania.

no longer possible, the Ure-ox, on the other hand, appears to have been more enduring; for a specimen of this colossal beast, which is preserved in the Museum at Lund, and had evidently been wounded while young with a flint weapon, shows that the Urus lived in Scania during the Stone period* (see Pl. XI. figs. 220, 222). This species, indeed, remained here a longer time, and was still to be found during some part of the Bronze Age, for the war-trumpet of bronze which is described in my work on the 'Bronze Age,' page 93, and sketched on Pl. IV. fig. 50, is evidently copied from a horn of the Ure-ox.

The people who built the tumuli, and who were a strong and robust race, had already appeared before the Bronze people, and during the proper Stone period. (Pl. XIII. figs. 236, 238.) They knew the use of fire; they cooked their food, and on their vessels soot is sometimes to be seen. They had perhaps learned the use of fire from seeing branches in the woods ignite from being rubbed against each other. They are said to have had tame cattle, perhaps even to have practised agriculture. (Figs. 180, 181.)

It was probably during this period that people of Semitic origin founded colonies in the western countries of Europe and in the south and west of Scandinavia, where they introduced, besides bronze,† the

---

* Nay, it appears to have been older in the country than the cave-bear itself; smaller beasts of prey had probably previously made their appearance.

† If we wish to understand the phenomenon of the *origin of bronze in Scandinavia*, it is quite necessary to realise the fact that *the best made* swords with spiral ornaments and short hilts, as well as

Phœnician worship of Baal. In the meantime, people of Cimbrian origin appear to have settled in Denmark and the southern parts of Sweden. Of them we have traces both in local names and in certain antiquities; for instance, the Cimbrian ox, cast in copper and evidently worn as an amulet.

We have already mentioned that the so-called Jära-Wall consists of various ridges which were raised one after the other, and which indicate inundations that had taken place at different periods. One of these is called the Cimbrian Flood, because it was after this inundation that a great number of Cimbrians emigrated from Scania and Denmark, and were beaten by Marius near Verona, 101 B.C. Ammianus Marcellinus relates (book xv. chap. 9) that it was a tradition amongst the Druids that some of their forefathers had come from the farthest islands on the other side of the Rhine, and that frequent attacks by the neighbouring tribes and an *inundation of the sea* were the first cause of their marching southwards.

Even during my time there were traditions about them in Scania, where it is said they assembled before the emigration on a plain which, during my youth, was still a heath, and called the Cimber Ground, situated between the villages of Gislöf, Aby, Isie, and

---

the small armlets, are the *oldest*, and that the workmanship by degrees became more and more deteriorated. The supposition that the oldest are the worst and that the bronze culture here has been more and more developed and improved, is founded on ignorance, or, still worse, on an unrestrained national vanity. It is painful to notice that several eminent authors of classical works have expressed this erroneous opinion.

the Baltic. The name of Cimbrishamn is likewise supposed to be derived from this circumstance.

By degrees the Scandinavian peninsula assumed its present appearance, boundaries, and people. The last immigration consisted of the Swedes, who brought with them the worship of Odin's Walhalla; but this period belongs to the Iron Age.

NOTES BY THE EDITOR.

Note 1, *page* 4.

Sir E. Belcher, in his paper ' On Works of Art among the Esquimaux ' (' Transactions of the Ethnological Society,' Ser. 2, vol. i. page 139), gives the following account of the implement with which that ingenious people make their flint tools. The handle, he says, ' is of fine fossil ivory. That would be too soft to deal with flint or chert in the manner required. But they discovered that the point of the deer-horn is harder, and also more stubborn ; therefore, in a slit, like lead in our pencils, they introduced a slip of this substance, and secured it by a strong thong, put on *wet*, but which on drying becomes very rigid. Here we cannot fail to trace ingenuity, ability, and a view to ornament. It is the point of deer-horn which, refusing to yield, drives off the fine conchoidal splinters from the chert.'

Note 2, *page* 40.

I confess it seems to me that the difference here pointed out is a matter of age and use. As the blade wore down, it was re-sharpened, and thus became shorter and shorter.

Note 3, *page* 53.

See also Judges xx. 16. ' Among all this people ' (the tribe of Benjamin) ' there were seven hundred chosen men lefthanded ; every one could sling stones at an hair breadth, and not miss.'

Note 4, *page* 63.

I have in my collection an almost exactly similar axe from Central Africa ; but the blade is of iron, and has rather straighter sides.

Note 5, *page* 105.

I need hardly say that many of our most eminent biologists would demur to this proposition.

Note 6, *page* 137.

Very similar dwelling-places occur in Scotland. Mr. Petrie has described one examined by him in the Orkneys. See Captain Thomas, ' On Orkney Antiquities ' (' Archæologia,' v. 34). A hollow was scooped out of the side of a hill, and walls were built of unhewn stones, converging towards the top. On the outside, smaller stones and earth were heaped up, so that the whole building had the appearance of a conical mound, about 115 feet in length and 55 in breadth. The central chamber, which was surrounded by several smaller ones, was about 40 feet long, 5 feet broad, and 10 feet high in the centre, communicating with the outside by a long, low, narrow passage, 18 feet long and 2 feet 8 inches high. Semisubterranean huts of this character are known in Scotland as ' weems,' from *uamha*, a cave. Several such, more or less subterranean, dwellings are described in the ' Proceedings of the Society of Antiquaries of Scotland ' (see, for instance, vol. iii. Part II. page 189), and Captain Thomas has figured (*l. c.* vol. iii. Part XII.) a group of ' beehive houses' in Lewis, which are still actually inhabited. These, however, are entirely above ground.

Note 7, *page* 141.

My friend Mr. Boyd Dawkins, in his memoir on the ' British Fossil Oxen ' (' Geological Journal,' No. XCI. page 183), boldly asserts that the cave-men of Perigord were ' a people more closely allied to the Esquimaux than any other,' and sums up as follows the evidence in favour of this assertion.

' The identity of four of the harpoons, or fowling-spears, marrow-spoons, and scrapers; the habit of sculpturing animals on their implements; the absence of pottery; the same method of crushing the bones of the animals slain in hunting, and their accumulation in one spot; the carelessness about the remains of their dead relatives; the fact that the food consisted chiefly of reindeer, varied with their flesh of other animals, such as the musk-sheep; and especially the small stature, as proved in the people of the

Dordogne caverns, by the small-handled dagger figured by MM. Lartet and Christy in the "Revue Archéologique" and in "Prehistoric Times," p. 255. This combination of characters is found, so far as I know, among no other people on the face of the earth except the Esquimaux; and therefore I cannot help believing that this people in South Gaul occupies the same relation to the Esquimaux as the musk-sheep and reindeer, on which they lived, hold to those now living in the northern regions.'

Since this was written Mr. Busk has shown that the *Ursus priscus* of our caves is undistinguishable from the Grizzly bear of the Rocky mountains. There is therefore some reason for the belief that the Esquimaux once inhabited Western Europe.

Note 8, *page* 161.

If the coexistence of ground and unground flint implements suggests doubts as to the division of the Stone Age into Palæolithic and Neolithic, *à fortiori* the very frequent occurrence of stone implements with those of bronze would compel us to give up the Stone Age altogether. The lesson, however, which such cases teach us is that of caution, not of doubt.

No one knows better than Professor Nilsson that every flint implement was rudely chipped out before it was ground, and some of them, as, for instance, arrows, were never ground. Moreover, the Palæolithic Age is not characterised only by the rudeness of the stone implements ascribed to it.

The absence of pottery, the presence of extinct animals, and the nature of the strata in which the implements occur, must all be taken into consideration. I have, however, already referred to these points in my Introduction.

Note 9, *page* 181.

Hearne does not, I think, deserve this severe reproach. We must remember that he was the only white man among this band of ferocious savages; that he was completely at their mercy, being far from any settlement, and had already suffered much ill-treatment at their hands. Any interference on his part would evidently have been useless, and the language in which he expresses his horror at the massacre is as strong even as that of Professor Nilsson: 'Even at this hour,' he concludes, ' I cannot reflect on the transactions of that horrid day without shedding tears.'   It is fair also to remember that Hearne was not a man who used strong language lightly. When some northern Indians met him on his return to the Fort, and plundered him of almost everything he had, he remarks quietly, that his load being thereby ' materially lightened, this part of my journey was the easiest and most pleasant of any I had experienced since my leaving the Fort.'

Note 10, *page* 215.

Professor Nilsson alludes probably to the Scotch proverb, ' Curri mi clach er do cuirn,' i. e. I will add a stone to your cairn.

Note 11, *page* 220.

The Norwegian peasants were not alone in regarding the Laplanders as scarcely human.   Regnard, in his ' Journey to Lapland,' thus concludes his account of them:—' Such is the description of this little animal, called a Laplander; and it may safely be said that, after the monkey, he approaches nearest to man.'   When Frobisher's crew, in 1576, captured an old Esquimaux woman, they took her for a witch, and pulled off her boots to see if she had cloven feet.   It is not necessary, however, to go so far afield for illustrations.   Down to the last century, and even now in out-of-the-way places, old women were regarded as witches, even by their own countrymen and countrywomen.

Note 12, *page* 251.

This alteration of the surface does, no doubt, indicate a certain lapse of time, and is a very good evidence of genuineness.   I have, however, some reason for thinking that, under certain circumstances, the process is not one requiring any great lapse of time.

INDEX.

LONDON

PRINTED BY SPOTTISWOODE AND CO.

NEW-STREET SQUARE

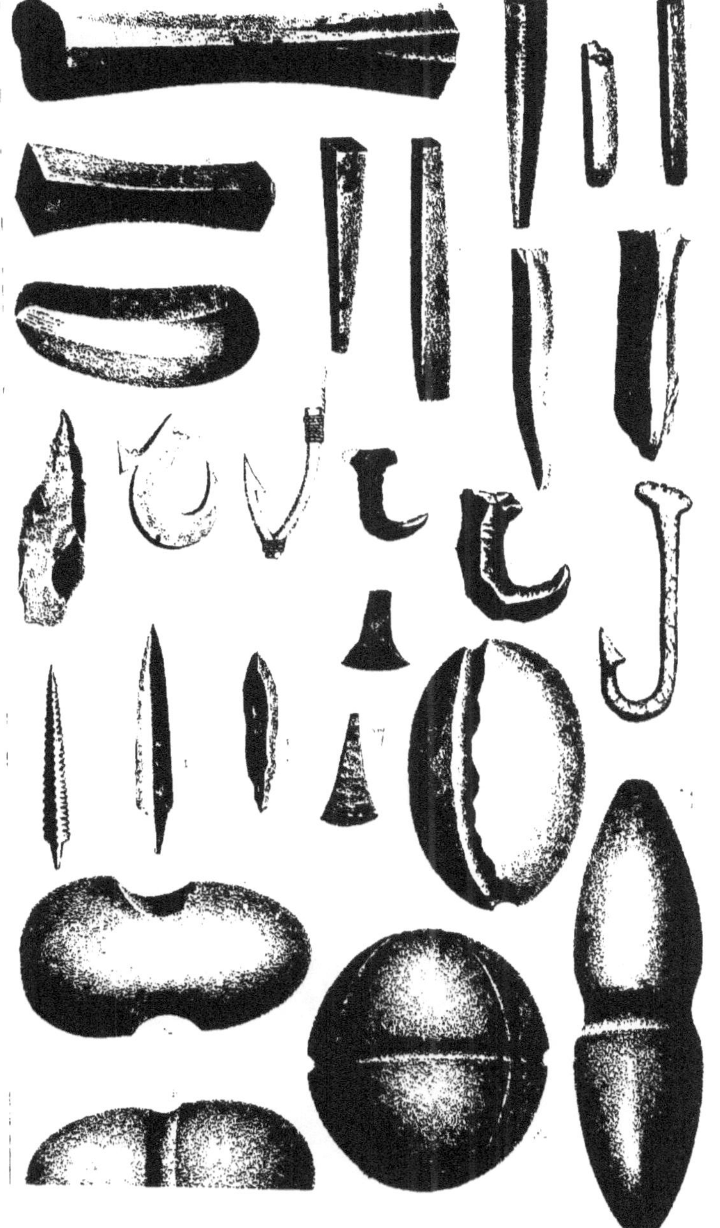

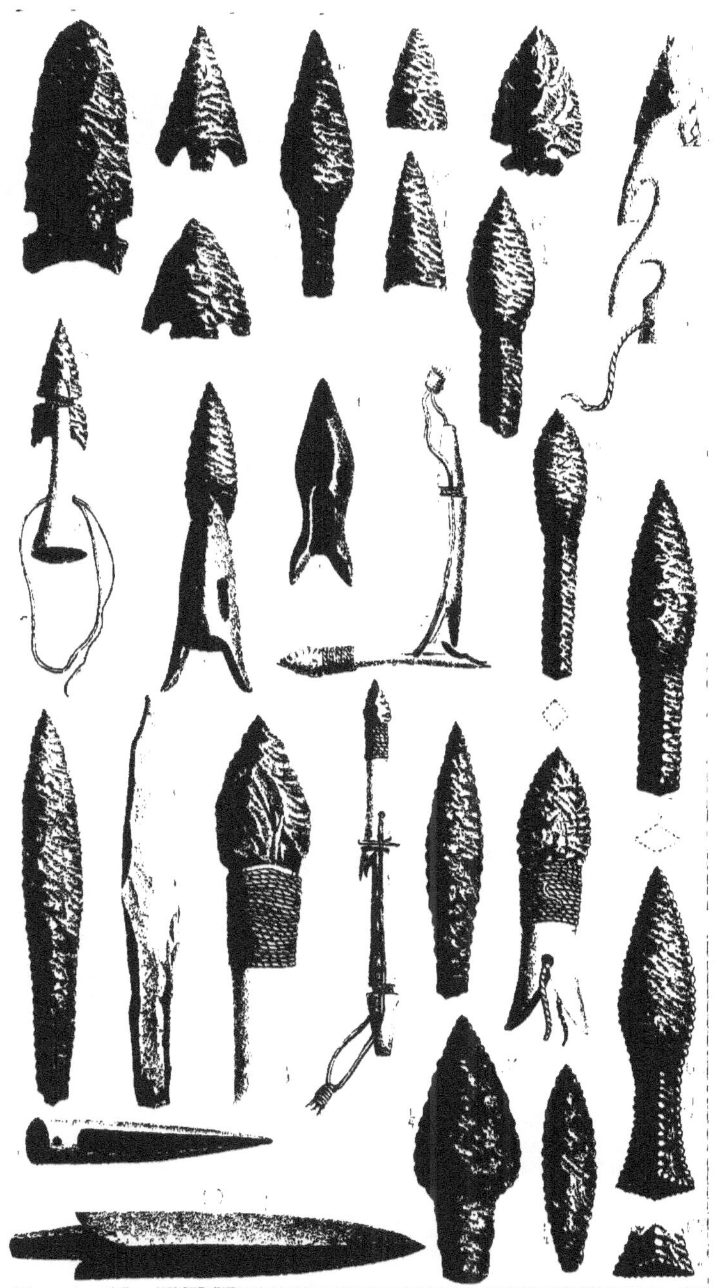

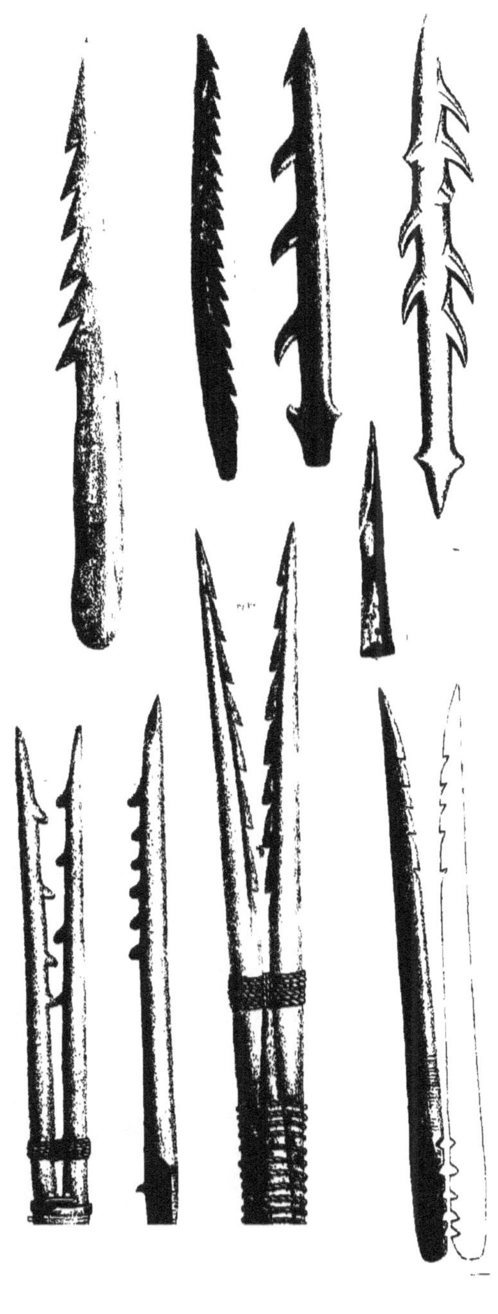

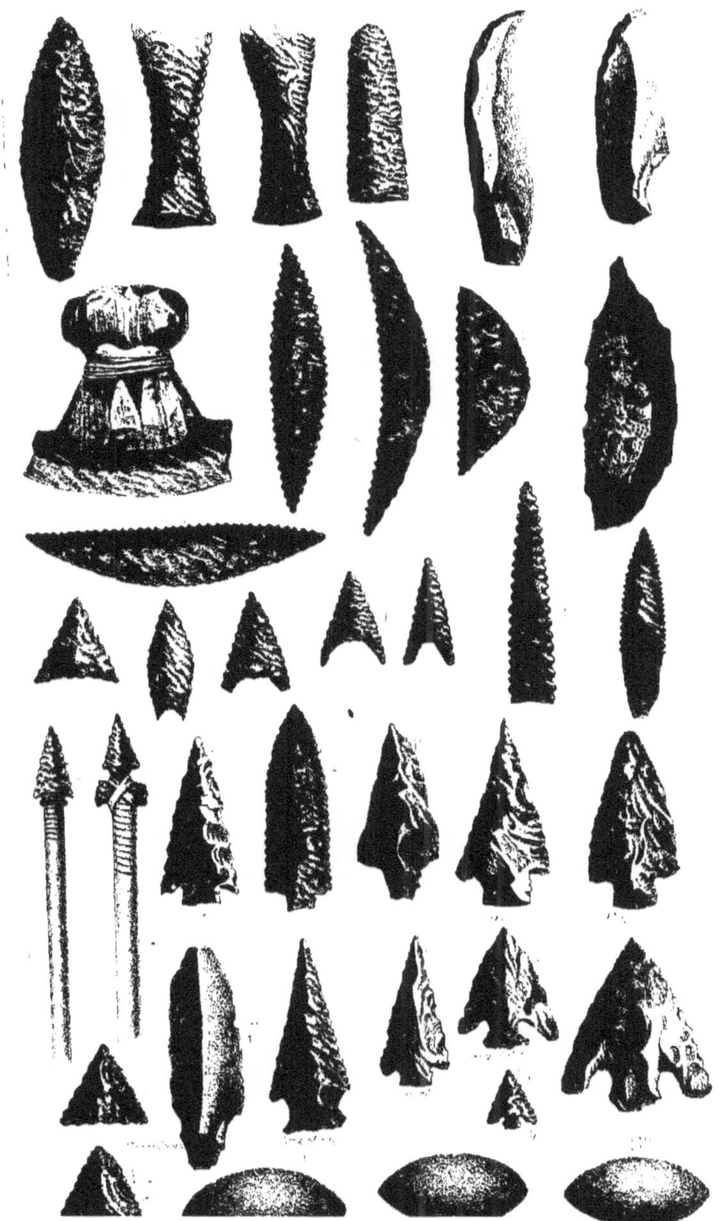

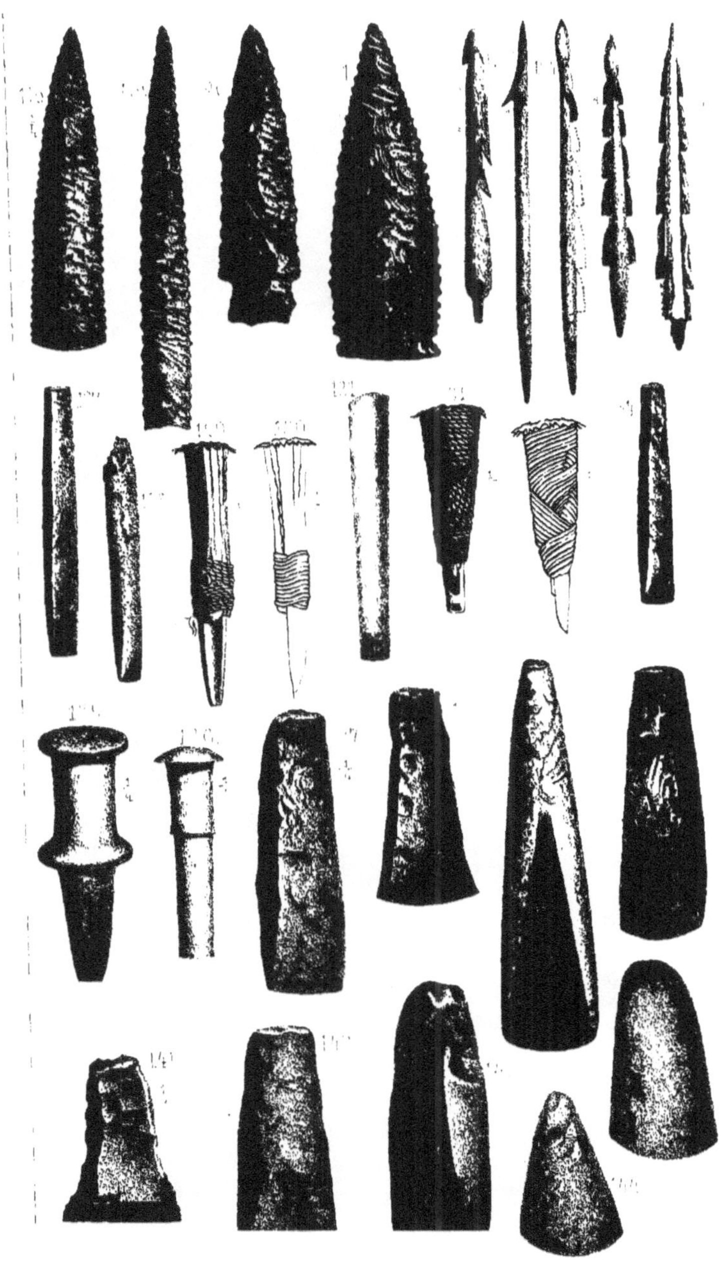

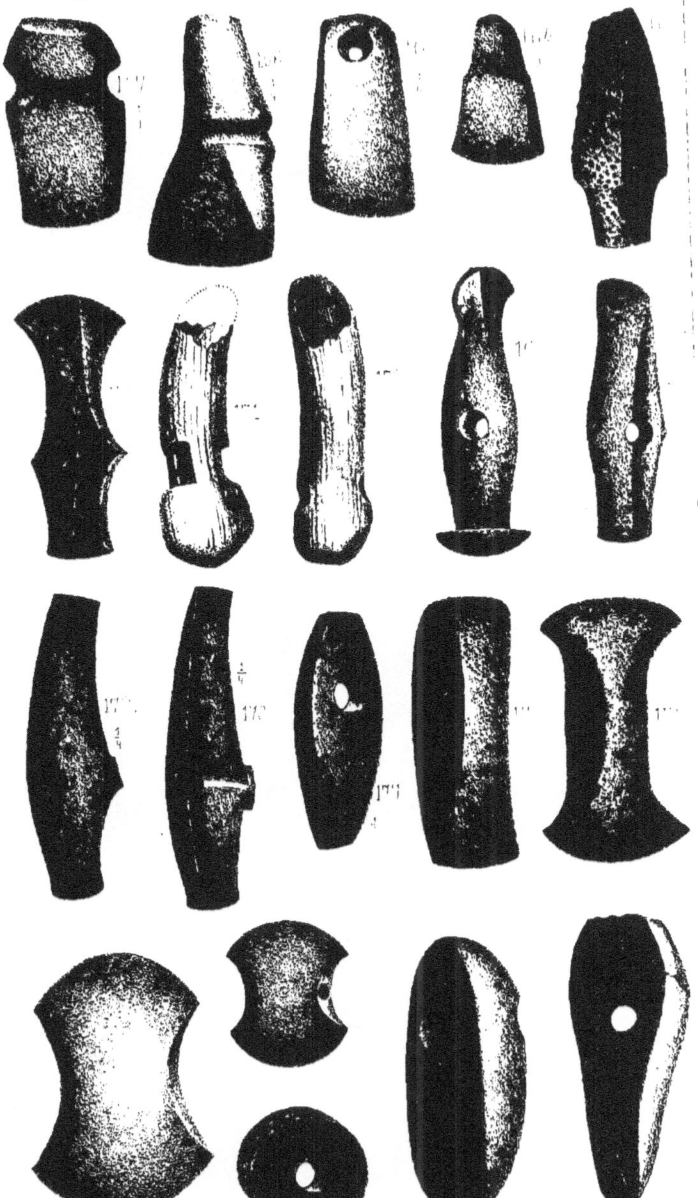

PL.VIII

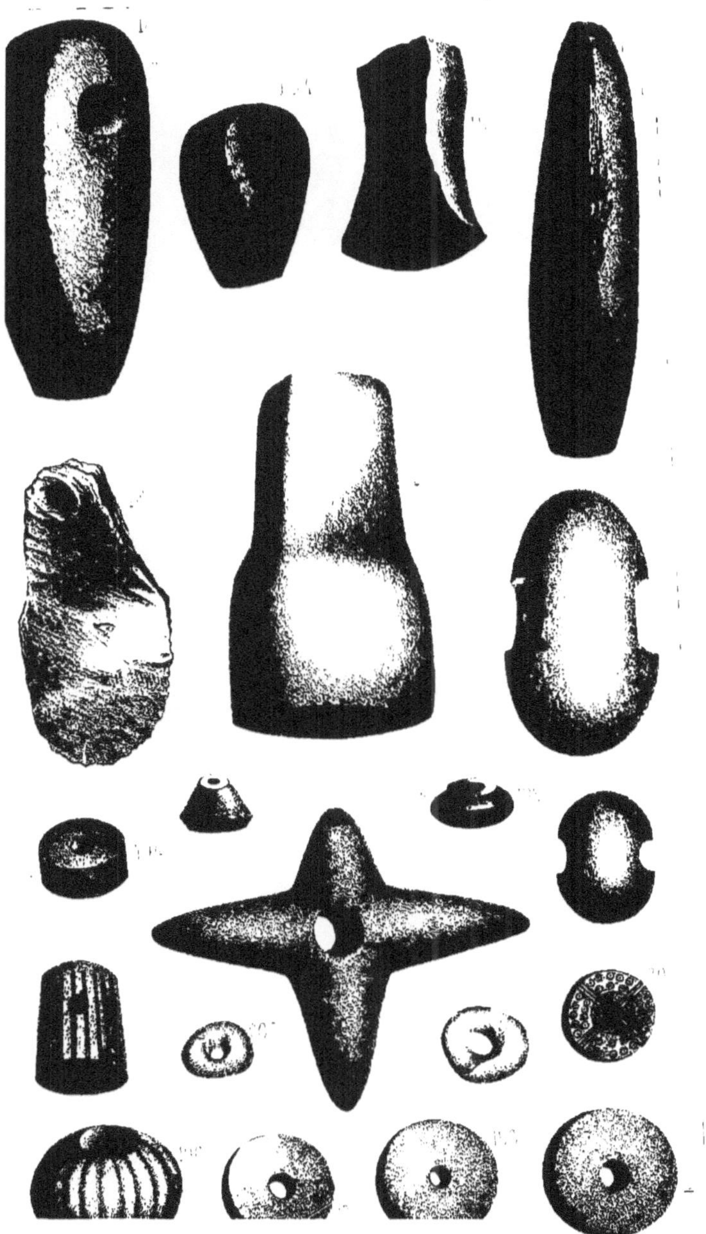

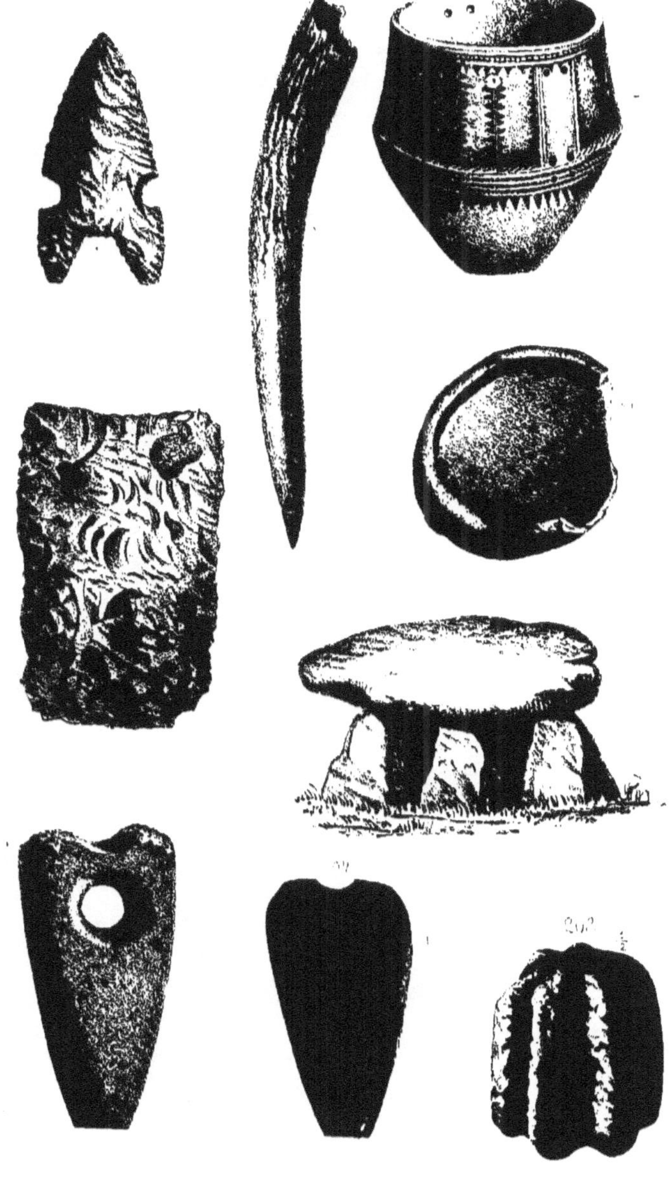

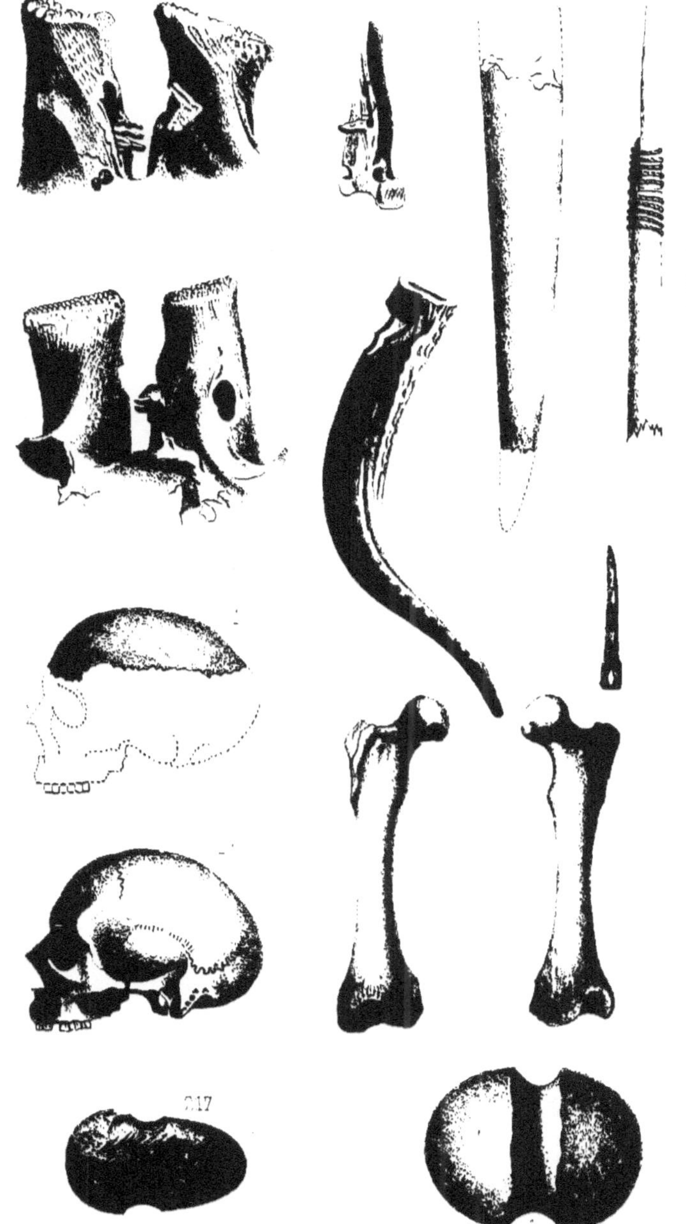

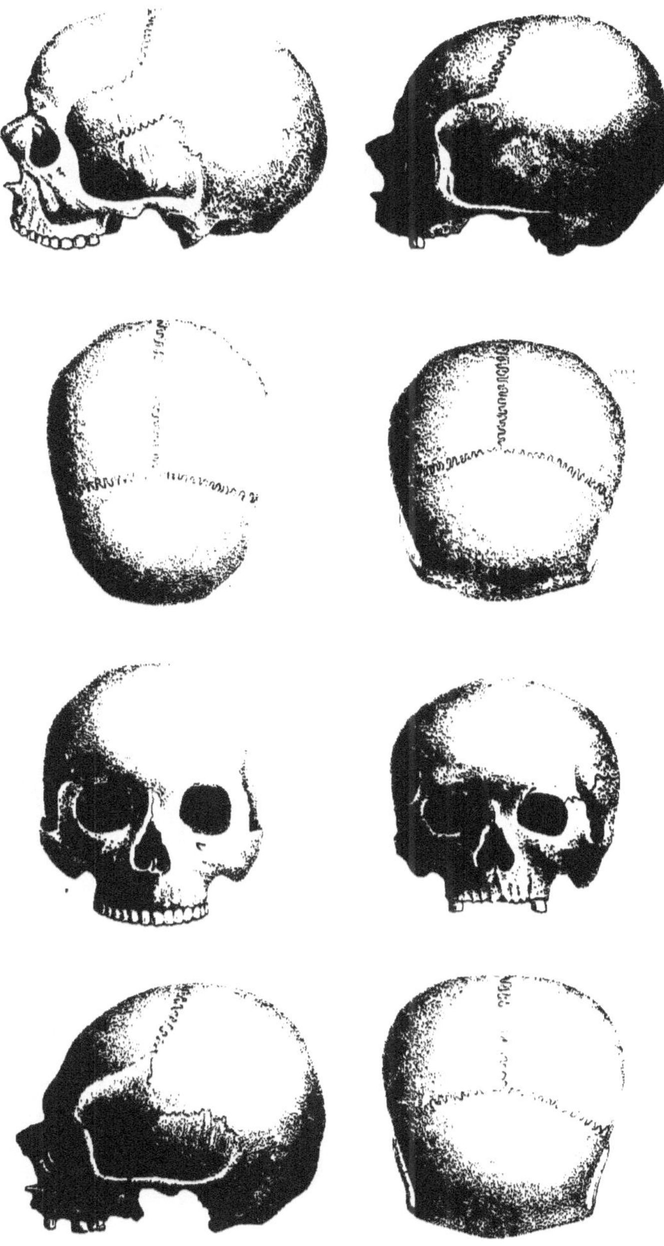

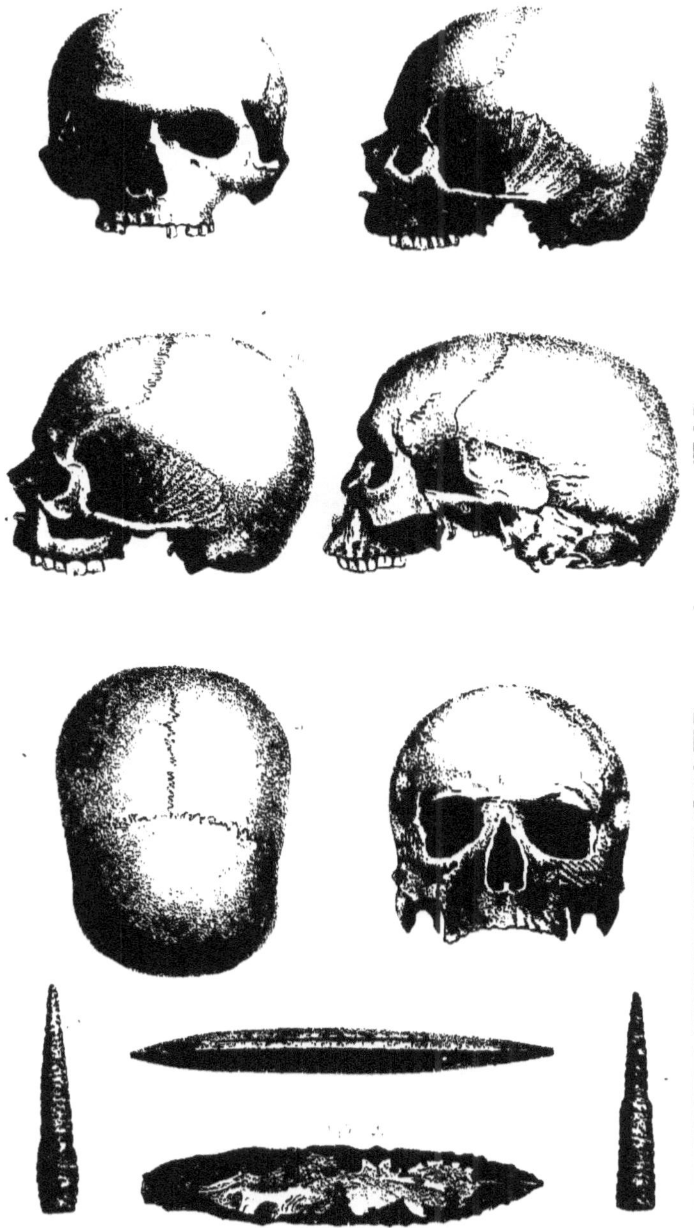

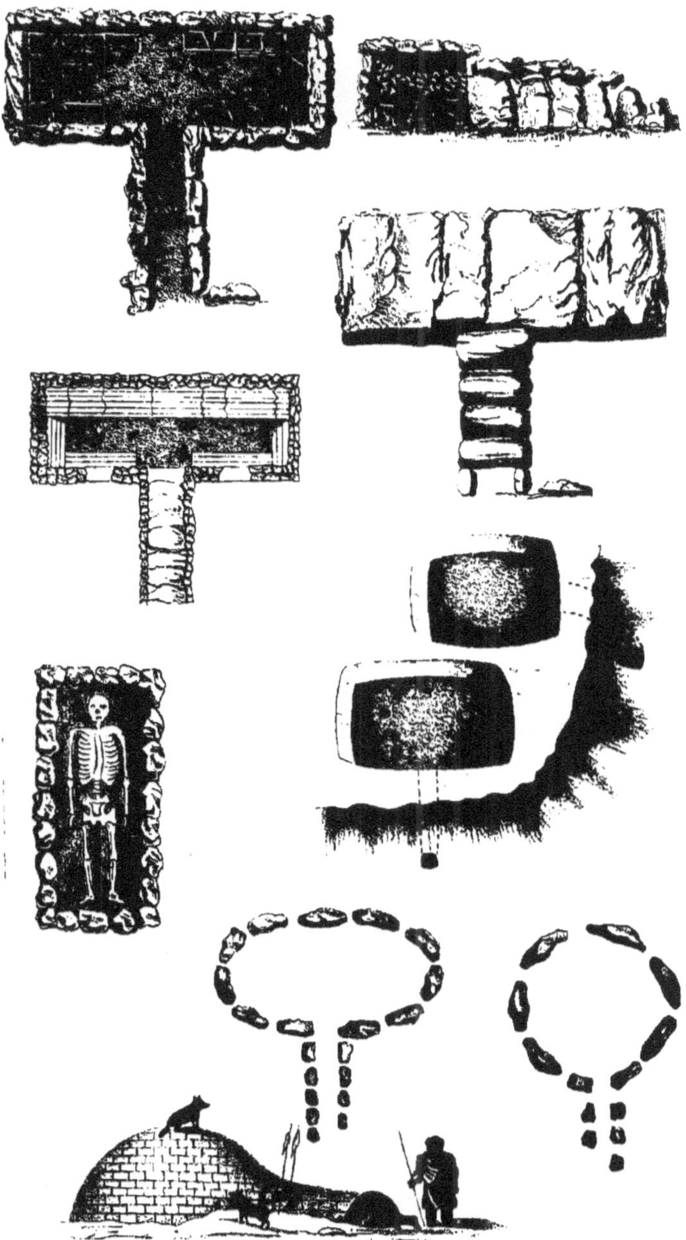

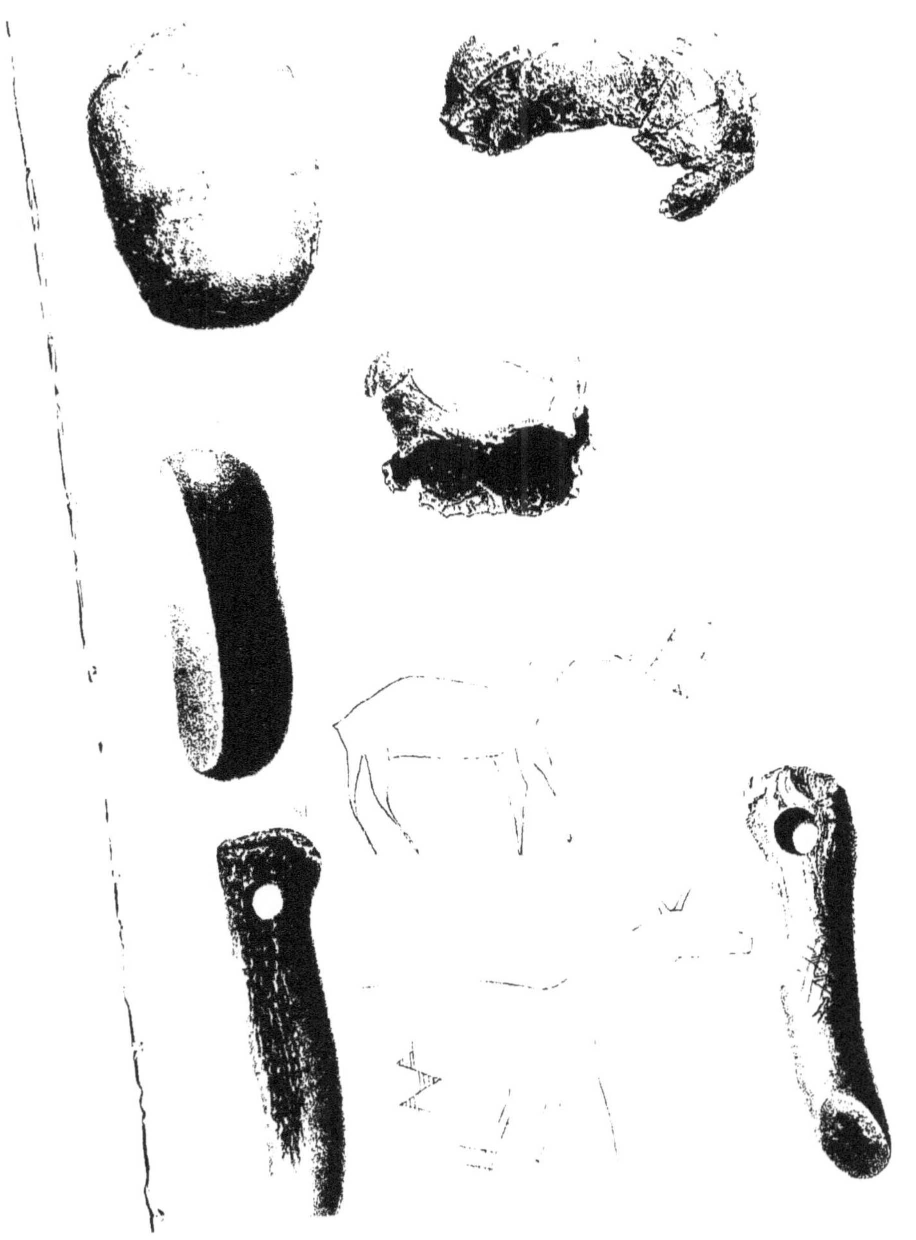

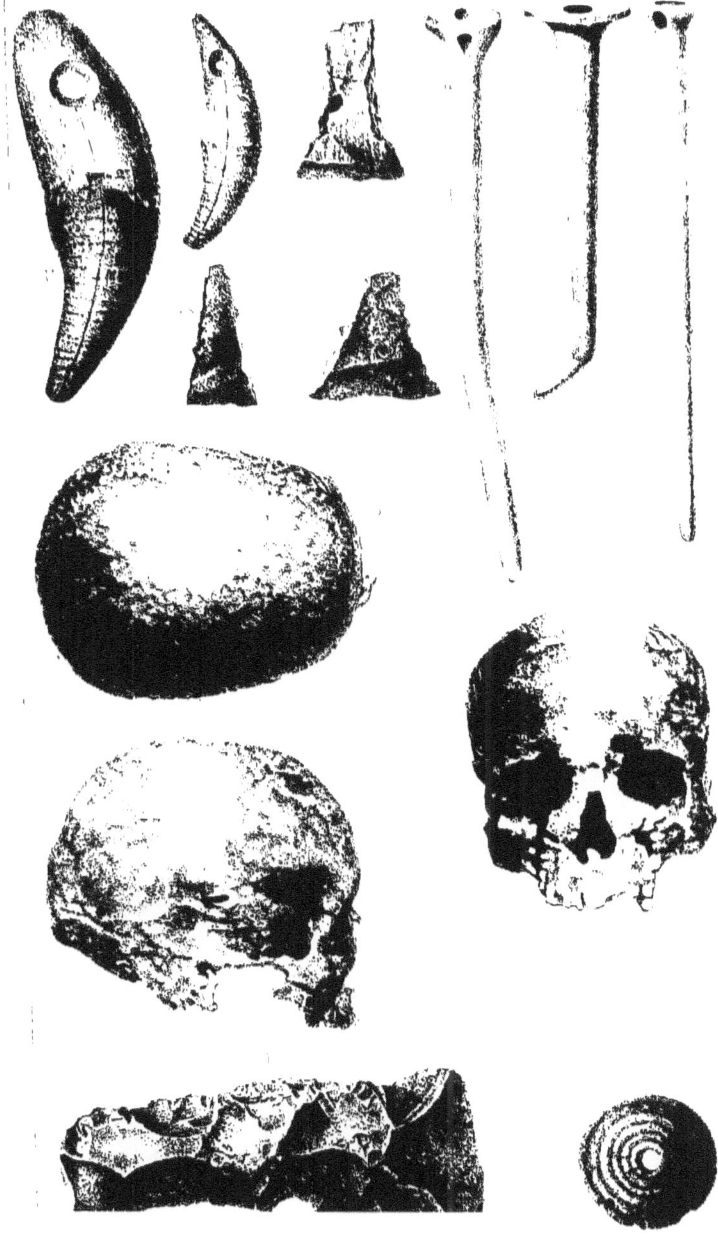

39 PATERNOSTER ROW, E.C.
LONDON: *January* 1868.

GENERAL LIST OF WORKS

PUBLISHED BY

Messrs. LONGMANS, GREEN, READER, and DYER.

Historical Works.

Lord Macaulay's Works. Complete and uniform Library Edition. Edited by his Sister, Lady TREVELYAN. 8 vols. 8vo. with Portrait, price £5 5s. cloth, or £8 8s. bound in tree-calf by Rivière.

The History of England from the Fall of Wolsey to the Death of Elizabeth. By JAMES ANTHONY FROUDE, M.A. late Fellow of Exeter College, Oxford. VOLS. I. to X. in 8vo. price £7 2s. cloth.

  VOLS. I. to IV. the Reign of Henry VIII. Third Edition, 54s.

  VOLS. V. and VI. the Reigns of Edward VI. and Mary. Third Edition, 28s.

  VOLS. VII. & VIII. the Reign of Elizabeth, VOLS. I. & II. Fourth Edition, 28s.

  VOLS. IX. and X. the Reign of Elizabeth, VOLS. III. and IV. 32s.

The History of England from the Accession of James II. By Lord MACAULAY.

  LIBRARY EDITION, 5 vols. 8vo. £4.
  CABINET EDITION, 8 vols. post 8vo. 48s.
  PEOPLE'S EDITION, 4 vols. crown 8vo. 16s.

Revolutions in English History. By ROBERT VAUGHAN, D.D. 3 vols. 8vo. 30s.

An Essay on the History of the English Government and Constitution, from the Reign of Henry VII. to the Present Time. By JOHN EARL RUSSELL. Fourth Edition, revised. Crown 8vo. 6s.

On Parliamentary Government in England: its Origin, Development, and Practical Operation. By ALPHEUS TODD, Librarian of the Legislative Assembly of Canada. In two volumes. Vol. I. 8vo. 16s.

The History of England during the Reign of George the Third. By the Right Hon. W. N. MASSEY. Cabinet Edition, 4 vols. post 8vo. 24s.

The Constitutional History of England, since the Accession of George III. 1760—1860. By Sir THOMAS ERSKINE MAY, K.C.B. Second Edit. 2 vols. 8vo. 33s.

Brodie's Constitutional History of the British Empire from the Accession of Charles I. to the Restoration. Second Edition. 3 vols. 8vo. 36s.

Historical Studies. I. On Precursors of the French Revolution; II. Studies from the History of the Seventeenth Century; III. Leisure Hours of a Tourist. By HERMAN MERIVALE, M.A. 8vo. 12s. 6d.

A

Life of Pastor Fliedner, Founder of the Deaconesses' Institution at Kaiserswerth. Translated from the German, with the sanction of Fliedner's Family. By CATHERINE WINKWORTH. Fcp. 8vo. with Portrait, price 3s. 6d.

The Life of Franz Schubert, translated from the German of KREITZLE VON HELLBORN by ARTHUR DUKE COLERIDGE, M.A. late Fellow of King's College, Cambridge. [*Nearly ready.*

Letters of Distinguished Musicians, viz. Gluck, Haydn, P. E. Bach, Weber, and Mendelssohn. Translated from the German by Lady WALLACE, with Three Portraits. Post 8vo. 14s.

Mozart's Letters (1769-1791), translated from the Collection of Dr. LUDWIG NOHL by Lady WALLACE. 2 vols. post 8vo. with Portrait and Facsimile, 18s.

Beethoven's Letters (1790-1826), from the Two Collections of Drs. NOHL and VON KÖCHEL. Translated by Lady WALLACE. 2 vols. post 8vo. Portrait, 18s.

Felix Mendelssohn's Letters from *Italy and Switzerland,* and *Letters from* 1833 *to* 1847, translated by Lady WALLACE. With Portrait. 2 vols. crown 8vo. 5s. each.

With Maximilian in Mexico, From the Note-Book of a Mexican Officer By MAX. Baron VON ALVENSLEBEN, late Lieutenant in the Imperial Mexican Army Post 8vo. 7s. 6d.

Memoirs of Sir Henry Havelock, K.C.B. By JOHN CLARK MARSHMAN. Cabinet Edition, with Portrait. Crown 8vo. price 5s

Faraday as a Discoverer: a Memoir. By JOHN TYNDALL, LL.D. F.R.S. Professor of Natural Philosophy in the Royal Institution of Great Britain, and in the Royal School of Mines. Crown 8vo. [*Nearly ready.*

Essays in Ecclesiastical Biography. By the Right Hon. Sir J. STEPHEN, LL.D. Cabinet Edition. Crown 8vo. 7s. 6d.

Vicissitudes of Families. By Sir BERNARD BURKE, Ulster King of Arms. FIRST, SECOND, and THIRD SERIES. 3 vols. crown 8vo. 12s. 6d. each.

Maunder's Biographical Treasury. Thirteenth Edition, reconstructed and partly rewritten, with above 1,000 additional Memoirs, by W. L. R. CATES. Fcp. 10s. 6d.

Criticism, Philosophy, Polity, &c.

On Representative Government. By JOHN STUART MILL, M.P. Third Edition. 8vo. 9s. crown 8vo. 2s.

On Liberty. By the same Author. Third Edition. Post 8vo. 7s. 6d. crown 8vo. 1s. 4d.

Principles of Political Economy. By the same. Sixth Edition. 2 vols. 8vo. 30s. or in 1 vol. crown 8vo. 5s.

A System of Logic, Ratiocinative and Inductive. By the same. Sixth Edition. 2 vols. 8vo. 25s.

Utilitarianism. By the same. 2d Edit. 8vo. 5s.

Dissertations and Discussions. By the same Author. 3 vols. 8vo. 36s.

Examination of Sir W. Hamilton's Philosophy, and of the Principal Philosophical Questions discussed in his Writings. By the same. Third Edition, 8vo. 16s.

Workmen and Wages at Home and Abroad; or, the Effects of Strikes, Combinations, and Trade Unions. By J. WARD, Author of 'The World in its Workshops,' &c. Post 8vo. 7s. 6d.

The Elements of Political Economy. By HENRY DUNNING MACLEOD, M.A. Barrister-at-Law. 8vo. 16s.

A Dictionary of Political Economy; Biographical, Bibliographical, Historical, and Practical. By the same Author. VOL. I. royal 8vo. 30s.

Lord Bacon's Works, collected and edited by R. L. ELLIS, M.A. J. SPEDDING, M.A. and D. D. HEATH. VOLS. I. to V. *Philosophical Works,* 5 vols. 8vo. £4 6s. VOLS. VI. and VII. *Literary and Professional Works,* 2 vols. £1 16s.

The Institutes of Justinian; with English Introduction, Translation, and Notes. By T. C. SANDARS, M.A. Barrister-at-Law. Third Edition. 8vo. 15s.

The Ethics of Aristotle with Essays and Notes. By Sir A. GRANT, Bart. M.A. LL.D. Director of Public Instruction in the Bombay Presidency. Second Edition, revised and completed. 2 vols. 8

Bacon's Essays, with Annotations. By R. WHATELY, D.D. late Archbishop of Dublin. Sixth Edition. 8vo. 10s. 6d.

Elements of Logic. By R. WHATELY, D.D. late Archbishop of Dublin. Ninth Edition. 8vo. 10s. 6d. crown 8vo. 4s. 6d.

Elements of Rhetoric. By the same Author. Seventh Edition. 8vo. 10s. 6d. crown 8vo. 4s. 6d.

English Synonymes. Edited by Archbishop WHATELY. 5th Edition. Fcp. 3s.

An Outline of the Necessary Laws of Thought: a Treatise on Pure and Applied Logic. By the Most Rev. W. THOMSON, D.D. Archbishop of York. Crown 8vo. 5s. 6d.

Analysis of Mr. Mill's System of Logic. By W. STEBBING, M.A. Second Edition. 12mo. 3s. 6d.

The Election of Representatives, Parliamentary and Municipal; a Treatise. By THOMAS HARE, Barrister-at-Law. Third Edition, with Additions. Crown 8vo. 6s.

Speeches on Parliamentary Re- form, delivered in the House of Commons by the Right Hon. B. DISRAELI (1848-1866). Edited by MONTAGUE CORRY, B.A. of Lincoln's Inn, Barrister-at-Law. Second Edition. 8vo. 12s.

Speeches of the Right Hon. Lord MACAULAY, corrected by Himself. Library Edition, 8vo. 12s. People's Edition, crown 8vo. 3s. 6d.

Lord Macaulay's Speeches on Parliamentary Reform in 1831 and 1832. 16mo. 1s.

Inaugural Address delivered to the University of St. Andrews. By JOHN STUART MILL, Rector of the University. Library Edition, 8vo. 5s. People's Edition, crown 8vo. 1s.

A Dictionary of the English Language. By R. G. LATHAM, M.A. M.D. F.R.S. Founded on the Dictionary of Dr. S. JOHNSON, as edited by the Rev. H. J. TODD, with numerous Emendations and Additions. Publishing in 36 Parts, price 3s. 6d. each, to form 2 vols. 4to. VOL. I. in Two Parts, price £3 10s. now ready.

Thesaurus of English Words and Phrases, classified and arranged so as to facilitate the Expression of Ideas, and assist in Literary Composition. By P. M. ROGET, M.D. New Edition. Crown 8vo. 10s. 6d.

Lectures on the Science of Lan- guage, delivered at the Royal Institution. By MAX MÜLLER, M.A. Taylorian Professor in the University of Oxford. FIRST SERIES, Fifth Edition, 12s. SECOND SERIES, 18s.

Chapters on Language. By F. W. FARRAR, M.A. F.R.S. late Fellow of Trin. Coll. Cambridge. Crown 8vo. 8s. 6d.

The Debater; a Series of Complete Debates, Outlines of Debates, and Questions for Discussion. By F. ROWTON. Fcp. 6s.

A Course of English Reading, adapted to every taste and capacity; or, How and What to Read. By the Rev. J. PYCROFT, B.A. Fourth Edition, fcp. 5s.

Manual of English Literature, Historical and Critical: with a Chapter on English Metres. By THOMAS ARNOLD, M.A. Second Edition. Crown 8vo. 7s. 6d.

Southey's Doctor, complete in One Volume. Edited by the Rev. J.W. WARTER, B.D. Square crown 8vo. 12s. 6d.

Historical and Critical Commen- tary on the Old Testament; with a New Translation. By M. M. KALISCH, Ph. D. VOL. I. *Genesis,* 8vo. 18s. or adapted for the General Reader, 12s. VOL. II. *Exodus,* 15s. or adapted for the General Reader, 12s. VOL. III. *Leviticus,* PART I. 15s. or adapted for the General Reader, 8s.

A Hebrew Grammar, with Exercises. By the same. PART I. *Outlines with Exercises,* 8vo. 12s. 6d. KEY, 5s. PART II. *Exceptional Forms and Constructions,* 12s. 6d.

A Latin-English Dictionary. By J. T. WHITE, D.D. of Corpus Christi College, and J. E. RIDDLE, M.A. of St. Edmund Hall, Oxford. Imp. 8vo. pp. 2,128, price 42s.

A New Latin-English Dictionary, abridged from the larger work of *White* and *Riddle* (as above), by J. T. WHITE, D.D. Joint-Author. 8vo. pp. 1,048, price 18s.

The Junior Scholar's Latin-English Dictionary, abridged from the larger works of *White* and *Riddle* (as above), by J. T. WHITE, D.D. Square 12mo. pp. 662, price 7s. 6d.

An English-Greek Lexicon, containing all the Greek Words used by Writers of good authority. By C. D. YONGE, B.A. Fifth Edition. 4to. 21s.

Mr. Yonge's New Lexicon, En- glish and Greek, abridged from his larger work (as above). Square 12mo. 8s. 6d.

Hawaii: the Past, Present, and Future of its Island-Kingdom: an Historical Account of the Sandwich Islands. By MANLEY HOPKINS, Hawaiian Consul-General, &c. Second Edition, revised and continued; with Portrait, Map, and 8 other Illustrations. Post 8vo. 12s. 6d.

Maunder's Treasury of Geography, Physical, Historical, Descriptive, and Political. Edited by W. HUGHES, F.R.G.S. With 7 Maps and 16 Plates. Fcp. 10s. 6d.

Physical Geography for Schools and General Readers. By M. F. MAURY, LL.D. Fcp. with 2 Charts, 2s. 6d.

Natural History and Popular Science.

Elementary Treatise on Physics, Experimental and Applied, for the use of Colleges and Schools. Translated and edited from GANOT's 'Eléments de Physique' (with the Author's sanction) by E. ATKINSON, Ph.D. F.C.S. New Edition, revised and enlarged; with a Coloured Plate and 620 Woodcuts. Post 8vo. 15s.

The Elements of Physics or Natural Philosophy. By NEIL ARNOTT, M.D. F.R.S. Physician Extraordinary to the Queen. Sixth Edition, rewritten and completed. 2 Parts, 8vo. 21s.

Dove's Law of Storms, considered in connexion with the ordinary Movements of the Atmosphere. Translated by R. H. SCOTT, M.A. T.C.D. 8vo. 10s. 6d.

Rocks Classified and Described. By BERNHARD VON COTTA. An English Edition, by P. H. LAWRENCE (with English, German, and French Synonymes), revised by the Author. Post 8vo. 14s.

Sound: a Course of Eight Lectures delivered at the Royal Institution of Great Britain. By Professor JOHN TYNDALL, LL.D. F.R.S. Crown 8vo. with Portrait and Woodcuts, 9s.

Heat Considered as a Mode of Motion. By Professor JOHN TYNDALL, LL.D. F.R.S. Third Edition. Crown 8vo. with Woodcuts, 10s. 6d.

Light: its Influence on Life and Health. By FORBES WINSLOW, M.D. D.C.L. Oxon. (Hon.). Fcp. 8vo. 6s.

An Essay on Dew, and several Appearances connected with it. By W. C. WELLS. Edited, with Annotations, by L. P. CASELLA, F.R.A.S. and an Appendix by R. STRACHAN, F.M.S. 8vo. 5s.

A Treatise on Electricity, in Theory and Practice. By A. DE LA RIVE, Prof. in the Academy of Geneva. Translated by C. V. WALKER, F.R.S. 3 vols. 8vo. with Woodcuts, £3 13s.

A Preliminary Discourse on the Study of Natural Philosophy. By Sir JOHN F. W. HERSCHEL, Bart. Revised Edition, with Vignette Title. Fcp. 3s. 6d.

The Correlation of Physical Forces. By W. R. GROVE, Q.C. V.P.R.S. Fifth Edition, revised, and augmented by a Discourse on Continuity. 8vo. 10s. 6d. The *Discourse on Continuity*, separately, price 2s. 6d

Manual of Geology. By S. HAUGHTON, M.D. F.R.S. Fellow of Trin. Coll. and Prof. of Geol. in the Univ. of Dublin. Second Edition, with 66 Woodcuts. Fcp. 7s. 6d.

A Guide to Geology. By J. PHILLIPS, M.A. Prof. of Geol. in the Univ. of Oxford. Fifth Edition. Fcp. 4s.

A Glossary of Mineralogy. By H. W. BRISTOW, F.G.S. of the Geological Survey of Great Britain. With 486 Figures. Crown 8vo. 6s.

Van Der Hoeven's Handbook of ZOOLOGY. Translated from the Second Dutch Edition by the Rev. W. CLARK, M.D. F.R.S. 2 vols. 8vo. with 24 Plates of Figures, 60s.

Professor Owen's Lectures on the Comparative Anatomy and Physiology of the Invertebrate Animals Second Edition, with 235 Woodcuts. 8vo. 21s.

The Comparative Anatomy and Physiology of the Vertebrate Animals. By RICHARD OWEN, F.R.S. D.C.L. 3 vols. 8vo. with upwards of 1,200 Woodcuts. VOLS. I. and II. price 21s. each. VOL. III. (completing the work) is nearly ready.

The First Man and His Place in Creation, considered on the Principles of Common Sense from a Christian Point of View; with an Appendix on the Negro. By GEORGE MOORE, M.D. M.R.C.P.L. &c. Post 8vo. 8s. 6d.

The Primitive Inhabitants of Scandinavia: an Essay on Comparative Ethnography, and a contribution to the History of the Developement of Mankind. Containing a description of the Implements, Dwellings, Tombs, and Mode of Living of the Savages in the North of Europe during the Stone Age. By SVEN NILSSON. Translated from the Author's MS. of the Third Edition; with an Introduction by Sir JOHN LUBBOCK. 8vo. with numerous Plates. [*Nearly ready.*

The Lake Dwellings of Switzer-land and other Parts of Europe. By Dr. F. KELLER, President of the Antiquarian Association of Zürich. Translated and arranged by J. E. LEE, F.S.A. F.G.S. Author of 'Isca Silurum.' With several Woodcuts and nearly 100 Plates of Figures. Royal 8vo. 31s. 6d.

Homes without Hands: a Description of the Habitations of Animals, classed according to their Principle of Construction. By Rev. J. G. WOOD, M.A. F.L.S. With about 140 Vignettes on Wood (20 full size of page). Second Edition. 8vo. 21s.

Bible Animals; being an Account of the various Birds, Beasts, Fishes, and other Animals mentioned in the Holy Scriptures. By the Rev. J. G. WOOD, M.A. F.L.S. Copiously Illustrated with Original Designs, made under the Author's superintendence and engraved on Wood. In course of publication monthly, to be completed in 20 Parts, price 1s. each, forming One Volume, uniform with 'Homes without Hands.'

The Harmonies of Nature and Unity of Creation. By Dr. G. HARTWIG, 8vo. with numerous Illustrations, 18s.

The Sea and its Living Wonders. By the same Author. Third Edition, enlarged. 8vo. with many Illustrations, 21s.

The Tropical World. By the same Author. With 8 Chromoxylographs and 172 Woodcuts. 8vo. 21s.

The Polar World: a Popular Account of Nature and Man in the Arctic and Antarctic Regions. By the same Author. 8vo. with numerous Illustrations. [*Nearly ready.*

Ceylon. By Sir J. EMERSON TENNENT, K.C.S. LL.D. 5th Edition; with Maps, &c. and 90 Wood Engravings. 2 vols. 8vo. £2 10s.

The Wild Elephant, its Structure and Habits, with the Method of Taking and Training it in Ceylon. By the same Author. Fcp. with 22 Woodcuts, 3s. 6d.

Manual of Corals and Sea Jellies. By J. R. GREENE, B.A. Edited by J. A. GALBRAITH, M.A. and S. HAUGHTON, M.D. Fcp. with 39 Woodcuts, 5s.

Manual of Sponges and Animalculæ; with a General Introduction on the Principles of Zoology. By the same Author and Editors. Fcp with 16 Woodcuts. 2s.

Manual of the Metalloids. By J. APJOHN, M.D. F.R.S. and the same Editors. 2nd Edition. Fcp. with 38 Woodcuts, 7s. 6d.

A Familiar History of Birds. By E. STANLEY, D.D. late Lord Bishop of Norwich. Fcp. with Woodcuts, 3s. 6d.

Kirby and Spence's Introduction to Entomology, or Elements of the Natural History of Insects. Crown 8vo. 5s.

Maunder's Treasury of Natural History, or Popular Dictionary of Zoology. Revised and corrected by T. S. CONBOLD, M.D. Fcp. with 900 Woodcuts, 10s.

The Elements of Botany for Families and Schools. Tenth Edition, revised by THOMAS MOORE, F.L.S. Fcp. with 154 Woodcuts, 2s. 6d.

The Treasury of Botany, or Popular Dictionary of the Vegetable Kingdom; with which is incorporated a Glossary of Botanical Terms. Edited by J. LINDLEY, F.R.S. and T. MOORE, F.L.S. assisted by eminent Contributors. Pp. 1,274, with 274 Woodcuts and 20 Steel Plates. 2 Parts, fcp. 20s.

The British Flora; comprising the Phænogamous or Flowering Plants and the Ferns. By Sir W. J. HOOKER, K.H. and G. A. WALKER-ARNOTT, LL.D. 12mo. with 12 Plates, 14s. or coloured, 21s.

The Rose Amateur's Guide. By THOMAS RIVERS. New Edition. Fcp. 4s.

Loudon's Encyclopædia of Plants; comprising the Specific Character, Description, Culture, History, &c. of all the Plants found in Great Britain. With upwards of 12,000 Woodcuts. 8vo. 42s.

Loudon's Encyclopædia of Trees and Shrubs; containing the Hardy Trees and Shrubs of Great Britain scientifically and popularly described. With 2,000 Woodcuts. 8vo. 50s.

Maunder's Scientific and Lite-rary Treasury; a Popular Encyclopædia of Science, Literature, and Art. New Edition, thoroughly revised and in great part rewritten, with above 1,000 new articles, by J. Y. JOHNSON, Corr. M.Z.S. Fcp. 10s. 6d.

A Dictionary of Science, Literature, and Art. Fourth Edition, re-edited by the late W. T. Brande (the Author) and George W. Cox, M.A. 3 vols. medium 8vo. price 63s. cloth.

Essays from the Edinburgh and Quarterly Reviews ; with Addresses and other Pieces. By Sir J. F. W. Herschel Bart. M.A. 8vo. 18s.

Chemistry, Medicine, Surgery, and the Allied Sciences.

A Dictionary of Chemistry and the Allied Branches of other Sciences. By Henry Watts, F.C.S. assisted by eminent Contributors. 5 vols. medium 8vo. in course of publication in Parts. Vol. I. 31s. 6d. Vol. II. 26s. Vol. III. 31s. 6d. and Vol. IV. 24s. are now ready.

Handbook of Chemical Analysis, adapted to the Unitary System of Notation. By F. T. Conington, M.A. F.C.S. Post 8vo. 7s. 6d.

Conington's Tables of Qualitative Analysis, to accompany the above, 2s. 6d.

Elements of Chemistry, Theore- tical and Practical. By William A. Miller, M.D. LL.D. Professor of Chemistry, King's College, London. 3 vols. 8vo. £3. Part I. Chemical Physics, Revised Edition, 15s. Part II. Inorganic Chemistry, 21s. Part III. Organic Chemistry, 24s.

A Manual of Chemistry, De- scriptive and Theoretical. By William Odling, M.B. F.R.S. Part I. 8vo. 9s. Part II. nearly ready.

A Course of Practical Chemistry, for the use of Medical Students. By the same Author. New Edition, with 70 new Woodcuts. Crown 8vo. 7s. 6d.

Lectures on Animal Chemistry Delivered at the Royal College of Physicians in 1865 By the same Author. Crown 8vo. 4s. 6d.

The Toxicologist's Guide: a New Manual on Poisons, giving the Best Methods to be pursued for the Detection of Poisons By J. Horsley, F.C.S. Analytical Chemist. Post 8vo. 3s. 6d.

The Diagnosis, Pathology, and Treatment of Diseases of Women ; including the Diagnosis of Pregnancy. By Graily Hewitt, M.D. &c. Second Edition, enlarged ; with 116 Woodcut Illustrations. 8vo. 21s.

Lectures on the Diseases of In- fancy and Childhood. By Charles West M.D. &c. 5th Edition, revised and enlarged 8vo. 16s.

Exposition of the Signs and Symptoms of Pregnancy : with other Papers on subjects connected with Midwifery. By W. F. Montgomery, M.A. M.D. M.R.I.A 8vo. with Illustrations, 25s.

A System of Surgery, Theoretical and Practical, in Treatises by Various Authors. Edited by T. Holmes, M.A. Cantab. Assistant-Surgeon to St. George's Hospital. 4 vols. 8vo. £4 13s.

Vol. I. General Pathology, 21s.
Vol. II. Local Injuries : Gun-shot Wounds Injuries of the Head, Back, Face, Neck, Chest, Abdomen, Pelvis, of the Upper and Lower Extremities, and Diseases of the Eye. 21s.
Vol. III. Operative Surgery. Diseases of the Organs of Circulation, Locomotion, &c. 21s.
Vol. IV. Diseases of the Organs of Digestion, of the Genito-Urinary System, and of the Breast, Thyroid Gland, and Skin : with Appendix and General Index. 30s.

Lectures on the Principles and Practice of Physic. By Thomas Watson, M.D. Physician-Extraordinary to the Queen. New Edition in preparation.

Lectures on Surgical Pathology. By J. Paget, F.R.S. Surgeon-Extraordinary to the Queen. Edited by W. Turner, M.B. New Edition in preparation.

A Treatise on the Continued Fevers of Great Britain. By C. Murchison, M.D. Senior Physician to the London Fever Hospital. 8vo. with coloured Plates, 18s.

Outlines of Physiology, Human and Comparative. By John Marshall, F.R.C.S. Professor of Surgery in University College, London, and Surgeon to the University College Hospital. 2 vols. crown 8vo. with 122 W

Anatomy, Descriptive and Surgical. By Henry Gray, F.R.S. With 410 Wood Engravings from Dissections. Fourth Edition, by T. Holmes, M.A. Cantab. Royal 8vo. 28*s.*

The Cyclopædia of Anatomy and Physiology. Edited by the late R. B. Todd, M.D. F.R.S. Assisted by nearly all the most eminent cultivators of Physiological Science of the present age. 5 vols. 8vo. with 2,853 Woodcuts, £6 6*s.*

Physiological Anatomy and Physiology of Man. By the late R. B. Todd, M.D. F.R.S. and W. Bowman, F.R.S. of King's College. With numerous Illustrations. Vol. II. 8vo. 25*s.*

Vol. I. New Edition by Dr. Lionel S. Beale, F.R.S. in course of publication; Part I. with 8 Plates, 7*s.* 6*d.*

Histological Demonstrations; a Guide to the Microscopical Examination of the Animal Tissues in Health and Disease, for the use of the Medical and Veterinary Professions. By G. Harley, M.D. F.R.S. Prof. in Univ. Coll. London; and G. T. Brown, M.R.C.V.S. Professor of Veterinary Medicine, and one of the Inspecting Officers in the Cattle Plague Department of the Privy Council. Post 8vo. with 223 Woodcuts, 12*s.*

A Dictionary of Practical Medicine. By J. Copland, M.D. F.R.S. Abridged from the larger work by the Author, assisted by J. C. Copland, M.R.C.S. and throughout brought down to the present state of Medical Science. Pp. 1,560, in 8vo. price 36*s.*

The Works of Sir B. C. Brodie, Bart. collected and arranged by Charles Hawkins, F.R.C.S.E. 3 vols. 8vo. with Medallion and Facsimile, 48*s.*

A Manual of Materia Medica and Therapeutics, abridged from Dr. Pereira's *Elements* by F. J. Farre, M.D. assisted by R. Bentley, M.R.C.S. and by R. Warington, F.R.S. 1 vol. 8vo. with 90 Woodcuts, 21*s.*

Thomson's Conspectus of the British Pharmacopœia. Twenty-fourth Edition, corrected by E. Lloyd Birkett, M.D. 18mo. 5*s.* 6*d.*

Manual of the Domestic Practice of Medicine. By W. B. Kesteven, F.R.C.S.E. Third Edition, thoroughly revised, with Additions. Fcp. 5*s.*

Sea-Air and Sea-Bathing for Children and Invalids. By William Strange, M.D. Fcp. 3*s.*

The Restoration of Health; or, the Application of the Laws of Hygiene to the Recovery of Health: a Manual for the Invalid, and a Guide in the Sick Room. By W. Strange, M.D. Fcp. 6*s.*

Gymnasts and Gymnastics. By John H. Howard, late Professor of Gymnastics, Comm. Coll. ‚Ripponden. Second Edition, revised and enlarged, with various Selections from the best Authors, containing 445 Exercises; and illustrated with 135 Woodcuts, including the most Recent Improvements in the different Apparatus now used in the various Clubs, &c. Crown 8vo. 10*s.* 6*d.*

The Fine Arts, and *Illustrated Editions.*

Half-Hour Lectures on the History and Practice of the Fine and Ornamental Arts. By W. B. Scott. Second Edition. Crown 8vo. with 50 Woodcut Illustrations, 8*s.* 6*d.*

An Introduction to the Study of National Music; Comprising Researches into Popular Songs, Traditions, and Customs. By Carl Engel. With Frontispiece and numerous Musical Illustrations. 8vo. 16*s.*

Lectures on the History of Modern Music, delivered at the Royal Institution. By John Hullah. First Course, with Chronological Tables, post 8vo. 6*s.* 6*d.* Second Course, the Transition Period, with 26 Specimens, 8vo. 16*s.*

The Chorale Book for England; a complete Hymn-Book in accordance with the Services and Festivals of the Church of England; the Hymns translated by Miss C. Winkworth; the Tunes arranged by Prof. W. S. Bennett and Otto Goldschmidt. Fcp. 4to. 12*s.* 6*d.*

Congregational Edition. Fcp. 2*s.*

Six Lectures on Harmony. Delivered at the Royal Institution of Great Britain before Easter 1867. By G. A. Macfarren. 8vo. 10*s.* 6*d.*

Sacred Music for Family Use; A Selection of Pieces for One, Two, or more Voices, from the best Composers, Foreign and English. Edited by John Hullah. 1 vol. music folio, 21*s.*

The New Testament, illustrated with Wood Engravings after the Early Masters, chiefly of the Italian School. Crown 4to. 63s. cloth, gilt top; or £5 5s. morocco.

Lyra Germanica, the Christian Year. Translated by CATHERINE WINKWORTH; with 125 Illustrations on Wood drawn by J. LEIGHTON, F.S.A. Quarto, 21s.

Lyra Germanica. the Christian Life. Translated by CATHERINE WINKWORTH; with about 200 Woodcut Illustrations by J. LEIGHTON, F.S.A. and other Artists. Quarto, 21s.

The Life of Man Symbolised by the Months of the Year in their Seasons and Phases; with Passages selected from Ancient and Modern Authors. By RICHARD PIGOT. Accompanied by a Series of 25 full-page Illustrations and numerous Marginal Devices, Decorative Initial Letters, and Tailpieces, engraved on Wood from Original Designs by JOHN LEIGHTON, F.S.A. Quarto, 42s.

Cats' and Farlie's Moral Em-blems; with Aphorisms, Adages, and Proverbs of all Nations : comprising 121 Illustrations on Wood by J. LEIGHTON, F.S.A. with an appropriate Text by R. PIGOT. Imperial 8vo. 31s. 6d.

Shakspeare's Sentiments and Similes printed in Black and Gold, and illuminated in the Missal style by HENRY NOEL HUMPHREYS. In massive covers, containing the Medallion and Cypher of Shakspeare. Square post 8vo. 21s.

Sacred and Legendary Art. By Mrs. JAMESON. With numerous Etchings and Woodcut Illustrations. 6 vols. square crown 8vo. price £5 15s. 6d. cloth, or £12 12s. bound in morocco by Rivière. To be had also in cloth only, in FOUR SERIES, as follows :—

Legends of the Saints and Martyrs. Fifth Edition, with 19 Etchings and 187 Woodcuts. 2 vols. square crown 8vo. 31s. 6d.

Legends of the Monastic Orders. Third Edition, with 11 Etchings and 88 Woodcuts. 1 vol. square crown 8vo. 21s.

Legends of the Madonna. Third Edition, with 27 Etchings and 165 Woodcuts. 1 vol. square crown 8vo. 21s.

The History of Our Lord, as exemplified in Works of Art. Completed by Lady EASTLAKE. Second Edition, with 13 Etchings and 281 Woodcuts. 2 vols. square crown 8vo. 42s.

Arts, Manufactures, &c.

Drawing from Nature; a Series of Progressive Instructions in Sketching, from Elementary Studies to Finished Views, with Examples from Switzerland and the Pyrenees. By GEORGE BARNARD, Professor of Drawing at Rugby School. With 18 Lithographic Plates and 108 Wood Engravings. Imp. 8vo. 25s. or in Three Parts, royal 8vo. 7s. 6d. each.

Gwilt's Encyclopædia of Archi-tecture. Fifth Edition, with Alterations and considerable Additions, by WYATT PAPWORTH. Additionally illustrated with nearly 400 Wood Engravings by O. JEWITT, and upwards of 100 other new Woodcuts. 8vo. 52s. 6d.

Tuscan Sculptors, their Lives, Works, and Times. With 45 Etchings and 28 Woodcuts from Original Drawings and Photographs. By CHARLES C. PERKINS. 2 vols. imp. 8vo. 63s.

Original Designs for Wood-Carv-ing, with Practical Instructions in the Art. By A. F. B. With 20 Plates of Illustrations engraved on Wood. Quarto, 18s.

The Grammar of Heraldry: containing a Description of all the Principal Charges used in Armory, the Signification of Heraldic Terms, and the Rules to be observed in Blazoning and Marshalling. By JOHN E. CUSSANS. Fcp. with 196 Woodcuts, 4s. 6d.

Hints on Household Taste in Furniture and Decoration. By CHARLES L. EASTLAKE, Architect. With numerous Illustrations engraved on Wood. [*Nearly ready.*

The Engineer's Handbook; explaining the Principles which should guide the young Engineer in the Construction of

The Elements of Mechanism. By T. M. Goodeve, M.A. Prof. of Mechanics at the R. M. Acad. Woolwich. Second Edition, with 217 Woodcuts. Post 8vo. 6s. 6d.

Ure's Dictionary of Arts, Manu- factures, and Mines. Sixth Edition, chiefly re-written and greatly enlarged by Robert Hunt, F.R.S., assisted by numerous Contributors eminent in Science and the Arts, and familiar with Manufactures. With 2,000 Woodcuts. 3 vols. medium 8vo. £4 14s. 6d.

Treatise on Mills and Millwork. By W. Fairbairn, C.E. F.R.S. With 18 Plates and 322 Woodcuts. 2 vols. 8vo. 32s.

Useful Information for Engineers. By the same Author. First, Second, and Third Series, with many Plates and Woodcuts. 3 vols. crown 8vo. 10s. 6d. each.

The Application of Cast and Wrought Iron to Building Purposes. By the same Author. Third Edition, with 6 Plates and 118 Woodcuts. 8vo. 16s.

Iron Ship Building, its History and Progress, as comprised in a Series of Experimental Researches on the Laws of Strain; the Strengths, Forms, and other conditions of the Material; and an Inquiry into the Present and Prospective State of the Navy, including the Experimental Results on the Resisting Powers of Armour Plates and Shot at High Velocities. By W. Fairbairn, C.E. F.R.S. With 4 Plates and 130 Woodcuts, 8vo. 18s.

Encyclopædia of Civil Engineer- ing, Historical, Theoretical, and Practical. By E. Cresy, C.E. With above 3,000 Woodcuts. 8vo. 42s.

The Artisan Club's Treatise on the Steam Engine, in its various Applications to Mines, Mills, Steam Navigation, Railways, and Agriculture. By J. Bourne, C.E. New Edition; with 37 Plates and 546 Woodcuts. 4to. 42s.

A Treatise on the Screw Pro- peller, Screw Vessels, and Screw Engines, as adapted for purposes of Peace and War; with notices of other Methods of Propulsion, Tables of the Dimensions and Performance of Screw Steamers, and Detailed Specifications of Ships and Engines. By the same Author. Third Edition, with 54 Plates and 287 Woodcuts. Quarto, 63s.

Catechism of the Steam Engine, in its various Applications to Mines, Mills, Steam Navigation, Railways, and Agriculture. By John Bourne, C.E. New Edition, with 199 Woodcuts. Fcp. 6s.

Handbook of the Steam Engine, by the same Author, forming a Key to the Catechism of the Steam Engine, with 67 Woodcuts. Fcp. 9s.

A History of the Machine- Wrought Hosiery and Lace Manufactures. By William Felkin, F.L.S. F.S.S. With 3 Steel Plates, 10 Lithographic Plates of Machinery, and 10 Coloured Impressions of Patterns of Lace. Royal 8vo. 21s.

Manual of Practical Assaying, for the use of Metallurgists, Captains of Mines, and Assayers in general; with copious Tables for Ascertaining in Assays of Gold and Silver the precise amount in Ounces, Pennyweights, and Grains of Noble Metal contained in One Ton of Ore from a Given Quantity. By John Mitchell, F.C.S. 8vo. with 360 Woodcuts, 21s.

The Art of Perfumery; the History and Theory of Odours, and the Methods of Extracting the Aromas of Plants. By Dr. Piesse, F.C.S. Third Edition, with 53 Woodcuts. Crown 8vo. 10s. 6d.

Chemical, Natural, and Physical Magic, for Juveniles during the Holidays. By the same Author. Third Edition, enlarged with 38 Woodcuts. Fcp. 6s.

Loudon's Encyclopædia of Agri- culture: Comprising the Laying-out, Improvement, and Management of Landed Property, and the Cultivation and Economy of the Productions of Agriculture. With 1,100 Woodcuts. 8vo. 31s. 6d.

Loudon's Encyclopædia of Gardening: Comprising the Theory and Practice of Horticulture, Floriculture, Arboriculture, and Landscape Gardening. With 1,000 Woodcuts. 8vo. 31s. 6d.

Loudon's Encyclopædia of Cottage, Farm, and Villa Architecture and Furniture. With more than 2,000 Woodcuts. 8vo. 42s.

Garden Architecture and Land- scape Gardening, illustrating the Architectural Embellishment of Gardens; with Remarks on Landscape Gardening in its relation to Architecture. By John Arthur Hughes. 8vo. with 194 Woodcuts, 14s.

Bayldon's Art of Valuing Rents and Tillages, and Claims of Tenants upon Quitting Farms, both at Michaelmas and Lady-Day. Eighth Edition, revised by J. C. Morton. 8vo. 10s. 6d.

Lyra Germanica, translated from the German by Miss C. WINKWORTH. FIRST SERIES, Hymns for the Sundays and Chief Festivals; SECOND SERIES, the Christian Life. Fcp. 3s. 6d. each SERIES.

Hymns from Lyra Germanica, 18mo. 1s.

Lyra Eucharistica ; Hymns and Verses on the Holy Communion, Ancient and Modern; with other Poems. Edited by the Rev. ORBY SHIPLEY, M.A. Second Edition. Fcp. 7s. 6d.

Lyra Messianica; Hymns and Verses on the Life of Christ, Ancient and Modern; with other Poems. By the same Editor. Second Edition, enlarged. Fcp. 7s. 6d.

Lyra Mystica; Hymns and Verses on Sacred Subjects, Ancient and Modern. By the same Editor. Fcp. 7s. 6d.

Lyra Sacra ; Hymns, Ancient and Modern, Odes, and Fragments of Sacred Poetry. Edited by the Rev. B. W. SAVILE, M.A. Third Edition, enlarged. Fcp. 5s.

The Catholic Doctrine of the Atonement; an Historical Inquiry into its Development in the Church: with an Introduction on the Principle of Theological Developments. By H. N. OXENHAM, M.A. 8vo. 8s. 6d.

Endeavours after the Christian Life: Discourses. By JAMES MARTINEAU. Fourth and cheaper Edition, carefully revised; the Two Series complete in One Volume. Post 8vo. 7s. 6d.

Introductory Lessons on the History of Religious Worship; being a Sequel to the 'Lessons on Christian Evidences.' By RICHARD WHATELY, D.D. New Edition. 18mo. 2s. 6d.

Travels, Voyages, &c.

The North-West Peninsula of Iceland; being the Journal of a Tour in Iceland in the Summer of 1862. By C. W. SHEPHERD, M.A. F.Z.S. With a Map and Two Illustrations. Fcp. 8vo. 7s. 6d.

Pictures in Tyrol and Elsewhere. From a Family Sketch-Book, By the Author of 'A Voyage en Zigzag,' &c. Quarto, with numerous Illustrations, 21s.

How we Spent the Summer; or, a Voyage en Zigzag in Switzerland and Tyrol with some Members of the ALPINE CLUB. From the Sketch-Book of one of the Party. Third Edition, re-drawn. In oblong 4to. with about 300 Illustrations, 15s.

Beaten Tracks; or, Pen and Pencil Sketches in Italy. By the Authoress of 'A Voyage en Zigzag.' With 42 Plates, containing about 200 Sketches from Drawings made on the Spot. 8vo. 16s.

Florence, the New Capital of Italy. By C. R. WELD. With several Engravings on Wood, from Drawings by the Author. Post 8vo. 12s. 6d.

Map of the Chain of Mont Blanc, from an actual Survey in 1863—1864. By A. ADAMS-REILLY, F.R.G.S. M.A.C. Published under the Authority of the Alpine Club. In Chromolithography on extra stout drawing-paper 28in. × 17in. price 10s. or mounted on canvas in a folding case. 12s. 6d.

History of Discovery in our Australasian Colonies, Australia, Tasmania, and New Zealand, from the Earliest Date to the Present Day. By WILLIAM HOWITT. With 3 Maps of the Recent Explorations from Official Sources. 2 vols. 8vo. 20s.

The Capital of the Tycoon; a Narrative of a 3 Years' Residence in Japan. By Sir RUTHERFORD ALCOCK, K.C.B. 2 vols. 8vo. with numerous Illustrations, 42s.

The Dolomite Mountains. Excursions through Tyrol, Carinthia, Carniola, and Friuli. By J. GILBERT and G. C. CHURCHILL, F.R.G.S. With numerous Illustrations. Square crown 8vo. 21s.

A Lady's Tour Round Monte Rosa; including Visits to the Italian Valleys. With Map and Illustrations. Post 8vo. 14s.

Guide to the Pyrenees, for the use of Mountaineers. By CHARLES PACKE. With Maps, &c. and Appendix. Fcp. 6s.

The Alpine Guide. By JOHN BALL, M.R.I.A. late President of the Alpine Club. Post 8vo. with Maps and other Illustrations.

Guide to the Eastern Alps. [Just ready.

Guide to the Western Alps, including Mont Blanc, Monte Rosa, Zermatt, &c. price 7s. 6d.

Guide to the Oberland and all Switzerland, excepting the Neighbourhood of Monte Rosa and the Great St. Bernard; with Lombardy and the adjoining portion of Tyrol. 7s. 6d.

The Englishman in India. By CHARLES RAIKES, Esq. C.S.I. formerly Commissioner of Lahore. Post 8vo. 7s. 6d.

The Irish in America. By JOHN FRANCIS MAGUIRE, M.P. for Cork. Post 8vo. 12s. 6d.

The Arch of Titus and the Spoils of the Temple; an Historical and Critical Lecture, with Authentic Illustrations. By WILLIAM KNIGHT, M.A. With 10 Woodcuts from Ancient Remains. 4to. 10s.

Curiosities of London; exhibiting the most Rare and Remarkable Objects of Interest in the Metropolis; with nearly Sixty Years' Personal Recollections. By JOHN TIMBS, F.S.A. New Edition, corrected and enlarged. 8vo. Portrait, 21s.

Narratives of Shipwrecks of the Royal Navy between 1793 and 1857, compiled from Official Documents in the Admiralty by W. O. S. GILLY; with a Preface by W. S. GILLY, D.D. 3d Edition, fcp. 5s.

Visits to Remarkable Places : Old Halls, Battle-Fields, and Scenes illustrative of Striking Passages in English History and Poetry. By WILLIAM HOWITT. 2 vols. square crown 8vo. with Wood Engravings, 25s.

The Rural Life of England. By the same Author. With Woodcuts by Bewick and Williams. Medium 8vo. 12s. 6d.

A Week at the Land's End. By J. T. BLIGHT; assisted by E. H. RODD, R. Q. COUCH, and J. RALFS. With Map and 96 Woodcuts. Fcp. 6s. 6d.

Works of Fiction.

The Warden : a Novel. By ANTHONY TROLLOPE, Crown 8vo. 2s. 6d.

Barchester Towers : a Sequel to 'The Warden.' By the same Author. Crown 8vo. 3s. 6d.

Stories and Tales by the Author of 'Amy Herbert,' uniform Edition, each Tale or Story complete in a single volume.

AMY HERBERT, 2s. 6d. | KATHARINE ASHTON, 3s. 6d.
GERTRUDE, 2s. 6d. |
EARL'S DAUGHTER, 2s. 6d. | MARGARET PERCIVAL, 5s.
EXPERIENCE OF LIFE, 2s. 6d. | LANETON PARSONAGE, 4s. 6d.
CLEVE HALL, 3s. 6d. | URSULA, 4s. 6d.
IVORS, 3s. 6d. |

A Glimpse of the World. By the Author of 'Amy Herbert.' Fcp. 7s. 6d.

The Journal of a Home Life. By the same Author. Post 8vo. 9s. 6d.

After Life ; a Sequel to the 'Journal of a Home Life.' By the same Author. Post 8vo.

[Nearly ready.

Gallus ; or, Roman Scenes of the Time of Augustus: with Notes and Excursuses illustrative of the Manners and Customs of the Ancient Romans. From the German of Prof. BECKER. New Edit. Post 8vo. 7s. 6d.

Charicles ; a Tale illustrative of Private Life among the Ancient Greeks : with Notes and Excursuses. From the German of Prof. BECKER. New Edition, Post 8vo. 7s. 6d.

Springdale Abbey : Extracts from the Letters and Diaries of an ENGLISH PREACHER. 8vo. 12s.

The Six Sisters of the Valleys : an Historical Romance. By W. BRAMLEY-MOORE, M.A. Incumbent of Gerrard's Cross, Bucks. Fourth Edition, with 14 Illustrations. Crown 8vo. 5s.

Tales from Greek Mythology. By GEORGE W. COX, M.A. late Scholar of Trin. Coll. Oxon. Second Edition. Square 16mo. 3s. 6d.

Tales of the Gods and Heroes. By the same Author. Second Edition. Fcp. 5s.

Tales of Thebes and Argos. By the same Author. Fcp. 4s. 6d.

A Manual of Mythology, in the form of Question and Answer. By the same Author. Fcp. 3s.

Cabinet Edition of Novels and Tales by By G. J. WHYTE MELVILLE :—

The Gladiators : a Tale of Rome and Judæa. Crown 8vo. 5s.

Digby Grand, 5s.

Kate Coventry, 5s.

General Bounce, 5s.

Holmby House, 5s.

Good for Nothing, 6s.

The Queen's Maries, 6s.

The Interpreter, a Tale of the War.

Elements of Maritime International Law. By WILLIAM DE BURGH, B.A. of the Inner Temple, Barrister-at-Law 8vo.

Papers on Maritime Legislation; with a Translation of the German Mercantile Law relating to Maritime Commerce. By ERNST EMIL WENDT. 8vo. 10s. 6d.

Practical Guide for British Shipmasters to United States Ports. By PIERREPONT EDWARDS, Her Britannic Majesty's Vice-Consul at New York. Post 8vo. 8s. 6d.

The Law of Nations Considered as Independent Political Communities. By TRAVERS TWISS, D.C.L. Regius Professor of Civil Law in the University of Oxford. 2 vols. 8vo. 30s. or separately, PART I. *Peace,* 12s. PART II. *War.* 18s.

A Nautical Dictionary, defining the Technical Language relative to the Building and Equipment of Sailing Vessels and Steamers, &c. By ARTHUR YOUNG. Second Edition; with Plates and 150 Woodcuts. 8vo. 18s.

Works of Utility and *General Information.*

Modern Cookery for Private Families, reduced to a System of Easy Practice in a Series of carefully-tested Receipts. By ELIZA ACTON. Newly revised and enlarged; with 8 Plates, Figures, and 150 Woodcuts. Fcp. 6s.

On Food and its Digestion; an Introduction to Dietetics. By W. BRINTON, M.D. Physician to St. Thomas's Hospital, &c. With 48 Woodcuts. Post 8vo. 12s.

Wine, the Vine, and the Cellar. By THOMAS G. SHAW. Second Edition, revised and enlarged, with Frontispiece and 31 Illustrations on Wood. 8vo 16s.

A Practical Treatise on Brewing; with Formulæ for Public Brewers, and Instructions for Private Families. By W. BLACK. Fifth Edition. 8vo. 10s. 6d.

How to Brew Good Beer: a complete Guide to the Art of Brewing Ale, Bitter Ale, Table Ale, Brown Stout, Porter, and Table Beer. By JOHN PITT. Revised Edition. Fcp. 4s. 6d.

The Billiard Book. By Captain CRAWLEY, Author of 'Billiards, its Theory and Practice,' &c. With nearly 100 Diagrams on Steel and Wood. 8vo. 21s.

Whist, What to Lead. By CAM. Third Edition. 32mo. 1s.

The Cabinet Lawyer; a Popular Digest of the Laws of England, Civil, Criminal, and Constitutional. 23rd Edition, entirely recomposed, and brought down by the AUTHOR to the close of the Parliamentary Session of 1867. Fcp. 10s. 6d.

The Philosophy of Health; or, an Exposition of the Physiological and Sanitary Conditions conducive to Human Longevity and Happiness. By SOUTHWOOD SMITH, M.D. Eleventh Edition, revised and enlarged; with 113 Woodcuts. 8vo. 7s. 6d.

A Handbook for Readers at the British Museum. By THOMAS NICHOLS. Post 8vo. 6s.

Hints to Mothers on the Management of their Health during the Period of Pregnancy and in the Lying-in Room. By T. BULL, M.D. Fcp. 5s.

The Maternal Management of Children in Health and Disease. By the same Author. Fcp. 5s.

Notes on Hospitals. By FLORENCE NIGHTINGALE. Third Edition, enlarged; with 13 Plans. Post 4to. 18s.

The Executor's Guide. By J. C. HUDSON. Enlarged Edition, revised by the Author, with reference to the latest reported Cases and Acts of Parliament. Fcp. 6s.

The Law relating to Benefit Building Societies; with Practical Observations on the Act and all the Cases decided thereon, also a Form of Rules and Forms of Mortgages. By W. TIDD PRATT, Barrister. 2nd Edition. Fcp. 3s. 6d.

Willich's Popular Tables for Ascertaining the Value of Lifehold, Leasehold, and Church Property, Renewal Fines, &c.; the Public Funds; Annual Average Price and Interest on Consols from 1731 to 1861; Chemical, Geographical, Astronomical, Trigonometrical Tables, &c. Post 8vo. 10s.

Decimal Interest Tables at Twenty-four Different Rates not exceeding Five per Cent. Calculated for the use of Bankers. To which are added Commission Tables at One-eighth and One-fourth per Cent. By J. R. COULTHART. New Edition. 8vo. 15s.

Maunder's Treasury of Knowledge and Library of Reference: comprising an English Dictionary and Grammar, Universal Gazetteer, Classical Dictionary, Chronology, Law Dictionary, Synopsis of the Peerage, useful Tables &c. Fcp. 10s. 6d.

INDEX.